Other books by the authors:

Emissaries of the Order of Melchizedek: Book I
by Antera and Omaran

Twin Flames: A True Story of Soul Reunion
by Antera

Emissaries
of the
Order of Melchizedek

Book II

Antera and Omaran

BALBOA.PRESS
A DIVISION OF HAY HOUSE

Balboa Press books may be ordered through booksellers or by contacting:

Balboa Press
A Division of Hay House
1663 Liberty Drive
Bloomington, IN 47403
www.balboapress.com
844-682-1282

Because of the dynamic nature of the Internet, any web addresses or links contained in this book may have changed since publication and may no longer be valid. The views expressed in this work are solely those of the author and do not necessarily reflect the views of the publisher, and the publisher hereby disclaims any responsibility for them.

The author of this book does not dispense medical advice or prescribe the use of any technique as a form of treatment for physical, emotional, or medical problems without the advice of a physician, either directly or indirectly. The intent of the author is only to offer information of a general nature to help you in your quest for emotional and spiritual well-being. In the event you use any of the information in this book for yourself, which is your constitutional right, the author and the publisher assume no responsibility for your actions.

Print information available on the last page.

ISBN: 979-8-7652-3966-7 (sc)
ISBN: 979-8-7652-3967-4 (hc)
ISBN: 979-8-7652-3968-1 (e)

Library of Congress Control Number: 2016906176

Balboa Press rev. date: 04/26/2023

Contents

Acknowledgements

We have infinite gratitude for the Beings of Light who illuminate our path with consistent love and patience. We also thank the readers of Book I who wrote to share their spiritual experiences from the writings. Special thanks go to Amy Chirp Schoenhofen and Rayceena Willy for reading and improving the manuscript.

Preface

What an exciting time to be alive! When we all chose to be incarnated now, we knew it would be a tremendous opportunity for both personal growth and service to humanity. This series, chronicling our story, is one of our contributions to aid the large evolutionary step we are collectively taking.

This second book of the series has taken years to complete, because of the many projects we have started and subsequent demands on our time. But finally, it is finished! We do hope to finish the next book in much less time.

We did not include another glossary. The one we provided in Book I has pertinent spiritual terms and readers may refer to it if a definition is needed. Indeed, it is always important to make sure words are understood in the way they are used whenever any uncertainty comes up and before continuing.

Once we met and realized we were twin flames, the adventures began, and we have followed our path of spiritual service while living in the real world through many challenges. It has not been an easy path, but it has been amazingly smooth and very fulfilling because of all the help we get from Beings of Light. These adventures have provided us with inestimable blessings and a precious education. Our hope is that by sharing this journey, everyone who reads about it will get the exact healing, insights, and transformation they need. This is what happened with Book I, and we are grateful for all the wonderful feedback we have received.

Our journey is unique due to Antera's ability, since childhood, to communicate with Beings of Light. These loving beings have been essential to all the choices we have made and projects we have created. We share their words throughout our story because they contain such a wealth of wisdom. Their words are timeless, applicable to the lives of all who are on a spiritual path. And the words carry energy. To get the most from this book, focus on the Master whose words you read. Your energy will then open and be uplifted to resonate more fully with him or her.

We are pioneers in many of our activities as we follow, to the best of our abilities, the requests and advice from the Ascended Masters, doing our part to smooth the path of humanity through the current chaotic period. These missions from the Order of Melchizedek have been consistently offered to us as intriguing opportunities, and always with love and respect. We have followed through with as many as we could, given our time limits in this 3D world. All projects and journeys have led us to expanded awareness in many ways, and through our work we open the way for others.

Thank you for reading! We are grateful for this opportunity to serve our beloved planet.

Antera and Omaran, 2022

Recap

This is Book II of the series, *Emissaries of the Order of Melchizedek*, a chronicle of the adventures of Antera and Omaran as they follow their missions, guided by Beings of Light. Book I started in 1998 after they were reunited as twin flames (see Antera's book, *Twin Flames: A True Story of Soul Reunion*, for their early story) and followed their tale through 2005.

The couple made their getaway from the dense energy of the San Francisco Bay Area, in central California, to live in the spiritual vortex of Mount Shasta in the far northern reaches of the state. The mystical mountain had been calling them for years. Going on faith that all would fall into place, they managed to purchase property and get a construction loan at a time when they had very little money in the bank, ending up with a 2.5-acre piece of land covered in manzanita thicket so entangled they could not even walk onto the property. But it called them strongly, and the 360-degree views were unparalleled.

Thus, they began clearing and preparing sacred ground and building a passive-solar house they designed themselves, in Golden Mean proportions. This huge project presented many learning opportunities as they were challenged to stay in the flow of Spirit while meeting physical goals. Omaran was the contractor, but he quickly found that his high standards of positive attitude and spiritual energy severely limited the pool of construction workers available. He got comfortable with firing people.

They developed more skills for cooperating with nature spirits. Antera's ability to communicate with non-physical entities allowed for many encounters with fascinating beings such as the Manzanita Deva on their new property, a native ancestor named Walking Stick, and a group from under the mountain calling themselves the Ancients. Omaran learned (remembered) how to move water underground when the new well did not produce enough for their needs.

Their quests took them on many hikes to explore all sides of Mount Shasta, while creating a Light Field over the entire area by making and connecting Light forms and clearing ley lines for more and healthier flow in the land. Along the way, they met various giant mountain spirits and other nature beings who were interested in supporting this land healing work. On one of these hikes, a large stone called out to Antera, asking to be the corner stone of their new house, so Omaran dutifully carried the heavy rock several miles back to their truck, without complaint. She painted it with the Golden Mean Spiral, and he attached it to the northeast corner of the foundation.

Pushing more limits, they decided, while building the house, to prove that they could live on Light alone. They gave up food completely for over a month, giving the cells of their bodies a powerful reset while learning how important food is to social interactions.

Even before the house was finished, they made a sacred area for ceremonies, consisting of a medicine wheel surrounded by a circle of sequoia trees. They got chickens, and a henhouse with a fenced yard was next. Y2K came and went without much disruption.

When the couple had settled into their new house, their focus went back to expanding their spiritual services and creating music. Antera became discouraged that more people had not awakened spiritually. Ever since she could remember, she had thought that by the year 2000 there would certainly be a mass opening as people woke up to what was really important and started their spiritual search. For a while, she decided not to teach any more classes until there was more demand. This didn't last long. They initiated more spiritual seekers into the Order of Melchizedek, lead ceremonies, and started developing a mystery school. With the completion of their first album together as well as Antera's first book, they rented out their home, bought an RV, packed up the dog and cat, and went on a West Coast book and music tour.

Along the way, they camped at many beautiful areas and at one of these, near Mount Rainier, Washington, they had their first direct, intense encounter with Divine Mother, who came through forcefully with Her desire to change the path humanity was taking. This was life-altering for the couple as they embraced Her energy.

The Land Healing Project was born from their love of the planet and desire to heal Earth, guided by Ascended Masters, angels, ancestors, and nature spirits. Silver Horse, a native ancestor, came to them in Sedona, Arizona, teaching some of the old medicine ways, and they did the first group land healing ceremony on Mount Tamalpais in the Bay Area. After that, the project expanded quickly, taking them on trips throughout the west to create permanent points connected in a grid, effectively sewing up California in a zigzag pattern.

The tour and all their trips had depleted their financial reserves, so they found themselves living in the San Francisco Bay Area again for a year to replenish supplies before going back home. It was such a relief when they made it back to the mountain!

Book II starts in 2005 after they have settled back into their Mount Shasta home and carries the story into 2008.

1

Into the Darkness

Omaran felt a little nervous, but he pushed that unsettled feeling in his stomach aside. He had made his choice to do this, and he needed all his mental focus for the task. It was too late to back out. He was sitting with Antera on the couch in their living room in December 2005, preparing for an inner journey to a location inside the Earth. Antera was not going with him but would be sending him energy from where she sat. The Masters had said they would not go there either, in fact, they had told him they could NOT go there. Doubt came up as he thought about that. Could he really do this? Was he strong enough?

It had all started with a past-life memory from hundreds of years ago, one he was still trying to understand. In that life, he had made some serious mistakes. He had unwittingly helped create an object that was designed to send debilitating energies to those who were trying to bring Light to the world. Though he had been coerced into this without knowing its true purpose until it was too late, he knew he might have been able to stop it if he had been more courageous at the time, even at the expense of his life. His actions were almost impossible to understand from who he was now, completely aligned with the Light.

To forgive himself more completely, he wanted to do something to undo the damage. He had a feeling that the object was still working, so he had decided he would try to disconnect it or somehow disrupt its power source. He had dubbed the place he was going, the Catacombs.

He could feel their dog Faith, a tan-colored lab-shepherd mix with a ferocious bark but a gentle nature, who was lying on the floor with her head resting on his feet. Samantha, their energy-sensitive tabby cat, was also close, lying on the couch. The animals were going to be his only companions on this adventure, both agreeing in spirit to accompany him and function as sentries and protectors, warning him if anyone appeared. They were both ready and waiting.

He recalled the conversation he'd had during the planning stages with the Ascended Master St. Germain, one of the great teachers Antera channeled. Since she was a small child, she had been able to talk with angels and other Beings of Light on the other side of the veil, and they had been her cherished teachers all her life.

St. Germain had asked Omaran, "What are you going to do once you get inside?"

"I'm planning on being as quick as I can, and I intend to use my Light Sword to cut as many cords as possible, which I see going to individuals around the planet," Omaran had answered. He had seen the object from a distance. "What I do after that depends on whether I've been spotted by anyone who doesn't want me there."

"How are you going to get to where you want to go? You certainly will not be walking. You need speed."

"I was thinking of creating a fast horse to ride in."

St. Germain had surprised him by replying, "Would you consider a fast race car?"

"That's a good idea."

"Speed will be of the utmost importance, and if you are seen by anyone, you do not want to linger. The whole time you are gone you will want Antera holding a protective space for you. I would also strongly suggest that you make yourself as invisible as you can."

Omaran was now ready. He felt he had done as much preparation as possible, knowing that it would be a daring task and possibly even dangerous, considering the beings involved with this malevolent energy. The time was now.

"Okay, I'm ready," Omaran said to Antera, as he took a deep breath and closed his eyes.

Antera said, "Good luck! I know you will be successful!"

He got behind the wheel of his etheric race car, which he had created using his imagination. Faith and Samantha settled onto the seat next to him. Not surprisingly, he seemed to remember exactly how to get there. The site was in Europe, and he traveled there in a few seconds. Then he drove right into the ground. Though non-physical, it all seemed very real. He intuitively knew there could be unwanted consequences if his mind wavered at all. At his destination, he saw, as well as felt, the targeted structure.

In the preceding days, he had seen it in his mind's eye several times, but in person it looked much larger and more imposing. It was shaped like a grey sphere with hundreds of tentacles attached to its surface and extending upward toward the surface of the planet, like a malevolent spider with a dark web. These cords, pulsing with some kind of dark energy, were no doubt attached to or aimed at people and organizations on the surface who were trying to make the world a better place. Clearly this harmful energy flow had to stop, and cutting those connections was the way to do it. There were so many that the job looked a bit daunting, but he hoped he could cut them in batches rather than one at a time and get out before anyone noticed.

Pulling his magical sword out of its sheath, he looked at its dazzling gold color. It had been a gift from the Masters a few years earlier, but he had never really used it. Until this adventure, he had wondered if he would ever need such a powerful tool. Now, he knew exactly what to do, and the sword became one with him, as if he were a trained knight in battle. The Light power of the sword pulsed through him, giving him more courage and strengthening his resolve. He took a deep breath and went into action, slashing at the cords ten or twenty at a time, moving as quickly as he could. The super-sharp blade easily sliced through anything it touched.

One section was soon finished. He moved in a clockwise circle around the sphere as he continued the deconstruction. As he cut, a part of his attention was listening for the sound of anyone approaching or warning sounds from Faith and Samantha. So far so good. He cautiously allowed himself to feel excited as he neared the end, with only a few more cords to demolish. With a final swing, he cut the last group, pausing only a moment to notice that the structure itself was deflating like a punctured soccer ball, its energy leaking out the holes where the cords had been. Its support was gone!

Not waiting to see more, Omaran gestured for the animals, and the three of them exuberantly jumped into the car and sped out in triumph. Done!

Arriving back home, he opened his eyes and saw Antera, who was still in deep concentration, sending him energy. He said, "I'm back, and I think it all went well!"

"Good to hear. But I don't want you to do that again. It was far too intense."

"Yeah. The biggest surprise was that no one came." He thought for a moment. "Well, they probably weren't expecting anyone. Or maybe it just wasn't being maintained any more. It was definitely still doing what it was designed to do, though. Now it is destroyed!"

"Wonderful! But why am I expecting to hear that there is more to do?"

"Yes. Well, the not-so-good news is that this is not the only one of these, it's just the only one I had knowledge of because of my history. But while I was there, I became aware of others like it."

They learned later, from the Masters, that while Omaran had been diligent at protection during the excursion, he had neglected to cover up where he came from, and he had left an energy trace which could possibly be followed. Antera and Omaran had never even considered that. Right away, Omaran looked for the tracks he had left and cleared them. He did want to go back into the Catacombs to find another of these dark structures, but not for some time, as other matters were pressing.

2

Mountain Release

Returning to their home on Mount Shasta in the fall of 2005 had been a huge relief to Antera and Omaran, after being gone for over two years. They had built this passive-solar home on the flanks of their favorite mountain. All the evergreens, fruit trees, and other plants they had lovingly installed on their 2.5 acres soothed and nurtured them.

But the energy of their home was definitely changed because the renters who had been living there had left energy imprints which felt foreign and disharmonious to the sensitive owners. In time, it would go back to feeling like their home, Antera and Omaran knew. They used all their tools of clearing and cleaning energy to speed up the process.

That wasn't all that had changed in their absence. The mountain itself felt tense, like it was also in need of release and clearing. This was confirmed when St. Germain told them that the Masters were genuinely concerned about the dangerous buildup of energies inside Mount Shasta. He asked if they would be willing to do some release work for their beloved mountain. Without hesitation, they agreed to do this.

It sounded like a new aspect of the land healing they had been focusing on for the last few years, so they were happy to learn a new way to work. Their Land Healing Project, which had taken them to many locations in California, with more to come, had been very fulfilling. It was wonderful to do Lightwork that was so effective at transforming negative energies into Light. The grid they had built in their state was stable and permanent.

St. Germain suggested that they both make staffs to use as tools in the venting of energy. They loved that idea! A staff just for releasing energy from inside the Earth! They knew wooden staffs had been used as power objects throughout history, but neither of them had previously thought about making one.

Within a day of this suggestion from the Master, while walking Faith, Omaran just happened to find some perfect oak limbs on the ground, which had fallen sometime in the past half year. He took them home, stripped the bark off and sanded them smooth to make the staffs.

During their travels and hikes, they had felt many vortexes where energy was spinning around and around, pushing energy either upward or downward. To release energy from below the surface required a spinning motion that was counterclockwise, and to bring energy from above downward a clockwise motion was needed in the vortex. For this project, the idea was to find vortexes that were already spinning upward and enhance their ability to release, making them more stable in the process.

Antera painted a spiral from the bottom to the top of each staff, to encourage the counterclockwise motion required for upward movement of energy. They had plans for much more elaborate decorations, but that was as far as they got when they felt a real urging to begin the energy releasing before it snowed so much that they could not get access to the areas they wanted.

It was mid-December when they embarked on their first releasing excursion. St. Germain had only given them a brief outline of how to do this, so they knew they needed to be creative and experiment. Often the Masters worked with Antera and Omaran this way, allowing them to try some ideas in the field before giving more advice and feedback.

Armed with their new staffs and other sacred objects, and accompanied by Faith, they headed for Black Butte, a small volcano next to Mount Shasta that, from a distance, resembles a pyramid. Their new-used Toyota truck, which Omaran had named Sky for its powder-blue color, was much better in the snow than its predecessor, Tan Man. Sky had four-wheel drive, essential for living in snow country.

"How close do you think we'll be able to get to Black Butte, with the snow?" asked Antera as they bounced along a dirt road with increasingly thick snow.

"Well, the snow's not too deep, and I think Sky can get us almost as close as if there wasn't any snow. Let's head for the north side first."

They were able to drive all the way to the Black Butte trailhead, which surprised even Omaran. "Wow, this truck is pretty impressive. Even with three 100-pound bags of sand in the back, Tan Man would not have gotten this far."

"This is a great truck. So where are you thinking to go?" asked Antera.

"We're northeast of the butte, and I'm hoping we can hike around to the northern area a bit further."

They parked and got out, loading up with their supplies. Antera said, "Lead on, the snow isn't too deep here."

They walked, punching holes in the white stuff with every step, enjoying the familiar pines, firs, and occasional cedar along the way. As their wandering took them up and over a small rise, Omaran mused to himself that one advantage of hiking in snow is that you can find your way back easily by following the tracks. The fact that he did not have to pay as much attention as usual to where they were going freed him up to sense energy as they hiked. He knew there was a vortex in the vicinity.

"So," he asked Antera, "do you have a fairly good idea of what we're going to do in the vortex when we find one?"

"We can wing it. We are looking for an area where we can release the energies that are stuck inside both Black Butte and Mount Shasta—the whole area, actually. As St. Germain was talking to me, I could see this disturbance extending out for many miles in all directions. But I believe we only need to do five or six releases to relieve the pressure for now."

"We aren't going to cause a volcanic eruption, right?" Omaran said, only half kidding.

"Ha, ha. No, we just focus on energy coming up and out. Do not picture magma!"

They trudged farther, though the snow got deeper, up to a foot deep in some shady areas. Omaran pulled his boot out of a deeper hole and said, "So, if I understand correctly, all we have to do is find an exact place where there is a vortex so that we can do some releasing, thereby saving this volcano from possibly blowing up. Is that about it?"

"That's about it."

"Oh good, I was hoping it would be easy, with no pressure."

After another mile, Omaran was drawn to a small area that was fairly flat. "See that area right over there? It feels pretty good to me. Do you sense anything?"

Antera stopped and sensed. "There is definitely some energy there. And if we're going to do two of these today, in these conditions, then I say let's go for it. We still have to do the work, hike back to the truck, and then go to another place."

"All right, then!"

They made their way to the small clearing, surrounded by conifers. Using their boots, they tramped out a circle in the snow and set out gifts for the nature spirits. Faith found a comfortable spot to lie down and watch, warm in her thick fur. They called in the four directions, stated their purpose, called in the Masters for their support, then started circling around and around counterclockwise. Gradually increasing their speed, they went faster and faster until they were running around the circle. They kept this up for about ten minutes, until they could feel a burst of energy out of the ground like a geyser.

They both felt that it was complete, so they stopped and tried to stand still. Dizzy, they grabbed onto each other in an attempt to regain their balance, almost toppling together into the snow. Standing in the center of the vortex, it felt like a powerful whirlwind, and they laughed.

"We did it!" Antera shouted.

"Woohoo!" Omaran joined in. "That was fun!"

There was no dry place to sit, and they wanted to get going, so they packed up and hiked back to the truck without delay. They drove around to the southeast part of the volcano and parked.

"We can't really go any farther. If we go all the way to the south side, we'll run into the dump, and I do not want to drive any further downhill because even as good as this truck is, I'm not sure we can get back up the hill. I think this area is going to be next."

"Okay, then," said Antera, getting out of the truck. "The snow doesn't look as deep here as on the north side, and we have plenty of time before the sun sets."

They hiked for about half an hour and found a place that felt like it might be a vortex. They were feeling lightheaded, as they usually did near a vortex, but they weren't entirely sure it wasn't because of the physical exertion. They both felt good about the location, however, so they set up and proceeded to do the same process, finishing up with the slow walk to a fast run for the final releasing.

The vortex opened and energy rapidly flowed upward. They stopped and stood in the center, holding onto each other to keep from falling as their bodies adjusted.

"Wow! That sure worked! Let's go home. This was a workout!" exclaimed Antera.

"I'm ready. I feel good about both of these," Omaran said as he started packing up. "If you have any energy left, maybe we can see if St. Germain might give us some feedback tonight."

"Let me rest a bit and have dinner, then we will see if I can. I am curious, too."

After dinner, they sat in meditation to prepare the space and lift their energy so Antera could channel. It did not take long for St. Germain to appear to her. He was a powerful being, and they were glad to have his council whenever he decided to come. Because Antera had the ability to contact many different beings by tuning her energy to their frequencies, she was often surrounded by a group in the inner realms, and would wait to see who wanted to talk, rather than calling one particular Master.

Before St. Germain spoke, Antera started laughing hilariously, saying, "He thinks it is very funny, the way we ran around and around today!"

St. Germain chuckled as he said, "Greetings . . . and thank you so much for running around in circles! We enjoyed it immensely. Yes, the circles are wonderful. These kinds of ceremonies are quite different from what you normally do, but I must say you came up with something quite creative. And it did create the vent. Yes indeed, we saw the vortex created and the energy flowed upward.

"Now I want you to know that you can do this anywhere. It is not something you have to do at a particular vortex because now you have the ability to open up that kind of a channel anywhere. That is what you did today. You did not find specific vortex areas, but you showed us that you could do this anywhere! And that is a good thing. It definitely was effective.

"The Mother Mountain thanks you as well as the Black Butte. They are well connected deep underground, and you were in areas that really needed some venting. But now you don't need to go to specific locations to do this, locations that were previously used as vents. You can create new vents!"

Omaran said, "I'm glad to hear that it was successful and especially that we can do this anywhere. That is really good news!"

"Good news, indeed!" St. Germain replied.

The Master went on to explain how to better use their new staffs and other tools that could be incorporated in future release ceremonies. Antera and Omaran were inspired to go out for more of this kind of work, but they knew they would probably need to wait until spring.

A week later, they were sitting in their living room to eat dinner. They had gotten back into the habit of having their evening meals there, because the dining room table was often covered by various projects, and it was comfortable enough to eat on the couches.

Omaran casually mentioned, "You know, we haven't had snow in over a week, not since before we did the releasing around Black Butte."

"Wait a minute . . . I know what you are thinking. But we need to wait until spring to do more field work now. It is winter!"

"I just think we could get in another releasing trip before a really big snow comes and we can't get out to Medicine Lake."

"Medicine Lake! We've never even been there, and the roads are probably not open now."

"I stopped by the Ranger Station today and they said they are. Apparently, there hasn't been as much snow out there as we've had on this side of the mountain," Omaran said. He had done his homework.

"Well, maybe . . . ."

Two days later they were on their way to the east side of the mountain. They were surprised at how long the drive was once they left Highway 89, but at least the bumpy road had been paved many years ago. Surprisingly, there was almost no snow and they stopped along the way to check out some unique volcanic terrain. Faith loved it, and she trotted around, sniffing inside caves and small lava tubes.

They continued their journey to the lake. It was smaller than they had anticipated, an old caldera that had eroded and filled with water. The area was sacred to some Native American tribes, and it felt peaceful and serene. No one else was there.

As they gazed at the lake, Omaran suggested, "Maybe we should do one on this side of the lake, and then head farther west for the second."

"That sounds good."

They had decided to do two release points. They hiked a short distance from the lake to a location that felt good, without pressure this time to find a pre-existing vortex. This made it much easier. Plus, they didn't have to tramp down any snow first. They could strike their staffs right on the ground, which they did to their immense satisfaction. After their intense running around the circle, they felt the vent open, and energy started gushing out.

"Ha, ha! It is so cool how this works," Antera declared as they clung to each other while waiting for the dizziness to fade.

Omaran laughed. "Let's go do the other one."

They drove the truck west along a rough dirt road, leaving the lake behind.

"I like that area up there," said Omaran, pointing up a ridge. "It looks like fairly easy walking."

"I wouldn't call it walking."

"Well, yeah . . . hiking, then. It doesn't look too steep."

And it wasn't. In fact, it proved to be a relatively easy ascent up the sharp volcanic rocks to the ridge. They found a lovely area between several large fir trees that seemed to be calling them. The fourth vent was finished just as a light rain was beginning to make its way through the fir needles and find them, so they headed back down to the truck. Driving back to the main road, they explored a bit, taking a different dirt road to see where it went.

"Stop! Look at all that obsidian!" exclaimed Antera as they came upon a hill that was covered with the black, shiny, volcanic stone, which they later identified as Little Glass Mountain. They stopped, got out and very carefully walked around. Some of the boulders were large, and they all looked extremely sharp.

"It's beautiful! I've never seen so much obsidian in one place!" Antera had an undergraduate degree in geology and had been on many field trips to look at rocks and landforms, but never had she seen a whole mountain of this special rock. It was thrilling.

The four vents they had created were sufficient for the time being, and there was already a shift in the feel of the mountain as some of the pent-up energies were harmlessly released. Significant snow arrived, and even Omaran agreed they would have to wait until sometime in the spring to resume this project.

3

Dad's Birthday Party

On the 24th of December, Omaran's father, Gene, had turned ninety years old. Gene's wife, Gerrie, had decided to put on a big birthday party in early January to celebrate this milestone, after the holidays were past. Gerrie invited family and friends, which turned out to be about 200 people, so she rented a large hall with a stage. She asked Antera and Omaran to write and perform a song about Gene's life for the party.

"Let's do something different," Antera said to Omaran when they were thinking about what to write. "How about something like hip hop or rap?"

"You think we could pull that off?" Omaran was doubtful.

"Well, not as ourselves. We'd need costumes, of course."

"So, you mean talk instead of singing? That would be different, all right."

"It will be fun!"

Omaran called Gerrie and asked her some of the details of Gene's life, to make sure he had the main facts straight. He found out, to his chagrin, that he didn't really know all that much about his dad's past. It was interesting that he grew up with this man yet only knew a small part of his story. It made Omaran wonder whether his kids knew much about his earlier life.

Antera wrote the highlights of Gene's life into lyrics, and Omaran put it to music. There was no melody, but there had to be a strong rhythm and arrangement. It really was a fun project. The costume box came out, and wigs . . . then some choreography.

A week before the big event, Omaran happened to be near San Francisco, so he drove up to see his dad and stepmom north of the bay.

Gerrie was out doing errands, but Gene was home. He yelled for Omaran to come on in when he knocked, rather than getting up out of his big recliner. Gene was a heavy man and had gotten even bigger in the past few years, making it hard to get around. He was also one of those people who has good things to say about everyone, and he was always delighted to have visitors. Even though he was undoubtedly uncomfortable, he had a big smile on his face and a ready laugh.

Omaran hugged him and sat down on the sofa. "Hey, big party coming up! I hear there are about 200 people coming. Are you looking forward to it?"

"Absolutely not," Gene said, his smile fading. "I can barely get out of my chair. I can't see well. I know I don't look good. I don't want people to see me like this, and I feel miserable. I really wish there was no party."

Omaran blinked, taken aback. "I'm sure that's got to be hard for you. I wouldn't want to do it either if I felt like that."

"I don't know why Gerrie wants to do this, but I haven't been able to talk her out of it." Gene shrugged. "I guess it's too late to cancel now."

Omaran nodded. "Yeah." He suddenly had a strong urge. "But guess what. Antera and I wrote a song for you that we're going to sing at the party, and actually, I have my guitar with me, and I'd like to sing it to you now."

"Why? You afraid I won't be around to hear it in a week?"

"No, Dad. It's just that when you hear a new song for the first time, it's hard to catch it all, and this one's got a lot of words."

Gene agreed to hear the song, so Omaran went out to the truck and got his guitar. He sang it and even remembered all the lyrics of the ten verses.

He was born in Topeka over ninety years ago . . .

"Bravo! I love it!" Gene clapped. "How did you know all that about me?"

Playfully, Omaran said, "What? I'm your son!"

Four days later, Gerrie called. She said, "I have some bad news. Your dad passed on this morning."

"What?" Omaran said. "What do you mean?"

"I mean he's dead."

Omaran was shocked. "What? Oh, no. What happened?"

"He got up out of his chair and fell. That was it, he was gone."

Omaran was momentarily stunned into silence. He sat down and tried to process the news. "Well, what will you do about the birthday party? It's next weekend! How can you get ahold of everyone?"

"The party is going to happen. I'm turning it into a memorial party."

Gerrie was a strong woman and could probably pull it off, Omaran thought. But what of all the other people who were expecting a birthday party? He didn't feel like celebrating and knew others wouldn't either.

"And I want you to sing your song," she added.

Omaran said, "I don't think so. It is a funny song, and we were going to dress in costumes and all that. I don't think we can do it now."

"The show must go on. You know he would want you to."

Omaran said, "We will think about it, but it would be hard. This is just too much right now."

"Well, I'll be counting on you. I have many more calls to make, so we will talk later. Can you call your brothers and sister?"

After hanging up and telling Antera the news, Omaran made the difficult calls to his siblings. Then he and Antera sat together to focus on helping Gene in his passing process. They saw that his spirit was still lingering in his home, in confusion, though his body had already been taken to the morgue. They talked with him, explaining what had happened, so he would have more clarity about what to do next and to help him move to the highest place possible.

Antera said, "He seems to understand what happened now." She paused, listening. "But he wants to stay and make sure Gerrie and other family members will be all right. Maybe you can assure him."

"You know what a strong woman Gerrie is," Omaran told his dad. "She will be fine. Plus, she has been preparing for your death for many years." This brought a stream of tears.

"He is also concerned about the birthday party," Antera added.

"She says the party will still go on, Dad. It will be a celebration of your life." To Antera he said, "I think he is happy about that. I see him smiling."

"Yes."

"I guess Gerrie is right about the party. My dad would want everyone to have a good time and celebrate his life rather than being sad."

"Okay, if you can do the song I can do it," Antera agreed. "I bet he will enjoy the party much more now."

Omaran nodded. "Last time I saw him he really didn't want to have the party, in his condition."

Even though his dad had lived a long, fulfilling life, Omaran would miss him very much. Gene was like a rock for all the family, steady and always there to support anyone. Omaran was very grateful he'd sung the song for his dad ahead of time, not knowing why he had been drawn to do that until now.

So, the party went on, and despite many phone calls, some people did not find out about Gene's death until they arrived. Antera and Omaran dressed in their costumes and did their hip-hop song about Gene's life. Many people shared experiences and memories, and it was truly a memorable evening. And Gene was there, enjoying it all from his unencumbered state.

4

Psychic Attack

Over the next few days at home, Antera and Omaran felt tired, as if they had been drained. The weather prohibited more land healing, and while they still had many things to keep them busy, their usual drive and spark seemed to be missing. They had been home from their tour for a few months now, and it was time to find work so they could pay the mortgage and keep their house. Omaran had really enjoyed this break from construction work, and he wasn't looking forward to doing that again, even part time. His body was strong, but even the thought of it made him tired. He really wished he had another way of making a living.

Antera was thinking about opening a practice using the SCIO, the quantum biofeedback machine they had purchased with money from the sale of their RV. It had helped both of them tremendously with their health while they had stayed in the Bay Area, and in the process, she had learned much more about the energy aspects of health as well as about psychic attack. When she ran the machine on either of them it showed that certain kinds of harmful energies were still coming into their space, so she continued to occasionally use the machine to cancel them out. She wondered if their current malaise might be related to these kinds of interfering energies.

One evening in mid-January they sat down to meditate together, hoping that a Master would talk to them. They got comfortable as they sat quietly and raised their consciousness to a higher level. Mother Mary appeared, wanting to speak.

Mary said, "I greet you, my cherished ones, and bring you the blessings of all who are watching over you and helping whenever they can. We very much want you to know that we are here for you."

Omaran put his hand on his heart and said, "Thank you. We feel that."

Mary went on, "We know sometimes you feel that the burdens you carry are too much. Sometimes you feel you can't keep going on as a Lightworker, carrying the Light for the Order of Melchizedek. I know how hard this can be at times, and how interfering forces can try to stop you and make you feel it is not worth the effort. This is all a part of being a Lightworker at this time.

"Your greatest defense is your connection with the Source of all energy in this universe. This cannot be taken from you, though many have tried. All Lightworkers who are still carrying the torch to the best of their abilities have been through so much. For eons, interfering beings have tried to cut off your connection to God, by changing your DNA or closing off certain neural connections in your brain and spinal cord, all to control the masses. But there have always been those who maintained their connection through it all. These are the Lightworkers! These are the bright lights!

"There will be times when you succumb and times when you soar above. Just know that this entire year will be up and down, because of the many turbulent energies coming toward the planet. You must continue on and realize that there will be some low days, and some difficult decisions. Allow the flow. Allow things to move forward gradually and steadily, and don't let obstacles sway you from your path. There will be obstacles—there is no question—and you want to go over them or around them but stay on the path. That is the primary task—not to get distracted, not to go so far around an obstacle that you take up another path, not to get so stopped by an obstacle that you don't move forward at all. Keep going, plodding along, knowing that the universe will provide you a path.

"Know that there is tremendous support all around you, every moment of the day now. We are never far because of the work you are doing, because we see your Light shining, and because we know that if we add to your Light, it will go somewhere.

"Remember, it is always darkest before the dawn. The last decade has been very dark at times. But you know it cannot stay dark for long. A decade is but an instant in the overall scheme. So just keep shining your Light. Keep holding that torch.

"I'm saying all this because I see that there has been a dip in both of your Lights, partly due to the death of your father, Omaran, and your grief. This is normal. And it is partly because of being around many people over the weekend who gave you energies which are not of the Light. You brought those energies back with you. Also, the overall Light that you shine calls in that which is not of the Light."

"That makes sense," Omaran said. "We are both feeling drained. Sometimes I do feel discouraged and wonder if all the Lightwork we do is really making a difference."

"Therefore, your choices are to keep on keeping on or to give up, as many have." Mary went on. "But I know you won't give up. If you have stuck it out this far, there's very little chance you will give up now. And I speak of all the Lightworkers who have come this far and are still holding the Light. You are the ones who are the heroes, holding the Light through the darkest of times.

"We support you in any way we can. Through the years we have watched your Light grow, and we have seen you learn some major lessons through some very difficult times, and still your Light shines. This is a sign of the true Light Warrior."

Omaran said, "Thank you so much for your support. No, we won't stop. And we will clear anything we brought home with us. Today, when I was feeling poorly, I took the time and brought in the Light. That changed everything! I know what to do, I just need to remember. I also need to come to grips with having to go back into construction after our trip.

"We do have a question. Antera has noticed through the SCIO sessions that we still have psychic attack coming in from unknown sources. Is this some kind of electronic warfare? And whatever it is, do you have any suggestions on the best way to counteract it?"

Mary answered, "This is a very specific thoughtform and coalition of energies that have been projected at both of you and many other Lightworkers, to impinge upon your thoughts. The purpose is to stop you in your work, even making you feel hopeless, or making you think that the work is futile. Just by becoming aware of it, its effect is decreased.

"It is being projected at many people who can make waves in the world, who can change the way people think, and make them freer. It is the free thinkers who are the most threatening to those who want to control others—it is those of you who do not watch the TV, who eat well, who are careful about what you put in your mind and your body. You are the biggest threat."

"Okay, thank you," Omaran said. "Are we doing enough to protect our home and property? We do call in the Light and power it up. I feel that we're creating so much Light here that we're pretty much protected, but perhaps I'm naïve in that."

Mary said, "Yes, I would say you are naïve. Every time someone comes to your house, they bring energy with them. And when you go out and come back, you bring energy with you. Unless you are so diligent that you cleanse everyone, including yourself, before they come in the door, every single time, there is always going to be an exchange of energy with the outside world.

"Your greatest tool is being a Pillar of Light and maintaining your connection as strongly as possible. That will make you safe. But you may not be able to hold it around the whole property. Others have lived here, and their energy remains. That may take a while to cleanse thoroughly."

Omaran was feeling better. He said, "2006 seems like it's going to be quite a ride. We're very grateful to be able to keep in contact with all of you."

"I would like to give you both my blessing, my embrace, and the love that is forever and abundant here. Be the blazing Light with all of your being, with your clear mind, clear body, and soaring spirit. I thank you once again and leave you with my blessing."

Two weeks later, a major setback occurred.

5

Compromised

Antera was sitting at her desk in her session room, running energy for a family member on the SCIO, when she heard Omaran frantically screaming her name. She ran downstairs and outside to the driveway where he was using the table saw to cut the wooden objects they used for the Land Healing Project. There was snow on the ground, but because of the urgency of his calls she didn't stop to put on shoes or a coat, dashing out in her socks.

Omaran was standing next to the saw, holding his hand, screaming, "I've cut my finger off! It's just hanging! I can't even find my thumb, it is gone! How did that happen? Oh, God, give me one second back! I'll never play guitar or piano again. It'll never be the same. What have I done? Why did this happen?"

It was a gut-wrenching sight. Antera felt his angst like a blast of cold wind. She looked at his left hand. The first finger was hanging only by a flap of skin, and the thumb was missing. The third finger was also deeply cut. He had turned the saw off, but he was clearly in shock.

"Okay, it's going to be all right. I'll take you to the hospital. Sit in the car and I'll be right back."

She ran inside and collected a jacket, shoes, and her purse. Her socks were wet, but she didn't bother to change them, putting her shoes on over them. Grabbing a clean dishtowel, she ran out and wrapped it around Omaran's hand, which, surprisingly, was not bleeding very much. He was pale but calmer now, deliberately taking deep breaths.

Antera put out a prayer for help as she quickly scanned the snow for his thumb. She thought there was probably a limit on how long fingers would survive on their own, if it was even possible to sew them back on. And there it was, about ten feet away, a lonely brown digit atop the white snow. It had a bandage on it from another injury. Scooping it up, she got in the car but realized she could not hold the thumb properly and drive, so Omaran held it in his uninjured hand.

"How much does it hurt?" asked Antera.

"It is just numb, really. I don't feel much pain," Omaran said softly.

"That's good."

The hospital was only a five-minute drive away, and fortunately the emergency ward was almost empty, and they took him in quickly, immediately cleaning his hand and doing x-rays.

When the doctor came in, he examined Omaran's hand and said, "I'm afraid all we can do is sew them up."

"What? Why can't the fingers be sewn back on?" Antera exclaimed.

"There are only a few microsurgeons in the world who could do that. And none of them are close. And even if one were available, it would be a very long rehab."

"He can do a long rehab," Antera insisted.

Omaran chimed in, "I can do a long rehab."

The doctor looked at the hand again, then at Omaran, seeming to consider it.

Antera said, "Please see what you can do. He is a musician and a carpenter. He needs his hand. We will do whatever it takes."

"All right, I'll make some calls and see if it is possible. But it is a long shot so don't get your hopes up." He left.

After sitting with Omaran for a few minutes, Antera went looking for the doctor to make sure he was still on the case. The emergency room area was small, and she found his office without much wandering. The door was open, so she was able to peek inside. He was talking on a phone while he held up the x-ray and described the injury in detail to, she hoped, a hand surgeon. She went back to wait with Omaran, and they both sent prayers for more help.

After a while, the doctor stuck his head in the room and asked, "Do you smoke?"

"No," answered Omaran. The doctor turned and walked away.

It wasn't long before he came back and said that an outstanding microsurgeon happened to be available at California Pacific Medical

Hospital in San Francisco, and would do it, provided Omaran could get there within six hours of the accident, after which the fingers would not take. This was 300 miles away, and it had already been over an hour since the accident, but Antera and Omaran were very happy that there was a chance.

As the hospital staff arranged for a small plane to take him, Omaran decided that he wanted to be fully conscious because the time factor may become important, and he wanted to be able to focus, meditate, and bring in all the help from Masters and angels he could summon. He knew he couldn't do that if they gave him pain killers, so these he declined when asked. Some of the initial numbness had worn off and the pain was about a four on a scale of ten.

Omaran said a tearful goodbye to Antera, who needed to drive to San Francisco because there was no room in the plane for her, and she would need to have a car to get home. The orderlies pushed him in a wheelchair out to an ambulance. It was 6:00 and the accident had happened at 3:45. They drove toward Weed Airport, about eight miles north.

The ambulance crew introduced themselves to Omaran as they sped to Weed. Mark, a dark-haired young man who looked to be in his early twenties, was driving. A second man, Steve, seemed to be in charge, directing Mark and making sure Omaran was all right. By the time they arrived at the small airport, it had begun raining, and Steve said that probably meant snow at the higher elevations where planes fly, but unless he got a call on his phone telling him otherwise, the plane was going to land. It was supposed to touch down at 6:20.

At 6:30 the landing lights turned on, and Steve said, "That's a good sign." When Omaran asked why, he said, "Because the pilot turns on the lights."

But ten minutes later, Steve's phone rang. As soon as he got off the phone Omaran knew the plane wasn't landing. "We're driving to Redding, aren't we?" He asked. Redding was at least an hour south of Mount Shasta.

Steve said, "Yep."

"We probably won't be there until 8:00 then." Omaran knew that would be cutting it very close.

Again, Steve said, "Yep. But there might be slight problem."

Omaran asked, "What?"

"Did you hear the siren a few minutes ago?"

"Yes," replied Omaran.

"Seems there's some guy speeding south on I-5, and they've tried to slow him with tack strips across the freeway, which is slowing the rest of the traffic. The guy managed to drive around them. So, there may be some traffic at some point."

Steve told Mark to head for Redding and to use the lights and siren continuously. Omaran thought that Mark was the perfect age to drive an ambulance when speed was of the essence.

As they started out for Redding, Omaran knew that if everything else went smoothly, it would be at least six hours before he was in San Francisco, so he began praying even more to his guides and angels for help, while he poured energy into his hand and the severed fingers. His intention was to add at least thirty minutes to the six-hour window.

About twenty minutes after they headed south, Steve, who was monitoring the chase, turned back to Omaran and said, "They got him, just a few miles ahead of us." Then he turned to Mark and said, "I'll guide you through traffic when we get there."

Mark said, "No problem."

In another minute they were in it. Mark used the siren, the lights, and the horn while Steve directed him, saying, "Get on the left shoulder. Now cut right. Get that guy out of there! Head for the right shoulder, cut back left . . . lay on that horn!"

In less than two minutes, Mark and Steve got through more than a mile of traffic. Omaran thought they were incredible! As they increased speed again, Omaran said, "If I'm able to get to San Francisco in time, it will be because of you two."

For the rest of the drive, he continued to meditate and charge up his hand. He knew he had to come to terms with the possibility that he may only have three digits on his hand the rest of his life, so he focused on being all right with that. Then, if the others were saved, it would be a plus. With tears streaming down his face, he silently declared, "This will not stop Antera and me from the work we are doing. We are stronger than this!"

They got to the Redding airport, found the plane, and Omaran was gently hustled on. There were two medical people for the flight, Tim and Scott, plus the female pilot.

Just as Tim began settling Omaran into an upright stretcher, the pilot said, "Tim, can I talk to you a minute?"

Omaran knew there was a problem . . . something in her voice. Tim walked off with her, and when he came back, he said, "We have to get another pilot because if she flew us down to San Francisco she would have to stay the night as she would have too many hours logged to fly right back. Another pilot is on his way over and it will just be a few minutes delay."

By the time the new pilot arrived and the plane was warmed up, it was 8:25, and they took off for the one-hour flight. Despite all the delays, Omaran was calm and surrendered his fate to the Divine.

About half-way into the flight, the pilot answered a call, muttered something, and hung up. He said to Tim and Scott, "They're not very happy in San Francisco with the speed this is going."

The pilot made some adjustments, and the plane picked up speed, knocking almost eight minutes off the flight time. After landing, Omaran was again put into an ambulance, accompanied by both Tim and Scott, who told the driver, "This is a Code Three. Use lights and make some noise."

For the first time since the incident had happened, Omaran began to relax just a little. He would know soon if the surgery could happen. When they arrived at the hospital and he got out, he was surprised to see all three of his kids and a daughter-in-law waiting for him. He cried with joy as he was wheeled in.

They got right to it, so Omaran assumed the fingers were still all right. It seemed like a miracle! It had been almost seven hours since the accident. After checking his hand, an orderly had to take off his wedding ring, which was excruciatingly painful. Omaran decided that it was a good time for morphine.

Two surgeons started working on the thumb before Omaran was even put to sleep. The team had four surgeons, led by Dr. Buntik, who he found out later was one of the two top surgeons in the world for this operation. The surgery took four hours.

It was almost midnight when Antera finally arrived. She had arranged with a neighbor to take care of the pets, packed bare necessities, and driven as fast as she dared. Knowing she would not be there when he arrived, she had called Omaran's kids, who lived in the San Francisco area, to see if anyone could be there for him. That they all dropped their plans and showed up was a testament to their love for their dad, and a big relief to her.

Sitting in the waiting room with the others, Antera closed her eyes for a moment to psychically see inside the operating room. There was Omaran, floating serenely above his body, and below, a group of surgeons and doctors working intently. She tried to contact Omaran to comfort him, but he did not respond, probably because of the drugs they had given him, so she just sent him love. Around the room, she could see a host of angels and Light Beings, so she knew Omaran was in good hands.

Dr. Buntik came out after it was finished and announced that it was successful. They had been able to reattach both the thumb and finger! He briefly described the procedure of attaching the bones, tendons, muscles, and the nerves, which were the most difficult. Antera and the kids were completely amazed at the technology, and so grateful.

The surgeon also explained, "I had to use two alternate arteries as he had apparently damaged the main ones."

"It's not surprising. He has been a carpenter for a long time." Antera replied.

When Omaran finally awoke, he said to Antera, "You know, I got exactly what I asked for. Because of all the love, quick work, an incredible number of people starting with you, and so many miracles involved with timing, I got that one second back. I am so blessed!"

The hospital stay was one week. They gave Antera a cot to sleep on, so she stayed with him, taking one drive home and back to get some clothes and food. She had packed very little, thinking she would only be gone for one night. She also brought the SCIO back with her, and discretely did energy work on Omaran in the hospital room.

His hand was completely bandaged and had to be elevated at all times. When they got home and the bandages finally came off, it was a rather shocking, even gruesome, sight. The hand was swollen, with probably a hundred stitches and many pins sticking out, holding it together. Plus, it was covered with dried blood.

Antera looked at it and said, "It looks like Frankenstein's hand."

"Yeah," Omaran agreed. "Can you clean it up a bit?"

She looked at it closer. "I'm kind-of afraid to touch it. But I will try. They said not to use any antiseptic on it, just water."

Trying not to rub hard, and avoiding pins and stiches, she wiped a bit of the blood off with some warm water and cotton swabs. It didn't look much better. "That's all I can do. I don't feel confident."

He needed the whole queen bed to himself, to accommodate all the pillows holding his hand up, so she moved a twin bed into the bedroom for herself. It was definitely going to be a long rehab.

Omaran needed to keep his hand above his elbow and his elbow above his heart, day and night. So, when he got out of bed and walked around, he had to hold his hand above his head. "Do you have a question, Dear?" Antera teased him.

She drove him three times a week to Redding for physical therapy, starting right after they got home. Alex, the therapist, was able to clean more of the blood off, to Antera's relief. The daily hand exercises began, starting slowly and building to longer and more frequent efforts. Omaran worked up to several hours every day, in addition to sending energy to his hand.

Two weeks after surgery, they drove back to San Francisco for Omaran's first post-op exam with Dr. Buntik.

"How are you doing?" the surgeon asked.

"Great!" Omaran said. "Alex, the hand therapist, thinks I'm doing well also, but we'll have to see what you think."

Dr. Buntik proceeded to take off the gauze, looked at the hand and asked, "Were they both completely off?"

Omaran said, "The thumb was, and the index finger was just hanging by skin."

The doctor examined it, took pictures, and praised his own work, saying, "Beautiful! Good, really good!" He paused, then said, "Crazy good! With the bandages off, you can even take a shower."

Omaran asked, "How long do I have to keep my hand elevated?" He had already asked Alex the same question two days earlier, and his answer had been two to four weeks.

"Oh, you can put your hand down now."

Antera said, "Are you sure?"

"Oh, he will put it back up. It will hurt too much."

Antera burst out laughing, and the doctor joined in. Omaran didn't think it was all that funny.

Back home, Omaran continued working in earnest on his hand exercises, working up to six hours per day. Antera had taken over all his jobs, plus taking care of him full time because he was unable to do much for himself. During the night, every time he moved, she woke up to help him change position, and make sure the hand was properly elevated. He was a deep sleeper and she a light sleeper, so she got very little sleep. But the healing was going well.

Antera was walking Faith one afternoon in mid-February when she realized that she was exhausted like she had never been before. It was hard work just putting one foot in front of the other. She was not just tired, but completely drained. The stress and lack of sleep from the whole experience had emptied her previously inexhaustible energy. Never before had she used up all her body's backup resources, the third and fourth winds. There was nothing else to draw from.

Faith was a sensitive, undemanding dog, and she seemed to understand that today's walk was a slow one. She trotted around, entertaining herself with the smells of wild animals and plunging into patches of snow. As Antera meandered, following Faith through the woods, she gave thanks for living in such a paradise, and that Omaran had gotten his fingers back. She suddenly felt the trees reaching their energy out to her, as if they felt her lack and wanted to help. It did help, and she soaked it up, thanking them.

When she and Faith made it home, Antera asked Omaran if he needed anything. He was on one of the couches with his hand propped up with several pillows, massaging his fingers. He said he was fine, so she allowed herself a few minutes of rest, lying down on the couch and closing her eyes before making dinner.

6

Melchizedek

Omaran was meditating on and off all day, between hand exercises, calling in huge amounts of Light to help with his healing and to speed his spiritual evolution. He had a lot of time to think about the injury. Was it karma? Psychic attack? What was the deeper reason? He was sure it was no coincidence that he had been making land-healing sculptures when it happened. It had effectively stopped their work for an indefinite time. He also knew he had felt irritable that day, not fully present, and he should not have been using a table saw. That was easy to see in hindsight.

Though the Masters had reminded them many times about being diligent in their psychic protection because the work they were doing tended to draw in opposing forces, he knew he had been lax. Why didn't he concentrate on that every day? He guessed that a part of him did not believe that it was necessary, no matter how many times he was told. And that had put not only him, but Antera, at risk. He knew he needed to learn the lessons from this, and fast.

After dinner, Antera said, "I'm getting a strong urge from the Masters. They want us to check in as soon as we can. Would you be up for that this evening?"

"Well, I'll have to check my schedule, but I think I'm free."

"And you're getting ornery. That's probably what they want to talk to you about."

"Ha, ha!"

Half an hour later, they prepared themselves for talking with the Masters. Antera said, "We are being taken up into the Realms of Illumination. No one has come forth yet to speak but we are being surrounded by legions of Beings of Light. This seems to be a critical moment. Are you all right?"

Omaran said, "Yes."

"I'm feeling a lot of energy, a lot of interest and activity. And Jeshua is our guide; he is holding out his hands to both of us, inviting us to follow him. We're walking along a Path of Light. All around us are Legions of Light led by Archangel Michael. He's the one I recognize, anyway. He's on a white horse with wings, galloping ahead.

"This is the place of Illumined Truth and Wisdom, the wisdom of the ages. In this place there can be no darkness, no falsehood, no illusion. Only truth that stands under the Light of the Spiritual Sun of the great Masters of the Universe. Now we've arrived and are in a vast space surrounded by golden and white Light. Many of the Order of Melchizedek are here, and we are surrounded by them. Melchizedek himself is sitting in front of us. Jeshua is taking us to him because he is the one who called us. Jeshua presents us, and we bow. On either side of Melchizedek are these huge angels of magnificent Light.

"He says, 'Rise and look me in the eyes.' And his eyes are like stars . . . infinity . . . the whole universe. In his eyes everything is exposed, nothing can be hidden."

Melchizedek said, "What do you see?"

Omaran answered, "I see Light. I see joy. I see and feel love."

"You see yourself! You ARE these things, do you understand?"

"Yes."

"Do you really understand?"

"I do, more with each passing day."

"Come forth, Omaran. Come forth into your absolute beingness. Come forth into who you really are. Do you see who you are?"

Omaran hesitated, then said, "I feel like I am what I want to be: a powerful, loving, serving being."

Melchizedek said, "There is no doubt. You have come full circle. You have been through the trials. You have been through the Fires of Purification. You have been through the Flame of Initiation and have emerged victorious. There is no more room for doubt! There is no more room for foolishness, Omaran! Claim who you are!"

Omaran sat up straighter. He could feel powerful energy pulsing through him. "I am Omaran the Christ."

It felt good to say that. He understood that Christ was a title associated with embracing the Christ Light, an energy of higher consciousness and healing. It was his goal, as he evolved, to become a Christed Being on Earth. Each time he proclaimed that he was a Christ it aligned him with those higher frequencies more fully.

"Trust your wisdom!" Melchizedek affirmed. "I recognize and acknowledge who you are. And by doing so, I expect you to BE who you are. I expect you to serve the way you have asked to serve. Do you understand?"

"I hope so. I know I've been asking to be a giant Beacon of Light. I've been asking to let the Christ Light come through me. I want to go into the Catacombs again and do more of that work, since we can't do land healing right now. I guess I'm not sure what I should be doing next."

"You are in the Realms of Illumined Truth. In this place you are the Beacon of Light. When you leave this place, you carry with you only a part of who you are. Therefore, it is essential that you maintain whatever connection you can to this place, to these Beings of Light, to the Order of Melchizedek and the Ascended Masters who support you in your work. This connection is essential to your success. If at any time you allow this connection to be compromised or severed, or rendered useless by doubt, lack of faith, or other forces, then you will not be able to serve the Light.

"As long as you maintain your connection to the Realms of Illumined Truth, the Spiritual Sun, and us, you have nothing to fear. You have no reason to wonder whether you are doing the right thing, for you will always know, in every moment, what the right path is for you. As long as you have your connection intact, you can go anywhere! You can carry the Light into the darkest places and come back without a scratch. You can carry your Light into the depths, as long as you maintain that connection.

"It is up to you to decide, task by task, whether you are strong enough to carry the Light and maintain your Pillar of Light. There may be times when you are not strong enough, and you will know by assessing your connection and how much support you have through your connection. Never allow that to be severed, even for a second, even for a millisecond.

"If you allow your connection to be severed by any means, then you will have compromised your task and yourself. I cannot stress this enough.

Then you allow harmful energies in, such as when you had your accident. By being a shining Light on the planet, you are a target. I'm sure you recognize that aspect of the work. Therefore, you must be very aware of what is going on within you and around you at all times. If you are not aware, then you will be susceptible. Understood?"

"Yes. I found that out the hard way." He wiggled his injured fingers. "But I still want to do the work. It is what I and we are here to do."

"Your work is extremely useful for the Forces of Light, but I want you to understand fully what you are getting yourself into. You do not have to take on any of these missions. But if you are strong enough and can do it, you can aid the balance of Light on the planet by delving into the source of much darkness. There are many missions, and very few Lightworkers.

"Now . . . let me see your Sword of Light."

Omaran chuckled nervously.

"I am serious, let me see it. Raise it up."

He grabbed his etheric sword and held it up with his non-physical hand.

The Master looked at it and said, "Do you understand the significance of this tool?"

"Not fully. I used it to do the catacomb work two months ago and it worked well. And just the other day I used it to help protect our property. But I don't fully understand it."

"A Sword of Light is different from a staff. A staff is used to create energy forms and protection, and to bring forth energy for a task. Your sword is different. Do I need to explain further?"

"I would like a little more explanation because I don't know how to use the sword correctly. When I go into dark places should I have my sword out? Should it be leading the way? Or does that draw too much attention?"

"If you are trying to not call attention to yourself, it is too late! There is much attention aimed at you and your mate. So, you may as well raise your sword and claim it. There is no more hiding. The time for hiding is gone for both of you. You both tried to hide for many lifetimes.

"I am going to refer you to Archangel Michael. He will show you how to use your sword. You can work with him over the next few weeks in your meditations. His sword sends out a blue-white light, like lightning. It is used to transform darkness into Light.

"When you transform the darkness into Light, you are not destroying or harming anything. And this, herein, is the key. Transforming darkness into Light merely transforms it into its original pure Light essence. Darkness has all been created. It was originally Light. Therefore, the darkness that you transform, you are taking back to its original form."

Omaran said, "Thank you for telling me all of this, I am honored."

"You have come a long way."

"I've had good teachers."

"Thank you for your work and thank you for coming tonight to my summons."

"It's my pleasure."

When Antera and Omaran opened their eyes, Omaran thanked her, and they hugged. He said, "I guess I need to get better at my awareness. When you channel these beings and I'm in their energy, it all looks so easy. I need to maintain that perspective and connection in my daily life."

"We sure don't want any more mishaps when one of us gets distracted and lets in harmful energy."

"No, we sure don't!"

7

A New Practice

It was a bright, sunny day in early March, six weeks after Omaran's injury. He had followed up with Archangel Michael as best he could, in learning how to use his sword. It was a powerful tool, and the more he learned and experimented, the more he realized that he had just scratched the surface on its capabilities and uses.

He was sitting on the couch doing his hand exercises while Antera did a session on the SCIO upstairs in her session room, the small bedroom they had thought would be a guest room when they built the house, but which had been repurposed. She finished and came part way down the stairs to check on him.

"How are your fingers? They certainly look better," she said as she poked her head over the railing.

He wiggled them. "I can bend this far. Alex says they are getting much better. But I'm really getting tired of these exercises."

Antera descended the rest of the stairs and went into the living room, sitting next to Omaran. "I bet. I remember you saying you could do a long rehab, though."

"Okay, okay, so I did. I'm not complaining."

"Good."

"Well, maybe I'm complaining a little bit. But it's not really about the exercises."

"About what, then?"

"We need to talk about our finances," Omaran said soberly. "I won't be able to do any kind of construction for a while, probably months. And our savings will soon be depleted. I don't want to lose the house."

On the day of the accident, Antera had decided that Omaran's hand was far more important than the house, so if they could not make their payments and they lost it, it would be worth it. They were self-employed and had no health insurance. But she didn't really think that would happen. She had always been taken care of, and her faith was strong, so somehow she knew that it would all work out.

She said, "I know. I'm looking at ways I can make money. I feel very confident about the SCIO now, and I think I will start doing this kind of session professionally." She had taken four weeks of training in Los Angeles last year and had practiced the complex software on the two of them and other family members for over six months. They were both very impressed with what the system had done for their health. She had been doing channeled sessions but preferred to teach others to get their own guidance rather than getting it through her. So, this seemed a good alternate session practice.

Omaran thought about that. "These sessions have to be in person, right? How would you build a practice here in this small town?"

"I'm thinking that all I need is an audience. If I give a talk about it, people will want sessions," Antera said. "In fact, that would be fun to do. I'm going to start working on a slide show now."

She abruptly got up, climbed the stairs to the office, and started working on her computer. She had never made a slide show before but thought it could not be too hard to learn the Power Point software.

In two weeks, she had finished the presentation and was happy with it, and next she had to figure out how to project it. The newest technology was a slide projector that would connect with a laptop computer and project the images onto a screen. They purchased a projector along with a big screen on a tripod, and she was ready to go out and give lectures. Now she needed to gather people.

Help came from an unexpected source. Her former employer and friend, Byron, had heard about Omaran's accident and wanted to help. He told a mutual friend, Stacia, who offered to hold an event at her medical office in the Bay Area, to help Antera start building a clientele. Stacia said she would send flyers out to her mailing list and set up a large downstairs room for an introductory evening.

Antera gratefully took her up on her offer, and it came together very quickly. On the evening of the event, the room was packed with people who were fascinated by the presentation and demonstration. Omaran helped schedule people for sessions, and Stacia allowed Antera to use the room over the next two days for them. Thus, Antera's new practice was launched.

On the drive back to Mount Shasta, Omaran reflected on how things had developed. "When I think about all that has happened in the past few weeks, I'm just amazed and so incredibly grateful for all the blessings we have received. We're surrounded by angels, both in the physical and the etheric."

"We certainly are. We would never have chosen this particular path, but I'm fine with it and once again I know we are being led on just the right journey for us. And for you, my Love, this must be a faith builder."

"I certainly can't disagree. No matter what happens we always seem to be taken care of."

"Seem to be?"

"No matter what happens, we're always taken care of."

Stacia let Antera use the room on weekends, so she drove to the Bay Area once a month to do sessions for two days, scheduling five to seven a day, each 1.5 hours with a half hour between them. These were long days, but worth it.

Wanting to find closer places to work, Antera also connected with a woman named Liv, who owned a new-age store in Redding, only a one-hour drive south. Liv, a warm, open-hearted person, was very excited to offer Antera an introductory evening as well as a room to use for sessions as often as she wanted it. So, she started going to Redding one day per week, then found a similar place at a chiropractor's office in Ashland, Oregon, to the north, and went there one day per week. With these three offices and a developing clientele over the phone—the sessions were effective at a distance as well—in a relatively short time Antera had enough business to cover their expenses.

But they both knew they were still under some psychic attack, and though they were diligent with the protection skills they had, there were times when they were vulnerable, such as when they were tired. On one of her monthly trips, Antera was hauling her equipment, which she had stacked on a dolly, from the car into her Bay Area office. It had rained the night before, and she was pulling the heavy dolly up some wet redwood stairs when suddenly her feet slid out from under her, and she fell hard on the deck. It was a severe blow to her spine, but she managed to get up.

Her only thought was that she could not possibly be laid up while Omaran needed her help. And she had to make her appointments. She managed to get the equipment into the room then found some aspirin and took two. Her spine had taken the brunt of many injuries earlier in life in gymnastics and dance, plus she had been thrown by a horse as a teenager. She hoped this one would not cause too much pain, but she could already feel a big bruise forming. It hurt to sit. But sit she did, making it through the day through the force of her will and with the help of an extra pillow on her chair.

When she called Omaran that evening and told him she had fallen, he exclaimed, "Oh, no! Were you pushed? Was it psychic attack? It's not like you to slip."

Antera thought about the incident. Earlier, she had deliberately re-experienced it over and over in her mind to release any emotional charge in the fall and help it heal, even going outside to touch the deck where it happened to clear any energy she had left there.

The previous night, she had slept in the truck alone on a street in the city, not realizing how stressful that would be. Knowing it was not only illegal but unsafe because the camper shell did not even lock, had kept her on edge all night. That she would not do again.

Not wanting Omaran to worry, she said, "I think I have just been tired and that makes me vulnerable. So, it didn't take much to throw me off balance."

"Well, protect yourself better and come home to me safely tomorrow. Maybe you can rest."

"I will. Don't worry. You just keep working on your hand."

As Antera hung up the phone, she thought about the land healing and other work they were doing. Why was it so threatening to those who didn't want humanity to move into higher consciousness? The Masters had told them over and over to be careful and protect themselves, and they were doing the best they could. It was quite a learning process. But they both agreed that there was no choice about whether they would continue or not. They were all in, no matter what. A couple of injuries would not stop them.

8

Achilles Heel

The first hints of spring were emerging on the mountain. Buds of new growth swelled with promise. Walking slowly around their property with Faith, Antera played her wooden flute for the nature spirits. She could sense them gathering and following her. These etheric beings seemed to especially love the tones of this wind instrument, even though Antera knew she was far from an accomplished player. Any tones seemed to please them. So, she continued to blow, making up simple tunes as she sauntered, avoiding the patches of snow that lingered in the shady areas. It was the first time this year she had done this.

She knew that keeping the nature spirits happy was important for the land and all the plants and animals of the area. She and Omaran had planted a couple hundred trees, including quite a few fruit trees, and because of the very poor volcanic soil, they needed all the help they could get, both physically and energetically. The nature spirits also helped to protect the property.

After finishing her rounds, she called Faith to go inside. It was quite chilly and the fire in the woodstove inside was welcome warmth. As she warmed her hands, she gave a silent thanks to the fire spirits.

"How did it go out there?" Omaran asked as he came out of the pantry. He had just put a load of clothes in the washer. Being able to put his hand down for short periods of time enabled him to do a few things around the house.

Antera was happy that he could do a few chores again but wondered if it wasn't too early. It had only been a couple of months since his injury and surgery. But she decided not to mention it, knowing that pushing him to take it easy with his hand would be met with resistance. "I think everyone's happy out there. They are all glad we finally came home."

"We are happy about that too!" He smiled and she smiled back, sharing their gratitude.

As Antera climbed the stairs to the office for work, Omaran tried to think of other things he could do, while he sat on the couch to do his hand exercises. He was so tired of sitting around! He yelled up the stairs, "Want me to go to the store for anything?"

"You can't drive yet!"

"Why not? It only takes one hand to drive an automatic. Alex said I can drive as soon as I feel confident."

"Do you really think you can carry groceries?"

"I can just take a basket out to the car. And you can help unload them when I get back."

"And getting money out of your wallet with one hand?"

He hadn't thought about that. "I will try that before going."

Antera paused as she thought about it. "Okay. There is a list on the fridge. Be careful. You don't want to set back your healing." She thought he would have to find out for himself if he was ready or not.

He was excited to go out, and a little nervous. It took two gloves, one on top of the other, to even begin keeping his left hand warm, and he held it close to his chest. It wasn't easy, but he successfully made his debut voyage to the store. This was a relief.

That evening, they sat to meditate together because they were feeling called by the Masters. Archangel Metatron, a powerful being they knew well, came through loud and clear as soon as Antera closed her eyes and took a few deep breaths.

He bellowed, "I greet you. This is Metatron of the Light. I come to you from a thousand suns! I bring you the pure Light of the Spiritual Sun!

"You are among those who have fought countless battles on this planet, throughout the history of humanity, thereby allowing more Light, more opportunity to expand the creative forces in this and all universes. You have both been the Light Bearers many times in your human incarnations and between lives."

Omaran nodded as he heard this. It did seem like a long time.

"The job that you and other Light Bringers have undertaken is far more difficult than any you have done before. It requires the expansion of your mind to embrace and overcome the limitations of the body. To be able to hold the Light in such an atmosphere, while being in the line of fire and drawing fire, is a difficult path. But it is one you have chosen and one you continue to walk.

"I come to you to give you my blessing and to make sure that you are indeed sure that you want to be at the front lines. It is not an easy place to be."

Omaran said, "Yes, it does feel like we are at the front lines. But we both want to be where we are. I know Antera has concerns about me and I have concerns about her health. But I believe we can do this. This is where we need to be. This is what we're here for. This is what gives us joy."

Metatron asked pointedly, "Is it giving you joy?"

"Well, it is, it really is . . ." Omaran felt as if he were trying to convince himself. "I really am excited about being able to bring the Light to places and situations where it is so needed."

"Omaran, I want to make sure that you are ready. There are many influences in your life, some of them positive, and others not. To engage, you must know your weaknesses. You must know where you are vulnerable and have the means to work around that. You must know how to avoid your soft places, so that your shields prevent any penetration. This is my concern. Do you understand?"

"What I understand is that both you and Melchizedek are concerned, so that makes me think that my enthusiasm probably isn't enough right now. I don't consciously know my weaknesses."

"If you know your vulnerabilities you can keep your field intact and protected. It is of prime importance that we know you can do this before we give you any more jobs that will insert you into dark areas."

"How do I learn my weaknesses?" Omaran was at a loss.

"You have had thousands of years to understand your weaknesses, Omaran. You know what they are. Tell me."

Omaran considered. "I think one would be my anger, which is less now, but still there. I'm not sure."

"Yes. What about your thoughts?"

"My thoughts, yes. They are more controlled, but I still allow some negative ones in. Wow!"

"In this work, there is no room for doubt, judgments, or other negative thoughts. Do you understand this?"

Omaran felt like he was really on the spot. It wasn't the first time the Masters had warned him, and he felt like he had worked very hard on these issues. However, he also knew there was more room for improvement. "I'm beginning to. I'm ready to get back to land healing!"

"I admire your courage, especially in light of your having been stopped so effectively. I admire this, yet I still want you to understand what you are dealing with."

"I think I'm beginning to get a better picture of what you and the others are saying. How do I become more aware? What should I do?"

"Awareness is one aspect of it, strength is another. You are not at your maximum strength. You are injured, and you have been compromised. This is why I keep saying I want you to realize what you are up against and not go into battle wounded."

"So, I have to be physically strong to shield myself? I know that during my recovery I've grown and healed a huge amount, maybe more than at any other time. I've been doing meditations several times a day and I'm getting stronger all the time. How strong are you saying I need to be before I can fully do this work?"

"Strong enough so that you are not vulnerable."

"Ah. Of course. Is there anything I'm not doing that I can do to speed up the process and get stronger?"

"You have emotional release work to do. This you avoid, but it is a part of your growth. As long as you are charged up with human emotional energy you are vulnerable. Emotions must be felt and released. Until you learn how and do it enough so that you do not build up this energy, you will be vulnerable."

Omaran shrugged. He did not want to hear that, but he knew it was true. "Okay."

Metatron went on, "It is the weak place of many Lightworkers. You live in a very emotional time on an emotional planet, and some of you are more emotional than others by nature. You happen to be a very emotional one, Omaran, and you have tried very hard to ignore it or squelch it. And this is your Achilles heel, your biggest weakness.

"Mastering the emotional body means being so aware of your energy that the slightest perturbation in your field is felt and acknowledged consciously in any moment. And the emotional body can be changing all the time. One brief conversation with someone can change it. Becoming aware of it allows you to master it, becoming aware of when your emotional body is not flowing freely. So, when I asked you about your weaknesses, this is what I wanted to hear."

Omaran laughed. "That's the only thing I didn't say."

"You see how it is human nature to avoid that which you need to address the most?"

"Yes. Thank you for bringing it to my attention again. I intend to walk this path, and I will do what's necessary."

Metatron went on to talk about the pyramid he hoped they would build on their property. He had been helping them plan it since long before they even bought the property. It would be a huge, expensive project, but they knew the funds and opportunity would happen at some point, especially because Metatron really wanted it built. They listened with excitement and hope.

9

Spiritual Intensive

April arrived, and Omaran felt like he could not just sit around anymore. Surely two and a half months qualified as a long rehab! He wanted to do more. The hand was partially functional, and he increased household duties to relieve Antera. Though she didn't complain, he was concerned about her stress levels with the responsibility of being the sole provider as she built her business, on top of caring for him. He was determined to use his hand as much as possible.

Shortly after his decision to do more work, Omaran got a call from a woman who wanted him to do a small construction job. She had called twice before and was turned down each time, but she had not given up. That was easily understood, given the difficulties of finding good workers in this small town. She begged him to come over and simply take a look, even knowing about his injury, and assured him he could go as slowly as needed. Finally relenting, he looked at the project.

Surprising himself, he said yes to the woman. But on the drive home, he felt a bit apprehensive—both of telling Antera he had accepted the job and of jumping back in a little too fast. But by the time he got home he knew he had to do both.

When he told Antera about it that evening during dinner, she protested. "Are you sure you're ready to go back to construction work? You're not completely healed. And you better stay away from table saws!"

"Don't worry, I will never use any table saw again, anywhere, anytime. I think I can do this. It isn't a hard job, and it is actually kind of interesting.

She has an outdoor gazebo with a wooden floor that looks like a sun with rays shooting out. She wants it rebuilt."

"And you promise that you'll be careful and only work a few hours a day? You don't want to hinder your healing."

"I actually think it will be good for my hand to move it more and try to grasp and hold things. I will be much more protective and mindful than I have been in the past. And I do need to bring in some money. You can't support us by yourself," Omaran said. "But you are coming close."

"We will make it! We kept our house, didn't we? I don't want you to start working too soon."

"It will be fine. If I can't do it, I'll quit."

Antera hoped Omaran would not overdo it, but she was also relieved that this meant he was closer to being able to get back to work. These few months had been especially difficult, and she did not let on to Omaran how much her spine still hurt from the fall she had taken. Much of the time, the pain was fairly intense. It had worked its way up from the sacrum to the mid-back to the neck, settling in areas of old injuries. She thought it was very fortunate she had such a high tolerance for pain, so she could keep working, but there was also a downside to that—she could put it out of her mind, and therefore not do anything to heal it.

The Masters did not let her get away with this for long, however. St. Germain was concerned and asked her to visit with him in her morning meditation every day for a while, if possible, so he could help her heal. Most of her channeling these days focused on Omaran, or it was advice about their work. So, this was an opportunity to take time for herself and her own healing. Off and on over the last couple of decades, she had gone through Spiritual Intensives like this, checking in daily for personal reasons for a few weeks or months, and always there was deep healing involved. She readily took up this request, deciding that no matter how busy she was, it would be worth it. It was all about priorities.

These meetings were precious. She and St. Germain talked about many topics. They had always had a good teacher-student relationship, since her first conscious memory of him visiting her when she was three years old. At that time, he had planted some seeds and imparted some concepts about her path and mission in this life, which had been so impactful that she had never forgotten. She had not understood what he had given to her three-year-old mind until she was almost forty years old, and then it had changed her life.

The Master was very concerned about her body and spent the first few days urging her to go to a chiropractor and improve her diet. Since Omaran's injury, they had let their normally strict diet get a little laxer, including some sugar and comfort foods. That was fine for a while, but now it was time to lighten up the body again to help the healing process.

Germain was gentle yet firm. "I suggest you curb the appetite now. Indulging in excess food will feed the pain. And most of your diet should be raw. If you want this body to serve you the best, you must follow its laws. This means not feeding the pain body."

"Yes, thank you, I'm ready to improve this and hopefully Omaran will also."

"If you desire higher consciousness, you must eat food that is higher consciousness, not food that supports lower consciousness and feeds only the pleasure senses. There are powerful mass thoughtforms around food, and these must be recognized to break free of them. Antera, you need to be the strong one and set an example for Omaran because he is more susceptible to those thoughtforms. It runs in his ancestral line.

"Thoughtforms about foods give a quick fix. They push people to eat unhealthy foods to feel good for a very short time at the expense of the overall organism. It is an illusion to think that food will supply an emotional need. Love, acceptance, and forgiveness come from the Divine, not from food. This is where people have been fooled. It is a great deception.

"And food affects people not only physically, but emotionally, mentally, and spiritually. Food has higher-dimensional energies also, not just physical. You take into your system all aspects of food and drink, all of the history, energy from all who have contributed to it including growing, harvesting, transporting, selling, and preparing. The energy of food is mostly ignored."

Antera found this to be very useful when she was tempted to eat something that was not living food. She started saying to herself, "That is low-consciousness food. I only eat high-consciousness food." Thus, she was able to turn it down more easily and walk away.

During these meetings with St. Germain, he also called in a special group of "Energy Healers" to work with her in the etheric realms, and bade her to call them, through his name, every day. When she did, she could feel them working, mending and fixing her spine and other areas.

One morning, Germain told her to be prepared for a big wave of energy coming toward the planet. He said, "When I say, 'be prepared,' I mean be open and clear and free flowing. Embrace the energy as much as you can, this will help. This energy will open areas in people that have been closed, and this can be challenging. Most will not know how to handle it."

"What specifically should I do?"

"Continue healing your spine. That is the area of constriction in your body."

"How long will the energy wave last?"

"It starts today and will be flowing over the next few days. It will stimulate a heightened awareness and sensitivity in you. Be sure to tell Omaran to be careful."

That she did, and he took it seriously, making sure he was paying more attention to his thoughts and feelings. He also started cleaning up his diet. There was much benefit for him as well from these sessions with St. Germain, albeit indirectly.

Antera noticed that during this intense flow of new energy, she could see and hear Germain much easier. It was like something had opened in her head. When St. Germain was with her, he focused his energy on areas of her head including her third eye, psychic ears, and the back of her head. It seemed he was trying to make it even easier for her to hear him, using the influx of energy to help her remove blocks and open more to the inner realms.

"Remember," he said, "what is really going on is in the inner planes, not in outer reality. That is just a reflection of what is really happening inside. The outer world is very engaging, but if you put all your energy there you won't be paying attention to what causes it all. Causality is becoming stronger as the veils thin, making it more and more important to put your attention on the source of activity."

Antera nodded. As she increased her awareness, she understood this more, not only in her mind as a concept, but in her direct experience. Sensing energy fundamentally shifted one's perception of reality.

She said, "But the outer world can be very distracting."

"Yes, I am aware of this," the Master said. "But Lightwork, by definition, is what you do on the inner planes, not what you do in the outer world. Some Lightworkers have forgotten this. Their lives are a reflection of greater battles going on inside. Trying to heal challenges in the outer world is like treating symptoms of a disease—it doesn't address the source. The source is on the inner planes.

"The inner and outer worlds are both important. It's just that most people are not conscious of the inner and what they are creating. Humans live equally in both. This is what waking up is all about, becoming conscious in the inner realms, and becoming a conscious creator or co-creator.

"To become more aware, look at the source of the outer forms. Look for whence the energy flow comes. If you see something happen in your outer life, where does it resonate with you? Where in your energy body? Track any disturbance back to its source—which could be an action, a thought, taking on energy from others or energy from your Higher Self or soul.

"As you become more aware of what is going on in your system, you become more conscious. It is all about energy flow."

St. Germain then asked her to look carefully at her energy field and find the area that wasn't flowing as well right now. She scanned her energy.

"I see a place in front of my body between the heart and throat chakras, around where the thymus is."

"What does this area hold?"

"Hmmm . . . pain . . . loss . . . sorrow." She felt deeper. "I hear, 'Don't leave me!'" These words opened the flood gates. Sobs started shaking her body. She said it a few more times, crying it out. This was from a long time ago, a past life of anguish when a loved one had gone away. After ten minutes of crying, the sorrow decreased, and the heavy energy lifted. She could breathe easier.

"You gave a piece of your heart chakra to the person who left. Now call back to you the piece of your heart you gave away."

On her command, a ball of Light came flying back and went straight into her heart. It took a few minutes to work its way into place, assisted by Germain, then slowly her heart integrated the energy that had been gone for so long. It felt full. She took a few deep breaths, feeling the difference.

Wholeness. That is what it felt like, having a whole heart again. And she hadn't even realized that it wasn't whole!

After a few days, the energy wave had passed, and her spine was feeling better. St. Germain started taking her to other places for her growth. On one occasion, she found herself in a rock chamber, or cavern.

"Do you recognize this place?" Germain asked. "You've been here before."

She looked around. There was a large rose quartz stone in the middle of the chamber. A sudden realization came to her. "This is the room you brought Omaran and me to inside the mountain! That was many years ago! I remember the rose quartz."

Eyes twinkling, he asked her to sit and gaze into the rose quartz. She focused on the beautiful stone for about ten minutes, and more memories started coming in.

Germain said gently, "There was a time, very long ago, when you came here often. You were a priestess."

As he prompted her, she saw pictures of that time, memories. The room seemed to shift in time. There were three flames that were kept burning at all times as source flames, Eternal Flames. Pink for love, yellow for wisdom, and blue for power, symbolizing the tri-fold flame of the human heart chakra. Each flame was ringed by stones, and this rose quartz that had held the energy of the Pink Flame was the only one left.

As she watched the scene from long ago, one by one people were escorted in and sat for a while in front of the flame they needed most, to balance the attributes in their hearts. She could see that as they sat, the flame would reach over and work on the hearts of the people, like it had a special intelligence. The effect was a very thorough healing and purification, and by the time the people left, they were visibly changed. Their hearts were glowing beautifully. When the three flames were in perfect balance, they merged into one flame and the person was attuned to oneness with the Divine.

What an amazing healing process! Antera watched more people be transformed into bliss. Then she turned to St. Germain and exclaimed, "I want to create a place like that again, in the physical world! What a wonderful temple of healing!"

He nodded. "Perhaps that will be doable, but it will need to be different now. At least you can incorporate some of this in your June event for initiates. But we will talk about that more another day. It is time to go back. Let us meet here again tomorrow."

The next day, Antera met Germain inside the chamber, which she began calling the Flame Chamber. Again, she focused on the rose quartz and was shown more memories of how the flames were used by initiates. He described to her more of the process and how it was involved with the Order of Melchizedek, especially when people went to higher levels of initiations.

Around the outer edge of the flames were other stones that focused energy, a rainbow of Light. This process for initiates and what had been offered here was clearly very complex and she did not understand it all yet. More memories would surface later when she was ready, she knew.

10

White Light Temple

Through May, Antera continued working with St. Germain almost daily. It was a highly transformational period leading up to her birthday, her time of greatest power and alignment. Within the radiance of the Master, it was easy to bring in her I Am Presence more and more fully, completing the merging between the soul and this higher aspect of her being. It was a culmination of all the lifetimes she had taken, a bringing together of the greatest purpose of the Light Bearer—to be a shower of the way, an example for others to follow.

Germain told her that this is what all true Light Bearers do. They travel the way and call others to do the same. He showed her others in the past who had pointed to the way but neglected to travel it themselves. Being completely genuine and living the teachings herself was of utmost importance. This created a purity of mind and heart.

Antera was learning and experiencing at an intense rate, going deeper with each lesson, even revisiting some she thought she had already mastered. Yet, new levels of understanding and experience emerged. She was so grateful to the Master.

Her monthly trip to the Bay Area for session work was in the middle of May, and Omaran was coming with her this time. St. Germain warned her to be vigilant with protection, especially since the daily sessions with him would not take place while she was traveling. He advised them to take tuning forks for sound healing and to use decrees several times a day, to keep their energy strong. It was always a shock to go to the city after being on the mountain because the energy was so much denser. It was like going into a thick fog. Fortunately, by following the guidance from St. Germain, they made the trip and came back intact.

In late May, St. Germain took her to a new place that was not inside the mountain. By this time, she had gotten used to going to the Flame Chamber for most of the lessons, so this was something new. Initially, it appeared to be a crystal temple. In front was a door that was very bright, almost too bright to look at even with her inner eyes.

"Go inside," St. Germain said. "I'll wait for you here."

"What? You aren't coming in?"

"No, this is a journey you must do alone."

She tried to see the door better. "What is this place?"

"Trust me, you will like it."

Yes, she trusted him. She boldly went through the door into the unknown. Inside was the most intensely bright White Light she had ever experienced, and she thought, "Maybe this is God! Goddess!" The Light was so bright that she couldn't see very much, but she noted that it wasn't hot like physical light. As she watched, a large shape slowly formed out of the Light in front of her. It was a statue of Divine Mother, the sacred feminine aspect of the divine. As it became more distinct, the emanations of energy coming off the statue hit her with force. The energy was intense, yet deeply loving. She started crying and sat at the feet of this form. It was like being nurtured in the greatest way, without words or concepts—just pure Divine Energy. She didn't want to analyze the experience, knowing this would take her out of it, but she knew at a very deep level that this was much more than a statue.

Without knowing how long she had been sitting there absorbing that energy, she suddenly knew it was time to get up and leave. On her way out, another shape formed out of the White Light over to the side. It was a terminal of some kind, like a subway station. Bright red tickets were sitting on a table, ready to be inserted into a slot. Beyond were various portals into other dimensions or places, beaconing her to investigate. Fascinating as this was, Antera decided she did not want to dilute the profound experience from Divine Mother, or get distracted from her integration of it, so she exited the temple through the door.

St. Germain was there waiting. He looked at her energy and smiled. "Was I right? Did you like it?"

"Wow. Yes. But I still don't know what this temple is or exactly what I was supposed to experience."

"Everyone has a different experience. Please tell me what you saw and felt."

Nodding thoughtfully, he listened as she described the Divine Mother statue and energy, then the portal she had seen briefly at the end.

"Hmmm, very good. This is a place you must go into alone, for healing. No spirit guides or others, save perhaps another human who has been there before, are allowed in. This is because of choice and free will. Human beings must face their creations alone so they can heal themselves. It is only pure White Light, so anything that is not Light can be exposed. And anything you see that is not Light is something you brought in with you."

"So . . . the statue was obviously made of Light, but does that mean the portal was not? Was it something I brought in? I didn't sense anything negative in it, just an invitation to go to another dimension."

"And you declined. Perhaps that was significant," he said noncommittally.

For Antera's birthday, they took the truck up the mountain and onto dirt roads until the rocks and ruts prevented going farther. Leaving Sky parked on the side of the road, they hiked across country to a special place they had only visited a few times. A medicine wheel, a circle of rocks with an equal-arm cross inside, had been built of rocks there long ago. Because it was tucked up in a canyon with large conifers all around shading it, it was still mostly covered with snow, making it difficult to find dry rocks for sitting. They settled for a wet log they could both fit on, covered by their jackets.

After lunch, they used their boots and sticks to dig into the snow and uncover the medicine wheel enough to see exactly where it was. After bowing with respect, they both walked around it then took turns standing in the center, gathering its energies. Omaran found a rock to sit on that was far enough away to give them each some privacy, and they settled in for meditation. Faith loved snow and found a perfect spot to lie down between them.

First, Antera marveled at the beauty of this place, and expressed her gratitude. As the peak time of her birth approached, in the early afternoon, she thought about the next year and what she wanted to focus on. The last month had been so transformational, working with St. Germain. But in some of the SCIO sessions she did on herself, an entity of some kind still showed up, in the form of an electronic device. She decided that for her birthday wish, she wanted to work on removing this once and for all, if possible.

She lifted into her Higher Self, and then asked for St. Germain. He appeared, with a group of Masters. It was her Council of Seven, the beings who had been teaching her for decades. There was a big "Happy Birthday!" from this loving group, and Antera realized that it was exactly the moment of her birth. Their timing was impeccable!

When all had settled down, she asked St. Germain if she could have any remaining electronic and other implants removed, even genetic ones, if there were any. She was so ready. He responded that the being to talk to about that was Isis, and he stepped aside. Isis appeared in golden glory, as she always did when she came to Antera, probably showing herself much as she looked back in the days of Ancient Egypt when she had been a teacher in the mystery schools there. It was how Antera remembered her and could recognize her now.

After her standard greeting, Isis went right to work, illuminating the device that had been flagged by the SCIO. She explained that humans were manipulated long ago by a group of beings to prevent humans from sensing Spirit, the source of energy. The pathways into the brain that should come directly from the Source were then used by this group to influence or control the thoughts of humans. When people built up Light, they started to overcome those false pathways and couldn't be easily controlled, thereby becoming a threat.

Isis said, "We have worked on implants in the past, when I was on the planet and your teacher in the pyramid temples. Do you remember?"

"I have some memories of those times, but I don't remember working on this."

Isis explained that pyramids are secure, protected places so it is easier to remove foreign objects while inside them—affirming yet another reason to build a pyramid on their property. "The device you still have can no longer influence your thoughts, but it can be used as a listening device, which I'm sure you do not want."

Over the next twenty minutes, the Master expertly built the flow through her spinal cord and realigned energy throughout her etheric, emotional, and mental bodies. This rendered the device nonfunctional. Antera relaxed into the birthday healing.

When Isis was finished, she announced, as if in the middle of a conversation, "And you know, the quickest way for you to grow is to help Omaran grow. You are tied together in soul."

Antera sighed. "Yes, I know I need to continue to help him, and I'm committed to that. I agreed to it." But, a part of her thought, this was her birthday, and she didn't really want to spend it helping him! That selfish objection did not last long, however, because she knew Isis spoke the truth. The better he did, the easier was her own journey. She surrendered and said, "Okay, tell me what to do."

Isis proceeded to give her the current mission. She brought Omaran's soul forward and showed Antera that he was surrounded by a network of subtle cords that had plagued him for a very long time. His feelings of guilt and low self-worth from mistakes he had made a very long time ago had allowed this, compromising him to the extent that those forces he was still attached to worked through him whenever possible. It was like the age-old battle between good and evil raging inside him. Isis further showed that at night when he slept, sometimes he was taken by the dark energies and sometimes by the Light. This was why it was so hard for him to heal and make consistent progress.

It all made sense to Antera, who had seen him make some progress through the years but had not understood why his healing always seemed somewhat temporary. Look at what he was battling against! No wonder he consistently turned on her when he got upset, no matter what the upset was about.

"That is a lot of cords," she said. "Am I to remove them?"

"No," Isis replied. "I just wanted you to see the situation more clearly. When he was involved with the dark occult arts, he was taken inside one of those dark stars in what he calls the Catacombs. That was when he was compromised, for eons to come. Part of his soul was taken and is still there. It is time to retrieve it."

"Wow. How can I help him do that?"

"Your task is to take him into the Light Star, or what you are calling the White Light Temple, the place St. Germain took you. It will take

54

repeated visits, but each time he goes he can retrieve part of his soul and put it back together. He will be able to undo a few of those circuits that were attached when he went into the dark star. He is fighting his way back and needs help now."

Antera thought about that. "I thought people had to go into the White Light Temple alone. How can I escort him?"

"Humans can go inside with one other human soul who has already been inside. Only higher-level beings may not go inside to help, so humans are sure to make free-will choices for their healing."

"So, to be clear," Antera said slowly, "my job is just to take him inside the temple and tell him what you told me about what to do inside there? What if he creates something dark? I'm not sure his thoughts can remain pure enough."

"Our brother Germain will give more instructions to you both when he takes you there. We would not ask you to do this if Omaran was not ready." Isis paused. "Now, perhaps you understand more about why your healing is trivial compared to what needs removing from your mate."

"Yes, of course I understand! Mine will be much easier once he is cleared! Thank you so much for showing me all this."

A few days later, after explaining it all, Antera and St. Germain guided an enthusiastic, though nervous, Omaran to the White Light Chamber. Germain told Omaran to hold a focused attention on what he sees because the White Light would be so bright and strong that it would mirror, or expose, anything not of the Light.

Antera went inside with Omaran while Germain waited outside. It was just as bright, almost like solid White Light, as she had experienced on her previous trips alone. She waited for Omaran to describe what he was seeing. After a few minutes of silence, she prompted him.

"What do you see?"

"I don't see anything, or sense anything."

Antera knew this meant his doubts and resistance were coming up. She helped him see an area of resistance between his solar plexus and heart. It was easy to clear it energetically while in this space, using some of the White Light that was all around. That made him feel better.

"Now what do you see?"

Immediately, he described in detail a metal cage around him, like he was trapped inside it. This was disturbing to see, because he could tell that it had been there a while, though he hadn't before seen or felt it. However, it came to him quickly what to do to heal this. From the White Light, he coalesced hundreds of flowers, all colors and types, layer after layer of them all around him. He simply reached out and took the energy as if it were solid, like white clay, and formed the shapes he wanted in his hands.

As he did this, he marveled at the process but didn't question it. The flowers quickly transformed the cage bars, replacing the metal with flexible strings of colorful flowers, winding all around. He could no longer see the bars! They disappeared. The cage vanished!

Omaran felt wonderful. He felt Divine Mother's presence very strongly as more flowers appeared without him directly creating them. "Flowers are the best way for me to protect myself!" Omaran declared. "Divine Mother is showing me!"

He continued to stand inside the multitudes of flowers, feeling bliss and joy as well as safety. He would never be trapped again! He glowed.

After a few minutes, time was up, and Antera gently coaxed him out the door, flowers and all.

He described what had happened inside to St. Germain, who was waiting. The Master looked pleased. Antera wondered if this meant Omaran had retrieved part of his soul and whether the cage had been related to the cords Isis had shown her. She hadn't seen either of those two processes happen. But Omaran looked radiant and had received a powerful healing, so she figured that was enough for now.

The next day they made a flower essence from comfrey flowers, which grew prolifically on their property. Its main function was to repair soul damage, and with his new-found appreciation for flowers, it seemed perfect for Omaran.

11

Call from the Masters

By June, they had caught up financially and their life on the mountain was almost back to normal and flowing smoothly. It was time to resume more of their spiritual service work. Neither of them could stay away from it for long. It was their mission and reason for being on the planet. So, when the Masters asked if they could take up their yearly event, Initiations into the Order of Melchizedek, there was no hesitation in saying yes! While they had been away on their book and music tour, they had taken a break from this work.

The perfect time was the Summer Solstice, a time of power as well as pleasant weather on the mountain. That would not be an easy deadline, but they thought they were up to it. The Masters put out a call to Lightworkers for the event, to draw in the people who would most benefit. Mother Mary described their call:

"We have put out the call to all those who are just awakening but who have been preparing for many years and many lifetimes on the inner planes. These are people who now know, deep in their hearts, what is meant by this. They understand that for a long, long time they have been working on the inner planes without their conscious minds knowing about it, taking classes that raise their consciousness and align them with the Forces of Light, and learning how to be a Lightworker.

"They will know by their intuition and in the depths of their hearts that this call is to be answered by them, and that they need to come to this ceremony to bring forth what they have been doing in the superconscious into the conscious mind, and into their life as they know it. And it will change their life.

"The second group we call are those who have been working for many, many lifetimes with the Order of Melchizedek, and they know perfectly well what they are doing. They are conscious of it. Some of this group want to give the pledge to the universe out loud in order to secure the rest of their life in service, to bring forth the Great Light into their lives, and to get extra help by consciously aligning with the order.

"Some in this group have strayed or have become caught up in the everyday activities and dramas of human existence. They have temporarily forgotten what their true priorities are, that they are brilliant Beings of Light, the Light Bearers who are here to help in his time of great change and transformation on the planet.

"These people are called to reawaken to their true priorities, their true mission in life. We need all of them to participate at this time of vast energetic changes and great awakening. We have looked forward to this time for centuries, even thousands of years.

"All of the Lightworkers who are alive today chose to be here to help, to hold the Light strong during these times when the Light is most challenged. This is their true purpose, and everything else in life is either a distraction from that or helps this purpose. It is up to each person to decide which activities are bringing the most good, radiating the farthest, and reaching the most people, animals, plants, or rocks.

"This is our call! It is a call from many Ascended Masters, from the Great White Brother-Sisterhood, from the cosmic Order of Melchizedek, and from Melchizedek himself. It is a call of awakening. We make this call from Mount Shasta where many of these sacred energies are found and projected out to other power spots on the planet! Through these lines of Light, the call is sent, and it is sent through the Network of Light."

Omaran started spending a few hours every day cleaning up the yard in preparation for the event. His hand was getting stronger and more capable of doing jobs like weeding. Spring had brought the usual influx of weeds and amazingly fast growth of everything. Because the growing season was short, everything grew faster, especially grass in the flower beds! The event gave them a deadline, and the yard was whipped into shape. Omaran was able to do most of the weeding and yard work while Antera did the event planning, promotion, and communication with initiates.

The event was highly successful and immensely satisfying to everyone involved. The power generated in the final ceremony was greater than any previous group. Michael, Antera's ex-husband, and his wife Jeen came up to help lead it and support the initiates. They lived in Redding, only an hour away. Michael had been involved since they did the very first of these in 1998 and continued to be an essential part of the work. As a working geologist, he was a perfect combination of the spiritual and the scientific, with a strong connection to the land and a long background in various spiritual practices, from Zen Buddhism to Native American teachings.

"You know," mused Omaran after everyone had gone and he had given in to the urge to rest on the couch, "it's almost like we never left. We got back into the midst of preparations for the event, and I almost feel like we just did this even though it's been almost three years since the last one."

Antera sat next to him. "It's a lot of work, isn't it? But the rewards more than make up for all the time we put into it. What a great group this year!"

"Yeah. I love the new people we meet and renewing connections to those we know."

"Now we can relax for a bit, right? I have a lot of catching up to do."

"Me, too," agreed Omaran.

"But maybe we can think about a trip for your birthday this year."

His birthday was about four weeks away. "Well, Love, you know I'm always up for a trip, but I don't think I'm quite ready yet to get back to the land healing. Before we can go out on the road for that again, I will need to cut some more of the wooden sculptures, and while I have thought of another possible way to do it that won't involve a table saw, I need a little more time."

"What are you ready for?"

"I'm definitely ready for the Tetons."

The Grand Teton National Park in Wyoming had called them before. It was a gorgeous and sacred area, and it hosted an Ascended Master Retreat in the inner realms, just as Mount Shasta did. These retreats were places where these Masters held meetings and taught classes for initiates and Lightworkers. When they had gone there briefly a few years before, they had fallen in love with the area.

"Oh? I wouldn't mind going there."

"Let's do it! We'll find a house sitter and off we go."

12

Old Wounds

Antera continued her spiritual intensive through June and July, checking in with the Masters every day. St. Germain took her back to the White Light Temple a few times, and often to the Flame Chamber inside the mountain, where he helped her gather more of the flames she needed for balance, primarily the blue flame of power.

One day when she tuned to the Master, he was in a different place. It looked like a banquet hall, decorated lavishly, and he sat at the end of a table with three others on each side. He gestured for her to sit at the opposite end, facing him. Germain was resplendent in robes of violet, blue and gold that sparkled as if they were alive. This was clearly some kind of special occasion.

Holding out his hands, Germain manifested a jeweled chalice. "Behold the Chalice of Wisdom and Knowledge!" It was shining with Light and gorgeous.

Then, to her surprise, he handed the chalice to Antera, saying it was a gift she had earned. Wide-eyed, she reached out. As soon as she touched it, she shot out and found herself soaring above the room, as if she could not contain the energy. It took a few minutes, but she finally managed to incorporate the high-frequency energy into her system, coming back down into the room where the others waited. Wow! What a rush.

Sensing that the next step was to drink the liquid inside, she peered at the golden elixir, took a deep breath, and drank it all. Nothing so dramatic happened this time. She observed a growing clarity in her perceptions, as if someone had given her eyeglasses she hadn't known she needed. The room and its occupants came into greater focus with details she could only see before as sketchy colors and shapes.

St. Germain proclaimed, "This is your initiation rite into the Realms of Illumined Truth."

"Thank you!"

"You are welcome."

She could see and identify all the beings now. They clapped, and there was a brief celebration. When the room was silent again, Germain asked if she wanted to go to her next level.

"Yes, of course!"

"It will require healing a deep, old wound."

She said, "Ah, of course. Okay, then. Show me the pain."

Whisked back in time, she was in Israel during Jeshua's life. It was his death that brought up the most pain, and she realized that many people who were there during that time shared that pain. It was like a major scar on the planet that had yet to heal completely. The Masters gave her many details of her life during that short, yet highly influential, time period and what was going on behind the scenes with Jeshua and his training and mission.

Over the next week, each day she learned more about her role in the drama and the pain she had been carrying. It brought up sobs and much gut-wrenching release. She'd had no idea there was still that much pain inside—after all, she had cried about Jeshua's death before. But just having more details of the situation and what had really happened brought up so much more.

When she thought she was almost finished with this round of healing, Jeshua appeared, and conversations with him brought closure and even more understanding and forgiveness. After that visit, she actually felt good about it, at least for now. From experience, she had found that it was best to never assume any healing was completely finished. Healing was layer by layer. But it seemed that this phase was complete.

Antera felt lighter and lighter, and she felt she needed time to integrate all she had gotten from these visits with St. Germain. However, she didn't want to take a break from the sessions with him yet. Sure enough, it wasn't long before another deep wound was revealed. A series of past lives were uncovered by the Master, all with a similar theme. In them, she was trying to protect sacred objects and knowledge that were threatened by those who did not understand their importance or did not want people to have that energy and knowledge. She knew she had been involved with many of the mystery schools that had existed on the planet through history, and many had been destroyed, so these memories made perfect sense.

Again, it took about a week of daily work to move through this pattern. One morning, Mother Mary came forward to help her heal this series of lives, showing her one after the other in more detail, when she and others were trying to hide or save sacred objects before the destructive forces, misguided people, or soldiers could get them. So much destruction! This was very painful to watch happen over and over. She had been successful in some lives, but against such overwhelming forces and with little warning, choices had to be made and much was lost each time. Statues of sacred beings were thrown down and crushed, scrolls were burned, temples were desecrated.

This brought up much more crying, as she was helped to let go of all that frustration and pain. Why were there always people who wanted to destroy that which brought Light to the planet? Was there no end to these dark forces? While going through this, Antera wept for all the lost sacred objects, wisdom, and culture, as well as what seemed like wasted effort.

Mary helped her forgive all the people who were involved in the destruction. Many of these people had no idea what they were doing, or they were just following orders. The ones who gave the orders were the hardest to forgive. Mary showed her that they were compromised by dark forces. Still, they needed forgiving. Everyone makes mistakes, and compassion is the highest road to take. Any who did such atrocities had no doubt been taken care of by their own karma. Once Antera was able to open her heart to forgiveness and compassion for the worst of the perpetrators, a weight lifted.

Making peace with this history also required that she let go of all attachment to material things, no matter what kind of energy they carried or what they represented. She saw that she had left energy behind in many sacred objects and places, and these bits of energy needed to be retrieved so she could release further. It took a few more sessions with Mary to pull back her energy and dis-attach from all those objects and locations.

What she was being asked to do was big. From now on, she was to create Light without any attachment to the outcome, and without holding onto any physical objects she created.

And she saw now that this was all very relevant to creating the current mystery school. Now that she had worked on this wound, she knew it would be easier to move forward with it. Deep inside, a fear had been lurking about losing it all, as had happened before. Why create the same things over and over only to lose them? It seemed like a lost cause. It seemed like madness. What if the world would never be able to bring sacredness and Light to the people? What if it has always been, and always would be, a lost cause?

But she really got it now. The mission is to bring as much Light as possible to places that are dark. Of course, bringing Light to places that are very receptive to it would be easy, but not nearly as useful! She knew now that she would continue to try, continue to do what she could, even if it was all destroyed—in fact, to do it knowing that it probably would be destroyed!

When the pain had been released, she realized that it may always be this way on the planet, but it would not deter her from creating new sacred objects and teaching the ancient wisdom. It was her soul mission, and despite the counter forces, she would continue.

"Okay! I get it!" She finally declared to the Masters. "Damn the torpedoes, full steam ahead!"

Both Mary and Germain laughed.

This had been yet another major healing, and she was relieved. In fact, she was more determined than ever to do whatever she could in the remainder of this life and then let it all go, just like the Ascended Masters do! They radiate Light out and hope it catches on, but they don't hold onto the outcome. She was so grateful to Mary and Germain for helping her through the healing process.

Now that she had gone through these latest two weeks of intense healing, she understood more of what the Chalice of Knowledge and Wisdom was all about. Now THAT was an initiation! Just by holding it and drinking the elixir, the chalice had brought up these old wounds for her to heal. It was terrific to find out more about her past and go through the healing, but she was super glad to be on the other side of it, and much lighter. From being on this planet so long, she suspected that there would be more of these wounds. For now, perhaps, she could take some time to integrate.

In her last session before their trip to the Tetons, St. Germain said he wanted to introduce her to someone who would be guiding her and Omaran while there—one who knew the area well and acted like a guardian there. She was introduced to Hiawatha! He certainly was not who Antera expected, but she was delighted to see him again. She had a deep connection to Hiawatha. He had first come to her in visions and dreams a decade earlier, then they had talked more directly. She knew him as a very wise soul and teacher.

She hugged Hiawatha, who appeared as a rugged Native American wearing deer-skin pants and vest, with some colorful decorative beads attached in spiral patterns. He smiled and said, "Hello, my daughter."

Pulling out a bowl of holy water, he said some preparation was needed before going to the Tetons. Proceeding with a ritual cleansing, he wiped her feet and hands, slowly, then splashed it over her whole etheric body. She felt very cleansed and purified, ready for anything!

13

Birthday Trip

On Omaran's birthday, after a two-day drive, they arrived at a campground on the east side of the Tetons, and they set up their tent and campsite quickly. The exquisite scenery was just as they remembered. The deep blue Snake River meandered through the valley at the base of the striking, jagged series of granite peaks. They took it all in silently.

"I want to go on a short hike," Omaran said.

"Now?" asked Antera. "It's after noon. But it's your birthday and if you want to go for a hike this late, that is what we will do."

"Yeah, we won't go far. It just feels like it would be wonderful to hike in the Tetons on my birthday."

Driving their car to a trailhead, they started out on a trail that led to a small lake, according to their map, though they knew they wouldn't make it that far. They passed a variety of deciduous trees in summer fullness, with many bushes, grasses, and other lush plant life they didn't recognize. Colorful wildflowers graced the open meadows. Plentiful water flowed across the trail in creeks that they crossed by rock hopping. It was stunningly gorgeous.

After about a mile they began climbing, and they were so taken in by the beauty around them that they continued without giving too much thought as to how far they were going. The temperature was quite hot and before they knew it, they had almost exhausted the two water bottles they carried. They kept going, not wanting to turn back just yet. When Omaran noticed the water getting low, he stopped drinking to make sure

Antera had some, knowing that she always needed to drink more than he did.

They asked some people they met on the trail how far it was to the lake and were told less than two miles more. They were enjoying the hike so much that they decided to make it to the lake. They had been climbing alongside a creek that was no doubt coming from the lake, and several side tributaries gushed off the canyon walls, falling and tumbling to coalesce into the larger stream. Suddenly, Omaran realized that he could go no farther without water. His mouth was bone dry and his throat raspy.

"I have to have some water," he said. "I'm just going to go up this tiny tributary a short distance and get some. Surely this is pure water."

"Omaran, you don't know if it is safe to drink, even if it is off the main creek."

"I know, but I can't go on without water. I'll just drink a little bit, only as much as I absolutely need."

He took off his hat and immersed his whole head in the creek. The water was cool and tasted as good as any he had ever drunk. It was perfect.

They made it to the small lake, sat on a rock in the sparse shade of a couple of small pines on the shore, and ate a snack. The water was a deep shade of green, and it held a perfect reflection of the rock ridge behind it. Knowing they had a long hike back, they only stayed about twenty minutes before starting back.

Their "short hike" ended up being close to ten miles. By the time they started making dinner at camp it was already dark.

"Thank you so much Love, it has been just about a perfect day," Omaran said softly.

"It was a great hike, besides the thirst. What do you want to do tomorrow?"

They had found out that to get a tent site in the coveted Jenny Lake Campground they had to be there by 7:00 am, which was the plan. "I think after we get our new camp set up, we'll take the ferry across the lake and head up into Cascade Canyon," said Omaran. "I can't wait to get back there."

"Me too, we've seen a lot of beautiful places, but that is one of my favorites."

The morning plan went smoothly. Procuring a campsite in Jenny Lake Campground, they set up their tent, caught the ferry and started climbing up the steep trail toward the canyon, all before 9:00 am. A stunningly beautiful waterfall rewarded hikers along the way, and for some people, that alone was worth the boat ride. For those who continued, the path became very narrow, climbing in steps cut right into the granite face to an overlook where most of Jenny Lake was visible. Antera and Omaran stopped to appreciate the expansive view across the valley before hiking into the high canyon. This was as far as most visitors went, especially those in flip-flops or carrying very little water. But the real treasures were farther on, in the canyon.

Cascade Canyon was sculpted by a glacier, forming a valley with a river bordered by magnificent sheer cliffs of granite on both sides. The plant life was rich. Animals were also abundant, including the occasional moose or deer grazing near the stream.

Omaran stopped for a moment to feast his eyes. "This is the most beautiful combination of canyon and mountain and stream I could even imagine. I think it's the most beautiful place I've ever been."

Antera nodded. They continued to walk for a couple of miles as the series of high peaks that made up the Royal Teton range, came slowly into view.

"Have you seen Hiawatha?" asked Omaran.

"He's on the other side." She pointed across the river. "He seems to be leading us farther into the canyon. He says we can follow him, but that if we feel drawn to some place along here, we may want to just go and sit."

"I'd like to continue on," Omaran said.

"Okay."

They followed the trail about two more miles, stopping often for the picture-perfect views and to drink water, of which they had plenty this time.

"I know we should be taking more pictures," said Antera. "But there is just no way that they would do this place justice. And I don't really want to take my eyes away from all the beauty."

They came to a fork in the trail. The highest Tetons, including the Royal Teton, which was the tallest peak, towered above them. Green and golden colors of the trees on their slopes rapidly seemed to diminish in size the higher they were, demonstrating the immense size of the peaks. Small streams bounced down rivulets cut into the mountains every few hundred feet. The river on the floor of the canyon continued to offer one spectacular view after another as it made turn after turn through high grasses and bushes, at times disappearing altogether. Wildflowers were in joyous dance everywhere they looked, and birds filled the canyon with a cacophony of melodic sounds.

They decided to stop and have lunch near the junction, sitting by the river, which was much smaller this far upstream.

"I feel drawn to the trail that is leading up to the left," said Antera, eating a handful of nuts. She looked at their small map. "And the one to the right goes around these mountains to the lake where we were yesterday."

"Me too. I'd like to stay closer to the Royal Teton."

Continually waving their hands to ward off the multitudes of flies, they finished their lunch and took off again. The trail got rougher and began to climb again into a canyon between the Royal Teton and a flat mountain on their right, which they were pretty certain was Table Mountain. They had seen it on a larger map and wondered if it was the same Table Mountain Godfrey Ray King had written about in his books.

They had been climbing for about an hour when Antera stopped and said, "Do you see that? Looks like there may be a cave up there." She pointed up the mountain.

Omaran looked. "Oh yeah, now I see where you're pointing. Wow, how did you spot that?"

"I heard it call and followed with my eyes."

"Of course you did. Now that I see it, I really feel it calling, too. Want to go up there?"

"Do you think we can climb up, sit a while, AND get back in time for the last ferry ride?" If they missed the ferry, there would be an additional two miles of hiking around the lake.

"Hmmm . . . it will take about thirty minutes to get up there. Yeah, I think we can. It will certainly be quicker going back because it is downhill."

Fifteen minutes later, they stood before a large cave opening, at least ten feet tall. Not really prepared to explore very deep, they sat just inside and marveled at how powerful the energies were. Soaking up this energy of the mountain, it felt as if they were inside a spinning vortex of forces, and it was not long before they were saturated and ready to leave. When they came out, they were both feeling a bit dizzy and had to be very careful walking down the steep, rocky slope.

Halfway down, Antera lost her balance on a loose rock and fell. "Ow!" Omaran quickly climbed back up to her. "Are you hurt?"

"My ankle." She examined it. "It is twisted, I hope not too bad."

"Can you walk?" Omaran was very concerned. It was at least a seven-mile hike back and he didn't think he could carry her that far. But he resolved to do just that if needed.

He helped her up and she gingerly tried to use the foot. "It hurts, but I have no choice but to walk back, so I will. Maybe you can just help me get the rest of the way down this loose, rocky slope."

By the time they got back to the trail they were no longer dizzy. Fortunately, Antera had brought walking sticks, on which she leaned heavily to limp along slowly. Omaran took her pack and piled it on top of his.

They hadn't gone far when Antera got a message from St Germain that he wanted to talk to them while they were in this area, if possible. So, they found a relatively comfortable spot to sit, from where they could see the highest peak of the Tetons. She tuned to the Master's energy.

St. Germain said, "I greet you and welcome you to one of our most sacred areas. Where you now sit is between two powerful vortexes and areas where many Ascended Masters gather frequently. The place you have been led to, and where you have been since you came off the trail, is an energetic pathway between the two, a ley line. We know you are following your guidance as we tell you where to go and as you listen to your guide, Hiawatha, and follow his signs. He knows his way around here in the physical world much better than we do.

"We spend our time in the heart of the mountain in front of you. There are many peaks on the top that jut out, but below the peaks they are all one mountain, one huge sacred area. We are very happy that you could join us here and gather these energies. Perhaps you could feel the strong pulse of the mountain up in the cave, for that cave connects directly into the heart of the mountain.

"Do you have any questions for me today?"

Omaran thought for a moment and said, "Would this river be a good place to be baptized?"

He and Antera had been musing about taking a spiritual bath by immersing their bodies completely in these waters, which they knew contained enhanced energies. They called it a baptism because the intent was spiritual cleansing and purification, like a rebirth. They had done this years ago in a shallow pool in a small creek on Mount Shasta, taking off all their clothes and dunking under. Though the water was cold, it had been invigorating at all levels. Because of the sacred energies in the Teton area, it seemed a perfect place to do it again.

"This particular trail that you have been on today is the most magical one here," the Master answered. "But the scenery is spectacular everywhere you go. The difference is the energetics. The waters that come down from this mountain are very, very charged up, as you might imagine. And if you could put it on your bodies, you would feel its electrifying force.

"For the baptism, however, you may want to go into a body of water that is not so cold. The idea is not to shock your system with cold, but to immerse yourself completely in water. So, you may want to look for some other area for that. But if you can get some of your body into this water, I do encourage that, because it is absolutely magical and will electrify your energy body and all your systems and wash away anything that is blocking the Light, throughout your electric body. So, if you go into it with that intent, you will gain much by using this water."

"We will do that as soon as we can get to the water. Is there any special place you suggest we go in the next few days?"

"This is such sacred ground. I believe the Native Americans who used to live here thought it was heaven and had a name for it that reflected that. It was renamed when settlers came through, as everything was. But your good friend Hiawatha has become acquainted with this area since he ascended and acts as a guide for many who come here and are consciously or unconsciously looking to gather the most important energies. And he is very knowledgeable, so if you have questions about the area, I suggest you ask him."

The Master then proceeded to open their energy, bridging their hearts and the sacred heart of the mountain. Great waves of purification flowed into their hearts as they resonated with this energy of the Ascended Master Retreat in the Tetons. Profound Divine Love in its purest form infused into their energy fields. When they thought they could not take any more,

St. Germain opened each of their crowns and fortified their connections upward, resonating to the I Am Presence. After about twenty minutes of this intense upgrade to their systems, he then worked on enhancing the DNA of every cell in their bodies to unveil codes that were long forgotten.

After St. Germain left, they sat for what seemed like quite a long time, absorbing and grounding what had just happened. It felt like they had been reamed out so only Love was possible. What a gift! Finally, they looked at each other and together said, "Yeah, we better go." With Antera's slow walking, they barely made the last ferry in time.

14

Laid Flat

It was their first night at the new campsite. Their neighbors, a man, woman, and girl, apparently did not know there was a rule to be quiet after 10:00 pm. They sat around their campfire long past the quiet time, drinking, laughing, and telling loud stories, mostly about times they got drunk and did stupid things. Antera and Omaran did not get much sleep.

The next morning, they decided to take a break from hiking to allow Antera's ankle to heal and to rest after the two long hikes, so they drove to a flat place close to the base of the mountains and found a beautiful area where they could sit comfortably in their camp chairs while they took in the dramatic rise that the mountains make on their eastern side. Hiding among trees and sagebrush, they were quite alone as they sat and meditated.

After a few minutes, Antera said, "St. Germain is talking to me."

"Oh, good!" Omaran responded, adjusting his posture in the chair. He had hoped this would happen.

"He's asking us to look at the mountain with our inner eyes and see the giant Pink Flame that burns inside. This huge flame carries the energy of Divine Love, and that is what we are to really get here, bringing it into our hearts and stoking up that aspect of the Three-Fold Flame."

Antera had been working intensely on her heart with St. Germain in the Mount Shasta Flame Chamber, so she felt the Pink Flame as very comfortable to her system. She went on, "He wants us to understand that everything that happens, including our loud campsite neighbors, is for a reason . . . a challenge for us to stoke our flame even more, to give up all judgment, all mental negativity that might come up. We want to encompass everyone we are around with the Pink Flame of Divine Love.

"We can call on these energies when we need them, to bring forth both the Divine Feminine and the Divine Masculine in all we do, think, and speak. When we notice that we are not loving enough, we call forth both parents: Divine Mother to nurture us and forgive us, to tell us that she is here always as a mother would be, holding us in her arms, giving us support and energy and pure Love and acceptance; Divine Father to give us his support and to show us the way, guiding us outward into the world. As we embrace both of these as the two aspects of Divine Love, this stokes up our flames.

"We call forth this Divine Flame from the center of the mountain, in the retreat. It is quite large, and it burns there continuously. We can call on it at any time, even after we leave here, now that we have been fully initiated into this Light."

"I can see it and feel it," Omaran commented.

Antera continued, "Germain also stresses that we need to make sure we are fully grounded at all times, because it is easy to go off into higher spaces here where the veils are thin, especially when we get up higher on the mountain. If we don't, we may twist an ankle or something."

Omaran chuckled. "Yeah, it's not like you to get ungrounded."

Antera smiled. "So now he just suggests we sit and take in the energies."

They sat there for a while, then drove to another spot to sit for a while. That night, back at the campground, their neighbors again presented a challenge. Knowing that they were in the process of amplifying their hearts, they listened to the loud, obnoxious talk going on at the next campfire. It was even worse than the previous night.

As they lay in their sleeping bags inside their tent, unable to sleep, Antera said, "Why doesn't the ranger come and tell them to be quiet?"

"I don't know. But that guy is getting more and more abusive and talking about things the girl should not be hearing."

"And his filthy language! I hope he will pass out earlier tonight. I've never heard anyone act like that in front of a child."

Omaran was trying hard to keep his heart open and his Pink Flame stoked, but the frustration was building. It was after midnight and the drunken party was still going on. Finally, he could not stand it any longer and he exploded, yelling with the full force of his lungs, "SHUT THE FUCK UP!"

There was silence. Antera was shocked, her mouth open. She could not believe Omaran would do that! He had completely lost it! And she had never heard him use that kind of language. Then the man came out of his shock and yelled back with some curses of his own. Suddenly it all seemed hilarious and Antera started laughing. Omaran joined in, and they laughed for quite a while, dissipating the energy. The neighbors went to bed.

The next morning, they left early for a hike, well before the neighbors got up. They wanted to go up toward the Grand Tetons from another side, using a trail to Amphitheater Lake. After driving to the trailhead, they had walked for only a few minutes when Omaran stopped suddenly.

"What's wrong?" asked Antera.

"I don't know, I just had an incredibly sharp pain in my stomach. I think I'm okay now."

They walked for a few more minutes. He doubled over with another sharp pain. "I think I'll just sit down for a couple of minutes. I'll be alright."

In a few minutes, the pain had passed, and they started up again. This time, Omaran was able to walk almost twenty minutes before it hit him again, but it was even more intense. "I have to stop. I'm just going to go off the trail a short distance so that no one will see me if they're walking by. I have to lie down."

He was soon very definitely sick, vomiting over and over, with diarrhea. Antera tried to make him comfortable, because it was clear that he wasn't going anywhere for a while.

Antera was pretty certain by then that she understood what was going on. "Omaran, I think you must have giardia from drinking the creek water the first day. That has to be it. There were warnings posted at the general store."

"Ugh."

Assessing the situation, she knew he would be here a while and may not even be able to walk back to the car later. She may need to ask some other hikers for help, because she certainly could not carry him.

"Love, will you be alright resting here while I go back to the car and get some more toilet paper for you, and a chair and book for me? I'll be fast. It will take maybe forty minutes."

"Just remember where to find me. I won't be going anywhere."

Antera took careful notice of where to exit the trail so that she could find him again. He was not too far into the forest. When she returned, he was still lying down. It was four long hours before he could begin to walk down the path toward the car, stopping every few minutes.

When they arrived back at their campsite, another surprise was waiting. Their tent was upside down! They both stared at it, at first thinking there had been a big wind, then realizing their camp neighbors, who had packed up and left, had probably done it to have revenge. Antera fixed the tent and sleeping bags, giving thanks that the people had not taken anything.

Omaran was sick through the night, and with the morning Antera was also violently nauseous. She hadn't drunk very much creek water at all, but apparently it didn't take much. All they could do that day was lie on a blanket in the shade of a big oak tree at their campsite.

By the end of the day, they were both feeling a bit better, and the worst of the illness had passed. They were leaving the next morning.

"Feels like we didn't get all we needed to get while here." Omaran commented. "Two days wasted!"

"Yeah. Bummer. But I have faith that we got the experience we needed to get, as always."

"I guess. At least we learned to pay attention when there are warnings about not drinking the water."

"It was just so hot!"

"Yeah, well, I'll never go hiking without enough water again. I just couldn't help myself at the time, I was so thirsty. Next time, we will turn around."

"We got so excited about the hike and the scenery," Antera said, "that we didn't want to stop."

"I've drunk water from other streams before and nothing happened."

"Me too. Guess we've been lucky until now."

15

Divine Father

After returning home and recovering for a few days, their bodies were almost back to normal energy levels, and it was time to see if St. Germain would comment about the trip. They had both noticed some shifts in the quality of the energy in their heads and overall consciousness from the experience but still felt like the illness had really set them back.

Antera brought St. Germain through in the evening as they sat in the living room.

He said, "I realize that a part of you feels you did not get everything you intended to experience on your trip, and that may be so, but we are pleased that you came back with the energies you did and pleased that you are able to hold them. If you do not work with these energies they will dissipate, and no longer be a part of you. But if you do continue to work daily with the Pink Flame of Divine Love and the I Am Presence and the effect on the center of your head, for the next couple of weeks, you will find they stay with you forever.

"You did come back with much more than you realize, and I hope you are not too disappointed that your expectations were not met. But I also hope you realize that everything happens for a reason, and there are very good reasons for all that happened to you there. Even though you got sick and felt that some of the days were wasted, they were not wasted from our standpoint. From looking at you we see that in the time you were sick you were able to counteract many transgressions against your bodies, and to delete certain negative energies in the cells of your bodies, through the illness. Illness is not always a bad thing. We know that suffering is not something you would ever choose, but sometimes it is necessary to get past some kind of block."

Omaran understood. He knew that for several months after his accident their diet had gotten less strict, though still far healthier than most people's diets. "Yes, it makes sense that we took on some toxins in our bodies. I hope they are out so we will have greater health once we recover fully."

"I see that you have already made some changes because of the illness. Getting your bodies back to a place of health and lightness is of utmost importance. For you to be of primary service to the Order of Melchizedek, you must have a body that can hold more and more Light. And usually this means eating a very strict diet, as the mystery schools have always taught."

Omaran said, "I think this peaceful feeling I have comes from being at the Tetons. And yes, there is a little bit of disappointment, but I don't think it's as great as it was when we first came back. Probably my biggest disappointment is how I lost it that night with the people next to us where we were camping. I really tried to send them love and not get upset, and then, boom! I just exploded. Obviously, that was not the most effective way to handle it. If you have any recommendations about what I should do if I'm ever in a situation like that again, I would certainly be open to hearing them."

"Omaran, I must admit that you had good cause there to be angry. There is nothing wrong with anger when it is properly placed. The mistake you made was in harboring that anger over a period of time rather than immediately speaking to them when you noticed they were being loud the first night. If you had handled it sooner rather than waiting so long, you would not have exploded in such a violent temper. Therefore, the lesson is to catch these things early before they become huge issues.

"I must admit we did get a good laugh out of the situation, and what you did was effective."

Omaran thought that some of the Masters probably didn't think his actions were all that funny, but he appreciated St. Germain saying that.

"But," St. Germain went on, "whenever you unleash anger in such a way it propagates, and that is a mistake. That is what you do not want to happen, because then those you target will take it out on someone else, perhaps the kids or the pets, and then they will take it out on someone else, and it propagates. It is not a pretty picture.

"So, I believe you know what to do next time. Handle it sooner and perhaps with a little more patience and understanding. There are many kinds of people in this world, many you would tend to judge as you judged them. It wasn't only about them being loud, you had a judgment on the kind of people they were, the way they were treating their children, and so forth.

"Remember, younger souls are doing the best they can. They do not know any better. To judge others as if they knew what you know is a mistake. That is when you start becoming intolerant and uncompassionate. Those people deserved your compassion, no matter how bad their actions, no matter what they said. They deserved your compassion. They deserved to be loved as everyone does. So, the only reason you had to be angry was if they were loud after the quiet hour."

Suddenly, St. Germain's voice changed. It was as if Antera was channeling Germain, and Germain was channeling Divine Father. They had experienced this before, when Antera was bringing through Mary and Mary spoke as Divine Mother. Both aspects of the Divine Presence, the feminine and masculine, were powerful forces rather than beings, and Omaran could feel the shift into this force as St. Germain spoke next.

"Omaran! This is Divine Father."

Omaran was startled and felt like he was shaking to his bones. He almost choked as he said, "Uh, yes?"

"I am calling you out to be an example of the Divine Father energies in your life. To be a perfect example of those male archetype energies as they are expressed through the human existence. Do you hear me!?"

"Yes, I do."

"Do you feel me!?"

"Yes, I do."

"Bring forth this Light! Bring forth the pure, unadulterated energy that is of the Christ! That is the form of Divine Father! May this power rage through you, may it shine forth into everything in your life, in the utmost purity, the utmost blessing, straight from the Source! There is no room for indiscretion! There is no time for any more practice, any more mistakes! No time for any more creation of thoughtforms that you do not want in your life! There is only time and energy for that which is the highest, most pure expression of the God Force.

"This is your decree! This is the time of awakening for everyone who has been waiting, the time of reckoning! The time of becoming the purest vessel, the purest conduit of the heavenly force. And there is no more waiting. Right now, everything that is not supporting this energy will be banished! It will be forcibly removed and transmuted. This may happen easily, or it may make you suffer, but it will happen. If you truly pay attention to all that is happening, if you truly tune in and maintain your focus on the Light and maintain your mind upon the Light and upon the flow of the Higher Will, then all will go very easily.

"But the moment you stray, the moment you have any thoughts or feelings that are not of the highest caliber and don't build your world full of Light, you will know immediately that you have strayed, that you have not listened. Then you will find things going wrong very quickly. There is no time cushion any more, there is no buffer. It has now been stripped away so that any time you transgress with your thoughts or deeds, there will be immediate repercussion. So, this is no time to make mistakes, that time is over. Am I being understood?"

Omaran said hesitantly, "I think so."

Divine Father continued, "This time is one of service for you. Paying attention to your intuition, your inner thoughts, and to the thoughts of God are your most important focus now. If you stray from that you will know immediately, and the sooner you catch yourself and bring yourself back to the most full, high energies of the Light, the quicker you will transmute the energy that was not in the flow. Standing in the Light is your service requirement! Standing in the Light at all times! I come to remind you of this.

"And the time has come to give up any lingering doubts and fears, there is no time for those! Banish them and stand in the Light! Stand your ground! Do not let any others determine your path for you. Do not allow others to take your time unnecessarily. Do not allow others to disrespect you. This means do not give up your power to anyone, not even in the little things, in the day-to-day things. Stand in your power! Stand in the Light of the Christ!

"I thank you for listening. I thank you for being here, and St. Germain for bringing me through. And I bless you with the highest Light, from the realms of ancient wisdom, from the realms of the Source energies. I leave you with these blessings."

And the energy left as quickly as it had arrived. Omaran felt like a whirlwind had come and gone. What was that all about? It seemed like the Divine Father wanted to get his attention, and He had! This was something he could not ignore.

Omaran opened his eyes and saw that Antera still had hers closed, with a slight smile on her face. Divine Father had touched on one of his biggest challenges, his feelings of unworthiness and not fully claiming his power. All his life, he had tried to be the nice guy, and that meant often giving his power away. Now it seemed he was being called out to claim his power and stand more fully in the Light. Was he ready to do that? Antera seemed to integrate all the Masters' teachings very quickly, but he felt like he kept going over the same lessons time and time again. This was a big one.

Antera opened her eyes and asked Omaran, "How do you feel?"

"Stunned," was all he could say. "I mean, this is Divine Father we're talking about. I can't possibly take all that in right now."

"Just take in what you can now and allow the rest to integrate in time, there's nothing wrong with that."

"Well," he laughed a bit nervously, "It didn't sound like there's a lot of leeway or taking my time in what He was saying."

"Yes, well it did sound like He was giving you a little push. But all you can do is the best you can do."

"Thanks. I know you're trying to help me, but I just need to work on this much harder than I have been. I know I'm controlling my thoughts much better than I used to, but this seems far beyond that. I just have to sit with this and reflect upon it."

"I think you just have to act upon it!" replied Antera as she got up and stretched.

Omaran stared at Antera for a few seconds. Then he nodded and burst out laughing. He laughed for several minutes, while Antera watched him with brows raised.

"What is so funny?"

The laughter slowly subsided, and he said, "That's what I do! I say, 'I need to reflect on it,' and then I don't! You called me out. And you're right, that's exactly what I must do, act upon it! Thank you."

16

Triple Seal

It was a typical summer in Mount Shasta, warm and pleasant, with temperatures in the eighties. In August, their trees gave plentiful peaches and then pears, of which they both ate freely. Excess fruit Antera cut up and dried on flat containers, covering chairs, tables, and most indoor surfaces. Omaran's hand was steadily strengthening, and he was able to increase the amount of seemingly never-ending yard work. His thoughts also returned to land healing, which had suddenly screeched to a stop because of the hand injury.

The land-healing grid in California that they had been asked to make had not been completed. They needed only one more point. Over the last few months, Omaran had thought long and hard about how to cut the wooden objects for the land-healing points without using a table saw. It was tricky, but he had an idea. Perhaps he could cut the shapes with his large beam saw using clamps. If he clamped the wood to a sawhorse, he could use both his hands to hold the saw. Yes, he thought this may work.

Omaran brought up the land healing one morning in late August, while he sat on the couch with his new laptop. It was his very first computer, and he was still learning how to use it, slowly and with some frustration. He could type using his right hand and two of the fingers of his left hand, and at least he was getting faster at that.

"I want to get going on the land-healing work again," he began. "And maybe create more release points around the mountain."

Antera was reading while eating breakfast, sitting on the other couch. Their dining room was rarely used for eating, except for when family or friends came over. It had turned into their music and project room, the table covered with various current endeavors. She said, "Yes, it is time. When I tune in to the mountain, it seems like there is more pent-up energy needing to come out, and more purification to do."

"Let's go out soon. This weekend?"

"Okay. Where to?"

"I'm thinking two more release points, one on the north side and one higher up on the west side where the majority of visitors go."

"I know where you are thinking . . . Triple Seal, right?"

He smiled. It was one of their favorite places on the mountain, and they had built a special Light Field there a few years before, a geometrical form made of Light that connected to some others encircling the mountain. "Where else? In fact, how is your schedule on Friday?"

"I should be able to go then. This will be our first time back there since we left on our tour."

"You're right. I can't believe it's been three years since we've been there. It feels like we were just there."

The phrase "washboard road" came about because of roads like the one they drove to get to Triple Seal. If they went slowly, they felt every bump and it felt like their teeth were going to be jarred right out of their mouths. If they drove fast, the suspension on the truck smoothed out some of the constant bumps, but then there was no warning for the bigger holes and very rocky areas that were too hard to dodge at the higher speed. It was a tough drive.

"Wow, I'm amazed that the truck can hold together. You'd think all the bolts would loosen up," said Antera as they jostled along. She added to herself that she should have worn a better bra.

"Sky is great! And the four-wheel drive really comes in handy. I don't think Tan Man could have made it again." Omaran fondly recalled his first truck, which, even though not four-wheel drive, had taken them on many dirt roads. He had sold it with 300,000 miles on the original engine, and yet there were three guys bidding on it.

"I think this road keeps getting worse. They must not be maintaining it." Antera was holding on with two hands, as best she could. She turned to look at Faith, crouched in the back inside the camper shell, and said, "How are you doing, girl? Hold on!"

They finally arrived at the trailhead and were surprised that they weren't the only vehicle there. "I don't know how anyone could get up here without a truck," said Omaran.

"But what a beautiful place! This is one of my favorite walks!"

"It certainly has a wonderful feel to it," agreed Omaran.

The trail started out in bushes and lupine, a low-growing shrub that still had a few blue flowers blooming. As they climbed, the bushes gave way to towering conifers, with little foliage beneath the trees. It was a beautiful hike, and they breathed deeply the rich smells of the forest. They had been originally introduced to the area by a friend during their six weeks of camping on the mountain in 1995. Back then, the trail wound through the woods much closer to their destination, with only a short cross-country hike at the end. The trail had since been moved to conform more to the land's natural terrain, making their hike mostly off trail, and discouraging many people from going there.

It took less than an hour to arrive at the place they had named Triple Seal. As they approached the valley, they stopped to gaze around. It was a magical place, with sacred geometry structures made from stones on the ground. Without a word, they put their packs down and began walking the area very slowly, pausing at times to take in the energies. When they felt complete, they sat in the center area to meditate in the shade of a small grove of ancient white bark pines, the oldest type of tree on the mountain, gnarly and twisted like elderly people, holding the wisdom of hundreds or thousands of years.

Faith wandered around with her nose to the ground, taking in all the new smells, then found a shady place and rested. After a few minutes of sitting quietly on the pine-needle covered ground, Antera said, "The trio of beings who are in charge of this place would like to speak with us."

"Great, I'm ready."

She said, "I see the Triple Seal Trio, three beings dressed in white robes, like the being I saw at Red Butte."

"I'm sensing great joy in them, just under the surface, ready to bubble over. They seem very friendly, very appreciative. I've been tuning to them twice a week."

"Yeah, they are very joyful that we are here and doing this work." To the Trio she said, "Today we're not only going to renew the Light Field as usual, but we're also going to do some releasing work. So, we ask for your help in locating the optimal spot to do this. We will do our normal ceremony, but if you have any other input, we would appreciate that. We want to go as deep as possible to release energies that need venting and to help the mountain stabilize."

She listened for a moment, before relaying what she heard to Omaran. "They are telling us to call down the energy of the sun into this area and to anchor it deep down inside the mountain. This will help them in their work. Let's do that now." She stood and raised her arms up, and Omaran joined her.

"We call forth the sun, and we call forth the Spirits of the Sun to anchor fully into this sacred place energies of renewal and peace. We make a connection with the source of energy for this mountain and a blessing for this place."

They lowered their arms. A nice breeze came up to refresh them, very welcome in the heat. Antera continued, "I see the three of them with their arms raised up and basking in this Light. I guess they can't call the essence of the sun for themselves like we can. It helps renew them, giving them hope and rejuvenation. They love it when people come here who are aware of the energies and who can help keep the energy going in this special place.

"They are saying that the most powerful time to come here is on the full moon, because the sun and moon are opposite. Then we can pull down the sun and pull in the moon and get a perfect combination of the two. They pull on each other."

Omaran declared, "We should come here on the full moon, then!"

"Today is the new moon. The sun and moon are aligned in one place, so we're getting a mixture of the two, making it a little harder to pull the sun's energy in."

"So, in the future, maybe we should schedule full moon days for hikes."

"Yes. I wonder if there's an optimal day for releasing energy."

"Probably the new moon."

"Yes, of course! The new moon would be optimal for releasing, so this is a great day for it. Let me see if the Trio wants to tell us anything else." She listened. "They are showing me particular movements, mudras, like a dance that's supposed to be done here. Not just walking like we do. I can see them doing a dance of some kind that creates a certain kind of energy."

"Like a Hopi dance, maybe?"

She watched with her inner eyes. "I don't know if the Hopi did this dance, but I've never seen it. I will try to copy it. Maybe we could bring a group of people up here and do it together. It would take a minimum of three people. That would really charge this place up and bc fun too! Plus, they have a sacred song for this place. Do you hear anything?"

"Yeah, I hear a tune." He hummed a few lines.

"It's like a mountain song."

They both got up and walked over to one of the rock structures. Antera showed him the arm movements, and they did their version of the song with the simple dance. The choreography evolved as they progressed into an impromptu interaction using their land-healing crystals, weaving around each other, and making connections. A grid of Light was formed in the center of the stone structure.

When finished, they both stopped and stood to survey their work.

"Wow!" said Omaran. "I think we did it."

"We definitely did something. We generated a lot of power, plus we brought in the power of the eagles!" During the dance, they had seen six eagles soaring right above them.

"Yes, that was amazing, wasn't it? The eagles seemed to be drawn to the energy we were generating."

After lunch, they went up the hill behind them to create the release point. As they climbed up to the spot they felt was the best place, Omaran remembered Jeshua's words from last fall. The Master had suggested, after watching them run faster and faster around to create the vortex, that they could ask the nature spirits to do that work for them.

"They can move around much faster than you two," Jeshua had told them. "Perhaps you could go around one time to give them the idea and then ask them to take over for you, explaining what you are asking them to do and why, and then you two will become the directors."

So, this time they tried this approach, inviting elementals to do the work. Jeshua had also explained that these etheric beings were excellent at doing this and they loved the idea of working with humans in ceremony. It worked! The elementals were able to spin the vortex much faster than Antera and Omaran had done by running around, and it was the strongest release work so far. They finished up for the day then retraced their steps, enduring the bumpy ride home.

17

Jade and the Golden Ring

Excited to finish up the release work for their favorite mountain, a few days later they drove Sky up the main highway and took off on a road that wound around the south side of the volcano. Parking at a small creek, they got out and hiked up the stream, one they had found during their six weeks of camping on the mountain over a decade ago. There were lush herbs and small plants along the water, and flowers in small meadows. A light breeze felt good on their faces. They were aiming for a particular area higher up that was calling them, one they had been to many years before. It seemed they were getting better at sensing where to go to open a vortex, and after thirty minutes of walking and a bit of wandering around, they found the place.

Because they had learned how to call in the elementals for help in the spinning portion of the ceremony, it went even more smoothly than at Triple Seal. Afterwards, they sat down for a drink of water in the shade of a towering fir and laughed at how they used to run around in circles, and how funny they must have looked to the Masters and other Beings of Light who were watching them.

"I can't call this work," Omaran declared. "Here we are, hiking on Mount Shasta to help the mountain and all the beings associated with it, and this is our service!"

"Couldn't ask for better," agreed Antera.

They expressed their profound gratitude at what they were asked to do and how they were thanked by the nature kingdom as well as the angelic realms. They knew, without a doubt, that they were among the most blessed people on the planet!

Antera changed her position on the ground to find more comfort. It always amazed her how easily Omaran could get comfortable. He could sit almost anywhere, not to mention that he could fall asleep just about anywhere.

Omaran suddenly said, "I think we should go back to Ash Creek Butte next and re-do the Light Field there."

"We haven't even finished here, and you are already planning the next one?"

"Well, it's been a while, and strengthening all of the fields is a good idea now that we have changed the energy flows."

"You mean with the new vortexes we created?"

"Yes, don't you think it has shifted the whole mountain? I want to make sure it is all still working."

"Makes sense. Maybe we can go next week."

It was ten days before they could get away again, in early September. Ash Creek Butte is another volcano on the east side of Mount Shasta. The other times they had been there they had not found an easy way up to the top, other than scrambling up a very difficult, steep slope. This time, they tried a new approach, following a rough dirt road to get a bit closer. In fact, on the map it looked like it would cut off at least a mile of hiking.

After some dead ends, they drove on an old dirt fire road, got as close to the butte as they thought they could, and parked. They hiked up a narrow canyon, hoping it would lead them up to the ridge, about 150 feet above them. This eventually led to a small snow-fed pond, like a watering hole.

"Listen," Antera said, stopping.

Omaran paused and put his attention on sounds for a moment. "I don't hear anything."

"That's it. Intense silence," she whispered.

"That's right!" He reveled in the quiet. Faith wandered off and laid down in some shade to wait for them.

They had always loved the quiet when they hiked high on their side of the mountain, but it was never like this. Other than the occasional chirp of a bird, this was near to total silence. It was marvelous. And yet the silence was so absolute that the inner ear noise became loud. It was quite different.

"Look, deer!" whispered Omaran as two deer appeared from around some bushes less than fifty feet away. The deer didn't see the humans, who had almost stopped breathing so as not to startle them. The deer took their time drinking at the pond and then moved off, seemingly unaware that they had been observed.

"That was awesome," Antera said. "I'm glad Faith didn't see them."

"It was a special gift from the area and the deer themselves. Thank you!"

They knew that deer on the mountain were not often seen, being very cautious and remaining hidden much of the day. This made it very special.

Gazing up at the ridge, Omaran said, "We aren't climbing quickly enough in this canyon. We'll have to go straight up."

It was now closer to a 300-foot climb in elevation, and their only choices were steep or steeper. They chose steep. It was not only steep, but loose scree made the climb slow, as they slid back partially with each step forward. At least the day wasn't very hot. By the time they made it up to the ridge, not only were they huffing and puffing, but they were pleasantly pleased to discover that they were almost half the way up to the top of the butte. This way was definitely shorter.

They rested to catch their breath, taking in the 360-degree view, then on they went. The second half of this journey was the most enjoyable because of the scenery. Out of the forest, everything was now open and visible, with only small bushes, stunted manzanita, and rocks to step around. Around the caldera ahead was the peak, and to the west, Mount Shasta towered magnificently. It continued to be an upward trek, but now there were a lot of distractions and beauty all around.

"I feel like I could just reach out and touch Mount Shasta," Omaran exclaimed. He stretched his arms out. "I love being at high elevations like this."

Antera smiled, taking advantage of the stop to sip some water before picking her way through some unique rock shapes. She marveled at the way volcanoes produced rocks of such interesting shapes as they cooled.

Finally at the top of Ash Creek Butte, Omaran found the can that contained a notebook and small pencil for people to sign. Less than a handful had added their names since they had signed it in 1999. They signed again with "2006" and then settled on some lumpy, sharp rocks to meditate.

Antera called the spirit of the mountain, saying, "Spirit of Ash Creek Butte, we are here to give you our gratitude and blessings for being here and holding this space. We are the ones who created the Light Field here for you and the nature spirits to hold. We are here today to reinforce that. We thank you so much for your beauty, your energy, for holding the ley line and anchoring it here. Please reveal yourself."

Omaran said, "I see her, a huge, wonderful being. I'm asking her for her name."

"I keep hearing 'Jade.'"

"Is there anything we can do here to help her?" Omaran moved closer to Antera so he could hear better against the howling wind.

"She says she is very appreciative of the work we're doing around the mountain. She appreciates being connected with the other places, and with the great Spirit of the Mountain. Her essence holds vast wisdom, and we can collect that quality here."

Antera paused, watching some pictures that Jade was showing her. "It is very interesting, how the major ley lines coming out of the mountain connect with each other."

"How so?" asked Omaran.

They had mapped one of the major ley lines coming out of Mount Shasta as it flowed through Ash Creek Butte toward the east. "Maybe I can draw it when we get home, on a map."

Antera shifted her position on the rock, trying to get more comfortable then deciding it wasn't possible. "Jade has a wand and she's showing me that she's connecting the energy flows way up in the air. I mean, way up there around the top of the mountain. It's like a golden ring, very bright."

"Should we visualize it?"

"Yes, we can make the structure stronger, like a halo around the top."

"What is its purpose?"

"I guess it's a part of the etheric structure of the mountain, so Jade is asking us to clear it out and make sure it maintains its clarity and beauty. Then it won't get contaminated."

Omaran said, "I'm seeing it as purification for the energies that come into the mountain from the universe. The ring purifies everything coming in."

"Yes, that seems right. I've never seen it before."

They both focused on strengthening the golden Ring of Light. For some reason, it was easy to see from this side of the mountain and this elevation. A distinct click was felt when they were finished, and they both opened their eyes.

The Light Field was then easy to reinforce, and with their work complete they said goodbye and thanks to Jade. As they started to follow Faith on their long hike back to the truck, Antera thought that next time they came here they would bring her a jade stone as a gift.

18

Conquering the Saw

Later that month, while Antera was upstairs working in the office, she suddenly heard a sound that made her involuntarily start. It was unmistakably the grating sound of a saw. She rushed downstairs, out the front door and around to the front of the garage where Omaran was in the process of using his twelve-inch beam-cutting saw to cut land-healing sculptures. As soon as he saw her, he stopped cutting and removed his ear protectors.

"Hey, Darling, what brings you outside?"

"Is that safe?"

"Well, I've got everything clamped down. The tabletop is clamped, and the wood is clamped to the tabletop, so yeah, it is. And I'm being very careful. I'm grounded, balanced, and working slowly and mindfully."

Antera relaxed a bit, folding her arms in front. It was chilly in the shade of the garage. "Okay, but what's the rush?"

"It's not a rush, but we are missing that last point in California, the one over on the coast west of here. I figured if we're going to drive all the way over there we might as well get a couple points in southern Oregon."

Just when they had thought the project was almost finished, with its zig-zag pattern along the coast of their state, the Masters had said it was exceeding all expectations of creating more stability and raising consciousness, so extending it into Oregon and Washington was the next step, when Omaran was healed.

"And when were you going to let me in on this new plan?" Antera asked.

"I was thinking about telling you tonight, after I had finished cutting and sanding these. But since you're here now I'm thinking this might be a better time."

"Okay, so what are you thinking?"

"So," continued Omaran, "we could head over to the coast, install a grid point in the redwoods, then, since neither of us has ever driven up the Oregon coast, we could continue on up into southern Oregon for a point on the coast then another on a loop inland toward Mount Bachelor. That would extend the zig-zag pattern and give the grid a strong point on a mountain. Good plan, huh?"

"And when do you see this trip happening?" said Antera, beginning to warm to the idea. It had been almost a year since they had been on a land-healing trip, but she had thought it would be a while yet because of his hand.

"Whenever it works, next couple of weeks or so. The weather is perfect."

"What about the animals? We could take Faith with us, but what about Samantha?" Samantha and Faith had joined them on the tour in their RV, but they no longer owned that.

"Maybe Samantha will be okay with a drive in the car. She did fine in the RV, and she is leash trained, so she could walk with us."

"Hmmm, cars are different than RVs, much less space. But it's a short trip so we could try it and see how she does."

Two weeks later, they were standing among some of the broadest, tallest redwoods Omaran had ever seen. These were much bigger than the ones in Marin County on the flanks of Mount Tamalpais, and the brown bark had a soft leathery texture that invited touch. The bark felt soft and pliable to their hands, and they breathed deeply the musty smell.

"These have always been my favorite trees," sighed Antera. "And not just the trees themselves; the giant ferns, the entire microclimate they create. I remember when I was a kid coming here on a camping trip with my dad and brothers. I fell in love with this area then. And my dad swore he saw a leprechaun peeking out from behind a fern. He was really quite excited by that and felt very lucky."

Omaran chuckled. "Wow. That's a side of your dad I haven't seen. I'm going to ask him about that next time we visit."

They stood silently, leaning in with their hands on a large redwood, feeling its pulse of energy.

"These trees are so nourishing, like they feed my entire system, from the physical body to the spirit," Antera whispered.

"It feels like we're in a giant cathedral," Omaran said as he gazed at the surroundings. "And the air is so fresh and clean. I almost wouldn't be surprised to see a dinosaur poke its head around one of these truly giant redwoods."

They explored the woods for almost two hours, taking in the delicious sights and smells, before deciding to look for a place to do their ceremony. Naturally, they picked a site near a large redwood. Faith found her spot and Samantha was tied to a small tree. These animals had been doing land healing their whole lives and were at home with the ceremony.

As they unpacked and set up all the ceremonial props, a process that was by now honed into an efficient and smooth cooperative effort, Antera suddenly stopped and looked around. She could perceive a crowd of nature spirits filing in to join the ceremony.

"What?" Omaran asked, noticing that Antera had paused to check out something in their environment.

"The elementals love the redwoods too. They are all around us, and more are coming. I felt a few come closer and perch on my arm when I unpacked my land-healing rock. I think they are very curious. And they seem to love the pets."

"Yes, now that I'm paying attention, I feel many of these little beings," Omaran said. He spoke to the elementals, "You are welcome to join us in this land-healing ceremony. Thank you for coming."

The ceremony required the cooperation and help of nature spirits, as well as Ascended Masters and angels. Some places seemed to have huge populations of these small beings of the etheric realm, especially where vegetation was dense, whereas other places had few. In some areas, nature spirits had to come from the surrounding countryside because of the sparse elemental population.

It was a powerful ritual. Another successful grid point was created and connected with the others, finally finishing the grid in California. On the way back to the car, Antera and Omaran stopped at the largest redwood in the forest. A sign said it was sixteen feet in diameter, and very old. What a presence it had!

They drove north into Oregon along the scenic highway and, hoping to find a path down to the ocean, stopped at a couple of pullouts to stretch their legs. But the sea below was much less accessible than in California, and there was no apparent way to get down the cliffs. Farther along, they found a motel right on the shore and they were able to take off their shoes and walk in sand and salty water. Samantha did not like the wet sand, so Omaran carried her most of the way. Faith loved it, running and chasing seagulls.

"You know," mused Antera as she did a quickstep to dodge a wave. "I do miss the ocean. During those years I lived just a few blocks away from it, I could hear the waves at night. First thing in the morning, I used to walk down and take a run on the beach, then dive into the water. It was so refreshing! Plus, my vegetable gardens there were fantastic. I could grow year-round." She had lived in Cardiff by the Sea, a small beach town north of San Diego.

Wind blew into Omaran's jacket, making it bellow out like a sail. He ducked his head and covered Samantha until the gust passed. "I love the ocean also. There is something very invigorating about it. Maybe I never mentioned this, but I lived right at the beach at the base of Topanga Canyon, just north of Los Angeles, back in the early seventies. At that time, there were still small houses right on the ocean. There is something special about hearing the waves hit the beach every few seconds, all night and day. I remember falling asleep listening to them." He closed his eyes and listened. "There is really nothing like it."

"Yes, very soothing, unless there is a storm and big waves." She took a deep breath of the moist, salty air. "Lots of negative ions, too, not to mention beauty. No wonder it feels so good to be here. But I wouldn't trade it for the mountain."

Omaran put his arms around Antera. "Remember our first walk on the beach?"

"Oh, yes, like I could ever forget that. It was really something. We hugged and were up in the stars."

They hugged, both thinking that after all the years together, holding each other was still so nourishing at all levels.

The next day they continued their drive north to find a site to create the first grid point in Oregon. Aiming for green areas on their map, which were usually parks, they stopped at a promising forested site and got out of the car.

"This is amazing," Antera said. "Such a thick forest. I can barely see any sunshine coming through at all."

"I love it. No underbrush. It's like a canopy or a wood cave. And I can't see it, but I can just make out the faint sound of waves crashing in the ocean not far from here." Omaran spoke in hushed tones.

"What a perfect place for this. Where do you think we should do the ceremony? Being seen by anyone won't be a problem." No one was in sight.

After a moment Omaran answered, "I think on the other side of that big fallen tree. If someone does wander by, they won't even know we're here."

Picking up their packs, they walked over and found that it was a beautiful spot, with tiny bits of light flickering in constant movement through the canopy as the wind made the trees dance. Samantha was content tied up to a branch of the log, where she quickly climbed on top to find a comfortable perch. She clearly did not appreciate being cooped up in a car for hours at a time, but she did appreciate all the new places and smells.

Nature spirits again contributed to the work, though not as many as in the redwoods, and all beings who attended created the point with powerful Lightwork. Buoyed by the excited group, Antera and Omaran continued singing as they walked back to the car, and a group of elementals lined up behind them, dancing and singing with them. It was such fun work!

Before leaving the coast to go inland, they spent one more night in a motel alongside the ocean and took another walk in the morning along an almost-deserted stretch of beach. As usual, occasionally a rock would call out to Antera as she passed, but she showed great restraint and only picked up a few. It was as if rocks were drawn to her everywhere she went, wanting to go home with her. Thinking about the plethora of rocks they had at home, Omaran gave her a look.

"What? I'm only taking a few," she said. "Don't worry! We have a car and plenty of room."

He replied with a shake of his head, but there was a smile on his face. Remembering other times when he had carried large, heavy rocks several miles on hikes, such as when she had found the corner stone for their house a long distance from the truck, he decided these rocks really were insignificant. But that didn't stop him from giving her a hard time.

After taking a windy road over the Cascade Range through gorgeous scenery, they spent the night in Bend, near Mount Bachelor, their next destination. Omaran had fond memories of taking his kids to Bend several times when they were just learning to ski.

The mountain was nineteen miles west of Bend, a short drive in the morning. It was raining lightly, but visibility was good. They had sent their intent ahead before starting out, to help them find the perfect spot and to alert the elementals of the area. This practice always made finding an appropriate site easier. Winding through the lower slopes and then starting to climb more steeply, they found themselves energetically pulled to the right down a dirt road. They complied.

They found an area they both liked, a short distance from the car, and quickly headed out. The forest was full of moisture and smelled of dense conifers. It had stopped raining, but the trees continued to drip onto the forest floor. Wearing their waterproof ponchos, Antera and Omaran gave thanks for the lovely, vibrant forest, and the mountain. This combination made for a very strong site for a grid point. They found a dry place under a log for Samantha, and Faith wandered as usual, oblivious to the water.

The ceremony went very smoothly. It was too damp to sit for long afterwards, but as they packed up, Omaran mentioned to Antera that a strange thing had happened during the procedure.

"When we were walking around, anchoring the energy in, it felt like someone grabbed my pant leg," he said. "I mean it was a real tug. I looked to see if I had brushed against a bush or something, but there was no bush there, so it must have been an elemental."

"The same thing happened to me!" gasped Antera. "It was a very strong pull. I thought maybe an animal had come up or something. It was that strong. It's the first time I've felt something physical like that."

"Amazing. I didn't know they could do that. I think they really wanted to get our attention."

"They got mine. I was concentrating on the work, so did not try to communicate with them, but how fun!"

"Well, we've got our name for this spot. The Touchers."

"St. Germain has said more than once that the elementals really like to play. I think we got a taste of their playfulness."

They loaded up the car and headed down the mountain in the direction of home.

"Well, we did it!" said Antera. "We finished the California grid and have started on Oregon."

"Who would have thought the project would continue? We thought it was just the California coast we were doing. Now the Masters want us to do the whole west coast."

"The work seems to be very effective. Next year maybe we can finish it for sure."

"It is a pretty incredible project," agreed Omaran. "We should be able to cover the rest of Oregon and Washington next spring, in a few short trips. But it's not like we don't have anything else to do. I'll keep checking in on all the points twice a week."

"How many do we have now, total?"

Omaran counted them in his mind before replying, "I'm pretty sure we've got twenty points now."

19

Solomon

Ever since they had found each other in 1994, Antera and Omaran had occasionally talked about acquiring a physical location to build a center for their spiritual nonprofit and mystery school. It had been an online, virtual center since before the nonprofit was formed in 1998. During the winter in early 2007, Antera had been getting some prompting from the Masters about building this physical form of the center.

"Wherever we end up with our center, I would really like to be able to see the mountain," Antera announced one day as she started a fire in the woodstove. There was a foot of snow on the ground outside, and on cloudy days their passive-solar home needed the extra heat of a fire. The center had become an ongoing conversation.

Omaran looked up. He was resting on the couch, after shoveling a path in the snow all the way around the house for Faith, as well as an area in the chicken yard so the hens could go outside and scratch. "Absolutely. How could we have a center in this area and not be able to see the mountain?"

"I'm thinking about a retreat, with guest rooms or cabins. Then people can stay together as they take classes, have initiations, and get healing. And it would need to be a large property, so we can finally build the pyramid Metatron has been asking for. We have been given so many ideas for it. Maybe it is nearing time."

Omaran thought about the town and its limited properties available. "My first choice would be the land right across the highway toward the mountain. If that is for sale, we would have a great view and I believe it is a large piece of property, maybe twenty-five acres or more."

"That's a beautiful area, but unfortunately it is on a mudflow from an old eruption. It doesn't feel stable to me. Even if that land were available, which I doubt, I wouldn't want to build there. You can move a seismologist from earthquake country to a volcano, but there are still places she just won't go."

"See, that's one of the things I love about you."

"What?"

"Your sense of humor."

"I'm serious!"

"I know, that's what makes it funny."

"Ha, ha. There must be a perfect property out there if we are to build this. Of course, only land in this town will work because the energies here are essential to the project. The other sides of the mountain have very different energy."

"We will see. Let's ask the Masters directly. Tonight?"

Later that evening, they settled into comfort and had a surprise visitor. Antera said, "Someone new is here. He says his name is Solomon." Neither of them knew much about Solomon, only that he was a king in the Bible and a builder of a great temple, but they were delighted to meet him. He spoke enthusiastically in support of the physical center they had been discussing.

Solomon said, "You have within your reach the manifestation of your long-held goals. I am holding a radiance over you now so that you may achieve them in this year if you so desire. If you choose to continue along this path and to make this manifestation completely real in the physical plane, there is no holding back now.

"This year is already in progress. If you embark upon your quest now, you will have time to not only complete it, but to fully anchor it and have it running successfully before the years of change arrive in 2011. But only if you embark now will there be this window of opportunity, and only if you embark now will I continue to impart my radiance upon this project."

Omaran said, "Thank you, Solomon. Your support is astounding and very welcome. But why are you interested in our small project?"

"It is not the size of the project," Solomon answered. "It is your energies, the combination of the two of you creating this together, under the radiance of many Ascended Masters and angels. This, along with your willingness to work hard, adds up to a tremendously fortunate set of energies.

"You have a shining star upon you now! Therefore, I urge you to begin talking about your vision, putting it into form in the energy planes, not in the physical world yet. You must see it as a completed project within the etheric realms first. Allow for the Will of the Divine to make changes to the outer form as you design it.

"This will be a floating form until it finds its physical home, but once the form is fully created, the home will be easy to find and build. It is the creating on the etheric side that is the work. This can be joyous work, creative work together. I believe in this project! It is worthy of my attention and gifts! All that you visualize will be amplified and brought into crystal clear focus. Do not underestimate your worthiness for my attention.

"In human form, you will always have some doubts. But purge those out as quickly as possible, knowing I have my radiance on this project and on you. You are under my eye. And I don't tell you that to make you nervous. I tell you that so you will understand the importance of this project and of moving ahead at this time. You have waited, thinking that it will become easier. But it is up to you to begin the work.

"I had help when I created my temple. Many people came from miles around to see what I was doing and to contribute. People gave me gifts. This flow came in, of wealth, support, and energy, because these people were touched by God in their hearts. And they knew if they contributed, they would be rewarded many, many times over. They would be blessed by the highest forces in the Universe.

"I ask you, what is your first step?"

"I believe Antera and I should start tomorrow evening with creating the vision," Omaran answered. "It seems to me that's the first step, and it's nice for me to know I don't have to be thinking of location yet."

"Indeed, indeed, indeed," Solomon replied. "The 'where' you may leave up to God/Goddess. The conceptual vision is the first step, and it will clarify over time. Tell me what you know of this vision."

Omaran described the mystery school and teachings. He knew this was Antera's part of it, but he wasn't sure about his specific role yet, other than the actual building process.

"Omaran, your task is to think about what contribution you want to make. This is your key to get out of construction. Do you believe me when I say this?"

Omaran took a deep breath and blew it out. "Oh, I want to believe you."

"But there are doubts?"

"Well, yes. I've tried several times to leave construction, but each time I find myself in a financial hole. So, I've always had to fall back on it."

"And each of those times you have not had the right thing to replace it with, have you?"

"Yes, you're correct."

"It seems you went out there thinking maybe something would turn up, rather than planning and creating something to take its place. I am asking you to plan and create something to take its place. I am asking you to create your dream and to build yourself a temple, a school where you can help others. I am saying there will be plentiful wealth to do this. But you must convince yourself of that, and the only way you're going to do that is to do it and find out, isn't it?"

Omaran was still doubtful but wavering. "Yes, it is."

"You don't have to know one hundred percent that it's going to be as I say. All you must do is have the faith to take the steps. All you must do is be willing to follow where Spirit guides you. Maybe you can believe in that."

"Yes, I can feel that."

"And maybe you can connect with that support every day in your meditations."

"Yes, I can do that." Omaran paused. "I have another question."

"I love questions."

"I'm sure I already know the answer to this, but I would assume that we should not limit the vision energetically. Rather than being caught up in details that are not possible to know until we get the property, is it best to think in terms of no limitation at all? Is the sky the limit?"

"Sky is the limit! The sky is always the limit. What can you embrace, what can you envision? Form follows function. So, the first step is figuring out what function you want to have. Then you can think about the size and form that is needed. For the immediate starting place, it is all right to start small, as long as you are always saying 'this or something better' and holding the door open for something greater.

"If you stay in the Divine Flow all the time, what you create etherically will be Divinely ordained. This will be a good exercise in always maintaining your connection when you work on this. And don't allow your human fears, doubts, and limitations to interfere, nor allow anyone else to tell you things are not possible. Don't waste your time! Immediately go to the Divine Source and rectify those kinds of thoughts. That is always the key when limiting thoughts come up or people tell you things that you do not want to accept. Simply go to the Divine Source and maintain your flow at all times.

"Is there anything else I can elucidate at this time?"

"No, I think you've given us very good, insightful directions to start. I'm sure there will be questions along the way."

"That is where your Divine connection comes in. Both of you have a good source of Divine connection. Don't think you don't, Omaran."

Omaran laughed nervously. "You must have picked that up. Sometimes I have been known to question my connection. I believe my doubts come at times when I'm not connected."

"Well, then, there's your solution! Stay connected! It is so simple! Whenever you have a doubt, say to yourself, 'Oops, I must not be connected,' and make that connection again. Doubts fall right away because with the Divine connection there are no limitations! None, zero, zilch! All limitation is from a lack of the Divine Light.

"I thank you for this audience, my dear friends."

Over the next few weeks, they talked more about what they wanted for their center, trying not to limit it. They decided they could probably do it with a minimum of twenty acres. Antera made some spreadsheets on estimated income and expenses, but the start-up costs were daunting, and Omaran wasn't sure how to make building estimates without knowing where the property would be. Just to start getting an idea of costs, Omaran met with a representative of the power company to determine an approximate cost of getting power to the area he had been thinking about, or property further up the mountain. The estimate came in at a million dollars, for only two miles of electrical lines! This put the project on a scale which he found challenging to embrace.

His doubts started to mound up. How could they possibly bring in donations or investors for this scale of a project? Neither of them had been involved with fundraising before. And how could they maintain a center of this size even if they managed to get it built? What other sources of income were there? Being in such a small town, it would depend on people coming from cities to attend events, and only in the warm months.

Omaran tried to do what Solomon had suggested. Almost every time he realized he was having a doubt, he turned his attention to his Divine connection. But sometimes that worked, and other times, not so much. It was an inner conflict of surrender versus will. Theoretically, he understood that nothing was impossible if his faith was strong enough. But in practice, his mind needed to conceive of how it could happen, before putting a lot of time and effort into the project. Faith was something he had struggled with his whole life, but it was also something into which he had put considerable healing time. How could he still have so many doubts, especially with Masters helping every step of the way?

Antera was very busy with session work, both using the SCIO and doing psychic sessions, and had little extra time to put into the center project, either. It was slow going. They were both getting discouraged, when an encouraging message came through from the Masters one evening in February.

As soon as Antera tuned into the channeling space, she was in the midst of a group of Masters having an animated discussion. It seemed they were excited about news they had received. St. Germain was the first to speak.

St. Germain said, "I greet you, and yes, we are excited! We have had some wonderful news and we are working now to incorporate what has happened into the framework of our individual missions and the missions that we are coordinating together. Metatron has arrived with a dispensation, and this is what we are excited about, because he has come to give us this bundle of energy, straight from the Source, from the great I AM. It is for humanity, and especially the Lightworkers, who are the cream of the crop of humanity. He is here to assist us to understand exactly what this means and how this will impact all of you. This is why we are discussing it, allowing it to unfold and to give us the insight we need to disseminate this energy to the beings who can most use it.

"I will let Metatron speak directly with you because you have tuned in right after he arrived, and we know very little more than you do. But we believe this to be a momentous occasion because it is something we have been hoping for, though we did not get our expectations up. I pass the voice to Metatron now."

Antera shifted her energy and tuned to Metatron, who said, "I greet you! This is Metatron of the Light, and I come to you from the Outer Spheres of Light. I bring you tidings from the innermost and the outermost Source. Omaran and Antera, it has been a while since we have spoken directly, and I address this to you as well as to the others here. I commend you for embarking upon a journey more aligned with your higher purpose than ever before, and for holding the Light for so long, until you could bring forth your I Am Presence on the planet. This is what you are doing through this project and through your constant devotion to your I Am Presence.

"I bring this dispensation for you and all other Lightworkers. It has just been granted by the Source of all energy for this universe. I bring it as a gift. I am the messenger. Because the energies of this year are helping Lightworkers move forward again, this bundle of energy I bring is specifically for the purpose of bringing into the highest expression in the physical the many spiritual centers that are springing up across the entire globe. I bring forth energies that will help them succeed, help them shine their Beacon of Light wherever they are, and help them connect with each other in cooperation rather than competition.

"It is the new paradigm. It is the paradigm of the Lightworkers, who have worked continuously through the ages to manifest these sacred centers. Finally, the time has come that these can be manifest!

"The dispensation has been given to help all of the Light Centers— yours included, Omaran and Antera. This dispensation is one you can tune to. I present it as a scroll to every group that is building or has built a successful center of spirituality and health. On this scroll, if you unwind it, are instructions for the full-blown protection from the Source for the manifestation of these centers in the highest good, and the magnetization of all those who can help and benefit from the services offered.

"The owners of the centers, as they become aware, are keepers of these scrolls. And they are to hold them in a sacred place. When they are able to read what is on the scrolls, they will have manifest all that was given.

"I make this declaration in the names of the most Holy Ones, all the angels, archangels, cherubim and seraphim, and the All-Mighty Source.

And I make this declaration in the name of all of humanity and the wonderful Earth, for all life forms on the planet and for the soul of the planet, for it is only through the work of this being, who over-lights this planet, that this has been made possible.

"It is through the work of the Divine Mother as well as the Divine Father, the combination of these two forces, that this is possible. I ask that each of the centers guard their scrolls within their hearts, for these are the scrolls of the teachers and healers. Perhaps you already feel the energy associated with this. If not, you will feel it over time. You will feel the acceleration like a fire has been lit, as people suddenly appear who want to take part and help.

"That is my message today. The dispensation has already been given to all the centers that are worthy, even those that have not yet been built. Some of the people involved will be aware of this and some will not. But the energy will shift. That I guarantee!

"I call forth high blessings to all of you doing this most wonderful work on the planet. And I will now be off."

Metatron left, and another of the group, Solomon, wanted to speak. So Antera shifted again to open to his words.

Solomon said, "Yes, I am here, and wasn't that a wonderful visit. I am so excited about this; you have no idea. We are all excited because we have waited for this particular dispensation for quite some time, to break through the barrier that has been like a glass ceiling to many Lightworkers in the building of their Light Centers or in the propagation of the activities they have been teaching and practicing.

"This will, indeed, help your center and put forth a new Light upon the project. It does not change the project, but there is more support! So here you have a perfect opportunity to run with it. And yes, I know how busy you are. Do not worry, I know you are going as fast as you can.

"Many of us are joining with you when you visualize and at the same time energizing all the other centers around the planet. It would behoove you to do the same. Send out energy to all the other Lightworkers who are creating centers, giving them energetic support, and it will come back to you. It always comes back. Doing this in the spirit of cooperation, as Metatron so eloquently described, is a very important part of this, and letting go of ego or anything that says, 'mine is the best one' or 'ours is the only way.' You know these concepts have caused many problems in the past. This is an age when everyone has their own expression. Some will be similar, some will be very different, but no two will be the same.

"So, Omaran, I know you were somewhat hesitant about talking to me tonight because you think you are not doing enough, but I see that you are doing quite a bit. I see these visualizations that you are focusing on every day. You've had a meeting of the board and informed them. It is progressing."

"Yes, thank you," said Omaran. He still felt somewhat lost with such a large project.

Solomon went on to give them more encouragement, and to describe better ways to visualize. He said to stay flexible in how the center manifests, at the same time making assumptions to put the plan together. It was an incredibly powerful set of messages, and Antera and Omaran were both inspired.

Over the next few weeks, Omaran still was not able to put numbers to the project. It could be bare land or property with some buildings to remodel. There were too many unknowns. And the longer he delayed, the worse he felt. He doubted himself, his abilities, and his worthiness of the attention and support from the Masters. Inertia set in, and he found other things to keep himself busy.

On good days, he felt optimistic and unlimited. But other times, he was stopped by the immensity of the project and its unknowns. He knew that his most important challenge was to stay tuned in to the Divine Energies, but his emotions got in the way, and he didn't spend the time in meditation it required. Overwhelmed, and remembering that Solomon had said this was the best year for it, the longer he waited, the worse he felt.

20

The West Coast Grid

Spring came to the mountain a little early in 2007, so Antera took a chance and pushed the frost date for planting the vegetable garden, at least putting in the plants that could take a light frost. Their location on the mountain only claimed seventy-two days of growing season, so timing was important. This year, she planted the fenced yard on the north side of the henhouse. The chicken and garden system they had installed was working well by alternating two large yards between chickens and garden. The chickens fertilized the area they were in, and the garden provided new scratch material and bugs for the chickens. They switched each year.

Antera loved putting seeds in the ground in the spring, watching them grow, and reaping the benefits of fresh greens and vegetables later. She thought about how there was nothing like food picked and eaten the same day. The life force was vibrant and could be felt as a living pulse when taken into the body. Sometimes she could sense the plants perking up when she came near. It felt like they actually wanted her to pick them so they could become a part of her body.

As she made little trenches for the seeds, she also thought about how good it felt to get her hands in the dirt. There was something very special about it, not only because it was so grounding, but because people had been doing this for so long that it was a big part of being human, a primal urge. When she thought of the many people who lived in cities and did not have gardens, she thought their lack of connection to the planet and the food they ate was probably why so many did not seem to care about the Earth. Why would anyone care, without the tangible connection of putting hands in dirt and walking in nature? She gave thanks yet again for living where they did.

Thinking about caring for the Earth drew her mind into their Land Healing Project, and completing the West Coast Grid, which is what they were now calling it. It had grown from the California coastal zigzag to the whole U.S. coast. Now that it was warmer, she knew that Omaran would soon start planning a trip to Oregon and Washington, to complete it. That meant it was also time to start painting sacred objects.

Omaran loved to plan trips, and when Antera brought it up late that afternoon as she wadded up newspaper to start a fire, he lit up. "Yes, I've been thinking about that," he said thoughtfully. "We could do the rest of Oregon and all of Washington in ten days, no problem, if we boogie."

"How many points?" She piled kindling on and struck a match.

"Probably eight, so we can zigzag between coastal and inland areas. One a day plus two days for driving should do it."

"I should have known you would already have it all mapped out," Antera said with a chuckle. She was glad he liked to handle the logistics, so she didn't have to. She was also glad that he didn't mind driving most of the way, leaving her with the navigation job. Maps were her friends, especially after all her field training in geology as an undergraduate. She added some small manzanita logs to the emerging fire, and the warmth felt soothing.

Omaran said, "We can head up through western Oregon and Washington for the coastal points, then go east through the Seattle area and down on the eastern side of the Cascade Range for the inland points."

"Sounds good to me if we can get a house sitter. I don't want to take the pets again. And I just planted many seeds, so I'll need to set up sprinklers and timers."

"I'll find a sitter. Let's leave in a week."

"A week! I'd need to reschedule too many clients. Let's make it two weeks. I do need to make a living, you know. Plus, I have a lot of painting to do to prepare."

"Okay, you got it." Omaran's spirits were lifted by thinking about a new trip. A house sitter was easily found, and everything fell into place.

Two weeks later they were back on their home-away-from-home, I-5, where they had spent the better part of a year driving from Mexico to Canada during their book and music tour. The road felt very familiar to them, and Omaran seemed have a sixth sense when it came to where the next coffee stop was. Antera couldn't figure out how he remembered places that all looked the same to her. The miles went by quickly as they listened to an audio book from the library that played on the car's cassette player.

"So, we are nearing our first location," Antera said as they drove through northern Oregon.

"I'm thinking we'll pull off in about twenty miles on a road that heads over to the coast, then we'll just look for the perfect place."

"Have you alerted the nature spirits?"

"I did that earlier as we were leaving, but that's a good idea to do it now, let them know we're an hour or so away." They pulled off the road and sent their intentions to find the perfect place on the coast, high enough so they wouldn't have to be concerned about the objects they buried ever washing away, and at the same time alerting the nature spirits that they were almost there.

It didn't take long to find a wonderful place to park that was very close to the ocean. "Look at that great hill that just rises out of nowhere. We could do the point on this side," said Omaran.

"It's beautiful! So many trees! But it might be too thick to walk unless there is a path that leads up to the top."

They loaded their packs and did find a narrow path that climbed up near the top. The foliage was much denser than they were used to in California. Green was everywhere, with lush growth of bushes and trees. Northern Oregon obviously got much more rainfall.

The path got narrower and narrower as they ascended the hill, as if it were giving in to the bushes. Pushing branches aside, it was slow going.

"At least not many people come here," observed Antera.

"Yep. I don't expect our ceremony to be interrupted," said Omaran. He stopped, seeing a slim opening to the left that resembled an animal trail. "Let's go off the main path here and see if we can make our way to that tree. I'll go first and see if it looks promising."

He went a short distance then motioned for Antera to follow. How he saw the way was a mystery to her, for she saw only continually thick forest and undergrowth, not a trail. But she had learned to trust his superior energy sense in the woods.

They came to a small area with fewer trees, less than ten feet diameter, and Omaran stopped. "This will be perfect!" He exclaimed. "The ocean is right over there." He pointed in a direction that seemed random to Antera.

"How do you know what direction the ocean is from this thicket? We can't even see the sun."

"I know what direction we have been walking, so it isn't hard."

Antera didn't say anything, but she was thinking it was very hard to keep track of directions when you were in a forest so thick without any reference. Sighing, she put down her pack and started setting up. The place didn't have big trees, but it was hardly devoid of smaller plants. Part of the ceremony required that they walk in a circle around the altar, and this necessitated some stomping down and moving of branches, which they did with apologies to the plants.

As with all forested areas to which they had been, there were numerous nature spirits, who at first watched and then participated as the ceremony progressed. By the end, with the final song, there was quite a chorus chiming in. Nature spirits love analog music, either played without amplification or sung live. The recordings Antera and Omaran played on the CD player were digital, but after an initial confusion about the music coming out of speakers, the elementals liked them and quickly learned the songs. This really spiced up the ceremony, making it more fun.

After the first point was finished and equipment was packed up, they slowly bushwhacked back to the car and headed north. Their goal was to find a motel close to the ocean, and that was what they found, with a restaurant. All in all, it was a great start to their land-healing trip. They fell asleep to the sound of the ocean waves lightly crashing on the rocks not too far from their room.

The next morning, they were up and on their way fairly early. They liked to get an early start so they could find their next location in time to finish the ceremony and get farther down the road. One point a day was what they were hoping for, and there were significant distances between them. Soon they were heading over a bridge west of Portland and entering Washington. They stayed on what was called the coast road, but they were surprised to see that it didn't go along the coast.

Antera was scrutinizing the folded map. She wore both reading glasses, so she could see the map, and sunglasses so she could see the road. Her green eyes had always been very sensitive to sun and glare. The overlapping glasses were a bit odd looking, but she didn't expect to be seen by anyone but Omaran. She said, "There are literally no roads along the coast in Washington. Hard to believe. Don't people realize how beautiful the ocean is? I guess we're pretty spoiled with our access to the coast in California and Oregon."

"It doesn't feel right," agreed Omaran. "But you know, very little of the population lives on the west coast of the state."

"Well, if they can't get there I can see why."

They drove for about half an hour and then started looking for roads that would take them into the woods, which seemed, if possible, even thicker than at the last site. The map did not show all the dirt roads, so they had to rely on being able to quickly slow down when they passed a road that looked promising.

"Let's try this one," Omaran said as he hit the brakes and turned off on a very narrow, bumpy dirt road. They couldn't go very far before it was too rough for their Subaru. It was really a great car on streets and in snow, with its all-wheel drive, but it didn't have a high clearance like their truck.

They stopped on the road and got out to survey the area. Deciding chances were slim that anyone would be driving in after them on such a rough road, they left the car there, took out the packs, and fought their way into the dense forest, making a path as they traipsed in.

"No problem with being hidden here," commented Antera. In some areas, this had been a major concern. "My gosh! This is like a rain forest!"

Omaran paused, looking for the easiest way ahead into the greenery. He said, "It isn't like a rain forest, it IS a rain forest. Too bad we left our machetes at home! Everything is thick and green. And it would be so easy to get lost. I can't see more than ten feet in any direction!"

"You better be able to get us back to the car, Dear."

"Don't worry, Darlin,' I know exactly where the car is. We won't go much farther. I think I see a small opening ahead."

They came to a clearing of sorts, very small but sufficient for their needs.

"Let's do it," said Antera. She looked around. "Look at the color of all that moss! Bright green, chartreus even!"

They soaked up the bright color. Omaran said, "Interestingly, I'm not feeling as many nature spirits here as I would have thought."

"Me neither. We will need to call them in."

"This isn't an ideal place, but it is probably as good as we can get in southwest Washington. I'm amazed at the difference from just going over the Columbia River. Alright, I'm ready. Let's concentrate for a moment on bringing in as many elementals to this area as we can."

After a few minutes, they were ready to begin their ceremony, and though there were not crowds of beings there, it was well attended enough to do the work. They left feeling much better about the area than when they had arrived.

Trying to retrace their steps, Omaran led the way back to the car. That was harder than anticipated. It was as if the forest had already regrown the path they had made coming in, and it had disappeared. Such regenerative powers! Wandering a bit, when he finally found the dirt road they had parked on, they were a hundred feet from the car. But they had made it.

With two points done, their next destination was the western side of the Olympic Peninsula. They had camped on the eastern side of this gorgeous peninsula in their RV, while they had been on tour, and loved it.

"Wow!" exclaimed Antera. "We thought we saw the ultimate of thick forest further south, but this may beat that. So green!"

"We are talking dense," agreed Omaran. "If there isn't a road that leads in, there's no way we're crashing this party."

"Crashing this party?"

"Just a figure of speech."

"I'm not sure it's appropriate for this."

"Just trying to keep it light, which may be the only light we're going to get. It's got to be dark in this forest."

"Hey!" Antera pointed. "There's a sign that says Mount Olympus that way. Let's turn there."

They drove onto a fairly smooth dirt and gravel road, but when they saw a sign that said the mountain was fifty miles farther, and the road started to get rougher, they decided to take the first side road that came up. It wasn't long before they took a chance on a dirt road that went a short distance before being swallowed up in a mass of green tangles. They kept going, despite some scratches to the paint job from branches, when suddenly, they were surprised by an opening appearing in the woods. They pulled over.

A short walk took them out into a meadow, and they did the ceremony out in the open. It was a pleasant change to be able to see the sky, even though it was cloudy. The spirits of the mountains, with their magnificent forests, lent their energy to the Lightwork.

Afterwards, they retraced their route back to the main highway and followed it all the way around the northern side of the Olympic Peninsula then around to the east side, enjoying the spectacular views of the inlet that separated it from the mainland and Seattle. They stopped for the night on one of the many picturesque islands. The next day, their goal was to get through Seattle and all the way to the eastern side of the Cascades.

"I love all the islands and bridges around Seattle. This is gorgeous," noted Omaran. He found a local radio station while Antera drove, and there was a weather report.

"It really is very lovely, for a city," she responded.

The announcer said, "There is a sun alert in the next few hours. Make sure you have sunglasses ready if you are driving."

"Did you hear that?" Antera laughed. "A sun alert?"

"That's hysterical! Only in Seattle," Omaran chuckled. "It makes sense, really, because if you don't see the sun for a few days, then it comes out suddenly, it could be blinding to the eyes."

Driving north from Seattle, they then found a road that wound through the Cascades toward the east, again through stunningly beautiful scenery. They could see tall, rugged mountains extending all the way up into Canada as they tried to find a road off the main highway to create a grid point, hoping there was time before nightfall. A promising road caught their attention and Omaran, who was back behind the wheel, was able to slow down and make the turn, heading southward and climbing fast into foothills.

"This road looks like it's going to climb up into the mountains a bit," he said.

"Let's do it. I think it would be good to have a mountain point here, to balance the coastal points."

They had found, by energetically tuning into them from home, that grid points they had created on mountains were much stronger and helped support other points. Streams of Light connected all points in the grid, so it was advantageous to have some in more solid areas, such as on mountains.

They climbed for about a half an hour on the windy road but did not find any place to park and get out. It seemed to be private land, as evidenced by the unending fences along both sides of the road, though there weren't many houses. Omaran was starting to get worried, because if they did not find a place soon it would be too dark. Surely there had to be some place!

Antera said, "I think we will have to go over a fence. There don't seem to be any openings here."

"You are probably right. But we may need to slide underneath instead of going over. At least this part of the state isn't wet, so we won't get too muddy."

They found a short turnout and parked, hoping Swan would be safe there. Climbing up a short hill, they slid under a fence and set up their ceremonial area on the only patch of semi-level ground they could find. Before starting the ceremony, they asked the local nature spirits and the Masters for protection and invisibility so no one, especially the owner of the land, would see or hear them. As long as they asked beforehand, they had found, so far, that this worked.

Finishing just as it was getting too dark to see, they packed up and retraced their steps. The point felt strong and well anchored.

The next day, they continued south on the road toward Mount Rainier, one of the most famous peaks of the Cascades. It was a long drive, but they were hoping to camp at the mountain. On their tour they had taken a few days there and had fallen in love with it.

It turned out to be a longer drive than expected, and daylight was dwindling, so they stopped at a motel and decided to camp the next evening and spend some extra time at Rainier hiking and enjoying it as well as making another grid point. Another strong mountain point connected into the grid would help all the points along the coast.

After a good sleep and more driving, they opted for stopping next to the mountain to do their ceremony. A perfect spot was found, off the highway about half a mile in a mixed grove of trees. The mountain wasn't visible yet, but its presence was strongly felt. As they got out of the car, nature spirits surrounded them, excited and ready to participate.

"Do you sense them?" Antera asked. "I guess they know what's going on by now. There's got to be hundreds of them here!"

Omaran stopped setting items out for the ceremony and opened his senses. "It's not like I'm really seeing them, but out of the corner of my eye there are fast images shooting by, and when I turn my head, there's nothing there. Of course, it takes me ten times longer to turn my head than it does for them to shoot by. But I do feel them, that's for sure."

"We will have a lot of help at this one."

And they did. The Light Form was created very fast with little effort from the humans. Giving thanks, they left the locals to their work of enthusiastically maintaining the site they had all created together. This was such rewarding work!

As their car once again headed west along the curvy highway, the east side of the mountain suddenly came into view. It was breathtaking, and they were already so close!

"This is very different than Mount Shasta," Omaran commented. "It feels like we're much closer to the actual mountain without having to climb it. Shasta looks higher. Maybe it's because this road is so high and we're much closer to the top of this mountain."

"I want to get out of the car and greet the mountain," Antera said. "This is extraordinary! I'm really glad we came in from this side. I noticed on the map that we can get higher and closer on this side."

Parking at the first turnout, they sat quietly for a while, taking in both the beauty and the energy of this powerful mountain. Then Antera said, "I'm also feeling some unsettled energies here. When we can, I think we should come back and do some release work similar to what we did on our mountain."

"I imagine we can do that later this year," Omaran agreed. "We certainly wouldn't want this volcano to blow up."

They got to a campsite late in the day and decided to stay two nights. The following day they took a long hike on a trail out of the campground in an area of forest that was bursting with life, greenery, water, and the many elementals who maintained the forest. They had sensed more of these etheric creatures this trip than ever before.

The following morning, they headed south again with a destination of Mount Hood in northern Oregon, another volcano of the Cascades. Driving over the huge Columbia River, Omaran remarked that it was so wide it was like driving over three consecutive bridges. On the east side of Mount Hood, it was easy to find open areas in the national forest, full of young conifers. It had obviously been replanted after a considerable amount of logging decades ago. There were enough old trees to still have a good feel to the area, and a grid point would help all the new growth. They completed the ceremony and took a back road to the major highway that led down the east side of the mountains.

"Wow! We have done it! We have sewed up the West Coast!" sang out Antera.

"Yes, we have," chimed in Omaran. "Even though it took us quite a bit longer than we expected."

"Well, your hand accident didn't stop us for very long. I mean, just a few months after that happened, we were out doing release work for our own mountain, and then shortly after that we were back on the road. I think that's pretty impressive!"

"That's true, it really is. Sometimes I forget the miracle of having two full, five-fingered hands. I'm just so grateful and still amazed." He paused, thinking. "So . . . what do you think is next?"

"I just want to get home and enjoy this completion for a while. It's been a long project. Pretty soon we'll need to begin planning this June's initiation event."

21

Errant Thoughts

Back home, they settled into their work, with Antera doing sessions and Omaran coming up with small construction jobs. He had decided that six hours a day was the maximum he would work, and he wouldn't even consider remodeling jobs that would take over a week. They were making their mortgage payments and doing fine financially.

Omaran continued to check in with each point in the West Coast Grid twice weekly, to give energetic support and make sure all was working as it should. When they connected with the Masters, they heard how pleased the Light Beings were with the grid, and that they were somewhat amazed at how successfully it was doing its work at transforming surrounding areas into Light. It felt like a job well done that would continue to do its work for many years.

On a warm evening after a sunny day in late April, they were sitting on the back steps outside, sipping some herbal tea. Omaran said, "Did you see all the chem trails today? So many of them! It seems like there are more and more. I don't like it."

"They can't be good for our health."

A couple of days earlier, they had watched a DVD about chem trails that had been loaned to them from a friend. There were days when the skies were full of these trails in an even, crisscross pattern that could only be deliberate, and not a consequence of normal air traffic. And these days, the color of the sky was no longer crisp blue, seeming to be hazy much of the time. This wasn't right. Plus, the evidence of metals and other toxic contaminants that had fallen to the ground from these emissions was disturbing.

Omaran felt frustrated. "I really want to do something about these. But what? Should I write the legislators? Pass out copies of this video?"

Antera shrugged. "Any of that would help. Education is always a good thing."

"I'm not sure if I want to put my energy into this, but someone needs to."

"Maybe we can ask the Masters about the highest path to take on this."

"Yes! Can you channel tonight?"

"Sure, when I finish my tea."

Half an hour later, Isis came through, first talking in more detail about the mystery school they were building and their history with these in the past, going back to Lemurian days. Their job now was to bring the ancient esoteric teachings to the current world, and to give practical tools for healing and spiritual evolution. Then the goddess asked if they had any questions.

Omaran was ready. "Well, thank you for all that information. I have a question on an unrelated matter. Is there anything that can be done regarding the chem trails? What can we Lightworkers do? This is very frustrating."

Isis answered, "There are many problems on the planet, and that is only one . . . problems that are out of your control. If you cannot change them, then you need to accept them. Those are your only options. If you get angry at this but you cannot change it, then you are only supporting it by resisting what they are doing. Do you understand that?"

Omaran said, "I do, I really do. But the frustration . . ."

"You need to either do something about it and channel that frustration into action or accept it and hope that others will act. There is no in-between. Being frustrated about it and doing nothing is nonproductive and will indeed make you more susceptible to those damaging frequencies. There is a certain wisdom in knowing what you can change and what you cannot. If you want to dedicate your life to dealing with these kinds of physical problems, that is very valuable—if that is your calling. There are many different vibratory levels where you can work on these problems.

"You can work on them on the physical level by writing your politicians and going along standard channels, and by copying the DVD and sending it out to certain people. Or you may work at higher levels of energy, as a Lightworker, to shift the planet itself to a higher level of vibration so that those kinds of activities are no longer compatible with the planet. As the Lightworkers and Ascended Masters shift the planet, those activities that no longer vibrate in the range of the planet, in this case the atmosphere, will not continue.

"Viewing the world from a Master's perspective, you see that everyone has their own path. Everyone is doing what they are supposed to be doing. There are no accidents. There is no way that the opposition forces doing these kinds of things are not fully known and fully matched by the Light Forces.

"But there are always reasons, and this is what you must remember, Omaran. There are always reasons for these things to happen and you may not know what they are right when they occur, but they will be clear at some point in the future. So, your faith is what carries you, your faith in knowing that the higher plan is in place and working. When you get upset by these things happening, it is because you do not have faith. Do you see this?"

"Yes. That thought did occur to me. Sometimes it helps to have some confirmation."

"Look at these things as if you were a Master. What would St. Germain do? What would Jeshua do about this situation? What are they doing? They are working on it! It is one of the many things they are working on."

"Thank you, that really helps me get a better perspective. I allowed myself to be affected by watching the video and temporarily forgot how Lightworkers work."

Isis went on, "Most of the people on this planet are raising their awareness and opening their hearts. The damaging activities cannot last in this environment of awakening. They will not last. I believe you will see many of the old structures breaking down because they are no longer supported."

Omaran felt better after Isis's advice. He really did know that he was committed to shifting issues through energy work rather than physical action. But it was still hard for him to not react in frustration when he read the newspaper and thought about world events. So much change was needed! How could people get away with the harm they were causing?

A few weeks later, Omaran was still struggling with his thoughts. He wanted so much to be able to stay centered and control his mind so it wouldn't go into judgment of politicians and people doing harm in the world. But it was difficult. And then there was the issue of his not moving forward with the physical center. He always seemed to have other things to do, so he ended up not doing anything. This, he knew, was also somehow connected to controlling his mind.

The center was moving forward in content, if not physically, through Antera, who had a long history of being actively involved with mystery schools in various cultures, including Lemuria, Atlantis, Egypt, Britain, and the Essenes. She knew it was a part of her mission to develop a place once again for people to learn about and experience spiritual evolution through esoteric teachings, and after all the personal healing she had done the previous year, she felt very good about it. With many ideas for classes, she was excited about a new concept called webinars, a way of teaching seminars on the internet. This would open the classes to many more students and solve the problem of living in a small town and trying to gather enough students to make it worthwhile.

To Omaran, one of the most challenging aspects of creating the physical center was funding. He knew this had been a stumbling block of his in other times of his life, taking various forms. This fear or belief in scarcity was also very prevalent among many other Lightworkers. Mentally, he knew there was really plenty to go around and all he needed to do was open to receive and visualize what he wanted, and the resources and people would come. It was simple in concept but difficult to implement right now.

This made him delay the energy work that manifesting the center required. It seemed he always had too much to do and not enough time, making him feel overwhelmed. But perhaps, as the Masters had said more than once, it was more about priorities than time.

More understanding came through the gentle words of Jeshua one evening. He spoke through Antera in a smooth, loving voice, coaxing them to raise their consciousness even higher.

Jeshua said, "I greet you my students, my brother, my sister, my beloved friends. I call you into this space of Light and Truth and Wisdom. In this space, all is known. In this space, you are the wise ones. You are purely aligned with what you call Divine Presence, Divine Mother, Divine Father. This is the place of union, the place of Spirit, beyond the realm of the soul, higher and more aligned with Universal Truths. Be here with me now, fully and completely, and allow this flavor of the cosmos to penetrate your beingness . . . a place of stillness and oneness."

Feeling an immediate shift in his energy, Omaran confirmed, "I feel this space, it's extraordinary." He felt that if he could stay in this consciousness, he could accomplish so much more.

"I call you here today because I see that, despite a few ups and downs, you are moving more fully into your empowerment and fulfillment. I don't mean at the soul level. I mean at the level of your I Am Presence. This is where you are aligned in your purpose and mission. This is your ultimate awareness. Though your soul may be continually working through its evolution, it is good to be fully present in the I Am, to remind you that you are not your soul any more than you are your body.

"You are the Divine! We are the Divine! Many of the little dramas you get involved in are not a big part of your divine nature. If you can keep this perspective, my dear ones, you will not be caught up in those dramas. You will not be swayed by mass consciousness, thoughts, or emotions. This is where you want to be, to move forward and fulfill your missions. From this perspective, you know what is most important and what is not, what is aligned with your I Am Presence, and what is not.

"You have come to a point in your evolution where there is no need to spend time or effort in activities that do not serve your higher purpose. When you are aligned with your I Am Presence, everything falls into place. There is not too much to do. There is just the right amount to do. It is only when you are working from the human perspective that you feel there is too much to do."

Omaran took a deep breath and responded, "I know that; thank you. But sometimes being here in the physical world trying to get so many things done while taking time every day for meditation and spiritual growth, it seems overwhelming."

"This state of turmoil that you are in is not permanent. It is temporary. It is essential to work your way through this into the place of having a perfected life, a life that is so full of Divine Presence that everything falls into place very easily whenever you start a project or do anything.

"When you are feeling overloaded it can be because you are taking on more than your part, or you are trying to affect things you cannot affect because they are not a part of your assignments. The errant thoughts and judgments, anything that is not aligned with this higher purpose, will have to go. You will have to streamline your thoughts and actions so that every action, every thought is aligned with this purpose. This is the only way to get it done.

"Think now of some thoughts you had today. Things you planned or thought about that were not necessary. If you can corral that wasted energy, control your thoughts, and move them into productive thoughts such as planning what is important to your purpose, you will find you have all the time you need to do everything you are doing.

"It is only the wasted energy, those errant thoughts that are anchoring into the drama, that give the feeling of not having enough time. Am I making myself clear?"

Omaran could already think of some wasted thoughts he often had. "Yes, you are."

"You need to have your mind on your work to do your work safely and efficiently, and you need to spend time planning that. But while you are doing things that do not require very much mental activity, you can put your mind to other uses. Plan ahead what you are going to think about in that time, rather than having unplanned thoughts."

"So, it's really using the mind as a tool instead of letting it take over and wander."

"Exactly. It's the wandering mind that disperses your energy. If nothing else, you can repeat mantras, prayers, or chants. If you have nothing you need to think about, use the mind in a positive way. This is the quickest way to progress and make your life easier."

Though he was thinking this was easier said than done, Omaran answered, "I will, thank you. Do you want to comment on the mystery school we are creating? Any advice?"

"Most of the mystery schools on the planet now are based on either channeled material that is very limited and not necessarily completely true, or on ancient teachings that have not been updated enough for the current times. There are, as yet, no mystery schools that can encompass both the mysteries that are still important from the old days, as well as new information that is needed for these days.

"This is why you must look to those old teachings but recognize that they will have to be modified somewhat for the energy makeup of the people who are here today. There are some parts of the ancient mystery school teachings that aren't even necessary now, or that are actually detrimental. So, you will need to be very discerning as you gather this material.

"When I last came to the planet, I was taught many of the ancient teachings, and I was taught from a young age to embrace all of them. That was my path, to learn about all these teachings and then to update them for the current people I was to reach. The people of that day were not ready for the strict teachings that I went through with the Essenes and other groups. I had to temper the teachings and just give the essence of what they needed to hear at that time. Since then, unfortunately, those messages have been distorted. But I simply give this to you as an example because as you delve into these ancient mysteries, you will need to bring forth only that which the current people who are waking up and needing guidance can handle.

"In this day and age, and in this country, people are extremely busy. So busy that they have very little time for their spiritual growth. Therefore, what you teach needs to accommodate these people and help them live a life of Spirit while doing their job and other activities. Little by little, you can help them break free of running on the treadmill. As they start to awaken, they will change their lives for the better.

"Helping people to open up in a balanced way, this is the key. Many schools of thought are not balanced. People learn to move into vast spaces and open their psychic abilities, but they are not ready for it emotionally or physically. And then there is power abuse, which has been a major problem on the planet. We know you will stay in integrity."

Omaran nodded. "I understand all that, and it makes sense to combine appropriate ancient teachings with what you Masters teach us. Thank you." His mind was errantly going back into overwhelm mode.

Suddenly, Jeshua laughed heartily. "Ah, but we are so serious."

Omaran let out a sigh and chuckled, realizing that he had been getting tense. "I'm sorry."

"Let us lighten up just a bit. After all, what good is being on the planet if you cannot enjoy it? Enjoy your senses. Enjoy what you are doing. Enjoy your life! Enjoy your mission! Enjoy your work!"

After Jeshua left and Antera came back to normal consciousness, she opened her eyes. Omaran was sitting across from her and still had his eyes closed, taking in the blessing Jeshua had given them. They always felt so wonderfully loved and uplifted after these "visits."

When Omaran opened his eyes, he said, "Wow, I feel good now. For a while there I was thinking this project is too big for us, too complicated. But right now, it seems perfectly doable."

"I will continue developing the classes and school curriculum. That is what I am good at. So don't be concerned with that. What are you working on?"

"Hmmm, well, not much right now. But I will think about it."

Antera knew what that meant. He had been procrastinating for months and would keep putting the project off. But she did not push Omaran. He would need to heal his limiting thoughts and doubts to progress. In the meantime, there was plenty for her to do, and now that web-based classes were becoming possible, they could have a successful virtual center.

"Maybe just going through this process of trying to create a physical center is so we can develop new skills or heal some things," Antera said.

"Hmmm . . . I never thought of that. You mean mastering my self-doubt and learning how to control my thoughts may be the whole purpose of this project?"

"It's just a thought."

22

Order of the Blue Snake

On her birthday in late May, Antera arranged to go out in the woods alone, as had been her tradition for decades. She loved the solitude and opportunity to write in her journal, meditate, ask for guidance, and think about the last year. Omaran liked to accompany her on these hikes, finding a spot for himself close by but out of sight and hearing.

Sitting on a patch of pine needles, Antera settled in to meditate and write her yearly entry into her journal. It was a warm, sunny day and a slight breeze kept it from being too hot. She was at a spot they had been to before, after a short hike through the forest, which they had been told by St. Germain was called Valley of the Holies, though they did not know why. It seemed a funny name, being hardly a valley. But it was somewhat flat compared with the rest of the mountain. The elevation was above 6000 feet.

After writing and meditating for about half an hour, Antera stood up and made her formal declaration of desires and intentions for the next year. She gave thanks for all that had happened in her life the last year, knowing that the time of birth is the most powerful moment of the year, resonating with all the other birth times in her life. Then she slowly walked back and forth in her area in a walking meditation, feeling how her intentions had been heard and opening to receive anything that was important for the next year.

As soon as she sat down again to meditate, a presence made itself known. Antera pushed it aside so she could continue her meditation, but it persisted. So, she turned her attention to the being to find out why. There were, in fact, a group of beings, all female, wearing beautiful flowing gowns in various shades of blue. They looked and felt angelic.

As soon as Antera focused on the group, her attention was riveted. It was like being shifted into another space, another dimension of reality, one she hadn't noticed until then, though she had been in this place for over an hour. Deliberately opening to this group now, and curious about why they had appeared, she said nothing for a few moments.

One of the beings, who seemed to be the spokesperson, started showing her pictures of an initiation ceremony where the angels in blue were doing an initiation of some kind for an unknown woman. The scene then rapidly switched to another ceremony, and another, each scene an initiation for a different woman, filling each with Light and the rapture of the Divine.

The scenes disappeared, and the leader turned back to Antera to see if she was understanding. She wasn't, and really didn't have a clue as to why this was being shown.

"You have come to a special place," the Light Being said. "A sacred place."

Antera nodded. "I do like it here. But why did you show me those initiations? Is this a part of the history of this area?"

"Not exactly."

Antera waited for her to continue.

"My name is Tara. And this group with me is dedicated to bringing more of Divine Mother's Light into the world."

Closing her eyes, Antera opened more of her inner clairvoyant sense. Tara was more visible here, and was revealed to be intensely bright and beautiful, no doubt an Ascended Master or high-level angel. Basking in Tara's energy and feeling her heart open in recognition as if she knew this being from long ago, Antera's eyes filled with tears of joy.

"Thank you for coming and showing yourself to me."

Tara smiled warmly. "The time has come for Divine Mother's energy to be more prevalent on the planet, and that is the goal of all of us. It is the lack of the Divine Feminine energy that has allowed so many problems and injustices to perpetuate."

"Yes, of course I agree."

"I know you do." She gestured to the other angelic beings. "This group is called the Holy Sisters."

"Holy Sisters?" Antera thought it was a strange name for a group of angels. "Are they a group of nuns or a religious sect?"

Laughing, Tara said, "No, they are not nuns or part of any religion. Divine Mother asked them to bring through a new aspect of her energy through this place."

"Through this specific place on the mountain?"

"Indeed. That is why it is called the Valley of the Holies. Since you first came here years ago, the energy has been building through the focused intent of the Holy Sisters, working tirelessly. This is the location."

"No wonder we like this valley so much!" Antera was impressed, but still wondering why all this was being told to her.

"The bigger group's name is perhaps more important. The Holy Sisters build and maintain the energy and it is almost ready to be taken out to the world by humans. The name of the group is Order of the Blue Snake."

Antera considered that. Blue snake? What kind of name was that, for devotees to Divine Mother? She could think of many other, more pleasant, names . . . White Swan, Golden Dove, Pink Rose. Feeling a bit like a rebellious child—this was a Master she was talking to, after all— she could not stop herself from expressing her resistance to the name. She retorted, "Snakes aren't exactly a well-liked animal. And why blue? That is a male color, and this is a female group, right?"

Again, Tara laughed, a silky, delightful sound. "I thought you may say that. But snakes throughout history, until the last few thousand years, have had extremely positive aspects. They symbolize the feminine, healing energy, transformation, and the kundalini. I invite you to research this when you get home.

"As far as the color, remember the Three-Fold Flame of the heart? It is made of three colors and aspects. Evolution of humans depends on developing all three in a balanced way: yellow is wisdom, pink is love, and blue is power. This is the blue you want to think about."

Putting this together, Antera understood. "So, the name means healing power?"

"Close enough. But more precisely, feminine healing power. It is about embracing or awakening the feminine power, the power of the healer, which is a distinct kind of feminine power that has been suppressed for a long time."

Antera thought about religious statues of Mother Mary, which often had a snake under one of her feet, like she was keeping it under control. This would mean she was suppressing her female power, which made perfect sense considering how the Christian church had successfully accomplished a massive suppression of female energy and women. She was starting to make connections.

A gust of wind blew her hair onto her face, and she brushed it aside with her hand. The dappled shade from the fir tree she was sitting underneath had shifted with the position of the sun, so she moved over, repositioning her body to stay in the shade. She closed her eyes again and Tara was still there, waiting.

Tara showed her a picture of a blue snake with orange eyes and said, "Here is the group emblem."

"Okay, that is nice. Is there a significance to the orange eyes?"

"The orange represents the opposite of blue and is a very physical color, symbolizing the projection of spiritual energies into the physical world."

"I see." Antera was taking it all in. "But I still don't know what all of this has to do with me."

"You are to be initiated into this order today, as the first human member, if you want. We are ready. If you decide to do this, you will then be able to initiate others, if you so choose."

This was unexpected, and Antera was a bit wary. It wasn't that she didn't trust the luminous Tara, but initiations were serious business, not to be taken lightly. She said, "What would happen if I did? What is the initiation, exactly?"

"It won't take long. You will have your female power enhanced. And by bringing this empowerment into the physical world you can help other women regain their power. Plus, you will have the honor of helping Divine Mother bring her upgraded energy more fully to humanity."

There was no choice, really. More empowerment was one of the things she was asking for on this birthday, and she knew the importance of the male-female balance. She gave her unequivocal consent and was excited in anticipation.

It was a powerful experience. The Holy Sisters surrounded her, and she was engulfed in a flame that was bright blue and taken through a series of profound expansions. To keep it sacred, she was asked not to share the details of it with anyone.

The whole process took less than an hour, but she realized that she had been preparing for it for about a year, starting with her spiritual intensive with St. Germain. Just as it wrapped up, Omaran walked over to her. It was perfect timing. He said, "Ready to go home?" He could see that she was radiant and smiling. "Looks like you had a good time!"

She burst out laughing and spun around in place a few times with her arms spread. "Yes!"

On the hike back to the truck, she told him a little of what had happened. He listened quietly, then said, "Fascinating! I want to be initiated! Is it only for women?"

"I don't know, but that is an interesting question. They only talked about women. But I will ask when I can. I'm really not sure about much. I need to integrate the initiation first." The power of her experience was pulsing through her as they hiked, and she knew it would take weeks to integrate and understand this blessing from Divine Mother.

23

Being the Experiment

Blue snakes had to be set aside for the time being so they could prepare for the Summer Solstice event, which took all their time in the weeks before. Omaran was cleaning up the yard and Antera worked on the content of the event and preparation for initiations. By the first of June they could palpably feel the energies building toward the group initiation. The people who heard and answered the inner call for this were all quite extraordinary individuals and Antera and Omaran loved meeting them, hearing their stories, and helping them to become conscious members of the Order of Melchizedek.

A week before, all the last-minute tasks were adding up. Antera had a to-do list a page long for this, and that didn't include all her other work, which had a page of its own.

"I think we need a cook," sighed Antera, as she thought about what she still hoped to finish before she went to sleep later that night.

"I got it tonight. You just keep working," Omaran put in helpfully.

"Well okay, but what can you make? A salad with avocado would be fine." She had always done most of the food preparation, and his skills in this area were questionable.

"I will put a scrumptious plate of something in front of you, never fear."

"Okay, I'll get some greens from the garden. Be right back!"

Antera ran out with a bowl to collect lettuce, spinach, and various other greens. A few peas were also ripe. She loved growing their food and eating it fresh, so the life force was strong. After depositing the bowl in the kitchen, she went back upstairs to the office until he called her to dinner. Sure enough, he had made a delicious salad with garbanzo beans.

Her sister Rose arrived a few days later, in time to help with preparations. Much of the ceremony and process had been developed by the two sisters together, and Rose always tried to make it to the mountain for this gathering. She was highly psychic like her sister and was happy to offer healing on all the initiates to prepare them for their initiation.

Antera's ex-husband, Michael, also arrived a day early and was promptly put to work, which he cheerfully embraced. The event went off with hardly a glitch, and Michael had to leave right after it was over. Antera, Omaran, and Rose were exhausted, sprawled out in the living room after everyone left, discussing how everything had gone while it was fresh so they could make changes for next year.

Antera decided to share a bit about the Order of the Blue Snake with Rose, and her response was very enthusiastic, saying, "I want to be initiated too! Let's go up there today! Is it a long hike? I leave to go home tomorrow."

Omaran echoed her with, "I'd kind-of like to be initiated into it as well."

"I thought that would be your response," Antera said to Rose. Turning to Omaran, she asked, "Are you sure you want to, Omaran?"

Omaran said, "I do want to, but we still aren't sure if men are allowed. I've had time to think about it since you were initiated. Honestly, a couple of times I have wondered if I really wanted to be initiated into a feminine order, but now I realize that we all have both masculine and feminine energies, and my goal is to be balanced in both parts. So, after giving it some consideration, I do want to if it is allowed."

Rose said, "Antera, can you channel Mary or someone to ask if men are allowed? It is the longest day of the year, so maybe we have time to go up there to the place where you were initiated."

"Right now? I'm drained from the event."

"We need to get feedback about the event anyway," Omaran said. "And Rose won't be here tomorrow. Please . . ."

"Please," Rose chimed in.

So, they set up and Antera opened to the Masters, first inviting St. Germain to talk about the event, then Mother Mary to answer their questions about the Order of the Blue Snake.

Soon after closing her eyes, Antera said, "Well, St. Germain is here. He's his usual ebullient self after ceremonies. In fact, a whole group of them is here."

The Master St. Germain congratulated them on the successful event and gave them some suggestions for next year. He added, "I hope you realize that you benefit as well. Every time you give this kind of spiritual service, even though you feel you have worked hard, you get benefit because it is completely done in love and with no personal gain, other than advancement along your own spiritual path. This creates purity."

After he had his say and answered some questions for them, he stepped aside for Mother Mary.

She said, "Hello my brother and sisters. It's wonderful to be here again and to speak with you. I am so grateful that you are doing the work that you are doing, and I am also very pleased that you are moving ahead with the Order of the Blue Snake, because it is a vortex of possibilities on the planet that will draw women into their power. You will find that as more and more people join, that vortex will become stronger. As people are added to the organization, the power of the feminine will grow, and grow, and grow.

"This is one of the wonderful ways that the energy of Divine Mother will find its way into the world. There are many ways that she is poking her fingers into the culture, and this is one of those fingers of Light from Divine Mother. She is poking her fingers all over the world, so to speak, and hoping that some of these activities will take, and humans will follow through on these opportunities.

"This order, though it is ancient in its essence, is a new order for these times. Its essence goes way back, but at this time it is so needed that we have a resurgence of this energy, new for the planet. The teachings are ancient, but they have been upgraded to be implemented in the current world, to fully bring forth these particular energies that are ripe. And so . . . BLUE!!!

"It seems the Holy Sisters do want you three to go up there. Simply go up there and receive this transmission of energy from them. They hold it in that place. Take your ceremonial and sacred objects. I suggest you go and be pleasantly surprised at what will happen. Do you have any other questions?"

Rose said, "The last week or so I've been craving blue."

"Well, as soon as Antera got her initiation you were immediately involved, both of you. And Omaran, as the first man to be initiated, we ask that you pay special attention to what happens within your system, because after all, this is slightly experimental. We want to know how this energy works in the male body. We know how it works in the female. So, we will ask you to pay particular attention so you can report on this, if you don't mind."

Omaran was excited. He could be initiated! "I am honored to do this. It's hard to express how pleased I am. I certainly will do that."

Mary ended with, "Let's go! I will see you there."

When Antera opened her eyes, Omaran and Rose were already thinking about what to take so they could start up the mountain quickly.

Omaran blurted out, "So what do we need to bring for the experiment?"

Antera and Rose looked at each other, then burst out laughing. Rose said, "Did you mean to say, 'what do we need to bring for the ceremony'?"

Omaran blushed. "Yes! Why did I say that?"

They would soon find out.

After a dusty ride on rutted, rocky roads, they parked the truck in the usual spot for this hike and started walking up the trail. Antera and Rose began talking about the initiation. Omaran wasn't really paying attention to them until he heard Antera talking about the possibility of leading others up to the area for initiation in the future. He and Antera had been up to the Valley of the Holies many times over the twelve years since they were first led there by St. Germain. However, the idea of leading others up there seemed to throw him a bit. It was not a particularly easy trail, and in fact for much of it there was no trail at all. He knew it would be his responsibility to get the group up and down safely. This responsibility began growing in his mind, distracting him from his surroundings until he lost his bearings.

They were about halfway there when he shouted, "Wait! We missed the turn. We need to go back." He knew they needed to be near the taller fir trees he could see off to the right in the distance, but he wasn't sure how to get there. Something was wrong!

Antera stopped and looked back. She was in the lead, followed by Rose, with Omaran in the rear and Faith trotting along between them. "Are you sure? This still looks familiar."

"Yes, we have to go back to that big log and turn there."

Antera knew Omaran had a much better sense of direction than she did, so she trusted him. He had only led her astray once, a few years ago, on Black Butte. So, with some hesitation, she turned around to where he said to go.

They all stopped in front of a very large field of sharp, volcanic boulders and stared for a moment.

Antera said, "We've never gone this way before. It looks treacherous."

"And I don't have good boots," Rose said anxiously. She didn't think she could do it. It would be climbing on hands and feet over the sharp, large rocks.

Omaran was gazing at some trees in the distance. "We need to get up there," he pointed. "I guess we missed a turn further back or something. But if we go in that direction, we will get back to the trail. I'll go first, and you two can slowly make your way behind me."

He took off, up the slope. Faith followed him with no problem, her toenails easily sticking to the boulders. Omaran was carrying a pack on his back, and a drum in his hand.

The sisters reluctantly started out also, watching Omaran get farther and farther away. They could see him pop up and down in the distance as he made his way over boulders.

Antera said, "I don't know what has gotten into him, he seems disoriented like there is something wrong. We've never gone this way before." She had good boots and was used to boulder hopping, but she was concerned about her sister.

They kept trudging on, heading for the trees he had pointed out. At this rate, Antera thought, they may not make it back to the truck before dark. Suddenly, a loud bang resounded among the rocks. It sounded like Omaran must have dropped the drum.

Antera yelled to Omaran, "Are you alright?"

"I'm okay," came the faint reply. They continued their laborious climb.

Omaran had slipped on the rocks and fallen. Shaken and a bit in shock, he just sat there. Faith came up and sniffed at him, concerned, so he gave her a pat for reassurance. He was very sure-footed and could not remember when he had last fallen. What was wrong with him? He also couldn't remember ever being so disoriented. He looked at the drum, which he had tried to save as he fell, and though it had made a loud noise when it hit, it seemed undamaged.

Assessing his body, he felt a warm tingling on his left arm, which had taken the biggest blow. Turning it over, he saw some blood dripping down his arm. Just a scrape. But why did this happen?

He took a few deliberate, deep breaths, slowly moving the air out and in. This helped him get centered, and then he concentrated on grounding. That felt better. Carefully getting up, he made sure he was in his body and in the here and now before moving again. That's when it hit him. He was going to be initiated into a female group. Women bleed, so naturally, he had to bleed as a part of his process of initiation! Suddenly, it made complete sense.

Less recklessly now, and with more respect for the volcanic rocks, he cautiously made his way over to where he felt the trail must be, and there it was. He waited in the shade of a large fir as he contemplated his fall. It wasn't long before Antera and Rose arrived. From here, it was clear that they had not needed to cut across the field of boulders. If they had continued the way they were headed, they would have ended up here much more quickly.

"It is not like you to lose your way, Omaran," Antera said. "What is going on with you?"

"I think this is all a part of my initiation." He told them what he had experienced, and his realization about being a man and needing to bleed.

Rose asked, "Did you feel lost and vulnerable?"

This caught Omaran off guard, and he had to think about that. He could own feeling lost, which was a very different feeling for him. He said slowly, "Yeah, I guess I did feel lost." He thought some more. For some reason, vulnerable was harder to own. Being a man who grew up during the days of John Wayne, being strong and in control was very engrained in his character. But he thought about how he had actually felt while wandering on the rocks directionless.

The sisters waited. He finally said, "And I admit I did feel vulnerable, too."

Rose said flatly, "That's how women often feel."

Omaran had to admit, at least to himself, that he had never thought of a woman's state of vulnerability before. It was a lot to think about.

Another thought came to him. "I think I also had to 'take the fall,' so to speak, for all the suppression of women by men in the past. There is a lot of bad karma accrued over the centuries by men. Perhaps my falling and bleeding is also to help make up for that in some small way."

"That all makes sense," Antera agreed. "Perhaps this is why Mary said your initiation would be experimental!"

She and Rose seemed to think this was very funny, and Omaran was trying to see the humor in it. Lost, vulnerable, bleeding, male karma, serious stuff! He had a lot to think about as they started walking again. He almost led them off trail again, but Antera was watching him carefully.

She said, "You just follow me and Faith for once, Dear."

He sheepishly complied.

There was still plenty of light in the sky when they arrived at the ceremonial spot. Rose and Omaran's initiations were just as profound as Antera's had been, and they were also told by the Holy Sisters not to share the details with anyone.

Afterwards, they sat on the ground to take it all in, saying little as they processed their experiences on their own. Before long, they noticed that the sun was setting and there was a definite drop in temperature. They still had to hike back to the truck before dark, so they packed up and started back, all of them feeling like they were on a natural high, very joyful and uplifted. Along the way, under a fir tree, was a pile of small branches that had dried in circles. Rose suggested they make crowns out of them, and they each chose one to fit their heads.

They nearly flew down the mountain to Sky the truck, and there was just enough dim light left to find their way, following Faith, who was a wonderful, reliable guide.

24

Blessings from the Mother

Antera wanted to return to the Valley of the Holies soon, so she could talk with the Holy Sisters and find out more about this Order of the Blue Snake. She felt not only more empowered since her initiation, but she noted that she easily held a constant higher perspective of her life. The joy she felt inside continued in a sustained way, unaffected by the outer world. This allowed her to take things much more lightly and see the humor in all the dramas people seemed to create. This new attitude, along with the feeling that she could achieve whatever she set her mind to, was marvelous, and just what she had asked for.

She had so much gratitude for Divine Mother, who she felt inside her in a close, personal sense, always present. The Divine Within had become very real, whereas before this phrase had only been a concept, just words. Now she knew what this meant experientially, to be one with the Divine. She had felt this several times before in this life, but not like this, so sustained. She had begun calling Divine Mother simply "Mother" so she could talk to this Presence. That differentiated Her from Mom, her human mother.

The Holy Sisters had said she could initiate others, but she did not have any idea how to do that. And there were other questions. Omaran was on board with another hike up there, so less than two weeks later, they were back on the trail. This time, Omaran felt normal and grounded, with no trouble finding the way. When they came to the place where he had taken them off trail across the boulders, they stopped for some water.

Omaran stood staring at the field of boulders, transfixed.

"Something wrong?" Antera asked.

"I cannot possibly believe I led us that way. From here it looks completely impossible, impassable."

"Well, you were the experiment."

He shook his head in wonderment as he packed his water bottle away and hoisted his pack to continue up to the valley.

After arriving, having lunch, and meditating silently for half an hour, Antera opened to the Holy Sisters. She described it for Omaran, saying, "I'm sensing the sisters around us, especially Tara. She says the initiation, for others, will be a process, not a single event, much like when we move into any kind of new level. There is a gradual process, and this initiation rite is the beginning of the process, which will then grow and build as initiates develop their female power. For some women—and men—this will take years. For others, who are already fairly empowered, it won't take as long to fully realize.

"It's about Divine Mother working through the human system in a way that has not been easily accomplished for a very, very long time. It has been deliberately blocked. This is a re-awakening of that female power, which may take a while. Divine Mother is very excited about this. She wants to see this spread as much as possible, so more and more people will realize this energy."

Omaran said, "I have been feeling it grow inside me, and all my healing work on myself and others has gotten stronger. And I feel it in other areas. I've been deeply affected and seem to have lots of power, but it is tempered by love. A perfect balance."

"They are pleased that you are integrating your initiation."

"Should we bring people up here to be initiated?" They had been thinking that they knew a few people locally who may be interested, and who could make the hike. But it would have to be arranged soon before it got too cold.

Antera said, "They say yes, for now. In the future that may change." She paused and listened. "Divine Mother is here to promote cooperation, healing, harmony, and peace. And She does it in a very powerful way, not in a wimpy way . . . I am feeling a huge force coming through me. Tara is bringing through Divine Mother."

Divine Mother said, "I do not accept anything but health and vitality and beauty and harmony and joy and Love! This is the natural state of being and I do not accept anything else! So, everything else will go! Everything will dissipate quickly and easily from the path of anyone who is initiated into this order. This is how my energy flows through you, this is how I project the Divine Power into the world, through all of you who initiate into this order and who embrace this energy and this power.

"IT IS THE POWER TO TRANSFORM THE WORLD! Do not have any doubts about that! There are no obstacles that can come in the way for very long of one who is a snake person, one who is of my bosom. I do not allow any obstacle; I do not allow any of the old patriarchal and paradigm energies to come in the way of my beautiful precious children.

"I say, use this power that comes through you from me and project it out to anything that comes in your path that is not of the highest order, that is not of joy and Love and Light and peace and harmony and health! Blocks will dissipate completely and very quickly if you use this energy properly. And I am telling you, THIS will transform the world! Very quickly. The more who can use this energy in the proper way—and I say that because I do not want anyone using it improperly, which will be impossible if they go through the initiation—the quicker it will propagate.

"This is a movement! And I, Divine Mother, the most Divine Energy that can come into the planet at this time, proclaim that this is so! I call for the Light of the most Divine Source to come through and bless everyone in the order and ask them to do the same for every obstacle that comes into their path.

"I hold all of you within my heart. I embrace all of you. This is not the power of the male force, this is the power of the female force, which means it is nurturing even though it is powerful. I hope you understand the difference, because when you are nurtured through love, harmony, and joy, you can transform anything that is not that way, rather than forcing your way through it or trying to change things physically, as the male energies have been doing.

"Let us propagate this energy! It is far more powerful than any other force that can be embraced as a human. It can be embraced by men as well as by women. Women are far more powerful in this energy than men, and therefore they will have an easier time of using it, but let us not forget that men have a female side as well and they can embrace my energies. I encourage them to embrace their feminine side, to embrace that which heals.

"And I envision this Blue Flame going out to the world at a very rapid pace. I invite all those who want to help in this project—to help spread this Blue Flame of healing out to the world—I invite you all to come and be initiated! Come and let me embrace you personally! I thank you all!"

Omaran felt the impact of these words, and especially the energy behind them, in his heart. He said, "I'm very grateful to be part of this order, thank you for the opportunity and the privilege."

Divine Mother responded, "Dear Omaran, you are the first male, and I am so happy that you went through with it. Remember that it is a process. It will take some time to fully integrate this energy and use it, but the more you use it for healing yourself and removing whatever blocks you have in your life, the stronger it will become. You did have to go through some initiatory experiences before the rite. What did you learn from those?"

"Well, I truly believe it was very important for me to go through all of that. I plowed ahead with my male energy and had to experience being powerless. I was wandering, I was lost."

"How could you have embraced your female power in such a circumstance?"

"I had to surrender, I had to just give up, and follow the flow. That's what I finally did."

"Yes. That was the awakening of this feminine power. You could have stopped and sat and asked for help, for direction, instead of wandering. Right?"

Omaran chuckled. It seemed obvious in hindsight. "Yes, that almost occurred to me. But in the state I was in, I didn't give it enough thought."

"I would also like to submit, my dear Omaran, that part of the reason for this was to show you that you have some emotional weakness. An emotional block was triggered to show you that you have unhealed trauma from the past, which made you go into that mode of losing your way and feeling lost."

"Yes, I do understand." He was near tears.

"Please feel my arms around you, my dear."

That put him over the edge, and his tears came out in sobs.

"Feel my nurturing energy. I love you so much. I want to give you the love you did not get from your mother. Just feel this love, you are so dear to me. Perhaps you could do some more forgiving of your mother. And just let me hold you, let me be your mother. I am your mother. I am your True Mother. Anyone else who is a human is only a brief and fleeting substitute and can only serve that purpose for a very short time. But I am always here. I am here to love you forever . . . forever! With never a disruption no matter what happens. I will not get sick. I will not die. I will not take my love from you; it will always be here, as it is here now. I thank you for being the first man to fully embrace this energy."

Omaran sniffed and whispered, "It's my pleasure."

"I'm so happy that you are part of this. It's been many, many years in the making and now it is starting to come to physical fruition. These Holy Sisters have been working here for a decade to build the energy up and to provide a place for me to fully come through. I thank the Holy Sisters, wonderful beings of Light!

"So please come again and contact me whenever you want. Bless you, bless you, bless you!"

25

Mount Rainer

There was much flow in their lives, with one project after another, but Antera and Omaran wanted to also fit in the first initiation for friends into the Order of the Blue Snake. The Holy Sisters had said all initiations needed to be on the new moon, so they decided on September, the soonest new moon to fall on a weekend, making it easier for people to attend. They notified a few people who might be interested and started planning.

In the meantime, they took another quick trip to the Northwest, this time to do release work on Mount Rainer. This volcano is one of the most likely to erupt in the Cascade Range. It is also very close to Seattle, a major city, making it closely watched by geologists.

After a ten-hour drive, they arrived at their campground on the mountain. It was as beautiful and impressive as they remembered from their last visit. The next morning found them high on the southeast side, enjoying the spectacular scenery and searching for a place to stop and do a release ceremony.

"I can feel the built-up energy inside this volcano, can you?" Antera said as Omaran drove the windy road.

"Yes, I can see why we were asked to come here. Let's help get this energy moving out!"

There weren't many side roads, but they found a place to pull off and park so they could scout the area. Spotting a trail that did not look much used, they packed what they needed and walked a short distance into the forest, soon finding a place they thought they would not be disturbed. The release ceremony went well, and many nature spirits joined in to make a strong upward vortex. The energy started pouring out and up.

"Well done!" Omaran exclaimed.

They continued driving around, hoping for a second location on the same side of the mountain. It took a while, but a dirt road finally showed up and they followed it into the forest a short distance and parked. After hiking less than a mile, they found themselves next to a small waterfall. The forest was lushly gorgeous with redwoods and ferns. They absorbed it all for a few minutes. No one was around, so they decided to make the vortex right there.

Sitting on a log afterwards, Antera laughed. "The nature spirits are still running around and laughing and singing the song we just sang. I see many of the same ones here that were at our first spot."

Omaran said, "I know, I saw them during the ceremony. As soon as we got in the car and picked out where we were going, they shot off for this area."

"It's amazing, because we didn't quite make it where we thought we were going, but they seemed to know where we would end up."

Antera closed her eyes to sense the energy. "We are being thanked by the Spirit of this mountain. Did you sense that being? It seems like a female presence to me more than a male."

"Yes, it seems female to me, too."

"Interesting . . . most people call this a male mountain. But there may be more than one deva here. This being is very grateful. I'm calling her the Angel of Mt Rainier. She has many, many nature spirits around here that help her. Oh! One of them I sense is the deva we talked to last time we were here, who called herself Lady of the Woods. She mostly resides in the woods, below timberline. She is so beautiful!"

"Is there anything else they want us to do here?"

Antera listened for a moment. "Not here. We just made Lady of the Woods' job a bit easier. She has been running around frantically, dealing with the effects of the energy that was built up inside the mountain. Now it has begun releasing. This mountain seems to voluntarily draw into itself negativity from the surrounding area, and there is plenty of that available from humans. Perhaps it drew in too much. The angel and all the devas have been overwhelmed. It is very good we came here. They do wish we would come back and do the other side. I'm telling them that we will try to come back for that, but we don't know when."

"We could make two more release points on the other side."

"Maybe," said Antera. She spoke to the Angel of Mount Rainier, "Hopefully by releasing this side, if you must erupt at some point, you can blow out this way where you're not going to hurt a lot of people and property. I know there are many animals on this side, but I think animals can get out of the way because they know an eruption is coming. People don't always get out of the way. They're pretty oblivious."

"Do you think it is getting ready to erupt?"

"I'm seeing a red fire really deep in the mountain, and it's strong."

"I hope this releasing helps."

"The more negativity we can transform and balance the better, and she does believe that we can do some energy work from home on the map. We can do harmonizing and balancing from a distance. It's not as effective but it all helps. There are other volcanoes around here, but this one seems to have the biggest fire under it."

Antera was shown how the volcanoes in the Cascade Range were all energetically connected underneath, including Mount Shasta and Mount Lassen, located the furthest south. Some of the negative energy from Rainier had been shunted all the way down to Lassen when Lassen blew in 1917, then some was sent to Mount St. Helens to release in its more recent eruption of 1980.

"It's all very interesting," she said. "The angel says she will blow off as much steam as she can through these two vents we created. She's very, very grateful. Her normal color is blue, but she's got this red fire under there. We need to help soothe the fire element. It wants attention, and it loves to consume. So, we need to be careful, because when a volcano erupts that is just the fire element consuming. It loves to blow out fire and transform the landscape."

"We hope that's not necessary here. It's such a beautiful area, and we want to preserve it."

"Yes. Let's make sure the fire elementals understand why we don't want to change the physical forms here."

They both focused on the fire elementals for a minute, then Antera burst out laughing. "Ha, ha! All the nature spirits keep dancing and singing! That's what they like doing best. They will do the work, but afterwards they just want to party! Celebrating a job well done!"

26

Fatherly Love

Antera stared at her keyboard, wanting to work on her new webinar but finding the distractions too strong to set aside. Omaran was acting irritable again, and even though she knew it had nothing to do with her, he projected his frustration all over the house. The worst part was, he still, after all this time and all he had healed, tended to let pain fester inside him and stew in it instead of taking the time to confront it quickly so it could be healed.

She knew that he knew deep inside, after being told so many times by the Masters and herself, that whatever he was upset about needed to be addressed. But when she asked what was going on he snapped at her, so she had to let him process it in his own ponderous way.

"It would be so much easier if I wasn't so energy sensitive," she thought. But of course, she didn't want to be unaware of energy like most people. She just couldn't maintain strong energy shields between herself and her twin flame. Everything he felt, she felt. Over the years, she had tried putting up various barriers or shields but had found that anything between them was not only unbearable, but unsustainable. So, she ended up taking the brunt of much of his pain and all she could do was clear it out of her system as often as possible. She sighed, reminding herself that this was her soul agreement with him.

She thought, "He's like a porcupine. Nice a lot of the time, then for no apparent reason, suddenly the sharp quills come out and I must get out of the way. No! Cancel that thought!" She didn't want to label him that way because it might hinder his healing. She knew how powerful thoughts are.

Taking a few minutes to clear her aura, then to send him energy from Divine Mother, she got back to work. Her plan was to give him the rest of the day then ask again if he wanted help with healing whatever pain had taken hold of him.

That evening, after an uncomfortable dinner together with strained attempts at talking about benign subjects, Antera gently approached him, saying, "You have been out of sorts for a few days now, do you want to tell me what is bothering you?"

Overcoming his first impulse to lash out at her, he took a deep breath. He knew what was upsetting him, but he didn't want to share it. "No, I'm fine." He reached for his laptop to check email.

"Well, you have been very short tempered. If you want to talk about it, I can probably help. Just let me know." She got up and went into the kitchen to clean up after dinner.

Omaran sat for only a minute before saying, "All right, I do know what is upsetting me."

Antera came back into the living room and stood listening, without saying a word.

"I'm sorry I have been hard to live with," he began, then paused. "I'm upset about my daughter."

He had enjoyed a great relationship with his daughter until his divorce from her mother, and it had been very difficult ever since. He knew that over the years his ex-wife had poisoned her against him.

"What did she say?"

"She disowned me, said she does not want anything to do with me."

"Why?"

"Because of some memories she says she has that aren't even true! I know nothing like that happened. I don't understand how she could even believe I would act that way!" He was angry. "I know it is from her mom, but I can't do anything about it! I want to defend myself, but how, when she won't listen?"

Omaran had hoped he was finished with the suffering his abusive ex-wife had caused him, but with the current situation, again there was anguish. He really loved his daughter and did not know how to best handle it. He had always avoided saying anything negative about his ex to his kids. What was the highest path to take?

"Wow. No wonder you are upset." Antera said soothingly.

"I just don't know what to do." Tears came to his eyes, his anger melting into the sadness of loss.

Antera let him cry and stayed silent but moved to sit next to him and put her arms around him. It was rare he was able to get in touch with sadness.

After a few minutes, she asked, "Do you want me to channel for you on this? Maybe the Masters have some insight."

He nodded, so half an hour later they were set up, with a fan blowing on them to stay comfortable in the August heat.

They sat silently for five minutes, then Antera said, "I'm seeing Jeshua. He's standing behind you, and he's got his arms around you. Can you feel him?"

"Yes, I do feel him," Omaran whispered as he tried to relax and let his energy expand to higher consciousness.

"Jeshua has his hands on your heart, and he's showing me something there. It's a wound. He's calling some healing angels to work on it. The angels have come and are toning together to start a healing. I'm looking at the wound. It appears to be a blow to the heart, but pretty deep . . . a big bruise, like you were hit there with a blunt object. Jeshua is talking."

Jeshua said, "My dear brother, what a blow you have taken. Allow these angels of Light to soothe and heal this wound. You have been holding off on this for a long time. Are you ready?"

Omaran wasn't sure what he was ready for, but he said, "Yes, yes I am."

"Then let us look at this more closely. I breathe Light into it. Your heart, your whole chest cavity fills up with Light."

Antera described what was happening. "He's blowing on it. I see a bunch of little dark things scattering out as he blows on it, like fragments of something being shattered, something dark. The angels are picking up the pieces, taking them away, and transforming them to Light. He's still blowing Light on your heart . . . and one last blast. He says . . ."

"That is it for now. The angels will continue to clean up and take care of these fragments of the dark star, for that is what you had in your heart. This is from a long time ago. The blow you just received is a reminder, a trigger for this deep hurt, and this deep mistake you made. Do you understand?"

Omaran was breathing deeply, feeling the work on his chest. He put his hands on his heart area. "Yes, I do."

Jeshua said, "You have made two major mistakes throughout your lifetimes, times when you thought you were strong enough to take on a tremendous amount of darkness to transform it. But you were not strong enough, for there was much that opposed you. Because of that, you took a lot of that darkness into your energy field, and this is what we clear out now."

"I'm trying to understand these mistakes from long ago," Omaran said. "Did I get swallowed up and intrigued by the darkness and willingly take it in, or was it forced upon me?"

"Some of each. You have within you an energy pattern of failure. This is because you attempted to but could not overcome the darkness. This pattern was implanted in you. And it has repeated for you over and over, even in this lifetime. It has been reinforced by some people, and now you are being hurt again. It is only an energy pattern. Do you understand, though, how deep this goes?"

"Probably not, but I guess this isn't just about me and my daughter," Omaran answered. "This past week has been pretty interesting. For the first time, I'm grateful that this happened. As much as it hurt, I'm finally ready to do something about this."

"Do you recognize the pattern that I speak of?"

"Well, it could possibly be my fear of confrontation. If I've tried to do things before and failed, then if someone can raise this fear in me again, it's going to stop me and put me right back into that same fearful place. Is that part of what you're talking about?"

"Yes," Jeshua said, "because as long as you carry this energy pattern, those who sense it can produce powerlessness in you, by magnifying that pattern. This means it is a button to be pushed by anyone who wishes to have you powerless. It is a deep-seated pattern that underlies many of the other problems you have had in this and previous lifetimes. It has repeated itself many times.

"Every time you did not succeed at something, you added a new layer to that energy pattern, and it grew. Whenever you were told that you could not do something or that you had failed at something, it grew. Look at your current situation. This is not about losing your daughter. It is about failing as a father."

Omaran could feel the truth of that. "Yes. That was beaten into me for many years during my previous marriage. I thought I'd rejected that."

"Whenever anyone said that to you, it was simply reinforcing what was in you already, and they knew it. It was a deliberate effort to disempower you by reinforcing your own energy pattern and making you fail."

"Maybe I'm just naïve, but it's hard for me to conceive of someone doing something like that intentionally. Accidently hurting someone is one thing, but intentionally?"

"Believe it, my brother. There are intentionally cruel people on this planet. Let us look even deeper at this energy because it does go back a long way. Until you can fully break through it you will continue to have encounters with it. To be successful at anything in life, you must be able to break through this pattern. Look at it now and just think of it as a pattern of energy. Where is it located?"

"Two places that come to mind are my heart and my throat."

"Alright, now put a form to it, think about its appearance. What color is it?"

"Black, spiked, metallic. A hard ball."

"Now, pull it out in front of your throat and heart, and hold it in front of you. What does it look like?"

"Now it doesn't seem as hard. The one from my throat is almost soft and mushy. The one from my heart seems like a closed box. It doesn't want to open."

"The forms have consciousness. You can speak to them. What do you say?"

"I forbid you to be part of me any longer. I command that you return to the Light."

"Do you have a tool that might be useful?"

Omaran thought about it. "Oh! My Sword of Light!"

"Indeed."

"As I hold my sword in front of me, and the Gold and White Light pours forth, I command you both to leave me and return to the Light! You are no longer a part of me! Your time is past!"

He touched the forms with the tip of his etheric sword, and they exploded. The angels swept in and picked up the pieces. The pressure in his heart and throat was instantly relieved, and he took a deep breath.

"Good. What you just cleared out was part of the pattern that was magnified, in this lifetime, by those who made you feel like a failure. But there is still a kernel left from previous lifetimes. To work on this kernel, you can do daily affirmations to reprogram the wiring that holds it in place. How can you affirm the opposite?"

"I am successful in everything I do and have done!"

"Yes. Say that a few times and mentally tell it to go back along your time track. Any of this core energy that comes into contact with this affirmation of Light will be immediately dissipated."

Omaran declared, "I am a powerful son of God/Goddess, and everything I do in this lifetime is perfection! Everything I do is a success! I command that this energy travel back on my entire timeline, changing any darkness that it meets into Light! I send this energy back along my timeline to clear out this core energy that has become attached to me! I dissolve it! I am a perfected child of God/Goddess! I AM THAT I AM!"

Jeshua let Omaran sit in that energy for a minute, then said, "Do you feel how that shifted things?"

"My gosh, yes! I haven't been where I am right now for quite a while . . . wow!"

"Send it forward in time as well."

"I send this Light forward, through the remainder of this lifetime, and any other times! I am successful in everything I do! I send this Light forward to blaze the way! So that every step, every action I take, is an expression of Divine Mother, Divine Father!"

"Good! Now you are in your power! If at any time you do not feel like this, it means you have allowed someone to take your power. This is your natural state of being!"

"This is different than anything I've ever felt. Wow."

The Master said, "Now, from this place of solid power, look at your daughter. Look at her soul. Does she hurt you?"

"No. I get the feeling she's looking to me for some kind of help."

"And what kind of help does she want?"

"She needs the truth that I carry when I'm in this state."

"How can you give that to her?"

"I believe I must speak the truth from my heart. But I also see controlling cords directed toward her from her mom, and she doesn't know how to clear those."

"You can only help those who ask for help. Do you see a course of action? Move back into your power."

"Even though I haven't been very good at it in the past, I feel like I need to talk to her in person, with no blame. I need to show her clearly who I am and let her take what she can of that. I feel I need to let her know she has done some harmful things, but tell her, not from a position of weakness or feeling sorry for myself, as I have at times, but from a place of power. It's not the easiest way for me because I haven't been good at confrontation, but I believe this is what I must do to cement this strength."

"And are you up to the challenge?"

Omaran sighed. "That's a good question."

"Can you maintain this power and be in her presence?"

"I could certainly say yes now. But honestly, I don't know."

"I submit to you that if you cannot hold your power, it will do no good to speak to her."

"Then perhaps I could send her a letter. I think I could do much better in a letter because I would have time to think about what I wanted to say and maintain command of the situation."

"Omaran, you are a powerful being, and what you are attempting is not a walk in the park. This is a major challenge, and you want to plan your strategy so that you maintain your power at all costs even if that means separating from her temporarily. I believe your relationship will mend, but sometimes it is very important to break off physical ties for a while, to allow yourself a period of cutting cords and bringing yourself back to your place of power, so you can let go of victimhood.

"I think a written letter would be far more effective than speaking to her at this time, and that would be my advice. The written letter has traditionally given people the time to think it over, the time to grow and heal between writing and receiving. That is why it is used for these kinds of circumstances. What do you think?"

"I think that's a wonderful idea. I've felt your presence all week, and I'm very grateful for you and all your help."

"You are welcome, my dear one. You need to be very aware of your energy and not allow yourself to get sucked down into feeling like a victim or feeling like it is not a good thing to let your daughter go for a while. Keep your perspective and stay in your power, and you can see the higher path that spreads out before you. You can see how everyone benefits from certain courses of action. No one benefits from you feeling like you've lost something, when in fact you are gaining your power, and you are allowing your daughter to do the same."

"Of course," Omaran said, understanding. "If I'm trapped, how can she get away?"

"It is a mutual arrangement, so there is no loss. Do you understand that?"

"Yes, I do, I really do."

"I want you to really think about it because this is a concept to remember. I do believe you are up to this challenge, especially if you look at it from the higher perspective of the soul, who sees much more than what is going on in these moments of perturbations and dramas. The soul has a much higher plan here and has been wanting you to heal this particular drama for a long, long time. You have been losing a battle for many lifetimes, and now it is time to get on your horse, hold your sword high and be the Christed Being that you are!"

Jeshua led Omaran in some decrees, which he repeated loudly and with feeling, proclaiming his power. The words kept vibrating and ringing in the air as he sat for a few minutes of silence.

After the energy had settled, Jeshua continued, "In the future, you may find yourself falling into the old patterns, but now the major energy of them is gone, so only the habit may remain. If that happens, recognize that habits are only habits, they have no substance. Decide right now. What will you do when you find yourself falling into the low spots again?"

"I know what low spots you're talking about." Omaran thought about it. "I need to do something I've only talked about doing before. I need to stop right then, no matter what I'm doing, and do those affirmations to bring me back to feeling this way. The key is to do it immediately any time this starts happening, not ten minutes later."

"Very well. And you can check in with me at any time, to gather this energy that you feel right now, remember that. I will leave you in this space, my dear brother."

This experience was momentous for Omaran. He felt as if he just had a tremendous healing. Twice a day, he began chanting the affirmations that he had spoken to Jeshua. As he did so, he could feel his power returning and clarity coming back to this mind. He was very diligent about this for a few weeks, and remembered what the Master had taught him, feeling a change in his energy field and body. This release of the old energetic pattern that had existed in both his conscious and unconscious bodies allowed him to move into his power in a much greater way than he could ever remember. He also realized that his initiation into Divine Mother's energy had opened him up to this healing.

The next day, Omaran wrote a letter to his daughter, explaining his viewpoint and expressing how much he loved her. He said that it was best that they did not communicate for a while. It was heart-felt and genuine. He had given up his expectations of their relationship, even releasing whether they could be in contact ever again, and this he had never been able to do before.

After it was sent, it stayed on his mind for a week as he anticipated her reading it and wondered what her reaction would be. He had let her go, and though he would always love her and hope to someday reconcile, he knew he needed to give it up and carry on with his life. Whenever he thought about her, which was often, he would send her love then move his mind to strengthening his feeling of being successful in all he did and had done, as taught by Jeshua, to heal the pain that he had carried for many lifetimes.

It would be about two years of separation before dad and daughter were back together, and after a few more years of discovering each other and how much they had in common, they not only became very good friends, but they rediscovered the relationship they had had earlier in this life and took that to new levels of understanding and learning together.

27

Fiery Codes

"The Fiery Codes of Light!" Antera blurted out forcefully.

She had opened her channel and Archangel Metatron was blasting his energy through her, in his usual way. Omaran could feel the power of these words but didn't know what they meant, so he remained silent, waiting to see what she would say next.

She continued, immersed in Metatron's energy, stating declarations. "I repeat: the Fiery Codes of Light! We have brought them forth from our hearts and activated them! They give us the wisdom of the ages and allow us to move forward without any baggage from the past. They delete karma of our past so that we may move forward in joy and ease, without attracting anything new to stand in our way. We clear out everything from our path! We are beings of the Light; we are beings of the Christ! We are exemplary beings of the human realm and of all dimensions. Our expression in all dimensions is powerful, strong, full of Love, full of Light, wisdom, experience, and joy!

"We are powerful in all our expressions, and we call on that power now to be with us in our human expression, in our bodies, in our lives, in our homes, and in everything we do. As the Fiery Codes are activated and blaze forth to remove veils, we see! We hear! We are aware!

"We let go of all density, we let go of the human dramas, and we reach forward into the Light, into the most powerful part of our beingness, into the most powerful part of our highest expression, to pull down that Light into the physical. We reach down into the physical to pull the physical up into the highest level. We are Divine Beings!"

Omaran felt a tremendous force come to him through her words, almost taking his breath away.

Antera continued, "And the Fiery Codes are being activated fully, in our hearts, removing the veils from the core crystals in our hearts, removing the veils so that we see all, so we may love fully and completely, as Christed beings. We give thanks for these codes, we give thanks for this help during these times of tumult, chaos, and irrationality, to identify that which is not real, not stable, not loving!"

Metatron started speaking directly through her. "Everything that is not of the highest vibration of Love will simply have to go! There is nothing that is of the lower nature that can survive in these times when the vibration of this planet raises to such a high level that the lower nature must be dissolved, or there will be tremendous conflict within each being. This does not serve!

"Right now, the choice is made in each individual: whether to follow Love or to allow that which is not Love to rule their decisions, to rule their words, to rule their actions. There is always a choice in every moment. Every choice you make—even the smallest choices during the day—every choice has consequences. Every choice allows you to choose between the highest and most loving path and that which is not so high or loving.

"The accumulation of all these little choices creates a big choice, creates your soul's choice to follow the Light or not. And this is what is meant by weighing your heart, in many of the mystery school traditions, when the Guard of Death or the Guard of the Underworld weighs your heart to see how light it is. In the Egyptian mythology it was weighed against a feather, and if the heart was heavier than the feather, the soul could not pass. It is the accumulation of all the many decisions throughout your life that creates the heaviness or the lightness in your heart. This determines whether you go on or not.

"Right now, so much is happening! The energy is so intense that it is very clear when someone is not choosing the higher path. It is very clear when someone is choosing anger or acting out of fear instead of acting out of love. Anything that has not been healed will be a choice presented to you, a choice in the present moment of whether to heal or not.

"These choices are what you have now in the present moment. At this time in the history of your planet, there is no time for dwelling on past mistakes. There is no time for this. There is no energy for this. The power of Right Now is the power of forgiveness! You can forgive everything immediately and effectively. You can wipe out thousands of years of mistakes, of problems, of issues between you and other people, of anything you have done you wish you hadn't done, of any way others have harmed you. Right now, you may completely let those things go! You may wipe your slate clean! This is the power of this time! It is unprecedented! By your intention, you can do this, by focusing on forgiveness and Love.

"This is the key to your successfully crossing this time in history with joy and with Love. Anything you hold onto that is not of Love, will hold you back, will cause you DEEP pain. This is why it is so important now to let go of everything you are holding. Let go of any hurt from the past, whether it is a hurt you caused or a hurt that someone else caused you. It is time to wipe it clean. Just imagine that you are erasing it, erasing it! This is powerful! Never has an opportunity been here like this one! All around you may be chaos, with people shouting and having problems, but you may sail through if, whenever there is any pain at all, you simply allow it to be erased in the past.

"If there is no pain in your past it is very difficult to have much pain in your present, because almost all pain in the present is caused by the past. So, wipe out all cords to other people, wipe out all the angry words you have heard or said. Wipe out all the places you have been where you have left energy and allow yourself to come into this moment clean and pure! Be with the other beings who have come to this moment, who have also had their Fiery Codes activated, who will sail through these times, who will be the rocks, who will be the strong ones for the others who do not have the knowledge or the wisdom to help them through it.

"Right now, at this moment in history, forgiveness and grace are the keys. There are always a few parts of your life where it is hardest to forgive, hardest to let go. Those are the areas that need your attention now. In the past there has always been time in the future to deal with these things. Now there is no more time in the future, the time is now! The time is now to clear out all those little corners that have been denied attention, and you know what they are. You will be shown what they are throughout this chaotic time, and you will need to stay on your toes, you will need to be alert, you will need to watch and not allow your attention to stray into the past, or to habitually ignore what you are feeling."

Omaran took all this in, thinking that it wasn't only advice for him, but it was for everyone. As Metatron talked, he felt the energy of the archangel fill the whole room.

"As you evolve," Metatron persisted, "you become more aware and more responsible. You cannot push things under the rug anymore. You may not get away with many things that other people can seemingly get away with. In the end, they will not. But that is not your concern. Your concern is for you and your evolution, your ability to forgive, and your ability to wipe clean the slate—so that there is only Light, past, present, and future. There really IS only Light, it is simply a matter of recognizing that. It is a matter of recognizing that the Truth is all there is, and the Light is all there is. And anything that appears to NOT be Light is not real. Period.

"If something appears to not be of the Light it is not real! It is a construct designed to teach you something, or designed to maintain the many, many dramas that play out on this planet on a continual basis. But it is not real! The reality is Love, the reality is Light, the reality is Truth! If you put your attention on that which is not real, you are not putting your attention on Truth and Light. That is your choice. Put your attention where you want, and it will grow. It will magnify. Put your attention on your Light and it will become brighter. Put your attention on something unreal and it will become more powerful and stronger. It doesn't make it any more real, but it may take away from your Light because you have put your attention on it."

Metatron paused. Just when Omaran started wondering if he should say something, the Archangel resumed. "The Fiery Codes are almost completely activated at this time. These codes are ancient, they were placed with your soul when you first came to this planet. And now they are complete! Allow them to breathe into you, breathe into your system the perfection of your soul, the mission of your soul, the completion of your soul.

"And we thank you for being here, we thank you for being the holders of this Light! And whatever you desire, right now, state it."

Now Omaran knew he needed to make a declaration, and he was ready. "I, Omaran, with all my heart and soul, desire, most of all, to completely forgive all those who have harmed me in any way, with word, with action, in this and all my other lifetimes. I wish to surround them with Love, and I ask them for forgiveness for all the things I have done that have not been from Love. That I desire most of all."

"Embrace this with your Light. Embrace all of it. Now call those Fiery Codes, the fire letters in your heart, to help you transform this energy. You have taken into your energy field much darkness from the past, now you must transform it, RIGHT NOW, INSTANTANEOUSLY! THROUGHOUT TIME!"

"I call upon the Fire Codes within me," Omaran said, "to cleanse all the darkness I have called forth willingly. I ask now that it all be cleansed so that only the Light is a part of me, and I am only a part of the Light. And the darkness is no more!"

Metatron raised his voice even louder. "And take that energy INTO THE LIGHT! Allow it to send you even higher, allow it to become the MOST PURE AND BEAUTIFUL LIGHT, LIKE THE SUN! Allow it to give you more Strength, more Wisdom, more Love, more Spirit! Allow it to feed your soul in its purified form. In your powerful state you can transform the darkest energy into energy of the Light, with your conscious intent!

"Now, do you feel that?"

Omaran took a deep breath and adjusted his position in the chair. "Yes! Yes, I do."

"There is still a small part that needs to be transformed. Please continue working on this. Perhaps there is a part of yourself that does not want to give this up or is not ready to transform."

"Yes! I do. I want to transform this now."

"Do so with your intent."

"I call upon the highest energies of Divine Mother and Divine Father that I can bring in. I want all this darkness changed into Light. I want to forgive everything, and everyone, including myself."

"All you are changing is your energy. You will not change anyone else. But this needs to be changed within your energy field, which is now quite vast. You are changing your past! You are changing your attitudes. You are changing your feelings! You are letting go of any grudges!

"When you recognize that you are a Christed being, there is no lack of responsibility. Other people who are not so evolved can get away with things, but you may not. The trick to navigating this age is for Lightworkers to come together in solidarity and to focus their attention on the Light and only on the Light, and to do it together because that is so powerful. This is the trick for navigating this age, this is the transformative path!

"And now how do you feel?"

"I feel much better. I feel . . ." He suddenly chuckled. "I feel brilliant!"

"And you look brilliant! Now, can you maintain this?"

"Ah, well we'll see. I'm very grateful for all the tools I've been given. And I have been using them more than ever. I know what I must do."

"Sometimes you forget how powerful you are. Sometimes you forget that you are fully endowed with the Christ energies. It is easy to forget when you live a life of human drama, but now you cannot afford to forget, if you want to make it through these times and hold your Light strong. This is what is required."

"Thank you."

"I am METATRON OF THE LIGHT! And I give you my blessing, I give you Light to take on your journey, I give you remembrance of who you are. I give you protection, and I give you the Fiery Codes in your heart.

"May the Light be with you forever and forever. And may you always remember who you are! Shalom."

They sat for a few minutes, integrating. When they opened their eyes and looked at each other, Omaran said, "I was not expecting that. I love the Fire Codes!"

"I wasn't expecting it, either. He was so powerful coming through that I almost drifted off into another dimension," Antera mused. "But I managed to stay with it." She touched her throat. "My voice feels a bit strained."

"It's no wonder. You really were talking loudly and lower than your normal voice."

"I bet." She smiled. They bent forward and hugged, with the Christ Light swirling around them.

28

Anything Is Possible

As summer progressed to fall, they continued to be very busy, keeping up their property as well as all their other work and projects. Antera's clientele continued to grow, filling her schedule with as many sessions as she wanted, all by word of mouth. She also continued developing classes to teach as webinars, guided by the Masters for the Mystery School, and she was excited about all of it.

Although much headway was being made in gathering tools and preparing the body of knowledge for the school, progress on creating a physical center had yet to take shape. Despite many gifts and much encouragement from the Beings of Light, the energy just did not seem to be there to move it forward. They thought they still wanted to build this, however.

Solomon came to talk about it one evening in September. They had the idea of talking with Mary about something else, but over the years they had come to accept that these powerful Beings did not come to their beck and call. Sometimes another being wanted to talk instead, and it was always the perfect information they needed each time.

After situating themselves comfortably in the living room, Samantha on the couch next to Antera and Faith on the floor by their feet, Antera said, "I couldn't seem to call Mary in, and now I'm standing in front of King Solomon, ha, ha! I guess he wants to talk to us."

"Uh, oh," Omaran thought. He knew what was probably coming. Solomon had been talking to them every month or so, encouraging the project and giving them many great ideas. The last time, he had asked them to study the secrets of sacred architecture and power within buildings. They had read a few books on this since then, but it was quite a big topic and would take some time to really study.

Solomon started with, "I am a patient man . . ."

Antera and Omaran both laughed, easing some of Omaran's trepidation.

"But I do hope that you will put some more effort into this project so that we can see it moving forward. I have given you many tools and gifts to use and I will continue to hold these available for you, until it seems that you have given up or you have turned your attention away. It is my hope that you will continue to work on this project and draw forth the needed funds and expertise to build your center, and that it will happen fairly soon, because the window of opportunity that allows you the time and energies for this will not be open forever. It is still open, but if you do not take some action before the end of the year, the window may be missed because of the many changes coming on the path of this planet.

"But if the opportunity is not seized," the Master said soothingly, "there is no problem, it simply will not be manifest. There do not need to be any bad feelings or guilt involved. Something else will come along and perhaps someone else will seize the opportunity. Tell me how it is going."

Omaran said, "I realize we haven't done what we said we would do. It seems a bit daunting, I guess. That could be from a lack of faith from me. I've had that pattern in the past. What I'm going to say now is not an excuse, but I've been going through some deep healing lately, and have been focusing on that instead of the center."

"My dear Omaran, I'm not trying to make you feel guilty or feel that you have not measured up in some way. That is not my intent here. I'm simply telling you that the window needs to be taken advantage of if you are going to do it. If you do not do it there are no problems with that. Of course, we want to see it done and you want to see it done, but we all know how busy you have been. There is no reason for you to feel that you have not done enough. I know how much you do. This is not about that."

"Thank you."

"I see that everything you have gone through in this last year was essential! You have been breaking down barriers, letting go of attachments, letting go of energy-draining connections that have held you back in the past. I praise you for doing this, my dear man! And I do see that, because you are gaining new skills in the inner realms, you now have new ways of clearing out anything that blocks you or keeps you from moving forward. These are such valuable skills and if you use them, you may move forward very quickly with this project. Do you see this?"

"Yes, and thank you for saying all that. I really appreciate it."

"If you simply focus on the project every day, just a little, the energy will move forward again."

"That sounds wonderful."

"If this is what you still want."

"Yes, I do want this."

"Are you sure?"

"Yes. And thank you for reminding me to use my tools to help me heal the remaining fear that I have. I know that's what has been stopping me."

"What is the fear?"

"It's the fear of doing something big, and not feeling worthy of it. I have done quite a bit of work on this, but I still have some of this left. I need more faith."

"As you speak this, I see these energies dissipating away from you. I see Omaran, the one who embraces his power, coming forth from within; the one who has courage, the one who uses his Sword of Light to tap into any quality he needs!

"If you need courage, take out your sword and stick it into a ball of courage, sucking it up into your system. If you need faith, stick your sword right into a BIG sphere of faith and suck it right up into your system. Or you can ground into these things inside the Earth. Imagine different pools of substances that you need and bring those into your system. Use the Fiery Codes! When you do this, what happens to the fear?"

"It dissipates. It is gone."

"It is totally gone! Useless! Transformed into useful material. Fear is never something you want to embrace for very long. If you ever feel it coming up, you can replace it with a quality that you want, like courage or faith, and the ability to be sure of your path and to feel your vast power! There is no end to the power that the two of you can generate together. You are like twin Pillars of Light. I would not be here if I did not see this. So, I want you to see yourselves as you truly are.

"If you feel the fear of failure come upon you, tap into the energies of success! The energy of failure is from long ago, and no longer applies to this time. In fact, it did not apply to that time either. You both failed to hold together land that was destined to fall apart. There was nothing else you could do. And yet, you have held on to that as a failure."

Omaran knew he was referring to their experience in Lemuria, long ago, when they had been healers of the land with the job of maintaining harmony by sensing problem areas and sending energy to heal or dispel the discord. When the land broke up because of disharmony, despite all their and others' efforts, they had felt partially responsible.

Solomon went on to give them a pep talk, further encouraging them to continue with the project. Omaran could feel the strength of Solomon's words, and while in the energy of this Master, anything seemed not only possible, but easy.

After the Master left and Antera and Omaran opened their eyes, Omaran exclaimed, "Wow! When we are locked in like that with Solomon's energies, I feel like I could magnetize anything!"

"Without a doubt! And he mentioned using the Fiery Codes Metatron activated for us."

"I sure like the power in them, just the name lights me up. But back to what Solomon was talking about, building the center."

"Ah the center," Antera said wistfully. "I haven't forgotten, and I'm working on the classes. But we don't want to neglect the rest of it. We just need to spend some time on it."

"Well, maybe we will have more time now that the land-healing work is slowing down. We probably are going to want to put a few more points in, especially in California, but we don't have to do that now. I'm still checking in with all the grid points and I'll continue to do that, but I think the creation of new points may be winding down."

"Yes, it's been a fulfilling project, hasn't it?" Antera said. "And fun."

Omaran nodded and smiled. "Anything we do together is fun."

29

Overload in the Valley

Fifteen friends responded to the call to be initiated into Divine Mother's Order of the Blue Snake. Two weeks before the event, Omaran took two trips up the mountain to clear a walkable path for the group. Concerned that most people were not as experienced at hiking as he and Antera were, he used loppers to cut out a curvy, snake-like trail through the dense brush.

On the day of initiation, everyone met at Antera and Omaran's driveway, and they crammed into as few cars as possible. Six brave souls rode in the back of Sky inside the camper shell, bouncing around on a six-inch foam pad. The camper was not at all airtight, and quickly, after turning onto the dirt roads, became very thick with brown volcanic dust. But this did not dampen their spirits!

Walking, Antera led the group up the hill and Omaran brought up the rear to make sure everyone made it to their destination. One woman was recovering from a broken foot, and others had done little hiking in brushy, rocky terrain, so the pace was slow. But all were very determined and considered the hike a part of the initiation. No one complained.

To say the least, the initiation was very powerful, and each individual had their own personal experience, all profound and life changing. Now the order had a group of humans! At the time, Antera and Omaran didn't realize how big a success it had been and the amount of energy it had raised. But they soon found out.

A few days afterwards, they were already thinking about having a second initiation the next month, the last time possible before winter.

Generally, the first snow at that elevation wasn't until November, so they thought an October hike was safe, and they went ahead with plans.

However, a week before the event it snowed, very early and low on the mountain. Only a few flurries fell at their house, but they knew the Valley of the Holies would be covered in snow and inaccessible except by snowshoe, which ruled out any initiation there before next year. Surprised by this strange happening, they canceled the event.

"Maybe the Holy Sisters don't want another initiation so soon," Antera mused over dinner that evening. "Seems strange."

"Yes, I'm sure they could have prevented the snow if they wanted us to bring another group up there. I wonder what's going on," Omaran replied.

"I think I'll check in with the Holy Sisters during my morning meditation tomorrow and see what's up."

"Okay, that would be good. The temperatures are definitely lower than usual, and we've already had the first fire in our woodstove."

The next evening, she told Omaran what she had learned. "They don't want any more initiation ceremonies up there."

"No more ceremonies?"

"Apparently it built up a huge amount of Light and they do not want to attract that much attention to what they have created there. If we want to take people up just to meditate there, that will be alright, but no more initiations."

"So, what's the new plan?"

"They said we can create a place here on our property to do them. That will take some doing, so let's schedule the next one in spring after the snow is melted here. Apparently, we need to form an energy connection between this place and the valley, by taking rocks from here up to there and bringing rocks from there down to here. That will form a connecting path."

Omaran thought about making a new ceremony site on their property dedicated to Divine Mother. "I have an idea. How about dedicating that area just south of our lawn to it? It seems like a good spot, and it is already cleared."

They walked out to look at it in the waning light of the evening. When they had cleared the manzanita on the property for building their house, they had been guided to clear a small additional area in the thicket, hidden from view, without a clear purpose for it in mind.

"It's perfect!" Antera declared, picturing it as she walked around. "We can put a circle of rocks here for ceremony. I can do that. Could you put a really big rock on the south side for the altar?"

"Of course. Interestingly enough, I know the perfect rock. I saw it just the other day when I was walking Faith across the street. I will need some help getting it though, it will be way too heavy for me to get into the truck alone."

Antera remembered that her son, Orion, would be visiting soon. "Orion will be here next week. Do you think the two of you could get it in the truck?"

"We might need a third person, but he and I might be able to use a plank to reinforce it, and then somehow pull it up into the truck bed."

"Well, there you go, now you've got a plan. You love plans."

"That I do," he said, as the planning in his mind began. "At least we can get a good start on the area before it gets too cold and finish it next year."

With considerable effort, Omaran and Orion were able to get the rock he had picked out into the truck, using a plank to slide it in. When they got back to the house, they positioned the wheelbarrow to drop it in. Omaran was a bit nervous that the weight might collapse the wheelbarrow, but fortunately it held and the two of them were able to maneuver it out to the new circle of rocks.

And so, the new area was developed. Orion had brought some fruit trees from his garden in Oregon, and some flower bushes and herbs were added. The area was ready, but they still had to do the rock exchange between the Valley of the Holies and their property. As it turned out, the early snow wasn't followed by any more for a few weeks, so Omaran and Faith were able to go back up to the valley and make the exchange. Antera picked out three rocks from their property to take there, and Omaran brought back three bigger ones.

Shortly after this was accomplished, winter hit in earnest, and they turned to indoor projects.

30

Stable Places

It was in November that they got more information about the land-healing work. Apparently, the Masters did not think it was finished.

"St. Germain is here," Antera announced. "He's saying it has been a while, though he is always nearby. So much is happening. He's been very busy, and he knows we've been busy too. He's greeting us and thanking us for tuning in."

St. Germain said, "There are many things going on of interest. There are many paths that can be taken. So come with me into the higher realms. Expand your consciousness to a place where there is all the wisdom you need, all the guidance you need, all the flow of Divine Will, Divine Mind, and Divine Love. Everything is present when you expand to these realms, when you expand out to be within this illumined place. We surround you now with our blessing and support."

The two humans already felt very expanded, just from these few words from the Master, accompanied by the energy he gave.

"We see that you have jumped ahead, you have broken through some very old barriers, to give you the opportunities you have before you now, and to finally realize that which you have chosen to do while within the human sphere. You now have more skills on the inner planes, so you know where the flow is and what is going on in the realms of creation, which are far vaster, more complex, and full of more activity than the physical plane."

Antera and Omaran had been developing their psychic abilities to sense unseen forces more clearly. As they cleared all that was not Light and Love, these senses naturally opened. But they had also been doing some exercises to deliberately strengthen them, and this was producing great results, opening them to more awareness of what was really going on.

Germain said, "I have spoken to you before about how important it is for you to know what is going on in the inner planes before physical manifestation, which is the very last part of the creation process. Now you are becoming more aware of this inner plane activity, which gives you the upper hand in the creation process. If you are at the whim of the creation forces, you do not have control over them. As you gain control over those forces rather than letting them control you or act haphazardly, you are more in control of what you co-create.

"These creative forces have been very polluted because of all the thoughtforms and negativity from humans. The trick is to use pure creative energy without letting it get tainted by the surrounding thoughtforms. It is very important that you recognize these outer influences that are constantly at work, so you do not channel that creative energy into a form that is not what you want.

"This is why it is so important to keep your channel clear, channeling only the purest creative force throughout all your work, your thoughts, and your deeds. This is the way to maintain the purity you want and need for your projects. The more aware you are of the forces around you, of the people around you, of the thoughtforms around you, the easier it will be for you to maintain that purity. Because you can either avoid or transform anything that comes within the path of your Beam of Light.

"I have told all of this to you before. I tell you this again, in a slightly different way, because you now have more abilities on the inner planes to sense what is going on around you. You know if something has been compromised or something is not quite right, or if there is a person who is trying to interfere.

"I see now that you are charging up your center building project every day, finally concentrating on the energetic form of it, and working on bringing it forward into the physical." He paused. "And are you ready for this, Omaran?"

Omaran laughed nervously. "Yes, yes, ha, ha, ha . . . uh, yes. I know that I will have fears coming up, but I believe I'm finally at a point where I'm usually releasing them immediately. So yes, I honestly believe I can finally do this."

"My dear Omaran, I certainly do admire your spirit. Every time I ask you that question, you always say you are ready. I do admire that, whether it is true or not. The fact that you say you are ready helps to bring it about. I believe you are more ready now than you have ever been. And it is a joyous project, is it not?"

"Yes, it really is."

Germain went on with some suggestions about how to visualize, then he asked, "Now, do you have questions for me tonight?"

Omaran had been hoping he would ask. "Yes, about the land healing. We think we are pretty much finished with it, but perhaps we could do just a few more grid points in California, one near Sacramento, one south of San Francisco, and one inland from San Diego, our most southern point. Are those good to do?"

"I would say wherever and whenever you can do these, do them! The points are very powerful and a very good use of your time. I'm sorry to say that there are very few people who have your intentions of energetically healing the planet. Most people are so involved with their own lives they cannot even begin to think of spending time on anything else. So please do whatever you can.

"There are many forces on this planet that are trying to create catastrophe and disaster. These are what you are working against. You sneak these grid points in, and they break through the negativity and hold Light, which slowly expands out into the countryside, dissipating negativity.

"The more there are, the more quickly they will finally overlap in their area of influence until there is a solid area that is at least partially influenced by these points. Each of them shines out into the surrounding countryside for miles and miles, slowly but persistently canceling out negativity around it. Therefore, we say the more the better! After a while, there will be no areas along the West Coast that do not feel some force of that influence."

"Okay, we will fill in with some more points," Omaran said enthusiastically. "Is there anything else you recommend for the project, or is it pretty much complete?"

"I would like to see some points a little farther inland. That would be my highest priority right now. Anchor the whole grid farther inland into more solid ground. Go as far inland as you can get, preferably into the Rocky Mountains. I know that would require a long trip, but at some point, we hope to see this done.

"The land-healing grid is working very well. However, some of the points are not as strong as others. This has to do with where they are located. Those along the coastal areas are not as strong as the ones that are anchored into firmer ground. Therefore, we ask you to go to the Rockies, for that is the most stable area of the continent. By creating strong points in the Rockies, you will greatly aid the points along the coast as you connect them and sense which ones need help, sending them energy from the stronger ones. This will help the entire grid."

"How many grid points do you think we will need in the Rockies?" Omaran asked.

"Because of the strength of the area, you will only need three or four. But they need to be in stable areas. For instance, the Tetons, where you love to go, would not be a good place for a strong point because the mountain range is much younger there. You need to lock into the older, stable areas. Do the research when you are ready, to find the best places to go.

"And later, possibly, you could work your way across the country. We know that would be a big project. Hopefully you will be able to train others to do this work, so you do not have to do it all yourselves."

"Ah! So, the project continues. The whole country! That's big. But we will get on it. Maybe next year." Omaran took a deep breath and decided to think about that later. The country would be such a big expansion of the project, it was too much to contemplate now. One trip at a time.

He had another question for the Master. "That does bring us to one more thing. While Antera is painting the sacred objects, she comes under psychic attack. I guess there are forces that don't want this project. She says it comes in as flows of negative energy at her and she has been able to keep them at a distance, but it takes a lot of effort. I suppose that means the objects are powerful, but is there anything else we can do to protect her and make it easier?"

"I believe it will help to become even more aware of what is going on energetically, because you will recognize what is happening quicker, and be able to take action to protect yourselves. And as you get more and more evolved and have higher vibrations in your bodies, your bodies will not be affected as much. That is part of the process, really honing the bodies.

"I see that you did very well for quite a while there, but some of your dietary habits have degraded slightly of late. I do see a big difference when you are on the raw foods, and I believe you probably feel it too. The vital energy in raw foods so far surpasses anything else you eat. It puts into your bodies that fine vibration that creates bodies of Light and purifies the vibration of your bodies so that those negative vibrations cannot stick. They simply pass on through. That is why I urged you to go on this very pure diet. The negativity will stick to acidic or heavy foods that you eat. As you get lighter, you get lighter in body. Use all your tools! But diet is the quickest and easiest way to maintain your health at its optimal level and create a body that is impervious to any kind of damage or infection, whether energetic or physical."

"Thank you for the reminder. Yes, sometimes we don't eat as well as other times, especially when traveling."

"You also have many angels and other beings here to help you, and they do the best they can. I know you probably feel that sometimes you do not get the protection you would like, but let me tell you, these beings are working very hard to keep you protected. However, if there is something in you that brings on harmful energies, they cannot violate your agreements unless you ask them to. They cannot interfere with anything unless they are given permission."

"Okay. Thank you so much for your wonderful guidance."

"It is my pleasure to be here and to see the two of you doing so well and working with the Three-Fold Flames in your hearts, building them ever stronger so that all three aspects are the same size. Make sure that you maintain the Three-Fold Flame in its purity, in its balanced and harmonious state, because if you ever get one or another of the flames out of balance with the other two, problems will occur. That is when projects get compromised, or interfering energy has a way in."

"Yes, we are both still focusing on the Three-Fold Flame."

"You can visualize each of your projects having a Three-Fold Flame as well, to bring balance so everyone involved will have great wisdom to see the higher path, love to bring innocence, compassion and forgiveness into the project to alleviate any problems between people, and power so there is plenty of spiritual energy to fuel it, keeping it going in its most immaculate state and power to reach out to the world."

"What a great idea! A Three-Fold Flame for a project!"

Germain ended with, "I leave you with a blessing from all of us, and I thank you."

They sat in the energies that lingered from St. Germain for a few moments, then Omaran opened his eyes and stared at Antera for a couple of seconds until she felt him looking at her and opened her eyes. She stretched and took a drink of water.

Omaran said, "Well, so much for the land healing winding down."

"Wow!" exclaimed Antera. "The Rockies area is huge, but afterwards the whole country? They will both be long trips, long drives. And how will we take the time off?"

"Well, it's not like we're going to go right away. Winter is here, so we obviously need to wait for warmer weather to go to the mountains. Then we can start thinking about the rest of the country."

"We could enlist Michael for some help with the Rockies, He's a geologist. He could find the most stable places."

"Great idea," Omaran agreed. "And speaking about trips, I was thinking that, since we will be visiting your folks in San Diego at Christmas time, maybe we could do a few more land-healing points on our way back."

"St. Germain did say the more the better, even though we have so many in California."

"True, but there are none in eastern California. I'm thinking about driving up the east side of the Sierras. One place I'm thinking of is Mammoth Mountain, especially because of all the seismic activity and magma movement." He knew talking about earthquakes and volcanoes would go a long way toward getting her excited about the trip. "Also, now that I think about it, I'd love to get back to Death Valley again, which is also on the eastern side. And you know, we could go to Sedona, which isn't that far away from your folks' place either."

"Ha, ha! Sure! You have obviously been thinking about this."

"Maybe a little."

Antera got up and headed to the kitchen to make dinner. "It would be nice to connect directly with Silver Horse again in Sedona," she said.

Omaran took that as a go, and immediately started planning the trip. Land-healing trips were fun and fulfilling at the same time. And they were good at it, according to the Masters, who could see the effects more clearly.

This wasn't the first time they had thought the project finished only to be asked to do another phase of it because the Masters said they were so pleased with the results. What had started as a few points on the coast of California had grown to a zigzag pattern to stabilize it, then the whole U.S. West Coast, and now further inland and eventually the whole country!

31

Guardian of the Deep

They left the San Diego area the day after Christmas, heading east to Sedona, Arizona. They had brought materials for creating five new grid points on this trip, one at a wildlife refuge in southwest Arizona, one in Sedona, then back to California for one in Death Valley, another in the Mammoth area, and the last one near Reno, Nevada. That was the plan.

As they entered the wildlife refuge, they realized that being out of sight for the ceremony was not an option. There were some rocks, but no trees. Fortunately, they could not see anyone around as they drove in and parked. They picked a small knoll that rose about a hundred feet a short hike away, and in half an hour they had climbed up onto it. From the top, they had a 360-degree view of the surrounding area. Being winter, the weather was pleasant, but they could imagine how hot it must get there in the summer. They pulled off the ceremony without a hitch, not holding back in volume as they sang the ceremony songs.

As Omaran began digging a hole to bury the sacred objects, he quickly discovered a problem. When the shovel could not break the hard-packed ground, he was glad he had also brought a small pick. Even that did not penetrate.

After significant effort, he stopped and said, "I'm not going to bury anything here, I can't even break ground with the pick."

It was the first time a hole was not readily achieved. Antera looked over as she packed up all the ceremonial items. She said, "We can't just leave everything exposed, even if no one comes up here. Eventually animals would come and disturb the objects."

"Right." He thought about it. "Okay, I think I can move a couple of these larger rocks and roll them over the objects to cover them."

It took some effort, but finally he did it. "Only a two-footed animal would be able to get to them now."

"Great job. You know, this may not be the only time we need to use rocks to bury them, especially in the mountains."

"As long as there are rocks around, I think we'll be okay, and since mountains generally come with rocks . . ." They laughed.

As they were driving away, Antera said, "I didn't sense as many nature spirits here for this one. And I just realized that we didn't send our energy ahead. Maybe that is why. Too many distractions with our visit to my folks and all."

Omaran pulled off the side of the road. "Let's do it right now for the rest of the trip." They set their intentions and let the elementals know where they were going and when they expected to be there. After that, the rest of the sites were very well attended by the nature kingdom.

Driving on to the red rocks of Sedona, they decided they wanted to connect with Silver Horse before they made a grid point. Silver Horse was a Native American Ancestral Spirit who lived near Oak Creek. It was exciting to think about meeting him again.

Antera and Omaran entered a park by the creek, left the car, and hiked a short distance along the stream to the place where they had talked with Silver Horse before. They sat on some smooth river rocks next to the slow-moving water, in which there were beautiful reflections of the red rocks on the other side. The air smelled fresh, and they breathed deeply, relaxing as much as possible on the rocks in some meager shade from some bushes.

Antera closed her eyes and called Silver Horse. He was there immediately, as if he had been waiting for them. She said out loud, "The first thing he is asking us is whether we remember what he asked us to get when we were here last time."

Omaran said hesitantly, "No, I don't. Do you?"

"I don't either." She listened for a moment. "Oh! He is reminding us that he asked us to make medicine pouches."

"Oh, yes! I remember now," Omaran said sheepishly. "But we didn't do it."

"No, we didn't. He is saying it is even more important now because it will help us stay attuned to the land, especially with the land-healing work. We carry several items now, but he says we each need a personal medicine pouch for our sacred and power objects. And we should always have cornmeal or small stones with us for elemental gifts, every time we go hiking or land healing."

Antera listened some more, then said, "His group is like a tribe of guardians in this area, and they patrol along the entire river putting their energy in the water and in the rocks. This is the blood and lifeline of this particular area and the healing energies they put in the river flow out to bless the land.

"He is asking us to begin working with the waterways by going to their beginnings, the headwaters, and putting energy into them. We can program and power up small rocks or crystals and bless the water with them. The energy can travel very far in the rivers and help to heal and cleanse them as well as all the plants, animals and humans who are affected by them. The Rocky Mountains contain the sources of many rivers, so when we go there maybe we can find as many headwaters as possible."

"I like that idea," Omaran said as he pictured it in his mind. "Blessing the waters sounds exciting and fun! We love rivers! And maybe we would meet some river spirits."

Antera paused again to listen. "Also, Silver Horse says that as we climb high into the mountains, we can take advantage of the updrafts and send blessed herbs and sage into them, and the air currents will take the energy around the world, healing and cleansing the air."

"Just charge up the herbs and throw them upward into the air?"

"Yes, something like that. It is important to get as high in elevation as possible so that the energy will spread far. This will have the effect of supercharging the air. He says it is good, when possible, to add music such as a natural wood flute, or a drum, or chanting." Antera suddenly laughed. "And Silver Horse loves the sound of my flute! He wants me to keep using it, as it draws the nature spirits."

Happy with the new ideas from Silver Horse to expand their land healing and looking forward to trying them out on the next trip, they left the creek and drove toward the area where they had done the group ceremony for empowering Lightworkers a few years earlier. They found the location, a few miles from town, and climbed up a hill adjacent to the previous location. They had the idea of doing the land-healing ceremony in the same place.

It was a relatively flat area surrounded by desert vegetation and low bushes, about forty feet across. All the dirt and rocks were the rich red color so prevalent in the area, making a striking contrast with the deep blue sky. Upon arriving, they found large numbers of nature spirits waiting and willing to help, sitting in bushes or on red rocks, or flying about.

During the ceremony, they both sensed the Sedona Elders, the group that oversees the larger area of Sedona and its vicinity. Antera and Omaran were honored to see them again, and felt their approval of the work, though no words were spoken.

Afterwards, for the second time in a row, Omaran wasn't able to dig into the ground, nor could he move any of the rocks around. He finally was able to squeeze the sacred objects into a crevice between two very large rocks that weren't about to go anywhere. The objects dropped out of sight like a drop of water absorbed into parched, dry ground.

Their work in Sedona done, the next day they got an early start on their long drive back home. On the way up the east side of California, they detoured into Death Valley for their third point of this trip. As they dropped into the valley from high in the mountains that surround it, they felt a tremendous flush of energy. They took in the immensity of the valley, which was always impressive. The colors of the rocks and strata rushed into their eyes as the area itself seemed to greet them with a welcoming flow.

"I am so glad we've come back here," Omaran said as he drove the windy road down into the valley. "I really like this place! The look, the feel, the vastness, and yet flanked on two sides by mountains. Wow!"

"It is spectacular," agreed Antera, "especially when it's not hot."

They decided to go to the same area where they had held a group Winter Solstice ceremony several years earlier. Parking on the side of the road, they hiked half a mile across a field of rocks with an astounding variety of type and color and ended up in some mesquite bushes. To Antera's surprise, Omaran found the exact spot where they had been before. They set up and did the ceremony, noticing that, in addition to all the Beings of Light, many nature spirits attended from around the valley and surrounding mountains. For a desolate place like this, it was an amazingly good turnout. The sandy soil was easy to dig into.

Afterwards, they sat in some shade from the mesquite bushes, on a sand berm that was passably comfortable. Meditating in silence for a few minutes to sense the area, as they often did after a ceremony, they both felt very peaceful even though there was some activity going on with the nature spirits, who were excited to be a part of this point.

Antera felt a light breeze on her face and tried in vain to brush her hair back behind her ears, so it didn't tickle so much. She could feel something energetically happening in the area, so she focused on that to see what it was. A big shift of some kind was taking place.

"Do you feel that new energy?" She asked Omaran, hoping he could identify what she was feeling.

"Yes, I'm sensing this will be a very strong point for the grid."

"Right. I'm sensing the significance of the depth of this valley, and its function. It's so deep that it is easily connected to faraway places, and any energy we put in here can extend out all over southern California and much of Nevada. But there is something more going on."

Antera opened more, and suddenly she saw what it was. "There seems to be a large being rising to the surface from the depths of the Earth right now. He is just over there by that dead bush." She pointed.

"Who is it?"

"I'm not sure yet. He isn't speaking because our language seems foreign to him. But I can slowly sense what he wants to communicate . . . he is giant but has no form, more like a blob."

She listened again. "Oh, he says he was at our ceremony here five years ago and it really touched him. So, he came back to see us again! He hasn't worked with humans directly before, and that is why communication is mostly non-verbal. I'm translating as well as I can. Apparently, he has been around for a long time, eons, but he has always been in the core of the planet. This is the first time he has fully come to the surface and presented himself to humans. It is a new experience for him."

"Wow, we are honored to meet someone from the core," Omaran said.

"He is saying that he will be happy to help maintain the grid point we created here, and that we have chosen a very good place to do this ceremony as it is in the heart of the valley, and everything can flow to the south from here. Now that he has seen a land-healing ceremony, this work intrigues him, and he wants to help with the project. Working with us, if we want him to, will help him in his evolution."

Omaran said, "We could use some input from someone who knows about deep Earth processes. How can he help?"

"He is showing me this region from far above. This valley is energetically like a hub, which means it is directly connected to many other places. Some areas are on lines of energy, and others are hubs, like this one. This is a huge hub, and its influence extends all the way from here to far out into the ocean. There is also a connection with Lemuria here, still in place and flowing energy right under the ocean to buried land, and another connection with the opposite side of the planet, through the core."

"Maybe the Lemurian connection is what drew us here."

"Could be."

"Did he give you his name?"

"I'm asking now . . . .. He says we may call him the Guardian of the Deep. He is gradually becoming more visible. Though he is very tall compared with us, rather than the shapeless form he showed me at first, he is looking more humanoid-shaped. Maybe he is taking that form so I can relate to him better. I don't think that is his natural form." She paused for a couple of minutes.

"Okay, I'm understanding him better now. He is a fire deva, very evolved and powerful in his normal environment. What he wields is tremendously transformative fire energies. Whenever we are doing ceremonies that call for transforming something from one form to another, such as a harmful form to a more beneficial one, we can tap into this valley and call upon him to personally come to wherever we need the kind of force he has."

"Wow! That sounds very helpful!" Omaran was excited about this new possibility.

"Well, he says he also has a vast working knowledge of the underground electrical currents and their balance and flow. Humans have disrupted many of these flows, and unless humans can become more involved with helping to balance these flows, there will be more electrical storms. The Earth and the atmosphere must be brought back into balance. This valley is also an important area for the electrical conduction of the planet, and the electromagnetic field."

The Guardian of the Deep went on to explain that the fire element on the planet was quite out of balance and this has, in the past, caused many land upheavals. There will be more of these unless the fire is balanced. He said that one way he could help on the surface would be to teach fire elementals how to help disburse an overabundance of fire in a place by distributing it over a larger area, rather than letting it collect. There were some areas that were like pressure cookers, however, and it was difficult, if not impossible, to change them, especially if it would be interfering with natural processes. Since humans caused many imbalances, they would need to help heal them by working with the fire elementals.

"It sounds like we can put the nature spirits in any area in touch with the Guardian of the Deep, possibly by sending them here, to Death Valley," Antera described further. "He can teach them to help balance the area where they live. It will also help the nature spirits evolve and become more aware."

"Wow, that really opens up some new possibilities," Omaran said as his mind raced.

Antera listened for a minute then went on, "The nature kingdom will do what they believe must be done to bring balance back to the Earth. They would like humans to help, but that help has been so minor and sporadic that they will not wait any longer. They will let natural processes happen. But they truly want our help with as much releasing of harmful human energy as possible because all kingdoms are suffering—human, animal, plant, mineral, air, water, and all. They want our help!"

"I hear the cry for help," said Omaran sadly. "Hopefully our land-healing grid is helping, at least in the Western U.S. If we call him specifically, will the Guardian go to any area that needs transformation or more balance?"

"He says yes, if we call him, he will respond, because he sees how the land healing is working and he trusts us."

"How do we call him, specifically?"

"He is showing me that if we look around here and pick up a few pebbles to take with us, these will contain a special connection to him. We only need to leave one of these small rocks in an area when we call him, and he will respond."

This was all super interesting and gave them a lot to think about, but they were getting tired and needed to hit the road, so Antera ended the conversation with the Guardian, thanking him for all the fascinating information. Using their pockets, they collected a variety of small rocks from the ceremony site then hiked back to the car.

On the way, along the scenic east side of the Sierra Nevada Mountains, they decided to put two of the Death Valley rocks at the next grid site on Mammoth Mountain, a super-volcano that had been showing recent signs of magma activity, including thousands of small earthquakes. They called on the Guardian of the Deep as they buried the rocks after the ceremony, with the hope that he would be able to disburse excess fire energy in the safest way possible. Later, after they got home, they noticed that the frequency of earthquakes and other activity at Mammoth had greatly decreased, and it remained low for years afterwards.

They finished up this trip with one more point a little south of Reno, Nevada, in the eastern Sierras. It was a good, strong point anchored into the mountains, and they immediately connected it into the rest of the grid, especially helping the Central California and coastal points.

"My goodness, what an incredible year we've just had," commented Omaran on the final leg of their drive home.

"It just keeps getting better. And I have a feeling that the Guardian of the Deep is about to take this entire grid to a higher level," said Antera.

"So, I'm thinking next summer for our road trip through the Rockies. We'll be able to get ready by then. It will take several weeks of driving. I'd say probably three."

"Of course, you're already planning the next trip."

"Ha, ha! Yes, well, you know me."

"I know you love traveling."

"So, what do you think? Next summer, maybe July?" Omaran persisted.

"Yes, that will probably work. Gives us lots of time to prepare. I'll do some research and find out where the headwaters of the major rivers are so we can bless those too, as Silver Horse suggested."

"Yes, I really like the idea of blessing the rivers. What about the air blessings?" Omaran thought about the air currents, as Silver Horse had called them. "How do you suppose we find the right places for those, where the wind can carry the herbs upward? I have a feeling those will be more challenging than the rivers."

"We can just notice where the large birds are soaring in the updrafts."

"Oh, how obvious. That's a great idea, and I feel better already!"

"Don't worry about it, Omaran, we'll find them."

"Who, me? I don't worry. You obviously have me confused with someone else."

"Yeah, right."

32

The Healer Within

The first Order of the Blue Snake initiation in their new Mother Garden was planned for May of 2008. The circle of rocks and large altar stone, along with the fruit trees, herbs, and flowers, had been put in place in the fall, and the rock exchange with the valley was completed to prepare the ceremony site. The Holy Sisters said they would come down the mountain for the event, now that there was a pathway for them to follow.

The pace of this new energy from Divine Mother was increasing as the process evolved, and Antera and Omaran wanted more information about it, such as how to better use the energy and how to guide the other initiates in their own healing and healing of others. The energy was very powerful, and the possibilities were emerging as it was used.

Settling into their meditation postures in their usual places, Antera on the loveseat and Omaran on the couch at right angles to each other, they slowed their breathing to prepare for a connection. They both raised their consciousness to a higher space as they had done so many times. Omaran was good at holding this space while Antera channeled.

Mother Mary was the Master who appeared to Antera, so she opened to her words, which were always so loving and supportive.

Mary said, "I greet you and I am so, so excited about the prospects for the Order of the Blue Snake this year. The energy is building. Those of us who hold the Divine Mother energies are delighted that this is moving forward and coming into place. We feel there will be a wonderful group of people initiated this year and more each year. As they learn to use the energy of the Mother, they will spread so much Light on the planet!

"One initiate, able and trained in using this energy, can transform hundreds of thousands of people. It is so powerful, there do not need to be very many to make a huge difference! This is why I am so excited. This is marvelous, just marvelous! The energy does not die off with time or with space. This makes it much more powerful than most of the energies you used before in healings and meditations."

Omaran inserted, "Thank you, Mary, we are so happy to hear that."

"I want to remind you of one little thing, and that is your song for Divine Mother. We really want to hear that song, so we are hoping you will have it done before long. Shall we push that a little closer to the top of priorities? It will be an inspiration to those who are using the energy of Divine Mother and feeling the feminine power that is growing every day.

"I do like a good song because it elicits the emotions, and a thoughtform goes out to inspire people. Songs can bring up emotions and power in a beneficial way. Singing about Divine Mother is a most powerful way to do this. So, that's just a little reminder."

Omaran said, "Okay, we will get at least a rough mix of it done before the next initiation. Thanks for the reminder. We know how powerful songs can be." He thought about the song and how long it had been in the making, since long before they met the Holy Sisters. It was time to get back in the studio!

He asked, "On another subject, can you tell us any more about what happened when we did the ceremony in the Valley of the Holies last year, and is it all back to normal now?"

"Ah, yes. The Holy Sisters are back into their normal way of being. You see, they were a bit scattered by your ceremony there, and not through any fault of yours. It was so powerful that they had to leave the area, to draw the energy away from that place. They needed to send it into main ley lines to have it carried out far and wide, because you made some major shifts in that ceremony. I don't know if you fully understood this. The Valley of the Holies is not directly on a major ley line, so energetic connections needed to be formed to help the energy go out to bless other areas.

"But now the Holy Sisters are back and doing their normal ceremonial dances. They do look forward to the first annual hike up there for members, like a pilgrimage, perhaps this summer."

"Oh, that is a great idea, an annual hike! We will plan that. So, another question. If I understand correctly, this is the first time this energy has been on the planet. Or was it here a long time ago, and is this is just a renewal of it?"

"This is the first time that this energy has been here, because the planet has not been ready for it until now. The Holy Sisters have been developing it to make it available for more physical use, by physical beings. As physical members, you add human frequencies to it when you use it with your human consciousness, which is quite different than the consciousness of us, who are not in human form. So, in that way it is new to this planet, which is why we are not entirely sure yet just what can be done with it. So far, we are greatly pleased!"

Mary paused, then asked, "Omaran, as the first man to embrace this energy, what has it been like for you?"

"As I'm sure you're aware, I've been using Divine Mother's energy quite a bit, and it is very effective. I probably could use some help with what else to do or what to notice, as a man. I imagine you're watching the other men who have been initiated so far."

"Indeed. Keep in mind that this is the energy of the healer. That is what feminine power is, the energy that heals. Therefore, you have become more of a healer, have you not?"

"Ah! Yes, that's certainly true."

"This is how She acts within your system, especially with men. She awakens the healer within, because men generally don't act as healers, whereas women are more naturally inclined and therefore would not feel that aspect as much. But this is what I am finding with the men who have been awakened in this way."

"Gosh, that's very helpful. I certainly have noticed the healer awakening even more in me. I'm using more of this energy in my healing sessions. I've seen how powerful it is!"

The previous year, he had been instructed by both Jeshua and Mary in how to bring in the Christ Light for others, by allowing Jeshua to over-light him as he toned. This was a powerful way to uplift a client's energy field. Now Divine Mother enhanced these transmissions.

Mary said, "As have we. We hope more men will be drawn to join. Are there any other questions tonight?"

"Well," Omaran answered, "Antera and I were having a little discussion earlier about how, in almost every newsletter we send out, we say something about the accelerating changes happening. But it honestly feels different to me now. And more and more people are making predictions of what is to come—some good, some devastating. As I was saying to Antera, I'm feeling very positive about what is happening on the planet now. What do you think?"

"Indeed, there are many changes going on in your Earth's environment and in the core of your planet in relation to those environmental changes. All of this adds up to a tremendous opportunity for change on the planet and within every human, animal, plant, element, and nature spirit. All are being challenged to change. All are being challenged to grow and heal. This is a ramping up that is not going to level off for quite a while. It will keep getting more intense. This is as it has always been foreseen, so it is not a surprise.

"If you are feeling these changes, embrace them. Embrace anything that comes your way. This is the key to making it through these times and staying on top of the surf, so to speak. Many people will be pushed under. If you want to stay on top of these huge changes and influxes of energy, every day must include some integration time so you can embrace the new energies, allowing whatever comes up to be healed in some way. You don't ever want to push issues under the rug or think you will heal them later. There is no later. Now is the time to heal everything.

"Rather than getting distracted by predictions or people's thoughts about what is happening—because there are many different opinions and viewpoints about this—and rather than getting caught up into what is true and what is not, stay true to yourself. Be watchful and mindful of your own spiritual growth and evolution, always putting your healing at the highest priority in your life, because this is the only way to make it through these times without tremendous stress.

"If you look around you, you will see many stressed-out people, because they are not stopping for a moment to see what is really happening within themselves. You only need to know what is going on within your system. This is where the action is. This is where you can make the biggest change. If you neglect that, you will have stress. This is what is happening for many people now, and it will only escalate."

Omaran affirmed, "Yes, we have seen that with many people we know."

"As long as you are remaining centered, grounded, and aware of what you are feeling and what is moving in your energy field, you will be fine. If you avoid your issues or distract yourself, it will be much harder for you to go through these times. That is my advice. Does that answer your question?"

"Yes, very much so. And I would like to say, we are both so blessed and so fortunate to have all of you in our lives. We love you so much! I haven't had the opportunity to speak with you directly since I got lost going up to the Valley of the Holies, Mary, and it's really nice to have you here again."

"Oh, but I'm always within your reach. I do appreciate those thoughts and feelings. I always give you my wholehearted love and appreciation. It is because of you Lightworkers that we have come so far in the evolution on this planet without major consequences, such as Earth upheavals. Yes, there have been some and there will be more, but if you think about what was predicted before, the risk has been greatly diminished. Even though some may still happen, we know that it is because of the efforts of you and others like you that they have been at least delayed, and perhaps canceled. So, I appreciate you both for your part in this.

"Feel this blessing on you, because it comes from my heart and from the heart of Divine Mother, who loves you both so much."

When Antera was back fully, she started singing the refrain from the song Mary wanted them to finish:

Goddess is back and She is making some changes.
Goddess is back, the world will never be the same.

It was a song Antera had started years ago, then they had worked on it together, but they hadn't yet recorded it. Omaran chimed in for a couple of repeats, then said, "It is about time we finished that song, isn't it?"

"Yes. See if we can get some studio time next week, okay?"

"I will. Let's try to get a rough mix before the May initiation." He paused and took a deep breath. "It doesn't look like this year is going to slow down at all."

"Slow down? Is that what you were expecting? Funny man! I just keep adding to my list. Speaking of which . . ."

Antera jumped up and bounded up the stairs to the office to get her to-do list. It was a large tablet with the first two pages full of items, some of them checked off as finished. It seemed that items were added at about the same rate as they were marked done, but she was used to that. She added the song. And they did manage to get a rough mix finished in time to play it for the new group of initiates.

33

The Grid Comes Alive

In early March, Antera was sitting at the dining room table painting sacred sculptures, singing along with their Land Healing CD while she worked, to imbue them with the needed frequencies. Omaran had just cut a batch out of wood, in his new safer way, and he had taken over the job of the base paint so all she had to do was paint the symbols, nine of them on each.

Last year, she had discovered that each sculpture had a genie assigned to it by St. Germain. She could feel one of these beings come in at some point during each painting process. Upon asking about them, St. Germain had said they oversaw the points in the field, staying there to coordinate all the elementals who maintain the sites.

But the idea of people in the past enslaving genies, such as the myths about confining them in lamps or making them guard a place against their will, caused Antera to wonder about the use of genies in this project. When she asked St. Germain, he had assured her that these were volunteers who wanted to be a part of this project because they could see how beneficial it was to both humans and nature spirits. Plus, there were personal benefits for them. They evolved more quickly if they participated, and it opened many new avenues of exploration and learning for them.

Antera learned that genies are more evolved than elementals and worked with all four elements rather than just one. This made them especially proficient at managing the sites. Therefore, as she painted, she welcomed the genie who came in for each object. The genies had shown her and Omaran a special symbol to represent them, and this was one of the symbols she painted. They were a fun group, and each one had a different personality. There were female and male genies, and she found herself painting the genie symbol a little different for each gender.

They had also discovered that there was another genie who lived on their property, assigned there by St. Germain. His name was Tutut. Sometimes he hung out on top of the roof, and other times on a tree stump in their front yard. He loved it when she played her flute on the property, and he was very involved with all the elementals who lived here and the processes they carried out, as well as protecting the land.

"After this batch is dry, I want to do a second land-healing ceremony on our property," Antera said to Omaran when he came into the kitchen, next to the dining room where she was painting.

"You think we need another one here? We already have one."

"How about doing one inside the house?"

They had not done one inside before, and it seemed like a good idea, or at least it would be an interesting experiment. Omaran said, "Alright, let's do it this weekend. It will certainly clear our house, and that is important."

"Good."

Omaran thought about it. "But where would we bury the objects if we do it inside our living room?"

"Maybe we can just set them in the corner. No one will know what they are."

By Saturday, the objects were dry and ready. That evening they set up a ceremonial space in their living room and proceeded to do it right in their house. It all went very smoothly and seemed ordinary until they came to the last song. Normally, when they were doing this outside, sometimes they would feel the presence of elementals more strongly than at other times, coming in to help the genie. But this time, as they were singing and moving around the room, they both felt they were completely surrounded by many, many more elementals than ever before.

"My gosh," exclaimed Antera afterwards. "There were hundreds of elementals dancing around and singing with us! It was like the walls disappeared and we were in an amphitheater!"

"I know, I felt the same thing . . . and they're still here. Wow! You know what I just realized? Something changed with this grid. It is like it just came alive!"

"Alive?"

"Many of these nature spirits are from our other points! It's like the beings at all the points are now in direct contact with each other! I think that's why they were here, maybe they can bi-locate or something, be here and at their points at the same time. I'm just amazed!"

"Well, we did connect with all of them at the start of the ceremony," pointed out Antera.

"But we didn't ask them to come here and join us. They did that on their own, because somehow, they could!"

"Hmmm, I wonder if the Guardian of the Deep had a hand in this."

Omaran had been continuing his once-a-week check-in with all the points and the beings in charge, monitoring how they were doing. He visually remembered what each site looked like. It was getting to be too much to remember as the number of places increased, however, so he had recently made a list. It was very interesting to recognize some of the beings from other places, who had joined this ceremony. What a development!

That night, Antera did not sleep. There was so much energy swirling around in the house that her body was buzzing as if she were lying on a vibrating bed. She looked over at Omaran, soundly sleeping, oblivious to what was going on in their house. What a gift, to be able to sleep like that! With a lot of time to think about it during the sleepless night, she decided she would not trade her finely tuned nervous system for his, because even though it meant conditions had to be perfect for her to sleep, it also came with enhanced psychic senses.

As she thought about what was going on, she realized that they had done this powerful ceremony and created a Light Form right in their living room, directly below their bedroom! It was way too much energy for her to relax. Plus, now that the grid was in full communication, maybe it meant that elementals would be visiting their home at other times! What had they been thinking?

The next day Tutut, the genie who lived on their property, came to her and explained more about what had happened during the ceremony, from his viewpoint of nature. He said that the grid sites were now not only connected through the lines of energy between them, but also it allowed the nature spirits to directly communicate from site to site! And they could, through these connections, even travel between them, as they had for the first time in this ceremony. Normally, most elementals were confined to and concerned with only their local area, so this was highly significant. It was a major step along the elementals' evolutionary path.

When Antera shared that with Omaran, he said, "Wow! So now this project is providing an opportunity for nature spirits to evolve quicker. And I think my job of moving energy from stronger points to weaker ones just got easier, too." The possibilities for this grid began dancing in his head, and he wondered what would happen on their Rockies trip.

"Yes, the connotations are exciting, but I do need to sleep. I'm going to ask the Masters if there is a way to move this new point elsewhere or do something with it. It was an experiment and worth doing once inside, but we can't keep it here!"

Later, the Masters confirmed that it would be possible to move the point to a place outside and gave her directions on how it could be done. She and Omaran moved it right away and the house calmed right down.

34

Goddess of Liberty

With the Spring Equinox of 2008 coming up, their focus also turned to having a global meditation, as they frequently did on the solar power days, the equinoxes and solstices. Each event had a different theme, determined by the Masters, highlighting an important issue for the current time. This time, when the two of them sat to receive information about the equinox, Antera was contacted by someone new.

"A being is here, and she looks like an angelic figure, quite beautiful, yet she exudes a strong presence. Oh, she is pointing to the Statue of Liberty in New York and saying she is the Goddess of Liberty! I've never really seen her before. She carries a torch and has a crown, probably a bit like the statue. What a delight! She wants to say a few words."

"Great!" Omaran said enthusiastically.

Liberty said, "Hold your focus on the wisdom and power of true liberty and it will transform this nation, and afterwards other nations, into a higher expression of it. Liberty was the first concept that this nation was built upon, and it was the most important concept of all! As this nation rises up from the gutter into a more enlightened state, which is the hope of all of us, liberty and freedom will shine again."

"Yes! We want to help with that. How can we help?" Omaran asked.

Antera listened to Liberty some more, then said, "First, she is concerned about the Statue of Liberty. There is some kind of threat to it, or something is wrong with it physically. I'm not exactly sure what the threat is, but she is concerned because it is a symbol that is very important to this country and to the world. It is her symbol, her statue. She says that it is an expression of the highest values and if those values have been eroded, the statue will also erode.

"She is a very real being and personifies the archetype of liberty on Earth, holding a constant blaze of Light. She holds her torch and blazes out these concepts and values for everyone."

Liberty talked again, saying, "These values have been degraded from 'liberty for all' into 'liberty for a few,' and I am calling for help to focus on the true and pure concept of liberty, liberty of beingness! I need your help to augment what I am doing to build this energy and spread it around the planet as a positive mass thoughtform. There are many people on this planet who are enslaved in some way, even in this country.

"It is time for more freedom within. Because when people are free inside themselves, they manifest freedom in their outer lives. If there is no freedom within, no thought of freedom and liberty within, you cannot manifest it in the outside world. So, I want to build that thoughtform."

Building thoughtforms, which are pictures or forms made from repeated and powered up mental energy, was a process Antera and Omaran had done with groups many times before. The focused group energy made this kind of work much more powerful than the two of them could do alone.

"Liberty is quite concerned," Antera said. "She just wants us to know that she's here and very active. You know, I'd really like to go see the statue."

Omaran agreed, "Me too. I'm sure we will, some day. I saw it a long time ago but looking at it again now that we have met Liberty would make it much more special."

"I guess the equinox meditation will be about the pure quality of liberty, then. I like that!"

"Me, too. I'm grateful she came. As a group, can we also do something about the physical issues? Something to make the statue stronger or protected?"

Antera thought about that and mentally sent the question to Liberty, who was still present. "She says that we can put up a strong energy of protection around the statue. I'm seeing how this can be done . . . yes, I get how."

"Does she show what the physical issues are?"

"Yes, she is showing me some cracks in her statue. I'm not sure if they are physical cracks or etheric, or even if this is a projection into the future . . . she says these are partly already manifest and will get worse if nothing is done."

Antera paused, watching pictures from Liberty. "I can see dark threads of energy aimed at it, causing this damage, and eroding the statue's integrity. It really looks like psychic attack on it. Some of the energy is coming from people in other countries, and some is coming from people right here in our country. And some is being deliberately sent by those who know how to wield damaging energy, while the rest is being unconsciously sent by people doing things to undermine liberty by abuse of power."

"Wow, I understand her concern. It's hard to believe that people would want to weaken the Statue of Liberty!"

"Yes, it is. But we will do what we can with the group energy to protect it and prevent more damage."

The equinox ceremony was focused on building the pure quality of liberty on the whole planet as well as strengthening and protecting the statue. A few hundred Lightworkers joined together in a virtual group, and Antera led a meditation to create these thoughtforms, resulting in some major shifts that made liberty and freedom more accessible to everyone, both personally and collectively.

A week later, Antera and Omaran heard from the Goddess Liberty again. She thanked them and the group profusely, saying that negativity had been pulled out of the statue, which had been a target of many who wished to squelch the liberties of others.

Liberty said, "The statue has come to be a very important symbol for this country and for my energy of liberty. You revitalized it at a very deep level. This, then, rekindles feelings of liberty in this country. For you see, the statue radiates this energy to all who see her. This benefits the people in this country and around the world."

35

Hotah and the Fairy Queen

Omaran casually asked, "And how's your research going on the headwaters of the rivers in the Rockies?"

Antera saved her work on the computer and turned toward Omaran, who was sitting at his desk next to hers in the office, paying bills. He rarely came in to work there, whereas she was at her desk many hours each day. It was a bit distracting to have him there, especially because he wasn't quiet, but fortunately she was good at switching her attention quickly.

She said, "I have a good list of the rivers. Now I just need to see how close we can get to the headwaters of each one. For some, it is very hard to determine where they actually begin because maps differ. Other headwaters are way up in the mountains and won't be easily accessible. But I'll continue to work on it."

"Ah. We may just have to get as close as we can."

"Maybe when we get in the field it will be completely different from the maps."

"I know you are very good with maps so I have confidence you can get us there," Omaran said flippantly. "And have you heard from Michael about the most stable areas in the mountain range?"

"You know how thorough he is. I'm sure he is still working on it. Hopefully he will get us something in the next week or so."

"That would be great. Do I sound anxious to start planning the trip?"

"It goes without saying." Antera turned back to her work.

"As soon as I know where we're going, I'll be able start preparations." He sealed an envelope and stamped it, then waved it in the air expressively.

"I really want to go to the Tetons for a visit, even though we won't be putting a grid point there because the range is too young. I can't imagine being that close and not going there."

She chuckled and turned back to him. "Okay, okay, I want to go there too. It's one of my favorite places ever. And I'm thinking about Yellowstone. I've never been there. Surely, we can take a few days to camp in those two places. We should probably camp as much as possible, to keep the costs down."

"Oh, yeah, I think we'll be camping most of the time, except on the days when we know we'll be doing the long drives."

"There are going to be many days with long drives. This is the West we're talking about."

"That's true. Well, in July we will still have long days and plenty of light, so we should be able to camp mostly," agreed Omaran. "We can take some quick and easy meals to fix so we don't have to eat out. We'll just allow as much flexibility as we can and I'm sure it will work out."

"So, I'm guessing you have somewhere else you are thinking about going. Am I right?"

"I'm glad you asked." He swiveled his chair to face her and leaned forward. "I've been thinking, now that we've been asked to do the Rockies and then the rest of this country, we can think about doing this work in other countries, like the British Isles. We could go there in the fall."

"Ah! No wonder you are excited. It would take a few weeks to make a grid on those islands."

"I think three weeks ought to do it. Maybe you could teach a class, or we could have an event while we are there, to help pay for the trip."

Antera thought for a moment. "I've never been to England. Most of my ancestral line is from Scotland and England, plus I have many past lives there. I've always wanted to go." Another pause. "I have a client in southeast England who could possibly help us plan an event or set me up with psychic healing sessions."

Since she had added psychic healing to her session offerings, there was no shortage of clients. These sessions were more popular than the SCIO sessions, and her practice had expanded fast by word of mouth and repeat clients.

"That would be great!"

"In fact, she just mentioned about a month ago that if we were ever going to be traveling to the British Isles to let her know, as she could book sessions with people she knows."

"I just love the way it all works when we're in the flow," said Omaran.

"I've never been outside the U.S., you know, except for Tecate and Tijuana, which some would argue isn't really Mexico."

"You're going to love it! I've done some traveling but I've only been to Europe once, when I was in the crystal business looking for sources. We went to France, Germany, and Austria. That was so long ago, seems like another lifetime."

As they talked about going to the British Isles, it wasn't surprising that they were overheard. One morning in late March, while Antera was doing her morning meditation, one of her spirit animals said he wanted to speak to both her and Omaran. His name was Hotah, and he was an owl who had been presented to her by St. Germain himself, years before. This magical animal had been one of her animal companions since then, and he often perched on her left shoulder.

She remembered how St. Germain had handed him to her. She'd had the impression he was loaning this owl to her, telling her at the time that Hotah had been a spirit friend and teacher for a number of others, including the famous magician, Merlin.

"But I'm not a magician," she had said, objecting half-heartedly. She had instantly taken to the owl and was really very pleased and honored to have him as a friend but questioned whether she deserved such a prestigious animal.

St. Germain had laughed and said enigmatically, "Aren't you?" He had winked and was gone.

When she had opened to Hotah to see if he would talk to her, she had been surprised when his voice came through with a strong English accent, and he spoke in a tone that was almost professorial. She was smitten with him, and he had been with her ever since, teaching her more about the elements, elementals, ceremonies, and energy flow. He also helped her see the higher perspective and further open her inner vision.

This was the first time, however, he had ever asked to talk with Omaran also. She told Hotah she would ask Omaran to join her in the evening, then got up and went into the session room to prepare for her first appointment.

That evening, Omaran and Antera sat in the living room to see what Hotah wanted. As soon as Antera tuned in, Hotah was ready.

"Hotah is here, and he wants us to fly with him, to England!"

Omaran laughed, "Ha, ha! No wonder. I can see it."

"So here we go, flying there very quickly . . . into a forest. It looks like I'd imagine a forest in the days of King Arthur would have looked, long ago. It is a magical place, deep and dark from the thick foliage . . . .. We're coming to a clearing which has a stone circle in it, and some beings are standing around the circle, many different kinds and shapes of beings. They appear to be nature spirits. It is like a fairy ring, and they've invited us, so Hotah is taking us closer.

"There is one being who seems to be in charge. She has a long gown and a tall staff in her hand and a crown on her head, like a queen. She's welcoming us. Hotah is sitting on my shoulder and urging us forward, so we're walking into this circle. The sun is coming in right here and nowhere else. It's a dark forest, so this clearing is really a special place. I don't think it's a physical place. She's bowing to us, so we bow to her. She is asking us when we will be traveling there."

Omaran was experiencing it as it was described. He answered, "Maybe in half a year. We are still planning."

"The queen is very sweet," continued Antera, "but some of the others aren't so sure of us. She is confident that this is a very good alliance. That's what she says, that we are making an alliance with her and her kingdom . . . she seems to be aware of what we are planning on doing on their island, the land healing as well as the Divine Mother work. Maybe Hotah already told her."

"An alliance sounds good," Omaran confirmed excitedly.

"Oh, I just realized that she's in charge of the whole island! Not only this forest . . . that makes her an important being. She's looking forward to meeting us in person, but she wanted to connect with us before we go. I'm not really sure what this alliance means."

There was a pause as Antera listened and watched the scene at the fairy circle progress. Omaran sat patiently.

"Well," said Antera, "now she's showing me that there are tremendous energies flowing all through the land. This island is really a critical place on the planet, very pivotal energetically, and it's vitally important that when we go there, we connect our continent with this island. There is more of a connection than we know, and not just through history, even though that is important because many of the first settlers in our country were from the island. But there's something very special there that I'm trying to put my finger on. The Fairy Queen is insistent that we really understand the importance of the British Isles."

"I've been feeling that," Omaran said. "Due to the grid we're doing here, as soon as we decided we were going to the United Kingdom, I got a thought that part of our purpose may be to energetically connect these two places."

"I think you are right. She is showing me lines of energy, perhaps ley lines, that come from the middle of the island—that is where this fairy circle is—and go all the way across the ocean into our country. So, energy spreads from there over to North America. However, there is something wrong with the way it's working now. It's not flowing properly. In fact, there's something wrong with many of the energy flows on the planet, as we know. One of these ley lines is landing somewhere on the East Coast, further north than New York."

"Boston? New England?"

"It looks like further north, maybe even as far as Maine. I don't know those states over there very well, and anyway, she is showing me raw land without cities or states marked! Maybe from long ago. Another line goes to a more southerly area around the Carolinas or Georgia. It creates a triangle.

"The queen is saying that we can build an energetic alliance between the land-healing grid that we've created on our continent to the one we create over there. The major ley lines on the British Isles are ancient and the energy is still flowing, though it needs to be refreshed and cleaned out. Some people are still aware and using it. Those islands are so magical! But because there are so many people and roads everywhere, many of the old lines have been disturbed and this means some loss of the magical power that was there before.

"Even though the lines have been disturbed at the surface, deeper inside they are still very much intact because they've been there for such a long time. There is still a lot of power for people who are sensitive to the energies."

Omaran said, "I have a couple of questions."

"Okay, go ahead."

"Will the Fairy Queen help us find the best places for grid points in all four countries?"

"She's saying the countries don't matter. Those are artificial separations. The important part is that there are two main islands. We can do grid points in any locations. She just wants to make sure we get the central area where the ley lines that go across the ocean start. Those are what she is asking us to clear, and maybe some others, using our crystals like we've done in other places."

"I see. Well, we can certainly do that," Omaran said.

"She's going on about how everything used to be aligned in a certain way so that different places were connected and enhancing each other and there was a feedback loop going on. But now, well, there is significant degradation in the flows and how they function, even though some people have worked to correct them.

"The ley lines carry Earth energies, but they affect the atmosphere over the island as well, and because of the flow problems, some of the air elementals have gotten trapped or stuck, and they can't do their work anymore. One other thing that we can help with is freeing them up. She says we can free them from the old ways and bring them more into current times. They didn't have time to evolve quickly enough, so they're calling out for help. I hear some of them saying, 'Can you free us up? Can you help us?' We aren't experts on that but maybe we can help."

Omaran said, "Does she have any suggestions on what we can do?"

"She says she will be guiding us when we are there. She will let us know when we are at a spot where there are beings calling for help. And the benefit is, once we have freed these beings, they may help us in our land healing. There are many kinds of elementals represented here in this circle because they all want help from humans and there are very few humans who can help them." She chuckled. "And here we are, barely knowing what we're doing in that regard, but they still really want our help."

"It shows how desperate they are if they're calling us," Omaran agreed.

"But we can learn! I just want to assure her that yes, we will do what we can. It's one of the reasons we're traveling there, besides doing the land healing and gathering our roots and seeing all the beauty and wonderful places we've heard so much about."

"Well yes, so much of our culture comes from there. Now we have more reasons to go."

Antera looked more closely at the other beings around the circle. "You know, some of these are fairly ancient beings, and a few are saying they've worked with me or you before. They seem familiar. I'm sure we've both lived in the British Isles in numerous lifetimes. We're going to work with them again. I'm telling them we don't have the skills we probably had back then, but we're learning."

Antera paused again, listening. "They seem to be in awe of Hotah. They're being very pleasant to us, but Hotah is drawing a lot of reverence. I'm looking at him and thinking, 'Who are you, really?' I know he's quite a magical bird. But here they know and revere him. The beings have been asking him permission to talk to us, like he's in charge."

Omaran said, "Well, what did you expect from Merlin's owl?"

"Ah, yes, there is that. He's really at home here, and apparently famous among this crowd. It's really cool."

"I'm wondering how we are going to find this spot. Or do we need to?"

"Hotah assures us that he will guide us."

They ended their unusual session with Hotah and the Fairy Queen, which had made them even more excited about going to the magical islands. And Antera had a renewed understanding of and respect for Hotah, her magical owl friend.

36

Running Bear

"I've missed this mountain," sighed Antera, as she sat on the ground, gazing at a field of poppies.

She and Omaran were enjoying the energy from a ceremony they had just completed on Mount Tamalpais, north of San Francisco. It was the same place they had done their very first land healing with a group back in 2005, but this time the site was finally made into a permanent part of the grid.

"Me too," Omaran said wistfully. "I'm so glad to be back here. It is very special."

They were leaning against a large granite boulder in the shade of a madrone tree. The tree had strikingly beautiful red bark that contrasted with its emerald leaves, which were fluttering in the wind.

Omaran asked, "Is the Angel of Mount Tam here? Or anyone else?"

"I'll tune in and see." She rummaged in her pack to get out the digital recorder, then sat upright to raise her consciousness into a space where she could sense unseen beings. She took a couple of deep breaths and shifted to get a little more comfortable.

"Well," she said, "there's a beautiful being here who says she is one of the Angel of Mount Tam's helpers. She seems to be overseeing this area, and she has been here since the first time we did a ceremony here. She's sitting up on that rock behind us. Her job is to watch over this place and orchestrate things. I'd call her a Deva of Place, and she has quite a few elementals who work for her.

"She is excited about something. Oh! They want us to do an Order of the Blue Snake initiation on this mountain. They want us to anchor the Divine Feminine energy here."

"That's a great idea! And we know quite a few people in the Bay Area."

"They are also very happy we came back to do this land-healing ceremony today, and to fully connect this site into the grid. We need a name for the grid, don't we? We can't keep calling it the West Coast Grid now that it is expanding. It can just be the Land Healing Grid. But that isn't a proper name."

"Well, we'll think of something else. We now have almost thirty points in it! It's getting harder to remember all of them when we connect them together."

"It has gotten big, and soon to be bigger." Antera turned her attention back to the deva and elementals. "She is doing something interesting with the Light Form we created, shooting way up in the sky and distributing the energy from it. Her helpers take pieces of the Light, as if it were solid, and carry them high up, then take them off somewhere else. Then they come back and get more. It's like a distribution system. They have a special pattern of movement, like a choreographed dance while they come and go."

"Fascinating!" exclaimed Omaran.

"It is! And the pieces of Light are, well, like what I might call fairy dust. Everything it touches is transformed into positive energy."

"How far does it go?"

"Their area is only around this mountain. I wonder if this happens at some of our other grid points and I just haven't seen it before."

"Or perhaps it's just here, because this mountain is special, and it has mostly upward energy."

They sat in silence for a minute. Omaran opened his eyes and watched the leaf shade patterns moving on the ground. He gaged the height of the sun and figured they could stay for another hour at the most before hiking back.

Then Antera said, "There's something going on with the Guardian of the Deep connection. The fire spirits are wondering what to do with this rock we gave them from Death Valley."

"I guess we weren't very clear about that. I kind of thought they would just know what to do with it. Maybe we need to be more specific."

Antera said to the fire elementals, "We invite you to learn from the Guardian of the Deep, who is a very evolved fire deva from deep inside the planet. We met him in Death Valley, where the rock came from."

Omaran added, "Think of the rock as a phone line to him. He has a lot to teach you about safe fire distribution, like how to balance the fire element so it isn't too hot, which might be destructive."

"Now they are excited about this," Antera described. "They are flitting around, wondering what to do with this new communication. It's exciting for them." She giggled. "They are funny!"

"Seriously, I do hope they understand why," Omaran said. "I mean, we know all the elements need to get back in balance, and that is why we do this work. Tutut told us that the Guardian is an alchemist, so he can transform the energies and teach the fire spirits at all the grid points how to do the same thing."

"What we hope for is to release the stress in a way that doesn't cause so much damage. Earthquakes are the biggest risk here, and I'd like to see more slow earthquakes, so the stress gets released in lower frequencies that don't damage buildings as much."

"And," Omaran said to the elementals, "by working with us and the Guardian of the Deep, you can evolve to a higher level of beingness. This is a quick path of evolution."

They were silent for a couple of minutes. Antera felt the Angel of Mount Tam coming closer, and she allowed the angel into her space to talk.

The Angel of Mount Tam said, "Thank you so much for doing this and for being who you are. I want you to know how deeply appreciative I am of all this work you are doing. I have truly missed you! Very few people have so much reverence for my mountain. Even when you are not doing ceremonies, when you walk through my woods and look at my vistas, you are spreading Light. I'm very happy to have you here again.

"I'm very much hoping you will do your Divine Mother ceremony here, because there is a strong female energy on my mountain. Many people in this area would benefit from that initiation. As you know, there is already a very strong connection between Mount Shasta and Mount Tamalpais. You yourselves have made much of that connection possible by going back and forth, and there are others who do that as well. And that connection will make it easier to do this ceremony."

Omaran felt deep love welling up in his heart and said, "I just have to say something. I have as much gratitude and love for you and this mountain as is humanly possible. And we're so very grateful for all you've taught us about land healing. You've given us inspiration to continue on. You've given us so much love, and this place will always be special to me."

"Yes, I know how you feel, dear Omaran. This mountain is very heart centered and touches many people. This is the energy that we hold for the whole Bay Area. So, thank you for visiting here whenever you can and maintaining this connection. I so appreciate it, and I bless you for this."

Antera paused, then said, "She is finished, and now she is showing me a Native American being who wants to say something. He wants us to know that there's a very strong Native American presence here that could be acknowledged as well, since we're acknowledging energies." She laughed, and Omaran joined her. "I guess we're attracting many beings who want to talk to us today. Anyway, he's really happy that we have such a great Earth connection. This was a special spot to the natives. He is expressing thanks and reminding us that the natives were the first ones to really appreciate the land and do ceremony to keep this place in harmony, so there's a strong connection with us in that way.

"This being was called because of our ceremonies. He's really interested in what we're doing, and grateful that we're bringing back some of the old ways and combining them with new ways. Do you sense him?"

"Yes," Omaran replied. "I just want to add that I've felt his and others' energies during my years on this mountain, without thinking about it consciously. His energies feel very familiar."

"Hmmm," Antera said. "Well, now he's saying that we are the answer to their prayers. They have been praying for help with healing and preserving the energy in this area. They are so grateful because of that."

"We're just very blessed to be the conduits."

Antera said, "He calls himself Running Bear, and he's in charge of doing ceremonies here. He says he is part of a clan or tribe, who go back to when there were grizzlies here. I didn't know there were grizzly bears here. Were there?"

"Oh, yeah."

"Okay, so he is talking about grizzlies, not black bears. This is the bear power they have, which they use in their ceremonies. Running Bear says they call on the bear power even though there are no physical bears here anymore. And that you can do that too, if you want. He is telling you that you could have a bear totem if you want and harness the bear energy."

"I would love that! What do I need to do?" Omaran sat up straighter.

"Well, just open to it, I guess . . . maybe you used to be a member of that clan and had bear energy before, because I'm seeing a connection between you and bears."

"I feel it! I feel the power of the grizzly in me," Omaran said excitedly.

"Yes, grizzly power . . . really, one of the most powerful animals on the planet."

"I feel right now like I am part grizzly."

"Running Bear says," Antera related, "that when you want power you can call on the power of the grizzly. It can bring you more power than you could probably ever want. You can use it in all your spiritual work, in everything you want to do. This is the totem animal that has been given to you in the past, and it is now time for you to embrace it again. It is being offered to you now."

"I accept whole heartedly!"

Antera watched for a few moments, then said, "They're doing a ceremony around you . . . shaking sticks and rattles, dancing around you. You are being initiated into the Running Bear Clan. Around their necks they have bear teeth and claws, symbols of bears. On the ends of their staffs, they have carvings of bear heads. I wonder if you could harness the energy of the bear in your staff."

"Oh! As they are doing this, I see a bear coming up the hill . . . a big one. They're calling it and making way for it. It's huge! And now it's up on its hind legs and roaring! The bear is asking you, 'Are you up for this? Can you accept my energy?'"

Omaran was thrilled and quickly replied, "Yes!"

"The grizzly is challenging you, and it's almost like you have to prove you're compatible or worthy."

Omaran affirmed, "I am ready for this! I embrace your energy."

"The bear is strutting around you, checking you out."

Omaran could feel the bear's energy very strongly. It was as if he knew this spirit animal yet was not ready for their meeting until now. The bear energy ran through his body like electrified blood. His breath was coming fast.

"Running Bear is saying that you need to take the name of this bear and use it only in this clan and when you use the grizzly power. The name is one you have to get yourself; I'm not allowed to get it for you. What is the name of this grizzly?"

Omaran took a deep breath and focused on the bear, waiting to be told. It only took a moment. "I got his name!" As soon as he said the name out loud, something inside shifted.

"When you said his name, the grizzly turned silvery white. It literally changed the frequency of the grizzly. I guess you passed the challenge! The bear is moving behind you now and putting his paws around you, giant claws and all."

Omaran was joyous. He could sense the spirit animal behind him, and the hug. It was more than a hug . . . like a merging of energy.

"And Running Bear says, 'Now your blood runs with the blood of the clan.' You are like blood brothers . . . brothers with the bear energy. That's a very powerful energy, whew! So, the bear will walk by your side and be there whenever you want power and bear energy. They are still doing some kind of energy work around you to anchor it in and continuing their dance with rattles. How's that feeling?"

"It's fantastic!"

"The dance is finished, and I think they are waiting for you to say something."

Omaran cleared his throat. "I am honored and extremely glad that you made me a member of the Running Bear Clan. I will carry this energy with the utmost pride and use it for the highest good. I will call on it in ceremonies. On behalf of my bear and myself, I am truly honored, thank you!"

"Okay, they're celebrating! Now you need a bear tooth or claw for your medicine bag!" Antera opened her eyes and gazed at Omaran. "Oh, yeah. I see that bear energy in you."

Within a few weeks, Antera found a grizzly bear claw for Omaran. It was a replica made of resin, because it turned out to be illegal to possess real claws, and the thought of taking a claw from a real bear wasn't at all pleasant, anyway. But Omaran loved it and started wearing it around his neck as a symbol of his spirit animal.

37

Home Is Where the Center Is

Antera wondered if the new bear energy was too much for Omaran to integrate. Shortly after they got back home, he fell into an irritable darkness. After a week of his being on edge and with no apparent healing going on, Antera was feeling frustrated with him. When he was like this, they could not communicate effectively, and she had to be very careful when saying anything to him lest he turn on her.

Clearly, he had something to heal, but if she asked him why he was upset he denied that there was anything wrong—like he could hide it from her! It amazed her that he still, after all this time they had been together, could act like she was his enemy. He had plenty of tools to heal himself, but first he needed to become aware of something to heal.

Sitting on her cushion in the meditation room, she took a deep breath and asked for guidance on how to keep her heart open even when he was energetically lashing out. At least he hadn't invited any demons in this time. Those beings were very hard to deal with. But he picked up entities of the common sort quite frequently, especially when he wasn't paying attention, and they loved to pick fights and amplify his pain. She knew that entities jumped from person to person, but only came in if the person had something that resonated with that kind of energy, such as anger, guilt, or sadness.

Antera was very glad she hadn't taken a body that was ruled by the emotions, like Omaran had. Her mind was much more in control in this life, and it seemed so much easier! She had experienced plenty of lives when that wasn't the case, though, and even earlier in this life she'd had her share of emotional upsets. But wow, nothing like Omaran, who seemed to change his mood with the moon phases.

Again opening her heart, she relaxed. She did some release work on the frustration energy, so that would not interfere. Then she put up stronger psychic protection, knowing that would help. It was so much harder to protect against negative energy coming from Omaran than from anyone else.

St. Germain came to her in response to her request for guidance. He said he wanted to speak to Omaran and asked her to channel for him later that day. She said she would, and then the Master spent a few minutes uplifting her energy, helping her out of the density and into higher vibrations of Divine Love.

When she saw Omaran, after he came back from running errands, she told him that St. Germain wanted to talk to him. That got his attention. He knew he hadn't been balanced of late. He had neglected his daily meditation and had not been feeling good. Was that why the Master wanted to talk? He decided to spend some time alone that afternoon to do some introspection and maybe some healing to make sure he was ready.

After dinner, they sat in their usual places in the living room. The days were getting longer so it was still light outside, but they lit a candle anyway, to enhance the atmosphere.

It required a few minutes to make the connections, then Antera said, "St. Germain is here and helping me raise my vibration a bit higher. He's looking at both of our energy fields, encouraging us to rise into the level of the Higher Self, to merge with the Higher Self."

After a few minutes, St. Germain quickly got to the point. "I greet you! I would like to explain why I came in so forcefully this morning to give you the message that I did. You see, I have been watching you and noticing, Omaran, that over the last week you have not been fully present. I would like you to become more aware of when your energy is not fully aligned with the present moment, because then you can catch the energies before they become all-encompassing or change your outlook on life.

"Your outlook on life is normally a good one, so whenever it isn't good, it is time to ask the questions: Is anyone influencing me? Is there energy in me that is detrimental or causing me to lose my focus on the Light, my focus on my goals and what I want in life? Once you recognize what is happening, you can pull yourself out very quickly. Tell me how you did that today."

Omaran said, "I think the first thing I consciously did was take responsibility for allowing myself to resonate with negative energies. And yes, I felt it coming this past week, as I spent less time in meditation. So, after I took responsibility, I used some of the healing tools I have, including the Violet Flame.

"I remembered something you said to me the first time we climbed Black Butte, and I was influenced by some heavy energy that made me feel lost and confused. It made a big impression on me. You said afterwards that I had a hard time because I resonated with that energy. I do understand that the way out of these moods is to raise my overall energy so I no longer resonate with the heavy energy. So that's what I did."

"Very good," affirmed the Master. "So now, if you could just do that a little earlier! When you allow something like this in, it stops the flow. It creates a barrier or a repulsion. So, it is very important to keep the channels pure and flowing outward in a loving and Light-filled way. This does not only affect you, Omaran, it affects many people if you get pulled under, so to speak. It is up to you to catch this as soon as possible. I do see that you are getting much better at this, but it's been days! That is why I came in. When a Lightworker is refusing to see something for days this is cause for intervention because there is no time to lose right now.

"I know I have been saying this for years, but we are in the end times of this cycle and things are happening very fast. If you do not pay attention, you can attract something you do not want into your space, like an accident or sickness. Do you know what I mean?"

"Yes."

"This is why you MUST catch these things early and deal with them immediately, before they have a chance to create thoughtforms that go out into the universe and call things you do not want. I know you know this."

"Thank you so much," said Omaran sheepishly. "As soon as I heard Antera say that you had come in, I knew I had to do something immediately. That, right away, had an impact."

"I'm so glad that you took it seriously and acted. Nip these things in the bud as soon as the negative thought comes up!"

"Yes, I see that."

"Now," said St. Germain, "I'd like to talk about the center. What's happening with the center?"

Omaran was relieved to move to another topic, even this one. "Honestly, when I think about it, I keep envisioning the property that we found further up on the mountain, even though you mentioned we could probably do very well with a smaller piece. It just doesn't seem to be coming together for us."

St. Germain said, "For sure, the energy has changed around the center. This is something you just need to pay attention to, because if the energy is not behind it, the focus and the goals can change. You are building the center, through classes and other activities. You are building it here! You already have two ceremonial areas on your property, and other plans in mind. So, keep the focus of building the center in whatever form it is to take. That is the wise thing to do. If you were King Solomon and had plenty of gold at your disposal, you could build whatever you wanted. But because you don't, I suggest you continue building it as you are doing, with people. Does that make sense?"

"Oh yes, it certainly does," Omaran said, relieved. "Thank you, that takes the pressure off."

He had been feeling bad about not putting in the effort needed. And he knew those feelings of guilt had been lurking behind his upset over the last few days. In fact, it had been bothering him since Solomon had started coming to talk about it. He hadn't realized what a burden that had been until now, and he already felt so much lighter after giving that up! He inhaled deeply and blew it out forcefully.

St. Germain went on to a new subject. "And it is truly wonderful that you can use your hand on the keyboard."

"Yes, I've been so incredibly blessed!" Omaran said. Because of his hand injury, he had given up guitar and transitioned to keyboard. He had bought a very fancy keyboard with many more sounds than he would ever use, and he was amazed at the new music coming through. "I don't know who is influencing me, but I've never written like this before. There is a new quality of sounds. I'm very grateful. Please pass my thanks along to whoever is helping."

"Now wait a minute, Omaran. You are fully capable of communicating with who is helping you."

Omaran chuckled nervously. "Okay, okay, yes. I know that."

"Tune in right now and call forth your muse. What do you sense?"

"Well, I sense a very colorful, large being, at a huge keyboard. But maybe I'm wrong . . .."

"Trust yourself, Omaran. Get rid of your doubts, now," the Master coaxed.

Omaran opened his senses more and waited before responding. "I just got the sensation that when this being plays the keyboard, rather than sounds coming out of it, it's like waves of energy coming to me . . . and then coming through me. I really have understood for a long time that the music comes through me. But this is different, what's happening now."

"This being is someone you know."

"Someone I knew?"

"Yes . . . knew and know. I suggest that when you are sitting at your keyboard call in his help consciously. This will activate the connection even further, and your ability to communicate these musical vibrations. What are you sensing?"

"Well, I have my doubts about sensing who he is."

"Just knowing that there is a being working with you who is a musician of high caliber who can put high frequencies into the music, if you want, will help you in your compositions. You do not have to know his name to have the connection, but sometimes it is a very good thing to know who is working with you and to know the purpose of the connection so you can be more conscious of it."

Omaran nodded. "What about the lyrics? Are they coming from the same muse?"

"There is not only one being working with you. Sometimes the words come from elsewhere. The being we are talking about with the music is strictly an instrumentalist, not a vocalist. But he plays many instruments and can make many different sounds. And do you sometimes wonder why you wanted that fancy keyboard?"

Omaran thought about that. The decision to spend so much on this instrument had perhaps looked irrational on the surface, but he knew he needed it. "You know, I don't think I'll ever use all the functions, but there are sounds in there that I just had to have."

"Indeed. That was his influence, to get you to open to other sounds, other ways of making music. This new connection was possible because you have removed some blocks that you had in your energy system. Your flow of music was blocked for some time. Correct?"

"Hmmm, yes," Omaran said slowly. "Oh, my gosh. I've worked hard on unblocking my crown recently."

"Do you have any other questions for me tonight?"

Omaran switched mental gears. "Just one. When we go to the Rockies, I'm thinking of doing five grid points because the three or four you suggested just don't seem like enough."

"Dear Omaran, I do admire your enthusiasm. And you like to overdo things, don't you?"

"Yes, I do. I just want to make sure it is rock solid. Plus, I want to have really good reasons to go from Canada all the way down to northern New Mexico. It is a long road trip. But we will love every minute of it!"

"It is perfectly okay to do five but four is plenty. You also have blessings for the creeks and the waters, so you have a lot of other energy work that you can do. It is not only about putting in four points."

"That's wonderful," Omaran said, his mental wheels spinning. "And we are looking forward to being at the Tetons again, as well as visiting Yellowstone."

"Yellowstone . . . it will take a lot of work to get that one cooled down."

"Any suggestions? I've been thinking four release points around the area and burying rocks from Death Valley and calling on the Guardian of the Deep. That's as far as we have planned for there."

"You want to go all the way around the caldera?"

"I know it's a big area. Maybe we need more release points than four, but I was trying to get it encircled somewhat."

"That will add quite a bit of time and distance to your trip. But you do not need to encircle it. What would be most effective would be to get to where the critical area is. Now, even the critical area is rather large there, so what is your goal?"

"I understand that the area could possibly have a major eruption, so our goal is to, hopefully, help release these energies in a less damaging way . . . perhaps downward toward the core of the planet. Or to even have some of those eruptive energies transformed into other forms of energy."

"That is a big goal. I would submit that sending that energy down into the core of the planet is not something you want to do. You do not want to make the core unstable. There are easier ways to do this. For example, you can use a map. You do not have to visit every place in person when you are doing that kind of work, releasing and harmonizing the area. This can be done with a map, and with your intent. I know that you love to go out there, but if you really wanted to cover Yellowstone, you would have to spend your entire two weeks just there, and I don't believe you want to do that. You can put on a map any number of wonderful objects. There are few limits to what you can do on a map, and there are big limits to what you can do in person. So, are you gonna work smart, or are you gonna work hard?"

Omaran chuckled. "I think I'll go for smart."

"Ooookaaaaay! You may want to visit it once to get pictures and take them home to do the serious work. You will need to locate it on the globe and use the pictures to create resonance with the place."

"I like it!" Omaran exclaimed. "Should we put one physical release point somewhere around there?"

"The pictures will be enough to create resonance, but if you want to do one because you will feel better about it, then you go right ahead. Bury some magical objects, that will create a stronger resonance. Take some rocks from there, more resonance. Be creative. The stronger the connection the better."

"Thank you, that's wonderful."

"Is there anything else?"

"No, again thank you so much for coming to Antera and getting to me quickly."

St. Germain finished by taking them both into higher-frequency spaces, to get closer to their Higher Selves, or I Am Presence, as he called it. Whenever he did this, they both soared into the realms where anything is possible, and answers to any questions were immediately available. It was a state they loved, and it was so easy to get to with the Master's help. And Omaran had snapped out of his upset.

When they opened their eyes, Antera said, "So, we won't be building a physical center after all. I admit I feel lighter now, too."

Omaran nodded. "I guess you were right. It was probably a good exercise for us, especially me, to overcome doubts and fears, whether we ended up building it or not. I hope I got the healing I needed. And St.

Germain is right, we've been creating it here on our property all along. I like that!"

"I'm surprised we didn't see this before. When I really think about not only the creation, but the maintenance of such a center, it feels so heavy, like a weight of responsibility. And to do it we would have to do nothing else! Of course, we don't want to do that!"

"Of course! Now we are free! Yay!" Omaran started laughed uproariously, and Antera joined him. They got up and held hands, whirling around, celebrating their freedom.

38

Council of Los Angeles

In early May, their second initiation for the Order of the Blue Snake was completed with a small group of seven in their home and new Mother Garden. It was such joyful work to see the people light up and open their hearts to the Mother energy. Once they did, their lives were changed, their male and female sides became more balanced, and they had a powerful tool for removing obstacles in their lives and healing at deep levels.

A few weeks later, Antera and Omaran headed down to southern California to see Antera's parents and to add a grid point in the Los Angeles area on the way. They drove into Griffith Park but found that a recent fire had burned in the area where they had been in 2005. Many trees and bushes were gone, changing the landscape considerably. Driving around, they toured the park searching for another place and found one area that looked promising further up the ridge.

"We can aim for that group of oak trees," Omaran said, pointing.

They packed up and started up the steep slope of burned sagebrush. The sun was hot, though it was only May, and they were soon sweating.

"I'm glad it's a weekday," Omaran remarked. "This place could really be full of people on a weekend."

"Yeah, maybe we should have driven around more and tried to come in from the top. This is very steep."

"I really don't think there's a way down from the parking lot up there, and anyway then we'd have to go uphill after we were done. I always like going up first, if possible, so the way back is downhill."

They hauled their packs up, and at the top selected a beautiful spot the fire had missed, which was mostly hidden and fairly flat. Hills blocked their view of the ocean, but its influence was felt in the moist air. The ceremony went smoothly, and they sat for a while afterwards to tune in to the area.

Antera suddenly smiled and said, "You remember that group of elders who talked to us before, the Council of Los Angeles, who oversee the whole area? They just gave us a big thank you!"

"Ah! Our pleasure. Is there anything they want us to know?"

"I'm looking at the Light Form we made from their eyes, way above. It is very bright! They are showing me how it affects all the land around here as it pulls in negativity. Quite a large area."

"Great! Do they want us to do more in this area?"

Antera listened. "They say, pretty much as many as we can."

"This is all we can do on this trip, but we will be back," Omaran promised. "Plus, we are doing two east of here next, and they will really support this point."

"That makes them happy, because they can already see the effects of the ones we have built."

"It makes us happy, too! And connecting with all these beings is so great. There's so much more going on than I had any idea of ten years ago. Wouldn't it be nice," he mused, "if when we came into each new life, we remembered at least some of what we had learned from previous lives?"

"Ah, Omaran would like the easy path, it appears."

"He would indeed."

"Okay, let's get serious," Antera said as she closed her eyes and opened her inner senses. "I'm seeing a being. She's calling herself the Deva of Griffith Park. She's a very beautiful presence, and she's very thankful for the ceremony we just did. She's explaining about the fire that came through the park, saying she had to allow it so it would transform some negative energy that had gotten focused here. The fire cleared some of that out, and she's so happy that we did this now because this will help purify it more quickly and maybe other fires won't be needed."

Antera paused for a moment. "The drought is also caused by disharmony, in an attempt to transform harmful energies." There had been a drought for a couple of years in Southern California, which even in normal years did not get much rain, so a slight decrease was important. "The deva is saying that it is so dear to her heart to see that there are a few humans who are doing this kind of work and helping. And she hopes it is not too late to retrieve this whole Los Angeles area. There is so much stress here, and there are forces at work that could cause much destruction. She has been asking for help, and here we are."

"We are happy to meet this deva and help," Omaran said.

"She's also on the Council of Los Angeles. I think it is interesting that there is a group of beings in charge of energy flow in such a large city."

"Yeah, must be a large group!"

"Big job . . . and I guess the council knew we were coming. They now understand the difference between what we did today, making the permanent point that connects with others, and the temporary form we made a few years ago. They're saying that what we created is very visible."

"That must be why we attract these beings when we do this," Omaran said.

"Yes . . . they want to call our attention to a lot of dense energy, especially in the downtown area. They are hoping this Light will spread out and really influence the land. Now they see how it works, getting established and more firmly anchored in, and how it is being connected with all the other points in the grid. I don't think they fully understood before what was going to happen."

Omaran said, "St. Germain mentioned that it takes a while for new places to anchor in, and for the grid to adjust and get used to the new energies. Please tell the council that in two months we will be finished with the Rockies, and once we put those points in and connect them with the others, all points will be strengthened."

"They hear you."

"Ah, yes. What about the Guardian of the Deep connection, did they mention that?"

"They are very excited about that connection. They're saying, 'Yes, this has potential!' Since we are not sure exactly how it works, we're just going to let that develop. I'm telling them that the idea is to let some of the stress from this area, especially the fire element, drain off into Death Valley where the Guardian will take it deep into the Earth and transform it, balance it. The Guardian said he would educate the fire beings of this area so that they don't have to create a physical fire to purify. Maybe there's a way to do it that is a non-physical fire, for example, using the Violet Flame instead."

"We know that there is a sense of urgency, and we will bring as much help as we possibly can to this city. I know the Rockies points we make will help."

"The council is saying that they've had to pull upward a little bit, going higher above because they were being bombarded . . . too much negativity, too much density. They are working from an even higher level. Their hope is that this area can go back to being the pristine paradise that it was long ago. This used to be a paradise but look at what's happened. However, they are in here for the long haul. They're still overseeing the whole area and hoping for the best."

"It's good they are hopeful."

"Well, frankly, there is a little bit of the 'too little, too late' attitude, really. Not about what we're doing so much, but what the people who live here are doing. Positive changes that were needed decades ago are being made very slowly. It's not that they're hopeless, but I'm not getting a good feeling from them. They are just very, very concerned, and have given up in some areas. They hope to keep the core of the good energy alive but let some of the older stuff go.

"It's really a bit sad to hear them saying that. But they are very, very glad for everything that anyone is doing to help and they're glad that we are here today."

"Well, they're certainly welcome and we hope it helps."

"Okay, I think that's it. The deva of the park is showing me a picture of a newborn baby and saying, 'out of the ashes is born the new.' It's a time of renewal for some of this area. She's still very caught up in the fire and the results of it and the rebirth, the renewal of vegetation and all that. And she has gathered a lot of help to rebuild the vegetation in the area, and that's what she's really working on right now."

After this land-healing trip and visit with family, they focused their attention on their annual gathering on the Summer Solstice. Each year, it seemed the number of initiates grew and this part of Antera and Omaran's service in the mystery school was very fulfilling. The next adventure was the Rockies trip, which was coming right up.

39

A River Spirit

The Rocky Mountains extend over 3000 miles in length from Mexico through Canada, a mountain range which is often called the backbone of the North American continent. This impressive spine protrudes upward with over sixty peaks higher than 13,000 feet elevation. Some areas are more tectonically stable than others, mostly because of the ages of the rocks and how long since they were pushed up to form mountains, and this was a significant factor for the land-healing grid. The Masters had asked for grid points to be made in the most stable areas so they would give strength to the rest of the points, especially those on the coast. Thanks to Michael and his geological expertise, the four best locations had been chosen. He had done his usual stellar job, sending them geologic maps and references along with his recommendations.

Driving through high mountains on curvy roads was going to take some time, plus the distances were rather great, so they had allowed three weeks for this journey in their Subaru wagon, Swan. A house sitter was arranged to take care of their house, plants, and pets.

The decision to leave on July 4th turned out to be a good one in terms of traffic, as many people were home celebrating the holiday. Starting their journey in the north, they headed toward Idaho, and drove late into the night the first day before finding a small motel for sleep. Unfortunately, it had not occurred to them that loud noises were also a part of this holiday, and they seemed to be in the middle of a fireworks display blasting all around them, even though they didn't arrive at their motel until almost 11:30 at night.

"I can barely believe this," said Omaran very sleepily. "It's close to midnight, and we're not even in the middle of a town, or if it is, this is really Small Town U.S.A., and we happened on the middle of their celebration. The fireworks are right above our heads."

Antera yawned. "I'm going to look at this as a wonderful welcome and a send-off for our trip! But I wonder what time they'll stop."

"Hopefully by July 5th," Omaran said. Despite the noise, he was asleep within a few minutes of lying down.

On the second day, they followed a river of the Lewis and Clark Trail through some spectacular scenery of northern Idaho. The river resembled a picture postcard, with trees hanging lazily out over the slow-moving water, a few fishing boats, and occasional fish breaking the smooth surface. The road meandered lazily around bend after bend of the river's path.

"This is gorgeous!" exclaimed Antera. "Let's stop and take this in."

"Should we do our new River Blessing along here?" asked Omaran as he drove.

"I know you're excited about doing them, but Silver Horse said to get as close to the headwaters as possible, and this is obviously a full-on river. We should be doing our first one in just a few days."

Omaran nodded. "Okay, I'll pull over when I find a place, so we can stretch our legs."

They stopped and enjoyed the serenity of the river scene for a few minutes. It was their practice to take off their shoes and submerge their feet in as many bodies of water as possible along the way as they traveled, so they found a couple of boulders next to the water to sit on as their feet dangled in the chilly water. This was very grounding and absolutely refreshing.

The first land-healing ceremony site was planned for that day in northern Idaho, if there was time, in an area near Lolo Pass, the highest place on the road. As they approached the summit, Antera suddenly said, "Stop as soon as you can! We don't want to go any farther."

"What? We're not even at the highest elevation yet."

"I know, but I just heard that we should not go any farther. I think we'll be out of the stable part of the mountain range if we continue."

"Ah . . . look, there's a road," said Omaran pointing to the left. He stopped the car on the side of the highway. "No one's behind us, so I'll just turn around."

"Go for it!"

Omaran drove onto the dirt road, and they proceeded for about a mile as they looked for a place to park. It was narrow, and hardly had room for two cars to pass each other, much less parking pullouts. They hoped to park and hike for a short distance to find a secluded place. The road got steeper and rougher, and while Swan was a good, all-wheel drive car, it was low to the ground, so Omaran drove very slowly.

Finally, a small knoll invitingly appeared next to the road, so they pulled off. Unfortunately, the slopes were very steep on both sides of the road, not allowing for any hiking. The knoll was close to the dirt road, and they knew it must be a well-frequented recreation area and cars could easily come by during this holiday weekend, but no other options were available. So, they took a chance and quickly set up the ceremony right there, far enough from the road so its energy would not interfere in the future.

Antera declared out loud, "Divine Presence and nature spirits of this area, we ask that other people be kept from here until we are finished. Give us a clean space and protection. Thank you!"

Omaran was especially excited about this ceremony, because it was the first time he would include his new staff. He had been working on this personal power object off and on for almost two years, and he could feel its presence throughout the ceremony, attracting beautiful energy and adding its stored power to make the work even more effective. The nature spirits were especially interested in it, gathering around it as they proceeded.

It was made from a white bark pine branch he had found on one of their hikes on the east side of Mount Shasta. This type of pine can live thousands of years, and that was the aged wisdom that was infused into his staff now, the wood carved with special symbols and topped with a crystal ball. It felt good in his hand, like an extension of himself, and he knew it took so long to make because he hadn't been ready to use it until now. The branch had sat drying against one of the large windows in their living room for months until St. Germain had prompted Omaran into action by asking him, "So how long are you going to let your staff sit in the window just weathering, Omaran?" That had motivated him into action, and it had been finished just in time for this trip.

The hour-long ritual was not interrupted, then literally just a few seconds after they were all finished, several loud three-wheelers came up the road, stirring up dust as they drove past. Antera and Omaran looked at each other with relief and gave thanks for the protection from intrusion during their ceremony. They sat in their camp chairs for a while to sense the shifts in energy, and a butterfly landed on Omaran's arm, staying there while they sat. Even when they got up to pack everything into the car, the butterfly did not budge.

"Wow," said Omaran, amazed. "I've had butterflies land on me before, but never one that stayed this long."

"That is really special," marveled Antera. "If we needed a sign that this was a perfect place and a job well done, I'd say that butterfly is it."

Before driving away, Omaran encouraged his little friend to fly off, with a farewell and thanks. Back on the road heading east, they crossed into Montana, looking for a place to sleep. They were hoping to camp and soon came across an RV campground that had a few tent sites. Upon inspecting them, however, they found soggy, rain-soaked ground that would not accommodate a tent. It was like a swamp. And Antera, whose skin was especially tender, discovered that the mosquitoes were voracious.

They went over to the manager's trailer to ask for options, and he very graciously offered them a small, funky cabin instead, for the same price. It had no bathroom and two somewhat functional fold-down beds. But at least the mosquitoes were kept out. They took it.

Before retiring, they wanted to do their vocal exercises and practice some songs for an upcoming show, so Omaran walked back over to the manager, an energetic man in his forties who introduced himself as Thomas, to ask if they could park in a corner and sing in the car.

"You are singers?" Thomas asked, suddenly perking up.

"Yes, we are singer-songwriters, and just want to practice our performance so we don't get out of shape while we are travelling," Omaran explained.

"Well, I can do better than that. I also happen to be the local chaplain, and I have a small chapel just over there. You can use that to practice. It has a decent sound system, and I'd love to hear some live music!"

Omaran was amazed. "Really? That would be so kind! Are you sure?"

"It's no problem, I'll meet you there in half an hour and get you set up."

Thomas did as he said, setting up the sound system on a stage for them to use. Omaran also found out that this manager-chaplain had a history in music, and was personal friends with a number of performers, including Marie Osmond and Dan Seals. He watched parts of their practice and clapped, very much enjoying it.

The next day it was finally time for their first River Blessing. Ever since Silver Horse had taught them how to do this, they had been looking forward to trying it out. After doing some research on the biggest rivers of the continent, Antera had printed out maps to what looked like the source areas of many of them that started in the Rockies.

While Omaran drove, she read the river descriptions out loud. "The first river is the Missouri, the biggest tributary of the Mississippi. It really isn't clear where it actually starts, there is sketchy information about it, but we are headed in the general direction of it."

"What? One of the largest rivers on the continent and we don't even know where its headwaters are? Hard to believe."

"Well," she continued, "the state of Montana claims that it starts where three other rivers come together in a big confluence. So, there is no spring. They even made a state park at that site to mark it. I guess we'll go there and see what we think."

"I think headwaters should be where the river comes out of the ground, not where other rivers come together. It doesn't make sense," Omaran complained.

"Well, this is coming from a man who up until this point in his life has never even thought about the headwaters of a river."

"Ah, yes, there is that. Point well made. End of complaints."

Antera had always loved rivers. Growing up in the San Diego area, it was rare to see water flowing above ground. Most creeks were dry except right after a rain. She and her brother had always been excited after any rain, running down to the local ditch to see if water was flowing. She hadn't seen her first river until she was eleven years old.

She now said, "We could always just ignore what the state of Montana says and choose one of the three tributaries on the map as the Missouri. They are all about the same length and maybe we can get to the source of one of them."

"No, no. I'll give this park a chance."

"That's big of you."

"Don't mention it."

Upon arriving at the confluence, the energy did feel very powerful. Wherever rivers come together there is a special energy that is felt by even the least sensitive people. Here there were three coming together, and it was so uplifting that as soon as they got out of the car and walked to the water, they immediately looked at each other and nodded, agreeing without a word that this was the perfect place for their first River Blessing.

"I stand corrected," admitted Omaran. "Even if this isn't the actual spring headwaters of the Missouri, I can't imagine a more powerful spot. Good job . . . both you and Montana!"

"I love it here!"

They took off their shoes, rolled up their pant legs, and stood on smooth rocks in the water. It was shallow and relatively warm compared with other rivers they had sampled this way. The morning sun was warm on their backs as they let the waters wash away the road energy. After a few minutes they put their socks and shoes back on and hiked a short distance along the shore to get away from people, warding off the plentiful mosquitoes.

They sat in a grove of small willow trees facing the river, their feet buzzing and feeling refreshed by the waters. The river here was already quite large, flowing swiftly. Birds expressed their joy in song as they flitted through the trees and along the water.

Antera said out loud, "We now call forth the Spirit of the Missouri River. Please take the blessings and energy we give you today upstream as well as downstream, to cover your whole basin. We give you these crystals, which are blessed with the thoughtforms that will purify and cleanse your waters and raise them to higher consciousness. Everything the energy touches will be blessed. Every drop of your blessed water that goes to crop irrigation will raise the vibration of the plants, animals, and humans it touches. This is a vast, vast project, and with our intent we infuse tremendous spiritual energies into this river."

The Spirit of the Missouri, who arose from the water dramatically as soon as she was called, as if she had been waiting for them, hovered majestically, listening intently.

Antera declared, "I see her! She looks like a giant flowing river with many branches. A whole river basin is formed and maintained by this beautiful and powerful being. This is a very evolved water being and she has been here a long time, thousands of years. The river is ever changing, never static."

They stood up, and while Antera played her flute, Omaran continued to focus on the energy, then hurled the charged-up blessing crystals as far as he could into the depths of the river. He also poured some sacred water they had gathered from other rivers into it. Once the blessing was given, the river spirit went into action, gathering to her hundreds of water elementals and giving them the task of carrying the blessings out. When the activity settled a little, Antera stopped playing and listened.

Antera said, "The river spirit is saying, 'Thank you so much, thank you for allowing me to upgrade my purpose and my abilities to hold the energies of this river. This gives me a higher evolutionary path to take. I manage vast numbers of water spirits, over a very large area, the whole drainage basin. I see that you call yourselves land healers, but you also heal the waters, the air, and the fire. All the elements.'"

"It's true," Omaran told the river spirit. "Thank you for participating and spreading this energy! This is our first River Blessing, and you are the most perfect river spirit to begin this new project."

"She goes deep down too," Antera described, "not just in the river but into the ground water. And this is her favorite place, right here, because it's magical with all these tributaries coming together into one . . . a sacred place. And in answer to our concerns about being at the headwaters, she says she will take the energy upstream as well as down. Thank you, thank you, all nature spirits who have been helping. Now we are finished with our work and will leave before we are eaten alive by mosquitoes!"

They gathered their things quickly and walked back to the car, only to find that it would not start. Omaran tried over and over, listening to it turn over but not catch. This had never happened before, and their mechanic had tuned it up right before the trip.

"Wait, don't drain the battery! Let's tune in a moment," Antera cautioned. "Maybe there is a good reason for this."

They both closed their eyes, and the Spirit of the Missouri spoke to Antera, saying she didn't want them to leave so quickly. She was so excited about meeting them and the River Blessing, that she had called on some of her helpers to stop them from leaving!

Antera described this to Omaran, then told the river spirit out loud, "We loved meeting you too, and your lovely river, but we really need to go on to other places now. We can always get the car started by popping the clutch anyway, so respectfully, we ask that you release it!"

Omaran tried it again and it started immediately.

40

The Pink Flame

The Tetons were nearby, and they had allowed a few days to camp in this part of the Rockies that juts up as an isolated short range in Wyoming. They pulled right into a campsite and reserved it for three nights. Fortunately, they had brought net hats to put over their heads, because the mosquitoes would have been unbearable otherwise, even with the natural bug repellant they had brought.

The first day in these gorgeous mountains, they went on their favorite hike up Cascade Canyon. After the last trip when they had gotten sick, they were very careful to carry a lot of water. Each time they hiked into this canyon it was like being transported into a different dimension. It was not only the physical beauty that took all their words away, but the tranquility and quiet that seemed like an outdoor cathedral. As they hiked, they gazed at the small river that slowly meandered back and forth around various trees, bushes, and small rock outcroppings. On both sides of the canyon, their eyes were drawn upward to a series of towering peaks that had amazing presence, as if they were alive. Farther up, billowing clouds and rich, blue skies soared on forever.

"Look! A moose!" Omaran stopped and pointed toward the river.

"I see it. A huge one."

They watched as it slowly moved along, grazing, its legs mostly in the water, in the idyllic scene.

"Hard to imagine a more beautiful place," Omaran said.

As they walked on, Omaran enjoyed the scenery but in the back of his mind he was also feeling a bit nervous about finding what they were calling a "fairy column." They knew there was one somewhere in this valley. It was going to be their first time doing an Air Blessing, as taught by Silver Horse. The doubts about his abilities, that still occasionally plagued him, were active. Antera never seemed to worry about these things, but his doubts were up in full force. What if he couldn't feel it? What if he could feel it but not find a trail to get there? Why couldn't he let go of these doubts and just relax?

The process would basically involve finding a fairy column and throwing blessed herbs into it, in the context of a ceremony to make it a sacred act. The air elementals would take the blessings and carry the energy high into the sky then far and wide in the atmosphere. These fairy columns were energetic rather than physical, but reason said that the fairies would take advantage of updrafts, which would probably be close to the cliffs rather than in the valley.

Omaran kept an eye out for any animal trails that may take them through the bushes toward the river, which was closer to the steep mountains on the southern side of the glacial valley. He had a good idea that the fairy column was somewhere close to the Grand Teton, the highest peak and where the most spiritual energies of the Master Retreat were. He kept looking, but the foliage was very thick with no way through.

He stopped, suddenly feeling an energy tug to the side. "I think we are close, so I'm looking for a trail."

Taking a few more steps, there it was, a barely discernable way into the bushes. He started in.

"Wait here and I'll check to see if it this trail goes through," he told Antera.

"You are kidding, right? You call that a trail?" But she didn't try to stop him, knowing he was very good at finding these small animal trails and bushwhacking through.

She sat on a small boulder to wait. The sun was hot and intense, and she wished she could have worn shorts and short sleeves, but her skin couldn't take the radiation after so much sun damage earlier in life. It didn't stop her from going out, but she always wore long sleeves, pants, and a big hat no matter how much she sweated.

Stomping noises preceded Omaran's voice as he made his way back to the trail fifteen minutes later. "Come on in! We can get close to the river this way," he proclaimed as he emerged, exuberantly successful.

Antera followed him slowly through the dense brush, and after about ten minutes it opened up and they could hear the rushing water getting closer. A huge granite boulder was sitting between them and the water, and though they couldn't see the top, it looked like it may be climbable.

"What do you think? Want to try to get to the top?" Omaran asked.

"You go first," she replied.

She was right behind him, and there were footholds and ledges that allowed a challenging but doable ascent. They were pleased to find that it was almost flat on the top, and provided a view above the bushes, with the river flowing loudly at its base, music to their ears. It was a perfect, secluded spot to stay a while!

Immediately, the shoes came off, and they both lay down on the hard surface, covering their feet with jackets to avoid sunburn. The many small crystals in the granite sparkled in the sun's light. They soaked up the spiritual energies of the place and recharged their bodies with Earth energy. Omaran fell asleep for a half hour, snoring lightly.

When he awoke, they decided to do the air blessing right there on the top of the rock.

"I hope we are close enough to the column here. It seems like a perfect spot. What do you think?" Omaran said, looking for confirmation. He was feeling more confident, and the place really felt powerful.

Antera answered, "It feels perfect to me! What a find! I think the actual column is nearer the cliffs, but we are close enough, at least as close as we can get."

They prepared for the simple ceremony, which included energizing a batch of prepared herbs and small crystals, then ending by throwing them all into the air. The wind gathered them, whisking some away, and the rest fell back down on the boulder.

They looked at each other. Omaran said, "I hope that worked. The herbs didn't go as far as I thought they would."

"I feel a lot of air spirits here, and they seem excited, so they got the energy."

He could feel them also, but still hoped they had done it right. They ate lunch, then decided to go back to the trail and continue hiking up the valley. After about an hour, another area drew them off to the side, this time with less bushes to force through, so they sneaked off toward the river when no other hikers could see them. A large fir tree next to the water looked like an optimal place to sit and see if Antera could bring through a Master from the retreat.

As soon as they got relatively comfortable, St. Germain was there and ready to talk.

The Master said, "Let me put you at ease. You got as close as you could to the fairy column that you were looking for, and that rock was a perfect spot. My blessings on you both and my thanks. I am glad you came back to this magical place. It is so, so dear to my heart.

"Now, that said, I would like to give you a few tips about improving on your ceremony technique. I would suggest that you charge up the herbs and crystals in a ceremony that brings the energies into them before leaving home rather than doing it as a part of your atmospheric purification ceremony. Then you would only need to put them out into the vortex of energy that the fairies create. Because they do create a vortex of energies that both sucks up and brings down. As they swirl around, they distribute whatever they get from below, up into the upper atmosphere.

"The site that you chose for the ceremony was tied into their column, which is higher up on the mountain. The fairies heard your call and created a connection to their main column which is in the upper reaches of these mountains. Therefore, the energy will be distributed. The fairies take the energy, they're not taking your herbs, Omaran. You understand?"

Omaran felt more at ease. "Now I do, yes."

Germain continued, "They take the energy you build in your ceremony and the herbs are a symbolic part of that. They are not the main part."

"Right, so it's similar to the tiny crystals that we put in the rivers," Omaran said.

"Exactly. I really like those little crystals that you use. And I want you to know the Missouri River Spirit is reporting back that what you did there was very successful. She wants you to know that she is very thankful and is spreading those energies far and wide."

Omaran said, "Thank you, please send her our gratitude."

Germain laughed. "Well, you can do that yourself."

"I will."

St. Germain then asked them to focus on the Teton Retreat Center and tune their energy to it. "Please connect the flame in your hearts into this mountain and this etheric retreat. This spiritual center is very active, and everyone in it is glad whenever someone comes here who is aware. So, tune to that now. This retreat is run by Ascended Masters, including myself, part time. I'm here today because you are here. There are places inside where you can go for deep nourishing and cleansing. I suggest you go there now. Feel yourself transporting up into a beautiful chamber deep inside the mountain, not high in the peaks, but deeper.

"You have been inside this chamber before. As you enter, you see the large Pink Flame in the center. You may walk into this Pink Flame and let it purify you completely. Why don't you do that now? Let it stoke up the Pink Flame in your heart."

They sat in silence for a few minutes under the fir tree, as they followed the Master into the Pink Flame with part of their consciousness and allowed it to permeate all aspects of their four bodies.

When they had soaked a while, the Master went on, "While you are in this Pink Flame, see before you any areas of your lives or your beingness that do not embrace this flame as easily as other areas do. Give a super saturation to those areas. Send them Love and acceptance. This is what the Pink Flame is all about—Love, acceptance, and compassion.

"And look inside your heart for any impurities that are there. They may appear as slightly dark areas, or very thin splinter-like objects, or thorns, or anything that is not of the Pink Light. Pull them out . . . as you allow this Pink Flame in your heart to grow, all those little areas of your life and of your heart can be removed, renewed, replenished, and stoked up anew."

He paused again, giving them time to clear their hearts. "Now, as you stand in the Pink Flame, see the group of Masters and angels around you. I am one of them. Feel our projection of pure Divine Love. Love so strong that nothing, absolutely nothing can remain hidden. And see what it feels like to be so loved . . . so loved . . . so supported."

The Masters and angels around them began singing and chanting, as they held this space. Antera and Omaran followed them as they chanted over and over, "I Am Love . . . I Am Love . . . I Am Love . . ."

As they chanted, the Pink Flame in their hearts grew and grew, so large that it reached out to the ring of Masters. A resonance between their hearts and the hearts of the Masters formed and started vibrating at a pure tone, within this pink energy. It was extremely intense, yet the vibration was so pure and loving, that it felt natural and easy.

After a period of time that they could not track in this state of awareness, Antera and Omaran felt the energy pull back in, and they were instructed to step out of the Pink Flame. They could see that their hearts were like blazing pink suns. They were escorted out of the chamber and back to where their bodies were sitting next to the river.

St. Germain said, "Give this Love to yourself. Turn it inward. It is easier to love others than it is to love yourself. So put it into the deepest recesses of your heart. Open a door right at the center of your heart and flood it. Very good, now tell me how you feel."

Omaran found his voice with some difficulty. "I feel completely at peace . . . I have no sense of my body. I feel like I'm a sun; like I'm a small sun."

The Master said, "Very good, Omaran, very good indeed. That is what this retreat is all about, in essence—building the heart flame into a beam of Love so strong that it gives you peace, that it permeates every part of your life, your physical body, your emotions, your thoughts. It permeates every part. I thank you so much for coming.

"This is a place you can visit from your home; you don't have to be here to visit, but it is always good to renew more strongly when you are here."

Omaran could only say, "Thank you so much for taking us inside."

"You are welcome, my good man. And now, keep this peace with you. Instead of allowing your anxiety or fear to drive you, let peace drive you, in a way that is not stressful, in a way that follows the flow, and allows Spirit to work through you much easier. It is important that you continue to build on your ability to broadcast Love to everyone, not only those people who agree with you or make you comfortable, but those who make you uncomfortable, those you do not like or want around you. You can still give them Love and acceptance. They need more of it than others. By permeating with this Divine Love, all judgment is gone and there is only Love for everyone and for yourself.

"My blessings upon you. Allow me to put my hand on your crown as you sit here and give you just a little more understanding about what it is like to be the Master."

After St. Germain left, they sat for a while and discussed the experience, deciding they would come here in meditations from home. But they also knew that the Teton Retreat was much stronger in person, so they hoped they would be able to travel here every year or two.

They reluctantly got up to hike back while there was light to do so, and before the last ferry left for the other side of the lake. A robin flew down and landed on the path in front of them, hopping along for about half a mile as if leading them back. This was very unusual behavior. They both marveled at the experience and talked to the robin as they walked along until it finally flew away. When they got back to camp, they were pleasantly tired from the long hike, and they slept well that night in their tent.

41

The Teton Retreat

The next morning, they awoke refreshed and ready for another long hike. This one would be more rigorous, up to higher elevation. The trail on the map looked like a very steep climb with many switchbacks, ending at Amphitheater Lake. It was the best way they could find to get closer to the Master Retreat without backpacking in overnight. They had attempted this hike on their previous visit but had to abort it about a mile in, because Omaran had gotten very sick.

This time, they were feeling healthy and raring to go. The aftereffects of their journey into the retreat the day before were still palpable, and they were hoping to go in again, from higher elevation. Antera could feel her heart singing as she started up the trail, leading the way, with Omaran close behind. They walked through the woods and over small streams, the lush smells flooding their senses.

Suddenly she could no longer hear Omaran behind her. She stopped and turned around. He had stopped and was standing with his arms folded over his chest. She could see that his aura had turned dark. Cautiously, she went back and approached him.

"What's up?" She asked.

"I'm not going up there. This is crap. I don't want to do this. It is not working for me, so stop pushing."

It was entities talking, she could see that. After their heart-opening experience the previous day, she wondered how this could happen, but not for long. She understood that when Light comes in, it exposes anything that needs healing. Perhaps something in his heart had been unleashed for healing. Unfortunately, however, he was not healing it. Instead, he had allowed these dark beings to take over, going on the attack. She knew from experience that engaging him in this condition was fruitless. It was something he needed to heal, and he wouldn't be open to any help from her. She said nothing.

He suddenly turned around and walked back toward the car, fuming. She stood there for a moment in disbelief, watching him go. "Okay, then, I'll go on without you," she called after him.

Turning to continue the hike, she hoped he would win his inner battle and catch up. His protective nature, she had a feeling, would conflict with the pain he was going through, and he would want to be with her to make sure she was okay. But after not making it the last time they attempted this journey, she was determined to do it with or without him.

It was a beautiful trail, winding in and out of the trees, nourishing her with each step. Open meadows on the steep mountainside were covered with golden and red wildflowers, more than usual because of abundant snow the previous winter. Views of the valley below and the winding Snake River along the base of the mountains were ever-expanding to the soul.

Even as Omaran turned and began walking back to the car, a part of him couldn't believe what he was doing. It had been quite a while since he had acted like this. And yet, when he thought about just turning around and hurrying to catch up with Antera, he couldn't do it. He walked for about ten minutes before he finally stopped and sat down on a rock.

He felt dizzy, and it had nothing to do with the altitude. He just breathed for a while, and even though he couldn't figure out what had brought this on or even what to do about it, he realized that he had to go after Antera. He decided he would figure it all out later, but right then he just had to go. He knew she would be safe on this mountain, especially with all the unseen help she had, but still there was a part of him that could not relax until he had caught up with her. It just wasn't right to be separated.

After walking for almost half an hour, he realized that she had, indeed, continued up the trail without him. He had been holding a small hope that she would be waiting for him, sitting on a rock somewhere. It was very steep going, and his pace was slow, but he was surprised when he hadn't caught up with her after two arduous hours. Finally, a young couple caught up and passed him and he said that if they see a redheaded hiker ahead, to please tell her that he was on his way.

Antera had a lot of energy, but she deliberately walked more slowly than she could, hoping Omaran may overcome his pain and catch up. The plentiful streams were tempting to drink, looking so pure, but she took no chances, instead soaking her bandana often and placing it over her head under her hat to cool down. She reminded herself about what had happened last time they tried this hike because of drinking from a tempting stream, and that caused her to lose all desire for it no matter how scorching hot the sun felt.

As she stopped to drink water from her bottle, a couple passed her. The woman said, "Are you missing someone?"

"Hmmm . . . maybe my husband?"

"We saw him a ways back, and he said he was trying to catch his wife. He is only a few minutes behind."

"Okay, thanks. Have a good walk."

She was relieved that he was going to make it after all. It was almost an hour later that he actually did arrive, while she was resting on a rock under the shade of a fir tree. Most of the climb was behind her, and she guessed that the lake was only a couple of miles away. As he approached, she watched his energy for clues as to his mood.

When he got close, he asked, "Do you have the electrolyte powder in your pack?"

She looked at him curiously. "Is that all you have to say to me?"

"I'm very tired." He wanted to say more, but he couldn't bring himself to do it. He was still wrestling with his anger.

She sighed and got out the electrolytes, handing him a packet, which he put in his water bottle. Nothing more was said, and they hiked together, frequently stopping for sips of water from their bottles. The elevation, combined with the heat, was very dehydrating.

He broke the silence by saying, "I'm better now."

She just looked at him, not saying anything, and hoped he would explain.

"I don't know what happened exactly, I wish I did. It's been quite a while since I've been that stupid. I think what happened is that the Pink Flame yesterday was so intense, it stirred up some very deep negativity in my heart. It had to be purged. That's why I got so upset. That's no excuse and even if that was the cause, I obviously must be able to deal with it and release it. I remember that the Masters keep telling us that if you bring in a great deal of Light it will attract its opposite. I understand that intellectually, but I still don't seem to be able to handle it when it happens."

"And?"

"That's all. Oh, and I'm sorry I acted crummy. As I sat on a rock after I left you, I felt completely sick at what I had allowed to take me over and knew I had to come after you."

"Okay." She could see that he had at least overcome the entities. But he hadn't healed whatever drew in that energy. If he didn't handle whatever had come up, it would come up again. But she said nothing. Right now, she wanted to focus on this amazing hike.

It was necessary to traverse several large snowfields to get to a lake on the way called Surprise Lake. They had climbed about 3000 feet and felt tired. They stopped at a waterfall at the far end where snowmelt fed the lake and ate lunch, taking in the absolute grandeur of the place. It was a perfect example of a cirque, carved out by glaciers.

But their goal was farther, a higher lake closer to the Grand Teton. They climbed along the waterfall, tromping through snow, and finally made it up to the next level. This lake was extremely pristine, still mostly covered with ice, and breathtakingly beautiful. They stood for a while, taking it all in.

"Want to go this way?" Omaran pointed along the shore.

"Yes, I want to sit down, and in some shade, if possible." She was feeling the altitude, and the lack of oxygen coupled with the heat had sapped her strength.

He led them around the shore then up a short distance, urging her on. "Just a few more feet up, to those small pines."

They collapsed on some rocks in the sparse shade and rested. Antera meditated on her I Am Presence for a few minutes. St. Germain came to her and invited her into the etheric retreat again. She began following him in another entrance, like a back door, but then silently asked if Omaran was invited.

The Master said, "I don't think he is ready. He is battling his demons and his heart isn't clear yet."

She said, "I do want him to experience this also. We hiked so far. Is there any way I could bring him along?"

"All right. Go back and get him. I will wait."

She opened her eyes and asked Omaran to get out the recorder because they were going inside the retreat again. She described to Omaran what was happening as the Master patiently guided them back along the corridor and into what he called the Chamber of Purification. The large room had walls that were cut from the native rock like a cavern and showcased a pool that was filled with gold-colored liquid.

"They are asking us to walk down into the gold pool. There are wide steps, plenty big for both of us. As we go in, we are immersed in the gold liquid, which is purifying us on a deep level, through and through. Our bodies are being purged by liquid gold in this pool of purification, so our bodies are turning clear, more see-through . . . we are in over our heads, and we keep going down. We can dance and swim and breathe underwater."

"I feel it, wow!" Omaran followed along, seeing and feeling what they were both going through as she described it.

"We keep going down, swimming down to the bottom of the pool, which is rather deep. At the bottom of the pool there is a large crystal ball."

"I see it. Looks like it is on a stand of some kind."

"Yes. I think we are supposed to put our hands on it. The depths of this crystal are . . . I keep hearing the words unfathomable . . . and it goes back in time. Time and space mean nothing here. As we hold our hands on this crystal, we get this intense radiance of Light and an intense energy of understanding."

They paused to take in the energy for a few minutes. She continued, "It's really all about purification because the more we understand about who we are and what we're doing, the more aware we are. The more we can bring forth our I Am Presence, the purer we are. The purer we are, the closer we are to the Divine. It all makes sense to me, does it to you?"

"Yes, I get it on a very deep level, way beyond words."

"The crystal is saying that only a few people get to come here, so we are very lucky to partake of this crystal's energy and the liquid gold."

"Wow, I feel like I'm being reamed out, clearing some last vestiges of negativity."

When they were finished with the transmission from the crystal and purification from the liquid gold of the pool, it was time to float back up to the surface and walk up the stairs and out. St. Germain was waiting for them when they walked out of the pool. They were radiant and found themselves dressed in shining golden gowns that seemed to radiate their own Light. They were overjoyed when they saw the Master, dressed in a purple and gold cloak and looking powerful and regal. They went down on their knees in front of him, in gratitude, and he put his hands on their heads.

St. Germain said, "Arise into your next level of radiance, my beautiful brother and sister. I thank you so much for coming here and having this ceremony and merging with the Flame of Love yesterday. I called you forth into the heart of this mountain, not only for your purification, but for your advancement into a new level of awareness and responsibility.

"Now, you may think you have plenty of responsibility, but I say to you, you have no idea what is coming, and how much responsibility you may be asked to carry for the Order of Melchizedek. We are calling on you to be so full of the Light, so full of the radiant Light of your Divine Presence that there is nothing that can faze you.

"I know you may also be thinking, Omaran, that you really blew it today. But I say to you, these are the kinds of trials you must go through, and if each time you are able to rise through and above them into a new level of awareness, then you are advancing. As you work to build your essence ever stronger in the Light, there will be those who try to stop you. There will be those who try to put up walls of resistance for you to sense, but these walls are not real. I say to you again, THESE WALLS ARE NOT REAL!

"This resistance is simply a smoke screen. Remember that you are Divine, you are the Light, you are the heavenly radiance of your Divine Presence, and there is absolutely nothing else that is real! It is time to set aside and throw asunder anything that is not aligned with this new level of awareness, with this new level of purification and radiance throughout the Universe!

"You have been given today the gift of the Teton Crystal and the radiance thereof. Let there be a memory of this instilled within your cells, instilled within your entire existence, from the physical to the outer dimensional levels!

"Let it be known in this proclamation that you have received these energies and will always carry them from now on! There is no resistance to this energy. Rise, my brother and sister, rise to your new level of radiance, your new level of awareness! Awaken to that which goes on around you and throughout this planet. Awaken to what is really going on so you may be of further service. Enlighten yourselves to finally raise up your awareness to the level of the golden core, to the Teton Crystal, to the Three-Fold Flame in your heart which holds the Christ Essence, which must remain completely stoked and available throughout your existence on this planet, and beyond.

"We give you this jump in your evolution because you are needed on this planet, and you have come so far. I ask that you hold this energy dear to your hearts, that you hold your I Am Presence dear forever, and throughout all space and time. You are timeless beings, you are space-less beings."

As Antera described what was happening inside the mountain, Omaran was able to follow along, experiencing it deeply in his soul body. They had been kneeling in front of St. Germain and they now stood up, and noticed angels flying all around them, singing songs of Love and Light. They both felt uplifted into the higher octaves of purified souls. The energy of the choir was almost overwhelming.

The Master then said, "And I say to you, remember this in the depths of your being and throughout your consciousness. Carry it with you throughout your days and into the nights, and with every word you speak and every song you sing. Let these angelic energies come through your voice, and project throughout the universe and into everyone listening! Use the sound waves and the power of sound, the Word! For this purpose, we bless you and we give you this gift. Take it out and project these healing frequencies, these angelic blessings throughout the world."

When the choir finished, St. Germain escorted them out of the Chamber of Purification, down a hallway, and up some stairs to the highest chamber of the retreat. This chamber was quite different. He opened the door to reveal what looked like a solid wall of granitic rock. Antera and Omaran found that their bodies were so pure they could move right through it, so they did just that, as they slowly entered the room.

"I ask you to sit here inside the rock. You will become the rock and it will become you. As you change your vibration to that of these beautiful minerals, they will give you information to further evolve the physical body to one that is more impervious to toxins, and less affected by the denser parts of your material world.

"Let this energy surround and penetrate your bodies in this realm and transmit it into your physical bodies sitting outside. Allow this energy to further raise the vibration of your physical vessels so that all those toxins and chemicals and lower vibrational energies may pass through without harmful effect. I will leave you now, and I fully support you being here at least ten minutes. Sit within this Chamber of Rock and merge with these minerals, and I will be back when you are finished."

They did as instructed, feeling more and more in tune with the minerals and crystals in the rock. It felt like toxins in their etheric bodies were being drawn out and a new level of purification in the physical was taking place.

When the Master came back and they exited the room, he said, "Very well, you are quite well done. I thank you for reaching this far up the mountain, though I know it was not easy for you to get here. I love you both dearly, and I know you are getting tired and need to be hiking back. I thank you once again for coming into the Teton Retreat, and now that you have been here in earnest, perhaps you can come back when you are not here physically. I leave you with my deepest Love and appreciation for all you have been through and all that you are doing."

St. Germain left, and they were quickly shown the way out by another being they didn't know and popped back into their bodies sitting on rocks under the pine trees by the alpine lake. There was so much to talk about, yet they had no words yet as they processed the experience. Before hiking back down the mountain, they each looked for a rock from that sacred place to take with them. Omaran found the perfect one. It was a heart-shaped rock with a dark area in the middle. To him, it signified his heart and the area he was working on healing.

They hiked the five miles to the car, much easier going downhill, and were so soaked with sweat and grime that they stopped at a hostel on the way back, to pay for a shower. The warm water felt unbelievably good. They treated themselves to a dinner at the local restaurant before heading back to camp, clean and fulfilled.

42

Yellowstone

Besides the Missouri, there are two other great rivers, the Yellowstone and the Snake, which have their sources in the Yellowstone area. Antera's research had given unclear results about where their actual headwaters were, however. Determined to find them and do a River Blessing on each, they got up early the next morning and headed north toward Yellowstone.

The Snake River source was easier to find than they had anticipated, and they stopped right along the road near its source, hiking along it for a while. Colorful wildflowers, as well as hungry mosquitoes, surrounded them as they scanned the area for a place to do the ceremony out of earshot of other hikers. They found a nice area away from the trail.

When they called the Spirit of the Snake River and distributed the crystals into the waters, they could feel her gathering her water spirits and spreading the energy upstream and downstream, in a bustle of activity. She was grateful and loved the blessing energies.

There were many rocks to sit on, so they stayed a short time to enjoy the experience, taking their shoes off and wading in the cool water. Such a beautiful river! Earlier, they had decided to take a few small stones from each major river home with them, to help tune to their energy, so that was a good excuse to wander as they gathered just the right river rocks.

Yellowstone National Park is on a super-volcano, called that because of the size of its potential eruption. St. Germain had told them they could do some healing on it when they got back home, to soothe it and help release the nonphysical build up. The plan was to take pictures of it at various places and create a large collage of the caldera, to send healing through a map. It was simply too large to do all the releasing in person.

In the park, they went to the ranger station and paid for two nights at a campground in the middle of the caldera, on the west side of Yellowstone Lake. There was still time in the day, so they drove to find the headwaters of the Yellowstone River. Its actual source seemed to be high in the mountains before it flowed down into the lake, not accessible except by backpacking. Other maps said it started where it comes out of the lake— again, surprisingly conflicting information on the beginning of a major river.

They decided it was good enough to catch it at the exit of the lake. Finding the trail to the river at that location did not turn out to be easy, however, so they finally stopped at a ranger station to ask.

The ranger behind the huge desk was a large man with a round face. He said, "Oh, that trail has been closed because of grizzly activity. You'd best take another one."

Omaran said, "Are you sure? Is it dangerous? That is where we want to go."

"Well, they are unpredictable, those bears. We don't want anyone to get hurt, and we don't want people to disturb them, either. There are plenty of other places to hike. Here is a map."

He handed them a folded map of the area with trails marked. Thanking the ranger, they sat in the car for a few minutes, getting their bearings from the map. They drove to the prohibited trailhead they wanted, and sure enough, there was a sign saying the trail was closed with a metal gate blocking entry. Since it was the only way to get to the place on the river they needed to be, they decided to go there anyway.

Antera wasn't really comfortable with the possibility of encountering grizzlies, knowing them to be vicious and unpredictable. She had seen black bears many times, because they lived in the woods around their home, but grizzlies were different. Omaran had a grizzly as one of his totem animals, so he was fairly confident in his abilities to sense them and remain calm. He called on his bear spirit to protect them by warning the bears away from where they were going.

"You lead the way, then," Antera said, not feeling entirely sure about this adventure.

"Don't worry, I'll have my senses on full alert."

His confidence was reassuring, and Antera had always trusted his animal sense. It wasn't a long hike, and most of it was not in thick forest, so visibility was pretty good.

Once they snuck under the gate, Omaran was surprised at how intent his senses became. However, it suddenly hit him that he was responsible for not only his own safety, but Antera's, and she trusted him. He immediately questioned his motives, as he wanted to be sure he wasn't doing this for macho or ego-based reasons. As they walked slowly along, he went deep inside and scrutinized what he was doing. There was only a feeling of safety and protection, down to the core of his being. His bear spirit was strong. He had no doubts after that, knowing it would be very good to bless the river.

After hiking about half a mile, Omaran suddenly stopped, focusing intently over to the right through the forest. "I sense something over there," he said.

Holding still, they waited, hardly breathing. Then they saw a large brown animal about 150 yards away, slowly making its way through the trees. It turned out to be a large elk, not a bear, so they continued onward. The ever-present mosquitoes were swarming around as they walked, so they had to keep moving.

Omaran continued to check energetically as to his sense of safety as they walked, and all seemed well. Less than two miles in, there was a perfect place close to the river, in a green meadow. No one was around, undoubtedly due to the bear warning, so they could do the ceremony without concern that others would hear or see. That turned out to be a nice advantage.

At this location, the river was already very large as it spilled out of the lake, and the presence of the Spirit of the Yellowstone River was strong, male, and waiting. They had put out a call to the river letting the river spirit know they were on their way, but they sensed that there may also have been some communication between him and the other two river spirits they had met. These beings maintain the energy of hundreds or even thousands of miles of river, so they could be anywhere along their waterway, and yet here he was, expecting them to arrive. It was impressive.

The ceremony went well, and afterwards they gathered more small rocks to take home, before hiking back to the car without seeing even a single grizzly. Omaran was sure that Antera was looking around and sensing as much as he was but neither of them brought it up, as to do so might call in the presence of what they wanted to avoid. There was a part of Omaran that was almost disappointed, but Antera certainly was not.

It seemed that the only place to get any supplies, other than junk food, was in West Yellowstone, a town situated at the opposite side of the park. Not realizing how far it was until it was too late to turn back, they drove completely around the edge of the huge caldera. At some point on their drive, they realized that having to drive around the whole area was actually a good way to get their energy around and into the entire place, and that this unintentional side trip was obviously no accident. They stopped for pictures along the way, for the collage at home, and caught sight of several animals near the road, including bison, elk, and one bear off in the distance. They watched in astonishment as several tourists climbed out of their cars and went on foot to approach the wild animals, even the bear, to get a bit closer for a picture.

They finally arrived back at the campground, which was very smoky from the many campfires. It was hard to breathe. That night, there were parties of people staying up past the 10:00pm quiet time, obviously drunk and very loud. One woman fell on her way to the restroom, then yelled out, "Damn that road for moving." Irritated as they were by the noise, they laughed out loud.

Antera was also feeling the restlessness of the active volcano. They were camped right in the middle of it, and it wasn't at all peaceful! The tectonic stress was very unsettling and would have kept her awake all night even if their neighbors had been quiet. Of course, Omaran slept as if he were in a quiet, peaceful place.

In the morning, she asked him, "So why do we need to stay another night?"

"I thought you wanted to do some hiking around here."

"I don't need to. I want to leave unless there is something else we need to do here. I'm sure there are lots of beautiful places to hike to, but I'm done with geysers and waterfalls and this volcano energy."

"Me too."

"Then let's get out of Dodge!"

They abandoned their campsite that morning, despite paying ahead, and set off for the next stable area of the Rockies, eastward toward the Big Horn Mountains in northern Wyoming. On the map it seemed like a good location for the next land-healing ceremony. Driving the curvy road through the mountain range was like going back through time. The variety of rock formations were strikingly beautiful, and there were signs along the road describing the ages of the outcrops. The higher the elevation, the older the formations, back to a Pre-Cambrian granite. This definitely fit the criteria of old and stable.

Near the summit, they parked on the side of the highway, grabbed their packs and walked into the forest. As usual, they didn't want anyone to see where they were going, so they hurried between cars going by, running to get out of sight in the trees.

Several antelope leaped through the forest ahead of them as they walked. An excellent place in the shade looked promising, a natural circular area, but as they were setting up, the local mosquitoes found them and attacked as if they were starving, and the humans were their first meal of the year. The essential oils Antera and Omaran were using to discourage them were simply not strong enough for so many. So, they repositioned to a sunny area, hoping that would make it more uncomfortable for the pests.

They were setting up when Omaran said, "I forgot the stools!"

There was a twenty-minute guided meditation as a part of the ceremony, and small folding stools made it a lot more comfortable.

"It's too far back to the car," Antera said, "and I'm already so uncomfortable with all these bites. I say, let's just sit on the ground. Grim and bear it! Ha, ha, I mean grin! Oh, boy. I'm going to look on this as a test of our ability to focus under adverse conditions."

They did pull it off, maintaining their concentration for the work by pushing aside the physical pain and itching. The ceremony was well attended by many elementals and Masters, despite the humans' discomfort. They were, once again, very glad that the elementals and other beings did most of the energy work.

When they were finished with the last song, and had given gifts to the elementals, Omaran got a funny look on his face and said, "What else could I have forgotten that would be even more important than the stools?"

"What?"

"The shovel."

"Oh, no!"

He always used a small shovel to dig a hole to bury the magical objects after each grid point was created. These objects were what connected the points energetically, a very important aspect of the project. They scouted around, but the ground was so rocky there was no way he could dig a hole deep enough without the shovel. So, he hiked back while Antera continued to hold the space of the ceremony, continually moving to discourage more bites. She sang the last song over and over, and he was back in twenty minutes. It was completed.

Following the road on over the pass, they started the search for a place to camp. A KOA campground was all they could find. It was the first time they had stayed in one, and they hoped it would be the last time. Even Omaran got little sleep because of the very close tents and continual traffic all night, as this campground was very conveniently located adjacent to an interstate highway. It was like camping in a city. But they did get showers and washed a load of laundry.

The next day was spent driving. There were a few smaller rivers along the way that they stopped to bless, though it was difficult to get close to most of them. It was very surprising that there was no easy access to such important natural features. Did no one care about rivers? Sometimes they had to park on the main highway or freeway and sneak down past a fence or other barrier to reach them. They even stopped caring so much if other people saw them, and if they could find access, they went about their business and ignored others.

Their goal was to get into Colorado, near Rocky Mountain National Park, their next planned land ceremony in a very stable area of the middle Rockies. Indulgently, they stayed in a motel in Fort Collins and got some much-needed sleep, anticipating the next day's mountain energies.

43

White Buffalo Calf Woman

Early the next morning, they were on their way west toward Rocky Mountain National Park, driving up a steep and winding canyon with a small river rushing right alongside, in many places only a few feet below the road surface. They saw an occasional person fishing and a few cars parked along pullouts, with sounds of children and happy adults playing in or near the river.

When they came out of the canyon they were almost immediately face to face with this section of the Rocky Mountains. They were already high in elevation, and the snowcapped mountain tops were visible. Soon they were in the park and surrounded by high, snow-covered peaks as far as they could see. The highway, claimed to be the highest elevation highway in the U.S., wound in and out of the curves of the mountains at elevations above 10,000 feet. At one point the road almost reached 12,000 feet. It was breathtaking.

Antera was watching their progress on the map, looking for the trail they had picked out. "It should be just around the next corner."

"Yes, this is it!" Omaran declared decidedly.

A small area of single-file parking marked the trailhead, with room for only four cars, and one place was waiting for them. Omaran smoothly pulled over and parked, they loaded up their daypacks with ceremony items, and they were off. As usual, they didn't know exactly where they were going, but they knew the place would be apparent when they saw it. The energy along the trail was so uplifting, they both felt like skipping along, singing, and laughing.

"It's like a fairyland! Can you feel it?" asked Antera, smiling and almost not able to contain the joy of it. "I've never felt anything like this!"

"I love it," agreed Omaran. "Feels like the nature spirits are leading us to the perfect spot."

"We are on the top of the world!"

After hiking only about a mile, reveling in the spectacular views, they both found themselves drawn up to a rock outcrop. Off trail they went, climbing rocks to get near the spot they had seen. When they arrived, they knew this was the place for the ceremony. The energy was very joyful as well as intense. They sat to meditate before setting up for the ceremony, glad for many things, not the least of which was the lack of mosquitoes. They leaned against a boulder and took off their shoes. The rocks made their feet buzz.

Shortly after sitting, Antera noticed that they were not alone. Many beings started to appear and make themselves known to her.

"It seems there is a spirit for each peak or group of mountains here; crystal beings . . . and they're just amazing. Ancient beings and guardians of this place are watching us. This is the heart, the central high point for the whole continent. I have a feeling this is a very sacred place, and it may be a very important point for the grid. What power is here!"

They were both quiet for a few minutes, taking in the special energies of the place.

Antera continued, "I keep hearing these low sounds, booming sounds of the mountains. Maybe it is the way they communicate with each other. But I'm hoping they can communicate in words to us!" She listened again. "I hear drumming, too. Maybe the Native Americans used to drum with the mountains, with the crystal beings here. Wow! Big drums to connect with these mountain beings!"

Omaran said, "This feels like a place that has been visited by Native Americans in the past, like they used to come right here."

"Yes, I see now that it was sacred ground for them, and they would come here to communicate with the mountain beings, right here. And there's also a fairy column right there on that rock where we can distribute the herbs, so it's a meeting of air and Earth. Oh! There's a Native American ancestor here, he calls himself Thundercloud. He is talking."

Thundercloud said, "You have reached the sacred place where we did our vision quests and found our connection to the Earth and to the Sky.

We came here to talk to the ancients, and to our ancestors, because the ancestors were so much a part of our culture, and our way of drawing forth energy and spirit into our lives. We came up here to drum and to call forth these great mountain beings, and to do our ceremonies. So, we are very happy that you have come here and chosen this place to do your ceremony. We honor you and we call forth the ancestors for you. They are coming from far and wide."

Antera said, "As he's talking, I'm seeing a lot of beings arriving, on horseback and on foot. They're spirit beings and the horses are white and beautiful. Thundercloud is summoning them with his drum, calling the sacred ones, the ones he calls the Shining White Ones."

Antera noticed one very bright being who stood out from the rest. The others were in service to her. She was stunningly beautiful.

"Oh!" Antera exclaimed. "It's White Buffalo Calf Woman, the being on the white horse. She came with a whole entourage around her! Oh my gosh! She's here to participate with us."

Thundercloud said, "We bring forth our most sacred energy and beings so that you may have the greatest effect in your ceremony today and bring these energies into it as well. We are calling for a vast healing! The world needs healing."

Antera and Omaran were in awe of White Buffalo Calf Woman. They knew of her, of course, as a famous Lakota prophet, and they knew she had brought many spiritual teachings to the natives long ago. But this was the first time they had met her in person.

Antera said to her, "We are so very honored by your presence and that you would participate in this ceremony."

Thundercloud continued to call up the ancient beings of the mountain range, and they slowly arose, emerging from peaks all around. They had not been called for a long time. He took out a special ceremonial pipe and lit it and gave an offering to the mountains. Then he blew smoke in each direction.

"I don't think the mountain spirits really understand what we are doing or why," Antera said. "I mean, they still have such a pristine place here, so why would we want to do an Earth healing? They are still so protected, high in the Rockies."

Omaran agreed. "Let's let them tap into our memories of what has happened to the planet, and what humans have allowed, especially to this country in the last two hundred years. Maybe they can see how far we've fallen from our connections with the Earth and Spirit, to understand why we do this."

"Okay," Antera said. "We call for their help in healing the land and to raise consciousness. They've been slumbering. We ask them to wake up into a new consciousness themselves, and to rise into a tower of strength, stability, health and vitality, the energies we want to spread over the land."

Omaran formally said to the mountain beings, "Our planet, and all of us, are evolving. So, we are all being asked to help the Earth make this shift. We need to let the greatest amount of Spirit and Light that can come through us to do so, until it permeates every atom of this entire planet. We are honored beyond words."

After a pause, Antera said to Omaran, "Thundercloud wants us to smoke the pipe. He is passing it around. It is an honor, like we are being included in this Mountain Clan."

"I would love to." Omaran held up his hands, took the etheric pipe and puffed.

Antera took it next and puffed. "They consider us one of them even though we're white, and I'm very happy about that. Thundercloud is communicating with the ancient ones in their language, so I don't know exactly what he's saying. Maybe he's interpreting what we said.

"I'm also hearing that it's not about preserving the old ways, it's about going into the new, and letting go. There will be changes and we cannot expect the old to stay around. It never does. This planet is ever changing. They are showing me pictures of land changes, especially on the coasts, and I think the mountain spirits understand that we want to draw on their power to strengthen the rest of our healing grid. We need their help to strengthen the whole West Coast because that's where we've worked, and eventually maybe the East Coast as well."

"We do understand that there will likely be land changes," added Omaran. "The most important thing is that the greater good for this entire planet, and all of us who exist upon it in every form, will come about. We are deeply grateful for what all of you have done. We are extremely grateful to be able to be here in the physical form and to help anchor all this in as we move into this greater age."

"White Buffalo Calf Woman is a huge spiritual presence, a beautiful goddess," Antera said with reverence. "Thundercloud is bowing to her, and she is now coming forward to talk to us."

White Buffalo Calf Woman said, "My dear ones, it is for you that we have waited and held hope for this sacred land . . . because of your connection to Divine Mother and Mother Earth, and the sacredness of the work that you are doing with the land healing and purification. We are grateful and relieved that you have arrived here, so close to the Divine energies of this planet.

"Yes, there are many sacred areas on this planet and this continent, but this particular area has the stability to hold this energy into the new age, to hold the beauty and the purity of Spirit into matter throughout the coming changes. I want you to know that this place is very special to me and to all of us, that we cherish it, and we cherish all who come here and sit on these rocks to see the grandeur of this place and appreciate the beauty of it. We ask that you carry forth this energy throughout your grid and wherever you travel.

"I send my blessing with you as a spokesperson for the entire Native American union. This is a union of all tribes and all peoples, and this energy must carry forward into the new times—of union, peace, Love, compassion, and healing. I give you my highest regards and the blessing of healing upon you.

"And I ask for you to spread this message far and wide. BY MY AUTHORITY DO I BRING FORTH THE SUPPORT OF THESE ANCIENT ONES AND ASK THEM TO PUT THEIR ENERGY INTO YOUR HEALING GRID! By my authority do they act, and will they act forever more as long as this is needed! They reach deep in with these mountain roots, they draw energy from deep in the Earth and they can pull up an unlimited source of energy. This is what I ask them to do today!

"As they rally their support, they take whatever part of my energy they need. For I have unlimited energy, and I bring forth a blast of energy from the Mother Earth and the Divine Mother, which is re-awakening upon the planet. I bring forth a silver energy of this spot and surround you with this energy of power and stability. I give my gift to these crystal rock beings. I give this silver energy to them as my blessing and my thanks for their help.

"And I send out through your grid a blessing of peace and healing, and a call to all Native Americans, those who are Native American by blood and those who are Native American by spirit. I send my call out to all of them and ask them to help in this healing effort, to awaken to a new level of awareness, to let go of the old ways that do not serve, and to bring forth the new ways. I am not saying to give up the ways of sacred activities, but I am asking them to give up old grudges, old ways of looking at others or judging others. The new way is the way of peace and acceptance and tolerance of everyone!

"LET IT BE KNOWN THAT I, WHITE BUFFALO CALF WOMAN, PROCLAIM THIS FROM THIS SPOT and out through the grid, to all of those who can hear my message. And I send it out into the future as well, to the future points that you will add to your grid.

"I will be holding this focus for a long time. I will not give up until I see peace, compassion, Love, and healing pervade this sacred land again! HEAR ME, all of you who have ears to hear. SEE ME, all of you who have eyes to see. CALL TO ME, all of you who have a voice to call. WORK WITH ME, all who have hands for work!

"My nation, my children, my clans, my peoples, hear me now! Receive my blessings throughout the land and let all barriers be gone to the truth, and to peace!

"During your ceremony, please include my blessing and these ancient ones. We will stay here throughout the ceremony, and I will have a part of my energy staying here as long as it is needed. I give you my blessing from the deepest part of my heart, and my gratitude.

"Now, let us see your work."

Wow! This was big! Antera and Omaran looked at each other with wide eyes, suddenly feeling like they were on the spot. This amazing goddess and hundreds of her helpers, ancestors, mountain beings, and other beings were all watching them and waiting for them to do their ceremony. It felt like an unexpected performance. The pressure was on, and they knew this was a test to see if their Land Healing Project was worthy of this attention and potential support.

Though they had done this many times, now they were a bit nervous. While they were setting up, Omaran suddenly stopped, looking embarrassed.

"What's wrong?" Antera asked.

He whispered, as if the beings couldn't hear. "I . . . forgot something."

"What?"

"The elemental blessings. I forgot them! I can't believe it. I need to go back to the car!"

"What? Are you sure? That will take a long time, and everyone is waiting. Isn't there a way we can wing it?"

"No, we must do it right. I have to go. I will go as fast as I can. It's only a mile and a half each way, so I should be back in less than an hour. Oh, boy. I'm so embarrassed. I hope they wait for me."

Antera took a deep breath and nodded. "Okay, Love. Don't worry, they will. Go!"

He fast-walked back along the rough trail, and all along the way felt as if he were being energized and lifted along. When he arrived back at the car and found the needed items, he got the message that there were more beings who wanted to attend, so he asked them to follow him back up.

Antera, meanwhile, had the task of entertaining the audience while waiting for him to get back so they could start. The crowd was being very patient. She climbed up some of the outcrops and talked with a marmot who was curiously peaking around some boulders, then focused on a bird who serenaded the group. She played her flute for a while, and the group seemed appreciative as they waited. After what seemed like an eternity, but was about forty-five minutes, Omaran came over the ridge, panting.

They finished setting up and pulled off their ceremony, perhaps more dramatically than usual. All the beings joined in the songs and chants and danced around them at the end.

Afterwards, as they distributed the gifts for the elementals, they realized that they had passed the test, even with the blunder. There was a feeling of both elation and relief. The beings then dispersed as the humans packed up to hike back to the car, feeling high on mountain energy. The fact that White Buffalo Calf Woman had not only attended the ceremony but offered her huge support for the project, was just so amazing and would take time to integrate.

"I'm blown away. And here we are, not even Native Americans!" Omaran declared. "But we know we have native roots in our soul histories."

"Yes, we've both been involved with that culture in past lives, and I really think that is as important as blood roots."

"Back in the sixties, when I was reading all the spiritual books I could find, I remember reading one about Edgar Cayce, who was quoted as saying, 'If you want to learn spirituality, study the Native Americans.' So, I began reading books on Native Americans right away, and in the second book I read about White Buffalo Calf Woman. You know how sometimes certain words or phrases just jump right out at you? Well, seeing her name had that effect on me. Something about her brought up deep feelings of love. And when she showed up today . . ." Omaran felt a lump in his throat, he was so touched. "Well, I'm just amazed that I could remember that I forgot the elemental blessings, I was so blown away by her being here. Instant tears."

"It's going to take a little time for me to take it all in," said Antera. "And what a time to forget the gifts for the elementals!"

"I am so sorry, how on Earth did you handle being alone and just waiting? At least I had something to do."

"I played my flute, sang a bit, walked around, and just enjoyed being in the company of such illustrious beings. What a blessing!"

Their feelings of lightness did not lessen as they drove through the park to their next stop, the headwaters of the Colorado River, located in the eastern side of the park. To get to the actual source, for the River Blessing, would require a fifteen-mile hike with considerable elevation gain. They decided that was too far, so getting close would have to do for this important river, which carries water to far-off areas such as San Diego. Hiking up the trail along the creek for about a half mile was far enough, and they found a nice spot near the water.

The thought of this tiny creek turning into the mighty Colorado River, which carved out the Grand Canyon, was staggering. They were still integrating from the ceremony earlier that day, and some of that energy went into the river along with the blessings. The Spirit of the Colorado River was very appreciative and let them know. What rewarding work!

Thinking that it had always been easy to find places to dry camp in a National Forest, they drove south along the west side of the park, looking for a promising dirt road heading off the highway. It was Saturday night, however, and the few roads they saw were already taken by other campers.

It had been a long, intense day, but there was no choice but to keep going. They stopped at a couple of motels, but they were very expensive and also full.

It was the middle of the night when they got desperate and went in search of a campground that was listed in their guidebook, down a side road. However, all they found at the end of the road was a barrier, and a sign that it was closed. By then, Omaran wouldn't take no for an answer, so he drove right through the sign and found a place to park. The tent went up quickly, though they were very sleepy. As they were sitting in their camp chairs stargazing, two other cars came down the road and followed their lead, driving past the barrier. They settled for the night.

44

Lifted by Fairies

"Leadville is the highest elevation city in the U.S.," Antera read from her notes. "That is where the source of the Arkansas River is. At least, that is what they claim."

They had gotten an early start, and Omaran was driving. They wanted to bless the Arkansas River next. There were numerous major rivers that started in the Rockies, flowing out in all directions. Knowing that river sources weren't always where people claimed, they kept their eyes peeled as they drove.

They were still many miles from Leadville, when they went around a big bend and Antera happened to see a very small sign.

"Wait! Did you see that?" Antera exclaimed. "Turn around! It said Arkansas River!"

"I don't see any river. Are you sure?"

She looked back. "Yes, there is a small creek. That must be it."

"That little, tiny creek?"

"Headwaters. Where it all begins."

"Humph," was all he said.

Quickly turning around, Omaran found a place to pull off by the creek and went a short distance down a dirt road so they couldn't be seen by passers-by. For once, they could actually see where it was coming out of the ground! Now this was a true headwaters, and a perfect place for the ceremony. The wildflowers were varied and colorful, and the creek made pleasant, soothing sounds as it bounced over rocks. The energy of the place was delightful, and the river spirit was very grateful as always.

With each River Blessing they did, they were more and more impressed with the multitudes of water elementals the river spirits managed all along the course of their rivers. It was hard for humans to fathom such an immense task. And the fact that these river spirits showed up when they were called, meant they were very aware of some of the activities of humans, at least these two particular humans.

Another fairy column had been sensed by Omaran along their route ahead, and it was near Aspen, at the Maroon Bells. Therefore, this became their next stop, to do an air blessing. He had been there thirty years before and loved the area. It had changed a lot in that time, however, and it took a long time to get there because cars were no longer allowed, and tickets were needed for a bus ride to the Bells.

It was worth all the wait and hassle. It was absolutely magnificent, and once they started hiking up the trail toward Crater Lake, they noticed that they were both hiking much faster than normal, as if they were being carried along energetically. It was a steep uphill climb at high altitude, but they felt like they were going downhill. They effortlessly passed several other groups of hikers.

"Wow, I could run up this trail!" Antera said.

"Me too! It takes no effort at all to walk. I'm amazed."

"Maybe we are in really good shape now, or maybe we are finally used to the high elevations."

"I don't think so. This is like we are being lifted up, like the fairies are flying with us."

"Ha, ha! You are right! I was enjoying it so much I didn't even notice, but there they are! I guess maybe they are excited about the air blessing."

"This must be what you felt like that time when you flew up Black Butte and I slogged along with what felt like a 100-pound backpack," Omaran said exuberantly.

They arrived at the lake quickly and found the fairy column. Many people were around, not surprising since the large outcrops called Maroon Bells and the scenic lake were spectacular. When they stopped, they stood for a few minutes taking in the views and breathing in the uplifting energy. But when they tried to find a secluded place to do their air blessing, it wasn't easy. Finally, they selected a spot behind some bushes, singing and chanting quietly for the ceremony as they tried not to draw people's attention. The blessing was given to a very joyous group of air elementals.

The fairies were busy distributing this energy when Antera and Omaran started back down the trail to the bus. Suddenly, they both felt very tired, dragging, even though it was downhill. Was it because they had practically run up the hill and the energy expenditure just now hit them? It was very strange. Antera decided to ask the fairies to help again. They heard the request, and even though it took them from their exciting new task of spreading the energy gifts, they sent some energy toward the couple, who immediately felt a lift and could have almost flown the rest of the way. It was immediate validation of the power and gratitude of the fairies!

After camping that night at Ruby Mountain along the Arkansas River, the next day provided another long drive. They treated themselves to a motel by the Rio Grande River so they could have showers. The energy of the room wasn't great, but they purified and uplifted it as much as they could, so Antera could bring through some kind of progress report and information from the Masters that evening.

St. Germain answered their call. "You have done a stupendous job! I am very impressed with how diligent you are, though I should not be surprised because you have always been so diligent in your work. Now, have you been feeling any changes since your trip to the Teton Retreat?"

Omaran answered, "Oh, my. Yes, I have. It seems much easier for me to hold a focus now than ever before. I still do fall into old patterns, but now when I do, they don't last long at all. I feel very different."

"I can see in both of your energy fields there is quite a change. I do believe this will take a while for you to integrate into your systems, so you may not feel it immediately, but I am very happy that you do feel some changes. Yes, you had a question?"

"I do have a question." Omaran was no longer surprised when the Masters knew this. "The Four Corners area has been growing in our minds. It seems like we are being pulled there, especially after what happened at the ceremony in Rocky Mountain National Park, so we're thinking about going to the Canyon of the Ancients. Should we just go there and sit, or do anything else?"

"The reason that you are being called there is that you have connected into some very deep roots of your own. As you know, you have both been

Native Americans in other lives, and these are the roots that I am talking about. You will find that you have left behind some energy there that needs to be collected to make yourselves more whole.

"To do that, you simply go there and follow where you are drawn, go to those places that call you. Absorb what is there for you to absorb. This would be a very healing thing for you to do, but also, it will make more complete the process that started for you in the Tetons and carried through to your encounter with White Buffalo Calf Woman. You may be aware that she is a very powerful being among the native tribes and meeting her was a great honor! And the fact that she came to your land-healing ceremony is almost unprecedented. Therefore, it is not only an honor, but a responsibility. She said she wished you to carry her message further if it is possible, to bridge the cultures.

"This is a task that you may or may not take on. However, it seems to me you have already bridged the cultures in the ceremonies that you do. They are very aligned with the old native cultures, not necessarily the newer ones, but the older ones before they became corrupted, as seems to happen with all civilizations. They were a very land-based culture, and they understood how to maintain the balance and harmony in the land . . . just as you did in Lemuria, just as you did in Atlantis, just as you did as Native Americans. This work you are doing is pulling all these different times of land-healing work together.

"By going to the area of which you speak, you may also come across some memories of others which need to be released and healed. You see, it is ancient memories and elders who still reside there in the inner planes, who call you. There is some inter-dimensional interference that needs to be cleared out because of the history of the area."

"Thank you for the confirmation," Omaran said.

"Some of these ancient beings have been hoping for centuries upon centuries for some help, by connecting with human beings who can do the healing process they need. And so, they call you. But you can choose which calls to answer, which projects to take on. I want to make it very clear that you are in demand and will feel called by many who would very much like your services, because it is a rare thing that you do. Do you understand?"

"I do, and we have noticed."

"You cannot help everyone. However, perhaps there will be ways in the future to shift large areas at a time. This you did long ago."

"Thank you so much."

"You are so welcome. I just want to tell you how joyous we are at the work you are doing and how very pleased we are with how it has been going. We see that you enjoy this work, so we are pleased. And you are receiving many, many gifts along the way. So, I thank you, and I leave you with my blessings."

45

Freedom for Hovenweep

For the final land-healing point, they drove farther south to the Southern Rockies in northern New Mexico, another stable area. On the map, they found a national forest in the target area, which usually meant easy access. But when they got there, fences lined both sides of the highway. They kept driving, thinking that it should end and become open land, but it went on and on.

"Are you sure this is a National Forest? Because all I'm seeing is fences." Omaran was getting frustrated.

"That's what the map says. I don't understand it."

"How dare they try to keep us out! This is public land!"

"Maybe ranchers are allowed to use it for cattle. But the signs do say no trespassing."

"Okay, that's it."

He pulled off the highway onto a narrow area of dirt on the shoulder, by a prominent sign that said the forest was closed. They figured it obviously did not apply to them. After such a long drive, they were going in. Just in case anyone driving by did not agree, they moved the car a bit to be in the shade of a small grove of trees, tucking it away so it was not so visible. Omaran was able to loosen the barbed-wire fence posts, and they squeezed underneath the fence by flattening their bodies to the ground, barely fitting, and dragging their packs under. They hiked into the forest.

The perfect ceremony site was not far from the highway. They found a group of rocks that had magical energies, full of nature spirits waiting for them. It was like walking into an arena. It was a very powerful ceremony, and the local elementals, as well as the regulars who usually showed up to these ceremonies, mimicked the dance the couple did, in a larger circle, going around and around. Antera noticed for the first time that the small beings were having to walk over the packs that had carried their ceremony supplies, because they had left them too close to the circle. From then on, they anticipated the larger groups and moved the packs farther away before beginning.

This turned out to be a very fun ceremony, and they got away with the intrusion into the forest!

The next stop would be the Four Corners area. This is where four states meet: Colorado, Utah, New Mexico, and Arizona. Upon arriving in Cortez, they went to the visitor center and a ranger told them all about the Canyons of the Ancients, the Anasazi and the legends around these people who had disappeared in the late fifteenth century, with no one really knowing what had happened to them. These people had built a sophisticated culture, with about 30,000 people populating the sandstone bluffs and mesas for almost 2000 years. At one point, they moved into carved-out bluff homes, as if they needed more protection, then all of them disappeared.

The very helpful ranger described how to get to the ruins, and when asked about campgrounds, he said the only one in the area was at a place called Hovenweep on the far west side of the monument. Though they were tired, and the drive did not sound attractive, it was either that or stay in a KOA in town. No choice there! The ranger called to see if campsites were available, but there was no answer. It was forty miles each way on a marginal road just to find out if the campground was open, but they took the risk.

The sun was low in the sky when they arrived at Hovenweep. A coyote crossed the road as they entered the campground, which they immediately decided was a sign of welcome, but they saw no other campers . . . no campground host, either. They thought it may be closed, but there was no sign. Finally, they found a small visitor center with a young ranger, who said it was all right to camp.

Touring the campsites, they obviously had their pick so they chose one that would provide some shade for the car. It was still quite hot, even with a thunderstorm that had provided a few drops of rain. The wind was significant, though, making them scout around for large rocks to put inside the tent so it would not fly away like a parachute.

The mysterious Anasazi ruins were impressive, the stones taking on a reddish color in the last light of the day. They hiked a loop trail around the canyon, marveling at the sophisticated stonework, mortared together only with clay. It wasn't easy to discern the function of some of the buildings which were tall, square structures that looked like towers. It was a mysterious place.

One area, slightly off the trail, drew them in, so they decided to check it out even though it was almost dark. Hoping that the waxing gibbous moon would be enough light to get them back to the campsite, they investigated. The area could have been a home long ago, protected by a canyon wall on one side, with a shallow cave for shelter, a juniper tree, and flat rocks to sit on and enjoy the view. They sat to feel the energy of the place.

"It feels very heavy and deeply sad to me," Omaran said. "Like something bad happened and has not healed."

"I feel that, too. It involves a large group of people, and they may be trapped here or something."

"I think they need to do some forgiving to free themselves."

Antera listened for a few minutes. "I'm sensing that there's some kind of a dimensional issue here, a dimensional warp that's holding a lot of beings. They're not able to break through. It's like they're trapped and don't know how to get out."

"Maybe that is why we were called here," Omaran said. "We may need to do some kind of a ceremony here to help them get out."

Antera tuned in more deeply. "There's also been a lot of pain and suffering and I'm sure that's part of why they got into this situation. But there's more going on here than that because the whole Native American culture is being asked to change. That's what White Buffalo Calf Woman was saying. There are many who are still fighting among each other or trying to hold their tribes and cultures separate . . . so many different little tribes, and they're not getting along. They're not sharing their heritage, and so it's still an issue.

"There's a group of elders here for this area and there are many different tribes represented here. It's not just the ancients, or the Anasazi. There are representatives from many different tribes here and they're asking us to do a ceremony, to help right what was wrong. They feel like there were some big mistakes made and like you said, Omaran, there's a need for forgiveness of themselves and each other. But also, they feel like they need to do something to atone and make it right before they can move on."

Antera took a deep breath, sensing the density. "You know, they're not happy with how things are going and how the descendants are living. The Native Americans are not living in a very up-tone way. Most are not living on the land like they used to, and many are halfway in the white culture. It's not a good situation. They feel it's because of mistakes they made way back, that this has happened to the peoples.

"I'm seeing them more clearly now. They're dressed up in these beautiful, colorful kinds of clothing, ornaments, necklaces, and headdresses, things like that. And they've been trying for a long time to right the wrong, but it hasn't worked."

Omaran said to the group of ancestors, "I'd like to say something. I have an idea about how you can really help now. Rather than trying to reach all the Native Americans, reach a few who are ready, who want to believe in the true path again. It doesn't take all of us here to bring about these changes, it only takes a few, truly dedicated ones, and others will follow.

"If Antera and I do try to reach Native Americans to deliver White Buffalo Calf Woman's message, we will no doubt encounter some opposition. Maybe with your energetic support, that can be overcome in enough people to have a powerful impact at the most crucial time in the planet's history . . . now!"

"Yes," Antera agreed. "They seem most concerned about mistakes they made and karma that needs to be released. We would have to do that in ceremony, perhaps tomorrow."

"Should we do it here or in another canyon?"

"They will come to wherever we do it, in the ancient lands. There's something about this area . . . it's impregnated with what used to be very spiritual energies, and that's why they settled here. They enjoyed that for a long, long time while they lived here. They were the most spiritual of all the tribes, but the others came to be jealous and tried to take their lands. That's when all the problems started. The Anasazi could have risen above it, talked it over, shared, and whatever needed to be done, but they didn't and that was the big mistake."

A dazzling chief stepped forward, wearing a large headdress, a colorful vest, and leather pants. "Their main spokesman is here, and he says his name is Red Feather," Antera described. "He's saying that they did not take the higher road, they went to a low level and fought, and were massacred. There were some really horrible, horrible things that happened. Because of that, the spiritual energies of this area were damaged, polluted, and this is one of the reasons they want to make amends, they want to clear it up if possible, and bring it back to a more spiritual center here. Because it used to be a very powerful, high-frequency place, and it has become very dense, because it's still holding that pain. If we can help release some of that really dense energy, then they will feel they can move on, and the uplifting energy can come back in here, if it is meant to be.

"They just need humans to help clean it up. They haven't been able to do it themselves. So, we have to decide how we're going to do that, and what kind of a ceremony we're going to do. He says he was contacted by Thundercloud, the being we met in Rocky Mountain Park. That's why he knows of us and would like us to do the same kind of thing here that we did there."

Omaran said, "Remember, I did bring an extra set of ceremony items just in case. We could do a land healing here."

"Okay, we will think about that."

Somehow, Red Feather convinced them to do a sunrise ceremony the next morning, a time of day rarely seen by Antera, and she wondered how she had agreed to this as Omaran woke her up at 5:00. They had decided to do a full land-healing ceremony, packing everything up the night before, so they left quickly without eating. There was barely enough light to hike.

A sunrise ceremony was a first. They weren't really sure if that meant they were supposed to wait until they could see the sun, or what. The site for the ceremony was hidden on the canyon wall, so the sun wouldn't hit there until much later. They decided to go ahead as soon as everything was set up and ready. At that hour, no one was around to hear, in case any other campers had arrived, or the ranger did rounds, so it actually was perfect.

They were the only two people, but the non-physical beings were a very large group, and they continued to arrive, finding places in the canyon just below where the ceremony was set up on a big, flat rock. For Antera and Omaran, it was like being on a stage. Chiefs and representatives from all Indian nations were there, including many they recognized: Running Bear from Mount Tamalpais, Hiawatha, Silver Horse from Sedona, and Thundercloud from the Rockies. From some of the others, Antera could feel a bit of skepticism, an attitude that said, "Show me that this will be worth the trip." They had been invited by Thundercloud and the others, and they came on their recommendation, but with doubts about the importance of what two white people would be doing.

It really was a powerful ceremony. Everyone was on board as soon as the Masters, nature spirits, and other support groups were called in. The singing and chanting were heart-felt but quiet just in case the rangers might be up early. A section of the ceremony was devoted to clearing karma associated with mistakes the ancestors had made, including fighting between tribes, and between whites and natives. This freed many of them up to move on or shift their work to a higher level. There was a huge release of dense energy with that process, and by the end of it, there was plentiful joy.

After it was all over, many of the beings dispersed. Antera and Omaran sat on the large rock to discuss how it went. Omaran said, "There was a lot of skepticism at first, but as soon as we opened our hearts, they did also."

"Yeah, and I think that's one of the things we do well. I mean, we're doing this out of the goodness of our hearts. It's just what we do."

She looked out at the group who were still present. "Red Feather is standing in front of us and wants to talk. He says, 'We are deeply in your debt, and we have gifts for you.' I can see behind him to the others he represents. They are all starting to really soar. There's this huge structure of Light we created, and they're floating off in it. That means they're free."

"During the ceremony," said Omaran, "I had a vision that there was a line of them, coming in one at a time and like you were saying, just soaring."

"It's like freedom! But Red Feather is laying some things at our feet here, and I think that's a tradition, to give gifts. Some very sacred things. He's unrolling a pouch or bag, like a medicine bag. I guess he was a medicine man when he was physical, a healer as well as a chief at the same time which made him very, very powerful. He's showing us something, some very sacred totem objects, amulets of some kind."

Omaran saw them, too. "I'm getting that there are two amulets and he's putting one on each of us, and we'll be carrying them with us like we carry other objects with us."

"He's putting them around our necks, yes. It's like being welcomed into the Native American heritage."

Red Feather put the amulet around each of their necks, as he said, "You are now part of us and as you carry these with you, others will recognize you better. When you go other places to do ceremonies, others will automatically know that you carry Red Feather's amulet, and this identifies you as being accepted by the ancients."

Antera said, "It's a wonderful gift that will help us in our future work, and we thank you so much, Red Feather!"

She saw that he wasn't quite finished. He unwrapped a beautiful crystal that also carried energy of the tribe. He had been holding onto it for a long time, but it was no longer needed. He wanted them to know that he was burying it to signify the end of a long period of suffering, now that they were freed. The karma was released, and it was the ending of a cycle.

Next, he took out a pipe, a symbol of sacredness for the Native Americans, saying that he wanted them to have this pipe. He also said they might want to get a real physical pipe for their future ceremonies. The pipe was made of bone or antler, and it had feathers on it.

"I think it may be his personal pipe!" Antera said.

Red Feather said, "I want you to have this and think of me when you do your ceremonies. Yes, it is my pipe, but I do have others. Thank you for accepting it. I will remain here as a Guardian, but my job will be much easier now, protecting the lands rather than contending with opposing forces and karma. I am joyful about this!"

Antera said, "We thank you so much, Red Feather, for these beautiful gifts. We will treasure them and remember you in all our land-healing ceremonies. And we give our blessings to all the ancient people, all the Anasazi, and all the ancestors of the current tribes. We thank you so much, and you owe us nothing. You are free! And to all the rest of you, we're saying you don't have to give us gifts."

Though she told them they owed nothing, they insisted on giving, because paying their debts was very important to them, and soon there was a large pile of items in front of them. It was a beautiful gesture, and they accepted it all, knowing they wouldn't be able to keep much of it.

Red Feather then said that the last gift was a red feather. This was a powerful symbol for the Anasazi and his ancestral line. He told them that if they could find a physical red feather, that would remind them of this.

Antera said, "Okay . . . thank you all and you are all released, you have no debt to us, you have no debt to the Earth, you are all free to move on as your spirit guides you. Listen to your soul, listen to your Higher Self, and go where you are guided."

At that moment, all the beings stopped and turned toward the east. The humans turned to see what they were looking at, and there was White Buffalo Calf Woman, making her entrance on a white horse. The crowd parted to let her through. She blessed all the beings around her, and they all wanted to touch her. She came up and dismounted with a flowing, graceful motion, to talk to the humans.

"You are now a part of us and a part of the new culture, the new way of being. You will help to spread this throughout the land. I call forth the energies of Divine Mother, Divine Father, Mother Earth, and Father Sky. I ask them to be fully balanced in each of you as you are blessed by this.

"I am so grateful to you for carrying forth this torch and shining your Light throughout the land, across the cultures, across the barriers that seemed insurmountable. They are breaking down fast as I speak, and as you travel the land. You are breaking down barriers you did not know you were going to break down!

"So, as you move forward on the rest of your journey and take this energy home, know that I send my blessings with you and out to every tribe, including the whites. All tribes. The whites are just another tribe. All the Native Americans and all the whites are one people. We are all one people. There is no need for separation or competition or fighting within ourselves, it only weakens us. It weakens everyone.

"To move into our new age of cooperation and harmony and peace, we must, we absolutely MUST cooperate with each other and love each other. This is my goal, this is how and why I have reappeared on the planet, as a symbol for the Native Americans and all people, to encourage this breaking down of barriers, and to bring forth the greatest peace and harmony to the land again. This ceremony today has played a major part in this.

"The area you are in here, which you call the Four Corners, is symbolic of the Native American issues. Here you see the Native American influence very strongly, but also you see the weakness, the in-fighting, you see many tribes together seemingly sharing, but not really sharing the land."

She turned to all the beings still present and continued. "Because of the release in the ceremony today we see that a big burden has been lifted, and I want all of you to notice that as this karmic burden is fully released, you are changed! Not only all of you here, but all the people you represent are changed, are uplifted to a new level of consciousness and back into strength, back into the power that was once yours, the power that you once held but abused, the power you once held but allowed to slip out of your hands.

"This karmic release goes very, very deep, and it goes back far, far into your history. This is not about the whites taking over, they were only a symptom! They came in because you had released your power, because you had relinquished that which you held sacred. You had relinquished your ability to live in cooperation and harmony and abundance. Taking back responsibility for the downfall of the Native Americans is what this karmic release is about, rather than being victims or blaming others or yourselves for what has happened.

"This is about forgiveness . . . forgiving yourselves, forgiving the whites, forgiving the land for not providing for you when you were in need at times, forgiving the imbalance that was created, forgiving the Earth for not giving you what you needed, forgiving Father Sky for not bringing rain when you needed it.

"Let all of this go now! This is the new age where all the Native American tribes will rise up again in power. Not power against each other, not power against the whites, not blame or anger, but personal power that comes from responsibility and joy in your own beingness and love for everyone . . . love and acceptance.

"Go forth, all of you, and take this energy to your tribes!"

She turned back to the human couple. "And you two will also take this to your tribe, to the whites, to those who have your ancestral lineage, so that you will also come out of feelings of being the perpetrators of many crimes upon the Native Americans. There is no longer any need to feel guilt or any other responsibility toward this. The karma you personally released today is the karma that the whites have upon the natives. All of that karma was released, and so now all peoples can move forward together.

"I want to impress upon you how important this is, because the natives here and the ancients had very deep group karma but there is also the white karma upon the red, and the guilt that is instilled in the white culture. This must be dispelled through forgiveness. It has been done today. There has been a major shift in this relationship between the whites and the reds. And I will submit to you that your abilities as land healers will be growing phenomenally because of this.

"We are moving out of that dense era and into one of Light. You have been instrumental in creating this shift today. The effects of this ceremony will be felt far and wide, and because of your Land Healing Grid, they will spread throughout the grid.

"Thank you again so much, you are so blessed, you are so blessed, you are so blessed."

She got on her horse and rode off. Most of the others also wandered off.

After a few minutes of silence, Omaran laughed and said, "After all this, I think we should call it Hovenjoy instead of Hovenweep!"

Right before the ceremony, on Red Feather's request, they had gathered small rocks and placed them on the altar to be charged up. These were to be taken out and distributed to other places to carry the energy of this meeting out farther, especially to other tribes. They started this new task by driving around the Canyons of the Ancients Monument and visiting each of the ancient pueblo ruins, leaving a rock at each, logging many miles of dirt roads.

The biggest and most famous of the ruins in the Four Corners area was Mesa Verde National Park, with dwellings inside high sandstone cliffs. The Anasazi had lived there only a short while, about 100 years, and it felt like it would be energetically much less important than what they had already seen. But for completeness, they thought they wanted to go there.

"I'd like to see Mesa Verde, but I think I'm done with these ruins, and we have a long way to drive yet today. Let's skip that one, okay?" Antera suggested.

"But Red Feather really wanted us to distribute these rocks all over this area, and this may be our only chance. Who knows if we will ever be here again? The sign said it's only fifteen miles to the visitor center, and it is spectacular the way they lived in holes along the steep cliffs." Omaran had been there many years ago.

They were both tired after getting up so early, but she reluctantly agreed to go. They reached the visitor center, and a new sign there said the actual ruins were another twenty-three miles! Coming this far, they continued. It seemed endless. Antera started complaining that it wasn't worth it, it was just too far.

Without thinking, Omaran blurted out, "I just want to get the rock out of the car!"

They both burst out laughing. Omaran had no idea why he had said that. They continued. When they finally arrived at some of the ruins, they were only accessible by guided tours, for which you had to buy tickets, and those were only sold at the visitor center, over twenty miles back! Not able to see the ruins after driving so far, seemed even more hilarious. No pull-outs along the road were available, so they stopped right in the middle of the road, and Omaran got out and hurled the rock off the cliff. Then they hightailed it off that unwelcoming mesa as fast as they could.

Before leaving the area, they decided it was important to go to the actual Four Corners, where the four states meet, thinking there must be something special worth seeing there. What they found was a small area with a few booths selling crafts made by local Native Americans. It was a bit disappointing. The heat was oppressive, so they buried a Hovenweep rock and left, wondering how the vendors could withstand it.

Tuba City had the only campground for hours around, so that was where they pitched their tent, hoping for a little sleep between noisy roads.

46

Oak Creek Wave

In the morning, they packed up and drove west. Antera drove while Omaran studied the map. He said, "You know, Dear, we can't possibly get this close to Sedona and not go see Silver Horse."

"I had a feeling you were going to say that. I was thinking the same thing. How far out of our way is it?"

"Not far," answered Omaran.

"Meaning a hundred miles? Two hundred?"

"Not that far. It will be worth it."

"It's okay. I'd like to go back and stick my feet in the water of Oak Creek."

Stopping in Flagstaff, they found an internet café to get email, stocked up on some food, then made it to their favorite campground by Oak Creek. They got the very last campsite available, and still had time to do a River Blessing on the small creek they loved.

As they sat in their camp chairs at night, listening to the crickets and frogs by the creek, they gave thanks for such an amazingly transformative trip. So much had happened! They would never be the same. From the Teton Retreat, to White Buffalo Calf Woman reawakening the Ancient Crystal Beings, to the sunrise ceremony at Hovenweep . . . what an adventure! And they had thought they were only going out to do some land healing! It was so much more.

Antera sighed, and said, "This country is so large, and the grid is only covering the west. I wonder . . .."

"I was wondering the same thing. It makes sense what St. Germain said about including the rest of the country in the grid."

"It's so big, hard to imagine doing such a large area. Maybe we could at least get a start on it after our trip to the British Isles in the fall."

"Yeah, maybe. You know, this trip will take a long time to fully integrate. So much happened, and I'm so deeply touched by everything and everyone we met."

She laughed. "It's funny, because everyone we met is non-physical, so to others it may seem like we were alone the whole time!"

"Yes, it would sound pretty weird to others. And yet, we are never alone. What a big group of supporters we have."

She leaned toward him. "I'm so glad we have each other to share this. Thank you for being here with me to have these adventures. This is something we could only do together."

They kissed. He said, "We are so blessed, and I'm so blessed to be with you."

"We are both lucky."

They were out of the campground early in the morning, and went to the famous Bell Rock, a prominent red outcrop, where they did another air blessing. They had sensed a fairy column there, and they had a fun time throwing the herbs into the updraft without anyone else seeing them. The next stop was the section of Oak Creek where they had always seen Silver Horse. There was a slight breeze, refreshing in the heat, and pleasant sounds of leaves rustling and water gurgling.

"Silver Horse is here," Antera announced, a few minutes after they had settled on some rocks. He appeared, as usual, on his horse, walking down the canyon toward them in the shallow water. "He says he wants to thank us for everything we've done, which is far beyond what he thought we would do. He has been at all our ceremonies on this trip."

Silver Horse said, "Your hearts have become much purer on this trip, and the blessings you have received are very evident."

"Thank you, we are very grateful for all you have taught us," Omaran said.

"I see the amulets you wear now, identifying you as Native Americans in spirit, and I honor that. But Omaran, Native Americans need to go barefoot! Ha, ha! I see you walking around like you never walked before!

Going barefoot is a very important part of being in contact with the Earth, and as a land healer, especially important!"

They had both taken off their shoes, and Omaran's feet were especially tender. "Yes, I feel sheepish about that."

"I am so happy that you have made the medicine bundles that I suggested, and that you are learning more about the sacred objects and how to use them. And I am deeply touched that you made the trip all the way down here to this place even in the heat of this time of year, to honor me. Do you have questions?"

Omaran answered, "Well, I think the things that are most difficult for us to find now are the fairy columns. How did we do this morning?"

"You couldn't go wrong here in Sedona, there are many fairy columns and you definitely hit one on Bell Rock. Other places do not have nearly as many. You can sense these, that is how you know where they are.

"I want to tell you," he went on, "that the wave of higher consciousness energies from your River Blessing came through here last night. I saw them and I felt them. They were powerful. I am so happy that I was able to experience that, and to see the shift of energies that happened. It was a wave of energy that came down the river and went on past. It was last night around 7:00 that I felt it at its peak.

"At first, there were a few little water spirits coming down, paving the way like scouts, and then the big deluge came through like a flood. This is how it felt to me. So, I want you to know that it was entirely successful, and spirits of all the other rivers are telling me the same thing. I wanted to feel it myself, and I am so honored and privileged that you did this on my creek, little as it is."

Omaran was very pleased to have more confirmation. "The size of creeks doesn't matter. You started this whole thing right here and we are honored that we were chosen to do this. It has gone so far beyond our expectations, and we are just going with it at this point. It's so wonderful. It feels like the possibilities are unlimited, so we are certainly going to keep doing this. I do have one question. When we drive past a river and don't have time for much of a ceremony, can we just throw a few crystals in? Does that help much?"

"All you need to do, once the crystals are fully charged up, is say a prayer and send them on their way. Call the spirit of the river, because if you do not do that the spirit will not appear. You have to call the spirit of the river, and when you sense the presence of the spirit there in front of you simply tell them what you are doing, say a prayer of blessings, and throw the crystals in. It does not need to take long. The charging up of the crystals before is what takes the time.

"All rivers and creeks can use it, as many as you can easily do as you are going through. Of course, you cannot get every creek or river in the country, or the world! But whatever you can do will help."

"Thanks. And one more thing. We are thinking about expanding the grid to the rest of this country, as St. Germain suggested. It suddenly feels more urgent. We'd be interested in your opinion."

"I have been urging this on you because of the effects of what you have done on this trip. So much more has happened, and now we see all the potential of this. If you could do the rest of the country, it would be tremendous! We don't want to put expectation on you, but the special ceremonies that you had on this trip that involved the Native Americans have been impressive. The Council is still meeting and working out ways to carry this energy out, from the ceremonies you did at the top of the Rockies and at the ruins. There are still deliberations being made about this because the shifts were great!

"There's a little bit of an upheaval right now while members of the Council figure out what to do next, like how to distribute this energy out to the world and how to upgrade their own service to one of higher purpose, more spirit and less bondage, less need and more giving. This is what we are doing now. We are very excited about all of this, and we know that more is in the works. I and the others you work with will keep you posted on this. Because of these big shifts, we are urging you to continue on in any way you can. But of course, it is your choice."

Omaran said, "We realize that. And our choice is to do more. We feel the urgency and it doesn't feel like a push or anything we don't want to do—we love doing this! This work is so extraordinary, seen from where we are in the third dimension, and a magnificent opportunity.

"So that brings up another question. If we take another trip, where are the best places to go? We aren't very familiar with the Midwest or East, especially regarding the Native Americans."

"Omaran, do some research. But areas will call out to you just as the Canyons of the Ancients called out to you. You have no trouble finding places, do you?"

"No, I really don't. If I get myself out of the way and relax and feel, I don't."

"I have no idea why you are still doubtful about your abilities in this regard! You are both strongly intuitive and have been able to find whatever you need. It is also a good exercise in following the flow, in trust and faith, and in keeping tuned in even while you are driving, even under difficult conditions, like having to get up before dawn, ha, ha! I was impressed, because I know that was difficult, you've never done that before.

"Now, you must keep in mind that Native Americans love sunrise ceremonies! So, you may be doing more of those, I'm afraid. It is a very magical time. It also allows you to do things before anyone else is around. I really had my doubts that you would do that. I told Red Feather, 'Oh, there is no way! You can ask, but there's no way it's going to happen.' However, you surprised us all pleasantly and it was a wonderful, powerful ceremony. Especially because it was almost a full moon, and the alignments—oh, particularly favorable.

"So, now I hope you are going to have a little time to enjoy yourselves at the end of your trip. I know you have a long drive yet. I also hope that the waters of this creek, that you have already charged up, may flow over you, and give you, in bathing, those higher energies that you imparted into the waters."

"We will get in the water tomorrow. Again, I would like to express our deep gratitude for the opportunity to be of service in this way. This means so much to us, and we are deeply touched. Thank you for everything you've done and for continuing to be there."

"As are we, very touched. I thank you from the bottom of my heart, and I mean that sincerely. I am very honored to be a part of your journey, to be able to communicate with you, to help you along your way, and to help define this journey for you. Many blessings to you, my wonderful brother and sister in healing this planet. And many blessings from all my tribe and all the other tribes around here."

Antera and Omaran got up and stretched, and tried to walk barefoot over the rocks, wincing. It would take time to toughen their soles. They put their shoes on and started back to the car, thinking about their next trip and when they could possibly get away again, and still pay their bills. As the trips got longer, they also got more expensive.

47

Nature Spirit Internet

They decided to leave a day earlier than planned, but not before taking a hike to the end of the West Fork Trail, about three miles each way through stunning red rocks and canyon walls on both sides of the stream. It was so picturesque. They took Silver Horse's suggestion and, as soon as they found a deep enough pool, immersed themselves in the blessed waters of Oak Creek. It felt incredibly refreshing.

Then it was homeward bound. The farthest they could drive that day was Las Vegas, but the only motels were casinos, so they kept going. Fortunately, there was a small town along the way that had one motel, so they stopped there, arriving around 10:30 pm.

Omaran had mentioned several times that he wanted to stop in Death Valley on the way, to talk with the Guardian of the Deep, but that idea had been rejected by Antera just as many times, because the temperatures there in late July could easily be over 120 degrees. However, when they awoke the next day, it was raining, a very rare event for the desert, so Antera had no further objections and they planned their route to the deep valley.

After a green smoothie in the motel room for breakfast, they hit the road early, hoping to make it all the way home that day. It turned out to be a mild 104 degrees when they arrived at their parking spot by the side of the road in Death Valley. Hot as it was, they hiked to the place they had done previous ceremonies, and where they had met the Guardian of the Deep.

The valley floor was littered with just about every kind of rock imaginable, many of them colorful. It was always so tempting to collect some. As Antera walked, she heard some call to her, "Take me home with you!" It took will power not to pick them up. She only stopped once to bend over and grab one.

Omaran said, "I knew you couldn't resist!" So she put it back down just to show him she could.

Settled into the meager shade of mesquite bushes, they called to the Guardian of the Deep to see if he would talk to them again. He appeared very quickly.

He said, "I've been expecting you, and I'm very honored that you would pay me a visit despite the adverse conditions. I did what I could to lower the temperature, but it is summer, after all. I hope the clouds help a little."

Omaran said, "Yes, it is better."

"I thank you for spreading my energy throughout your Land Healing Grid. I have learned so much from the beings at the other sites! They have communicated to me many things I did not know of other terrains, other places, other cultures of nature spirits. The grid has allowed a vast communication system to be put in place between the nature spirits of many different lands, whereas before, their focus was very local. Now they're all learning to communicate with each other in a new way that helps with the exchange of energy between the different land-healing sites so that areas that really need more healing than others can be addressed. And I understand that this is all part of the purpose of the Land Healing Grid."

Antera commented, "He looks very different than he did before, like he has evolved. He has more of a solid shape. Whereas when I first saw him he was amorphous, just emerged for the first time from the deep, now he has taken on a form. He's evolving because of this new information he's getting from other places in the grid. Okay, do you have questions for him?"

Of course, Omaran did. "Is it enough that the Land Healing Grid has been created now and come alive? I guess one of the reasons I felt very drawn to come here today is to see if there's some way we could work better with you. I'm sure you are aware that the stones we took from here six months ago have been placed at all the new grid points, to enable the fire elementals to communicate with you much easier. Any more suggestions?"

"First of all, it is not only the fire elementals I have been communicating with, but also all of the nature spirits. The fire elementals are my kin, but I am communicating with all of the other beings, and we are learning from each other.

"I have vast knowledge about the deep processes in this planet because I have worked in the core and other areas inside it. And that is why I am called the Guardian of the Deep. Now that I have emerged on the surface, knowledge and wisdom that I have carried for eons comes out to be shared with the nature spirits, and I do that freely. I do that because of this communication network that you have set up. Because this is more than a land-healing network, this is a communication grid that has, when it started to work like a telephone system, given me access to all of the others and they to me. You do not need to facilitate this process any more than you have because I am now in communication with these beings and by setting up this grid, I am able to use it to the purpose that you have set into the grid points, which is Earth healing.

"You are already calling me in to each of these grid points as you do your ceremonies, and I have come to each one of them you have created since we met. Therefore, I am familiar with all beings you call in, both of the spirit realms and the nature realms. There is so much going on that you don't know about. It has to do with the healing of this planet on a very deep level, because, you see, there are beings within the Earth—deep, deep in the Earth—who are working diligently to heal the numerous problems that there are with this planet.

"There are imbalances within the core, the crust, and the mantle. But I am primarily concerned about those in the core because those will affect the entire planet if they go so far out of balance that it disturbs the rotation and various other processes. We are talking about deep processes, important for all life here. Therefore, it is important I get the help from the surface to take to the deep places, as well as bring my knowledge and wisdom to the surface to communicate to those up here who are working from the outside in. Does that answer your question?"

"Yes, and that makes me extremely happy. We're both aware that there's much more going on in this grid than we have any idea about, and that is fine. We know our purpose is to continue to set these points and do the releasing that calls us."

"If you want to do more traveling, there are plenty of other places on the surface of the Earth that could use your help. But that is a major project and I suggest you look at how you could fund such a thing, because I understand the funding part of it now. I have learned this since I came to the surface, because there are things that you humans need to do that are fairly alien to my way of being; however, they are very important to you. Your physical needs need to be taken care of and that is done by the money. I do hope that you will call on help so you can work that out.

"Now, there are many areas that need your Land Healing Grid, to help the communication system between all the nature spirits on the surface and the deep areas. When you have finished your country and are ready to move out to other areas, please let me know and I can help you form an idea of where the most important areas are.

"In the meantime, I do enjoy you asking me to participate in your ceremonies whenever you are creating a new grid point. This allows me to really communicate with new areas and new beings, and set up a 'nature spirit internet,' you might say. You see how much I have learned!"

Omaran laughed. "I'm amazed!"

"I am also in command of many beings down in the core, so there are processes going on there that I am helping to facilitate. As you work this grid and add more points around the globe, you will see that the communication lines go through the core. Then we will be able to really make some changes within the core. That is why, at some point, if you could travel around to the other side of the globe and put some grid points in there, it would certainly facilitate what we are doing deep in the planet as well as on the surface."

"If everything goes according to what we hope, we should see you again in a few months, and we will talk about future trips."

"Well, perhaps at that time it won't be so hot for you, and you'll be able to sit here for a while. However, even then it is still going to be hot! This is a hot place! That is why there are not many people here. Any other questions?"

"I don't believe so. We are honored to have met you and to be working with you. It's a real pleasure."

"I do thank you so much. It is because of you two that I have evolved so quickly of late and have been brought forth into a new level of service. When you summoned me, I did not know what was going on, or what I was being called to do, because you weren't clear about that, but over time

I have found the need that I can fill for this planet—my new service. I am honored to be a part of this project that is far reaching and very effective. I thank you and we will definitely be in contact. Until we meet again."

They walked back to the car and cranked up the air conditioning. As they drove out of the valley, they marveled at how different the Guardian was from the last time they had seen him. It was as if he went from kindergarten to a Ph.D. very quickly!

After fourteen hours of driving, they made it home exhausted but were buoyed by the enthusiastic welcome they got from their pets.

48

Change of Plans

It took a few days to unpack and put everything away, and to recover their energy. It was so nice to be home. They had just gotten back to their normal routines and work when they realized they had better start planning for their trip in October to the British Isles.

Antera was meditating in front of the altar in their meditation room one morning, when her mind wandered to that next trip. There was something about it that didn't seem right, though they were both excited about going there. She had an unsettled feeling, so she opened to guidance to find out what was going on.

St. Germain was immediately there, saying that a change of plans may be in order. He asked if they could delay their trip to Britain and go around the U.S. instead. In fact, he requested that they do land healing around the country as much as possible before the presidential election in early November. The election was going to be close, between Barack Obama and John McCain.

When Antera told Omaran about this, he looked very thoughtful. He was much more concerned with the election than she was, but it had never occurred to him that land healing would affect it in any way. He said, "This election is critical. But I wonder what the land healing has to do with politics."

Antera said, "It makes sense to me that by clearing some emotional and mental pain it would help people awaken and make better choices when voting. Instead of voting from a place of fear or anger, or tapping into mass thoughtforms for their opinions, perhaps many will be more conscious.

We know it raises consciousness overall, and of course everywhere we go we shine the Light."

"I see. Yes, absolutely! Let's do it! This is way more important than going to Britain. We can go there next year. Our own country! Of course!"

"If we do it, how many weeks do you think we will need?"

Omaran's planning mind kicked in. "You know, it will probably be about 10,000 miles of driving."

"Woah. 10,000 miles!"

"Yeah, well, it is 3,000 miles straight across each way, and we will need to make a big loop, so I expect it will be at least that."

"Okay, and how much time do you think we need?"

"Hmmm, I think five weeks. That means, to be sure we finish before the election, we need to leave right after the equinox event in September."

They were both silent as they thought about that. It was only a few weeks away, and it seemed like they had just gotten home. Antera ventured, "And how will we pay for it? If I go that long without working, I'm not sure we will be able to pay the mortgage, much less the trip expenses."

"That will be a challenge. You know, Guardian of the Deep said to ask people for help. If our nonprofit organization can support the project, then donations will be tax-deductible, right?"

"Yes, we can run it by the Board of Directors to see if Center for Soul Evolution will make it an official project. Another challenge will be finding a house sitter for so long and on such short notice."

"Clearly, a lot has to come together for this to work."

"Yes, well if the Masters really want us to do this, they will need to help make it happen."

So, knowing that they couldn't pay for this trip themselves, they started planning for it anyway on the faith that somehow the money would be there when it was needed.

"I wonder if we could do a Blue Snake initiation somewhere on the East Coast while we are on the trip," Omaran said to Antera one evening during dinner, suddenly excited. "You know, we will be on the road during the new moon in October."

Antera considered the idea as she chewed her salad. "I can ask the Holy Sisters. Doing one here is very different from doing one away from the mountain, so I doubt they will allow that."

The next morning, during her meditation time, she asked the Holy Sisters about it. To her surprise, they said yes. But to make a strong pathway of connection energetically from the mountain to the ceremony site, some rocks from the ceremony site would need to be mailed and carried up to the valley, and rocks from the valley mailed back and put in place for two weeks at the site. Then, with intent, the pathway could be made.

It sounded like a lot of work, but when Antera told Omaran, he said, "No problem! You know what this means? If this works, we will be able to do this anywhere we can find a group who wants it. That's exciting!"

"Yes, it opens up possibilities. So to make it happen on this trip, first we need to find a place to do it. And there wouldn't be much time to promote it. We are leaving in a month! And we don't have a lot of people on our mailing list from the East Coast, either. How would we find enough participants?"

"It would be really good to get Divine Mother's energy firmly in place over there. There has to be a way." He was feeling a large flow of energy about this.

"Well, we can put it out there and let Divine Mother arrange it if She wants." She thought for a moment. "In fact, I do have a couple of clients in New York. I could mention it to them and ask if they know of a place for a workshop."

"Okay! I think it will happen!"

It was just a couple of days after that discussion that Antera happened to have a phone session with one of her clients, Laurinda, who lived in upstate New York. When finished with the session, Antera asked her if she knew any places around there to do workshops. Laurinda gave her several contacts and said that she would really like to do the initiation herself if it came about. But when Antera looked the places up on the internet they didn't feel right. The initiation required a private space outside for a ceremony as well as indoor workshop space.

She emailed Laurinda and asked if she knew anyone with a large house and yard who might be open to hosting such an event. Laurinda said she would like to do it in her home! It happened that she had seven acres and a room in her large house that could accommodate up to twenty-five people. In fact, she had been thinking about holding events there. Antera accepted it sight unseen as the perfect location, and the event fell into place very easily. Laurinda knew many people in the area who she thought may want to attend. Divine Mother worked very quickly to make it happen.

They did these initiations as a service to the Mother without pay, so this did not help with creating income on the trip. Antera decided to arrange for a few phone sessions from the road as well, to help with house costs. But there was still the cost of the trip itself, and as the departure date marched closer, they finally decided to do as the Guardian of the Deep had suggested and send out a request for donations. This was tricky, because they had found in the past that the less attention they called to themselves while doing the land-healing work, the less resistance they encountered and the smoother it all went. So for all the previous trips, they had told no one where they were actually going. To make the donation request, they would have to tell people their plans.

The solution that presented itself was to send letters to a select group of people they knew and trusted, rather than the entire mailing list. The Board of Directors of Center for Soul Evolution agreed to collect donations and support the land-healing trip as a spiritual project of the organization. The letters went out by snail mail, and they awaited the response.

Getting ready for the trip was a marathon. September was harvest time for fruit, and each year Antera preserved most of the abundant pears, peaches, and other delights from their trees by drying and freezing. So on top of session work, planning and packing, and getting ready for both an equinox event and the event in New York, she spent several hours a day cutting up fruit.

There was also all the painting and making of sacred objects to take into the field and preparing for the initiation itself and all its materials. Plus, they had already arranged to do their Twin Flames musical for a TV show at the local college, so they were rehearsing for that. There was simply no time for much sleep!

They had a running conversation about all they needed to do before leaving. In the first week of September, Antera proclaimed, "I'll figure out where the headwaters are of the major rivers we will be close to, if you can lay out our general route." She was leaning over the railing and shouting down the stairs.

Omaran was sitting on the couch downstairs, working on his laptop. He jumped right in. "Well, it seems to me it is most important to head north first, then turn south down the east coast, and finally work our way back west through the southern states. We'll be going in late September and while I don't anticipate any winter-type weather happening that early, we should definitely go through the northern states first."

"Okay, then, north first. Got it."

"And if part of our plan is to have a positive impact on the election," Omaran continued, "that is another good reason to go to the northern states first because there are a few swing states along that route."

"Okay. I've started a list of things to bring. And I know you'll lay out the perfect trip for us, you are so good at that. I'll get you the river info by tomorrow. How many River Blessings do you think we can do?"

"You get the list together and we will do all the headwaters we can."

"Oh, and how many sets of land-healing materials do I need to paint? So far, I have twelve."

"I'd like to take twenty-four. I've already started packing the elemental gifts and other ceremonial items."

"Wow, twenty-four? Well, then! We can do it! And just one more question. Did you get an appointment with Roger for Swan's check-up?" Roger had been their mechanic since they moved to Mount Shasta, and he had taken care of their Subaru since they bought it new in 2001.

"Yes, I'm taking it in the week before we leave. I already talked to him."

"Isn't that cutting it a little close?"

"He wants to see it right before we leave."

"Okay, then." She ducked back into the office.

49

Tutut

"Hey Love," Antera said, "can you take a bit of time this evening? I know we are both super busy, but while I was painting and singing to the genies this afternoon, Tutut started talking to me. I told him we would both talk with him after dinner."

"Of course!" said Omaran. "And I'll make dinner tonight. You are busier than me."

"Good! If you don't mind."

"Not at all."

After dinner, they sat to see if Tutut, the property genie, still wanted to talk. They both closed their eyes and shifted their awareness.

After a few minutes, Antera said, "Yes, Tutut is here. We haven't seen him for quite a while. First, he's asking me, 'What about the flute?' I haven't played it in a long time, and he says the yard needs it."

"Plus, you will want to play it while we are out in the field," Omaran added. "So you don't want to get rusty."

"Yes, I know, and for the Blue Snake initiation, too. I'm wondering if Tutut is going to come with us or stay here." She listened for a moment. "He says his place is here, and he's going to stay here. I see that one of the ways we resonate with the house while we're gone is for me to play the flute. Apparently, he can play his at the same time so there will be a kind of resonance if I tune in to him that way. This will be essential on this long trip. During our last trip, a hole was created in the energy field of the property, and some leaked out."

They had noticed, upon coming home from the Rockies trip, how the energy had changed in their house and property. Samantha had acted aloof as if she were disturbed that they had been gone so long, and even easy-going Faith seemed different. The house, property, and pets required some energy work to get all back to normal. They had wondered how to prevent this, and St. Germain had given them some good advice, telling them to bring a portable altar with them along with pictures of the house and pets so they could easily check in with them every day. He had said the pets need to feel the energy of their people every day. The flute connection Tutut was telling them about would also help.

Tutut had several other tidbits of advice for the trip. Antera described what she was hearing. "He wants us to call in the Ancient Crystal Beings of the Rockies in every ceremony we do. They are at the heart of the country, the most stable place. And he says to connect the points to each other as we do them, rather than waiting until they are all done."

"All good," Omaran commented, nodding.

"He is glad we're going to bless the Great Lakes. He says to just get the ones we can, especially the ones that flow into the others. We don't even have to get the St. Lawrence River, because it will get the energy from the Great Lakes, eventually. Energy will flow much more slowly through the lakes than it does in rivers, but it will flow.

"He's telling me something about the Black Hills. There's a being there who wants to meet us, so he's just pointing that out to me. It's close to the grid point we did there on the last trip."

Omaran said, "That area has been calling to me for some time."

"Apparently, we need to go there, but there are plenty of places to visit and there will not be time to do them all. We will need to pick and choose. Because of what we did on our last trip, we seem to have the attention of many Native American ancestors and they all want us to come to their areas. Tutut is saying that if we can just get to a couple of them that will have to do.

"He's pointing to a map, to the Great Plains, places where Indians were slaughtered. If we can't get to them, we can just include them in whatever ceremony we are doing. Are we going to Arkansas? Can we do a grid point there?"

"Yes, I want to connect in with the Atlantean crystal." There was a giant etheric crystal, made in Atlantis and moved to Arkansas before the land completely broke up. It was called the Crystal of Knowledge.

"And something in Texas. He's pointing to Texas now, a high place, a magical place for nature spirits. Hopefully we can find wherever that is. So what other questions do we have?"

"How close should we get to the actual East Coast? Should we just stay in the Adirondacks, Appalachians, and Smoky Mountains? They are all the same mountain range, right?"

"He's just saying yes, we should try and do some near the coast, higher elevation rather than lower, but to just look at a map. But he says those are not all the same range! They are separate, so don't lump them together. There are beings associated with each of them and they would not like that.

"But it is all right to skip Florida, which isn't critical. We are to get the body of the country."

Omaran asked, "Tutut, I know you will stay here, but can you also be at our ceremonies? Can't you be in two places at once?"

Tutut answered directly, "That is a very good question. I can be in two places at once, but I only send a very small part of myself to your ceremonies because my assignment is here. I'm also assigned to help you in this endeavor however I can, so yes, I do send a small part of my energy."

Omaran asked, "Antera has a feeling that the race issue is still very important in this country and that we may be addressing that, as well, on this trip. What are your thoughts on that?"

The genie said, "You might notice that you were asked to do this before the election and there are good reasons for that, which do have something to do with race, increasing tolerance, letting go of these old notions of hatred and superiority. This is all a part of the election and could be the tipping factor. Right now, we're not sure who's going to win, and if it can be tipped, we're hoping you will be able to do that by working on this very issue—by spreading the energies of higher consciousness, neutrality, and love for everyone. The energies of harmony, balance, wisdom, and insight will help to shift that. Even if only a few people feel it, that helps. And by a few, I mean thousands. All you need is thousands to shift some of the states and get the critical balance. Once there is some kind of shift it can propagate very quickly throughout the lines of ancestors."

"Through the ancestors?" Omaran asked, confused.

"Yes, you can do karma release, like you did in Hovenweep for the ancestors, which will then clear it for whole families, on into the children.

I'm talking about the karma around bigotry and thinking some people are better than others.

"You do not have to do a full grid point to shift karma and patterns of thinking. Yes, it would be nice if you could, but obviously you can't do that everywhere. Wherever you do make a grid point, it will connect to others, and you will get all the area between them because of the energy flowing between points. You can also stop along the way and shift energy where you feel it needs shifting."

"Thank you, Tutut! I had no idea you would have so much information about this project. But I get it now. All the nature spirits are deeply involved, and especially the genies!"

Antera opened her eyes. "I guess I'd better start playing my flute again! And I will make a portable altar cloth. I have an idea about sewing symbols on it."

"That sounds perfect," Omaran said. "I'm wondering what else we can do about the karma release. I got a picture of burying programmed crystals. Maybe we could add those to our agenda."

"I could program them on the SCIO like I do the river crystals. That is by far the most powerful way to program them. Then we could bury them wherever they are needed along the way."

"Good. I think we may have quite a few crystals of the right size. They don't need to be good quality. I'll find as many as I can among our boxes of crystals."

"And yet another thing to add to my list, ha, ha!" At this point, she could only laugh at the nearly impossible to-do list she had. "Don't worry, I'll get everything done."

"I know you always make your deadlines. You are amazing that way."

"We both do." She kissed him and scurried off into the dining room to paint again.

50

Hold onto Your Core

Omaran was feeling a bit overwhelmed with all that had to be done before leaving on their trip around the country. As he walked Faith through the woods one afternoon, with only two weeks left before departure, a sense of burden and too much responsibility came over him, and he felt very heavy. He tried to reason with the feelings, not letting them completely take over, as he had done sometimes in the past, especially during their book tour several years before. That trip in the RV had been very stressful.

Antera had told him many times that he could be busy without being stressed, that it was very subjective how people reacted or responded to situations. It seemed she was able to get huge numbers of things done every day without the feelings of overwhelm he sometimes had. She claimed that when she felt like there was too much to do, she made a list and just seeing it in writing made it seem more doable. But Omaran had resistance to making lists because of his time in construction when he had made so many, he never wanted to see another one.

Contributing to his unease, he had finally started using his staff, which was very powerful. But sometimes he felt like he did not know what he was doing, or that he was not worthy of wielding such power. Why couldn't he just do it and not second-guess what he was doing?

Faith, trotting along in front of him, suddenly sprinted into the bushes after a squirrel. Omaran was reminded about how animals are always in present time, not worrying about the future or analyzing the past, as humans tend to do. Faith had heard a squirrel's squeak and instantly was on its trail, even though she had chased countless squirrels in her life and had never caught even one. All the failures in the past did not concern her at all. This might be the time she actually caught one, and it was fun to try even if she didn't.

Omaran wanted to live his life that way, not being concerned about whether he was successful or not, and just enjoying the process. The Masters had taught him so much about self-doubt, and he reflected on those lessons. Somehow, that self-doubt was related to his feelings of stressing out when there was a lot to do. Did it all go back to not being confident enough? He sighed. He had already worked on that many times.

Veering off the trail, he found a boulder he often sat on in this area of the woods, and Faith followed, the squirrel forgotten. As he sat, he closed his eyes, took a deep breath, and called on Jeshua to help him let go of whatever was holding him back. Almost instantly, he felt a shift in his energy, like the heavy energy simply lifted off. The Master surrounded him, purifying his energy and helping him expand back to balance and harmony. He relaxed and breathed deeply, smelling the pines and firs of the forest combined with the ever-present dust during this dry time of year.

As he sat in Jeshua's energy, all seemed perfectly fine. If only he could maintain this feeling! He decided to ask Antera if she could bring Jeshua through soon. It was nice to feel his energy, but even nicer to hear his words.

That evening, Jeshua started out with, "My dear brother and sister of the Light, I come here tonight to speak with you about some things of importance on this world, and in your lives and the lives of many. The times ahead promise to be of unprecedented challenge and opportunity at the same time.

"This is already happening, and the key, as we have told you many times, to making it through unscathed, is to hold on to your core. Hold on to that which is real, that which is important, and let go of everything else.

"So what IS your core? Your core is LOVE, pure and simple! That is the only thing that is important. That is the only thing that you must hold onto. For some, everything else will be ripped away. For many Lightworkers, this has been occurring over the past few years or even a decade, in preparation for this time. But for many others, it is just beginning.

"That is why it is so very crucial that priorities be set, that you know what is important in your life and what is a part of that core of who you are and what you are here to do. Even that which you think you are here to do may be stripped away! It may have changed because of the ever-flowing ebb and tide of consciousness.

"I come here tonight to speak with you and to remind you of what is important, to remind you that you may have many plans, but do not hold onto expectation. This is the way to navigate through these times—flow forward from a place of the now, from a place that is current and not a part of the past nor a part of the future.

"As this moment in time gets more intense, more focused, many people will not be able to hold on to their core energy. They will forget about Love, they will forget about what is truly important, and they will forget about loving and helping each other. There will be many angry people! That is what I am referring to. There is no way around it.

"But there will also be the emergence of the star people, the people who hold the star in their hearts, who do maintain Love and caring for everyone. These people can look past those who are blaming and angry and see within those people the core of Love, and therefore help them by projecting this core of Love back to these people so they may, in turn, magnify their own cores.

"We have been speaking of these times for many years, and they are here. There is no more practice, no more waiting. All that so many of you have come to this planet to experience is in process. Many people have put words to the fact that they are here for these exciting times, but then when the challenges hit, they forget. They act like a victim, or they do not understand why things are happening the way they are.

"Everything that is not Love will be stripped away! Because only a heart-based person can thrive on the energies that are coming into the planet now. This will only accelerate.

"My brother and sister, I tell you this, though you already know it. I want you to pay even more attention to when you flow out of the place of Love so that you may correct it immediately. This is how you will progress upon your path, by maintaining your sense of Love—for each other, for everyone in your families, for everyone you know, and for everyone you meet on a casual basis.

"I'm not saying you do not do this already. But I want you to really focus on it because it is such a key to these times. People who are undergoing many dramas now, which will only increase, are having these dramas because of unhealed parts of themselves coming up—the parts of themselves that do not love. It is only that which is being stripped away. There are many changes coming and happening right now, and I only want you to stay on top, every day, not a single moment missed by flowing out to a place that is not of the heart! Am I bringing my message across?"

Omaran responded, "Oh yes! Yes indeed."

"Do you think that you do this most of the time?"

"I believe I do. I used to let negative thoughts come up then dwell on them. Now, I recognize them very quickly, and most of the time I turn my mind around quickly. However, I know you wouldn't be saying this if it wasn't very, very important."

"It is of utmost importance at this time for everyone, but few will be able to do it. Omaran, I have come tonight especially because I heard your call."

"Thank you for coming. I was not doing so well earlier today and after I called you, I felt much better."

"Did your self-doubt come up again?"

"I think that is what happened."

"It seems to be an overriding pattern. But you have tools you can use to build your confidence and let go of self-doubt. You can let go of the thoughts that say, 'Who am I to be doing this? What kind of power do I really have? I don't know what I'm doing.' That whole pattern is one of the things that will be stripped from you. Do you understand?"

"Yes, I think I do. Self-doubt is not Love, so it is not part of my core. I haven't thought of the doubts as another form of a block."

"Doubt and lack of confidence have been major issues with you, Omaran, since I have known you, for thousands of years. Major patterns take some work to heal. I hear you say, 'Oh yes, it is time to deal with these or there may be some chaotic energy.' But what I am telling you is, get rid of these or you will have major problems! Everything is being stripped away! If you do not clear it out yourself, then something will happen to make it worse, until you have to deal with it.

"The Universe will reflect it back to you in a major way if you hold onto that pattern. You have two probable futures ahead of you. One is a path of doubt and being unsure of yourself, so the universe comes in with a big blow to show you that you are nobody and that you really don't know what you are doing. The other path is one of confidence, one in which you work very diligently on this pattern with all the tools that you have, and you create that confidence in yourself that brings to you tremendous success. Now, you tell me, which path you would like to take?"

Omaran laughed. "Door number two!"

"I'm so glad you said that! We have spoken of this before. And little by little you are working on removing what is around that doubt. You want to love yourself without any expectation even while you work on what is holding you back the most.

"You have come a long way, both of you. This is a time when you cannot afford to skip the morning meditation and clearing. You have many psychic and energy tools that you can use. Every single day, spend some time using your tools to clear out deep patterns so they don't build up.

"You also can do affirmations about this. What would be a good affirmation to chant throughout the day to affirm your confidence and belief in yourself?"

"Ummm . . . I'm thinking . . ."

"I will give you time to think about it, but how about these? I believe in myself. I believe I can do anything I want to do. I love myself exactly the way I am. I AM the release of all self-doubt. I AM the perfection of my Higher Self, expressed in my life in every moment."

Omaran repeated the words. "Thank you, I like those."

"You may choose to replace negative thoughts with confidence, strength, success, the power to move people, the power to transform the planet, Love, and wisdom. So any criticism simply passes you by and does not stick. Any criticism you get is simply an expression of the person who criticizes and has nothing to do with you.

"Now feel what it is like to be confident, to know that you have skills no one else on this planet has. You are unique, as is everyone! There are some things only Omaran can do. You have all the skills, knowledge, power, wisdom, and Love that you need, to be tremendously successful and prosperous in everything you chose to do that enhances the Light on this planet. You have everything you need! And the sooner you realize that—and I don't just mean realize it in a mental sense, I mean really get it—it reaches in, fills your heart, your chakras, your central core, your grounding cord, and your antakarana. It is all about what you think of yourself.

"There are so many people on this planet who have been very successful at what they do with much less ability, training, and wisdom than you have. But they believe in themselves, and that is why they are successful. There is never a word out of their mouth that undermines their abilities. There is never a thought that undermines their abilities. They move forward with ease and grace, and of course, with work. But they believe in themselves. Can you feel that?"

"It's interesting. I can feel it but at the same time I can feel that part of me that has doubts."

"Where is it?"

"It's right in front of me, very close."

"And who put it there?"

"Probably me. Or if I didn't put it there, I allowed it to be there."

"And why did you put it there?"

"Safety, so I wouldn't get hurt again."

"If you can see this right now, you can remove it. Remove any doubt that you have, any limiting factor that you have put on yourself that is keeping you from being fully successful."

Omaran pulled out his sword and dissolved this energy of self-doubt. He knew how to do this. When it was gone, he could breathe easier, and yet another weight was lifted. Amazed that there were so many layers to this issue, he said, "It's gone now! Wow!"

"It dissipated. What do you fill the space with?"

"I fill in with the Christ Light and replace that energy."

"Good. Now do you feel more confident?"

"Yes!"

"Do you see how easy that process was?"

"Yes, but I think it is because you are here."

"I did not do it, you did. This is why I did not do it, to show you that you have these skills, and you may use them anytime to remove a doubt, lack of confidence, anything that stands in your way of being a vast Light on the planet!"

"I see . . . I do see!"

"I would like to say, Omaran, that many of the little things you get upset about go back to this core issue. Underneath, this is the issue, this is the fear. If you find yourself getting upset during the day and really look at what's underneath the upset, I think you will find that 95% of the time, it goes back to this very issue.

"You cleared out a major part of it, but there are a few other layers. If you find yourself upset, just go within and say, 'How am I doubting myself? How is this related to my fear of not being successful?' Do you see?"

Omaran said thoughtfully, "That is really helpful."

"But do you understand the power of your faith, and how that supersedes any doubt?"

"I believe so, because when I have faith, I am allowing my Higher Self to come through and then it becomes real! Right now I feel that."

"Good, very good. And whenever you do not feel this way, that is when there is work to do to get yourself back to feeling this way. Because the confidence that you feel right now is the truth. I know that Divine Mother really stirred you up around this very subject not long ago. She poured into you that which would stir up these deep patterns so you would bring them out and fully dismiss them once and for all.

"Do you have any other questions, my brother?"

Omaran said, "Right now, my only questions are about how to work more with my staff. We're trying to keep this next trip slightly under the radar to minimize interference. Is there any reason that I should not use my staff for this? Is using it going to cause more exposure than we wish?"

"Ah. I believe it's a little late to be saying you want to keep it under the radar. You have announced it to many people and used your staff already. There is really no hiding."

"In that case, there's no reason to not use it again."

"But you still want to take caution in how much attention you draw. If anyone wants to know where you are, they can find you. If you downplay what you are doing too much, then it becomes less powerful. So there is a fine line between doing the work in a way that is extremely powerful and yet not announcing that power too openly until after each ceremony is finished. This you will learn through experience."

Omaran was feeling very strong and unlimited. "So it's safe to use my staff to call in donations for the trip? I feel like I can create anything right now!"

"Yes! And now let me give you my blessing before I leave. By the Light in your souls, I wish you the very best."

As soon as Jeshua's final blessing was finished, Omaran jumped up and went upstairs to get his staff. He put out a call for donations, from a confident, powerful stance.

The response to the donation letters was wonderful. Checks arrived in the mail with amounts from $50 to $1000. Many people were happy to help with the project, and the amount collected was enough to pay for the trip expenses. Antera and Omaran were so grateful!

The Blue Snake initiation was set for the new moon, which gave them only a week to drive to New York, a push with all the stops they had planned on the way. This necessitated their leaving as soon as possible after the equinox ceremony.

On Wednesday, four days before their planned departure, Omaran took Swan in to the local mechanic, Roger, for servicing, and to make sure it was ready for the long drive. Before leaving it there, Antera talked to Swan and asked her to be sure to let the mechanic know if anything needed attention, so there would not be any problems along the way. Later that day, Roger called Omaran with the bad news that the car would not make it that far.

"Hmmm," said Omaran rather slowly. "Let me get back to you, Roger." Turning to Antera, he said, "It looks like we may have to find another option."

"Meaning?"

"It appears that Swan needs a new head gasket, which will take twelve days to repair and cost $3000."

"Well, besides not having the money for that, we can't wait that long." She eyed him. "You're not thinking about taking the truck, are you?"

"I believe Sky could make it. And there's really no other choice."

"You'll have to have him checked out right away or we can't do it."

"I'll call Roger back and take Sky over right now."

Sky was older than Swan, about twelve years old, but had a few less miles on its odometer. Omaran immediately took it in to be checked out. Roger said, "It's a Toyota, so the engine is better, but it has some weakness in the struts, shocks, and brakes, which will cost about $1000 to fix. I can have it ready for you by the end of Friday."

"Great, let's do it!" replied Omaran. He was already thinking that with the truck, they would be able to carry more.

The truck with its camper shell would certainly carry more, but unfortunately, the camper did not lock and there was no time to get that fixed. So they would have to use energy to seal it with all their stuff in the back. To help keep the old truck working on the long journey, Antera took pictures of it and sent them to her sister, who volunteered to do energy work on it daily. She also took pictures of their home and pets and printed them up to take with them.

Sunday, September 21, dawned and they had somehow managed to get everything together. Although they didn't get out as early as they had hoped, not until 9:30 am, at least they were finally ready to leave. Antera was running on two hours sleep, after a week of four to five hours each night. Omaran was only in slightly better shape with three hours of shut eye. So it would be a challenge to stay alert on the road. Omaran got behind the wheel.

"I think you're going to have to drive most of today. Even coffee doesn't work anymore, but I'll try and drive for short distances," Antera said sleepily.

"I got it covered. You can just sit next to me and enjoy the view. It's funny now, but I was almost looking forward to starting our trip just so we could rest a bit," said Omaran.

"You think it will be restful, driving across the entire country doing twenty-four ceremonies, diverting to headwaters of the major rivers, clearing out karma for the ancestors here and there, and who knows what else?"

"The word 'restful' can be very subjective, you know. And relative."

"It's hard for me to imagine."

"Then let me take you away from all this painting and herbs and fruit and classes and sessions and almost sleepless nights. Let's go for a drive."

To be continued in Book III . . .

Printed in the United States
by Baker & Taylor Publisher Services